THE
DOUBLE
MAN

THE DOUBLE MAN

WILLIAM S. COHEN
and GARY HART

WILLIAM MORROW AND COMPANY, INC.
NEW YORK

Some portions of this novel deal with real occurrences and actual events involving international terrorism, but the depiction of KGB and CIA operations within the Soviet Union and the United States is fiction and should not be construed as being factual—or even probable.

Library of Congress Cataloging in Publication Data

Cohen, William S.
  The double man.

  I. Hart, Gary, 1937–   . II. Title.
PS3553.O434D6   1985   813'.54   85–267
ISBN 0-688-04167-1

Printed in the United States of America

First Edition

1 2 3 4 5 6 7 8 9 10

BOOK DESIGN BY ELLEN LO GIUDICE

TO MEMORY

ACKNOWLEDGMENTS

The authors have benefited, in the telling of this story, from their association with many people. But, as apprentice storytellers, we particularly appreciate the seasoned ministrations of Tom Allen, a professional and a gentleman; our editor Maria Guarnaschelli, indefatigably cheerful and patient, and the source of boundless encouragement and advice; and Bill Adler, our friend and the fountain of many books, including this one. We also want to thank members of our families, our colleagues, and friends, who were consistently interested and supportive. Faults and shortcomings in this story are ours alone.

PART ONE

O who is trying to shield whom?
Who left a hairpin in the room?
Who was the distant figure seen
Behaving oddly on the green?

1

Friday, March 20

THE HEAVY METAL DOORS protecting the basement garage of the State Department Building rose slowly. The Secretary of State's armored limousine emerged, closely followed by a security car. The little motorcade turned right on C Street and passed in front of the building's brightly lit facade. The dozen or so late-night tourists and spectators who had gathered across C Street to get a glimpse of Secretary of State Woodrow Wilson Harrold were disappointed to find it impossible to see inside the limousine's dark windows.

One man, wearing a seaman's watch cap and pea coat, stood somewhat apart from the cluster. As the limousine passed, he followed on foot as far as the corner, where the two cars slowed but did not come to a halt at the stop sign, then quickly gathered speed as they swung onto 23rd Street, heading north.

The man melted into the dark shrubbery behind the National Academy of Sciences Building. He extracted a walkie-talkie unit from his pocket and spoke into it briefly. He then stepped out onto the sidewalk, hailed a cab, and directed the driver to National Airport.

As the limousine turned left onto Virginia Avenue, two of its passengers reflected contentedly on the success of the evening's state dinner for Soviet Foreign Minister Aleksandr Suvarov. Alicia Harrold and her daughter-in-law, Natalie, had just come from the majestic John Quincy Adams Drawing Room on the seventh floor of the Department, where the diplomatic function for Suvarov had been combined with a celebration of the Secretary's fifty-seventh birthday. In honor of his grandfather's birthday, the car's third occupant, Woodrow Wilson Harrold III (who had borne the burden of that distinguished name for all of five years) had been permitted to stay up till this very late hour of 11:30 P.M. Unconcerned with the success or failure of state functions, Woodie was banging on the glass partition behind the driver, demanding to use the car's telephone to make a surprise call to his grandfather. Secretary Harrold had remained behind to brief President Arthur Christiansen on the events of the evening. The squirming little boy had rumpled his grandmother's new silk dress, but Alicia was indulgent.

Any thought of personal jeopardy was far from her mind. Her husband had warned her of danger on several occasions, but Alicia had assumed he was simply repeating a litany the Secret Service required him to deliver.

Alicia Harrold's fifty-three years had been privileged ones, without danger or want. Like her husband, she had been born, reared, educated, and married in wealth. And wealth automatically brought security, which to her simply meant freedom from intrusion and treachery. Now, after two years in Washington as the wife of the Secretary of State, she was aware of a new definition of security: the guarding of precious lives and institutions from something called terrorism. Last week, at the National Cathedral, she and her husband had attended a memorial service for Bruce Dickinson, a young cultural attaché blown to bits in Lagos. She and Bruce's mother had gone to Sweet Briar together. "That's the sixth one we've been to this year," Woodrow had said as they walked down the Cathedral steps.

The threat of terrorism was visible all over Washington. The metal detectors in hotels, sometimes even in churches, the constant escort of large, silent men, the concrete barriers in front of the White House gates. The White House was the worst place, of course. Armed men everywhere, inside and out. Even antiaircraft missiles. She often commiserated with poor Lucy Christiansen, who had to try to call the mansion home. And outside, some maniac might jump out of a crowd and start shooting at any time. She had once said something about this to Lucy at a Cabinet wives' luncheon at the White House, and the President's wife had reacted angrily. Obviously the very subject was upsetting to her.

Right now, headed toward home, Alicia Harrold had her hands full with her overtired grandson. She looked at Woodie and smiled. At the dinner he had been a bit boisterous at first but, in response to a lecture from his mother, had calmed down and behaved like a little gentleman right through the baked Alaska. His father, a career Foreign Service officer who had just undertaken his most important assignment as Deputy Chief of Mission at the American Embassy in Belgrade, would have been proud. Then, throughout the endless toasts and speeches, Woodie had fallen sound asleep.

But now the little boy was wide awake. Alicia wryly recalled Suvarov's remark. "I am surprised you bring a child here," he had said in his heavily accented English. Then he had muttered something in Russian, and the American interpreter, obviously flustered, had translated: "He says Woodie is a very . . . very *active* child." Alicia had met Suvarov several times before. But tonight, she reflected, he had not been the coolly gracious diplomat. He had seemed ill at ease, unable to bring himself to say anything chatty or even civil to her. She had asked politely about Suvarov's grandchildren, and all he had said, in English, was, "I do not see them. I must always travel, correcting American lies about my country."

She must pass *that* remark on to Woodrow when he got home. Suvarov, she reasoned, probably just didn't want to appear too friendly. Not with the chill that had been blowing between the United States and the Soviet Union for the past few years. Still, Woodrow should know about it.

Alicia Harrold glanced over her shoulder. She felt a curious mixture of relief and apprehension at the sight of the State Department security car fifteen yards behind them. In model and manpower, it was identical to the Secret Service backup cars that protected the President and Vice-President: a new Mercury station wagon, with a flashing red light mounted above the center of the windshield and additional red lights on either side and near each headlight. The security detail consisted of an expert driver and a "shotgun" agent in the front seat, with two agents in the second seat and two more facing each other on bench seats in the rear. The head of the detail, riding shotgun in the limousine, kept in constant touch with the backup car through a compact two-way communications system. All the agents carried holstered .38-caliber Smith & Wesson revolvers. The agents in the backup car were also equipped with Armalite AR-18 automatic rifles, which could produce a devastating shock wound at five hundred yards after passing through steel plate. The backup car also carried an array of antipersonnel grenades, tear gas, and riot-control clubs.

As the low-slung armored limousine passed the Watergate Apartments heading toward Rock Creek Parkway, Alicia Harrold's

Episcopalian soul fleetingly pondered the nature of violence. She made no particular progress. It was a peculiarly masculine notion, alien to her. Still, she was glad the security car was there.

The limousine and its unrelenting shadow swung right onto the parkway. Alicia's mind turned from violence to thoughts of the pleasant evening. To Natalie she said, "Do you suppose Woodrow will ever take one little drink at one of these formal events, just once? He says even the tiniest sip dulls his mind or makes him nod off. He's probably afraid of starting World War Three in his sleep."

As the limousine slowed slightly before starting up the incline of Waterside Drive, Woodie fell to the floor of the car and let out a howl. Natalie bent down to pick him up, and reached for something to say that might distract him: "Look, Woodie," she said. "There's the Oak Hill Cemetery, where John Payne is buried. He wrote a famous song called 'Home Sweet Home.'" She began to hum the familiar melody.

At that moment, ten feet to the left of the accelerating limousine, a barrel used to hold sand for tire traction in the winter erupted with a deafening roar. The blast lifted the trunk section of the Secretary's limousine completely off the chassis and dropped the shattered body of Alicia Harrold onto the pavement of Waterside Drive.

Simultaneously, the motor and front end of the security car were blown fifty feet up the hill, to join the trunk of the limousine. The driver and the agent riding shotgun were mangled beyond recognition. The two agents in back were still alive but were blocked by the wreckage and the bodies of their companions. In what was left of the limousine, Natalie, the chauffeur, and the chief of the security detail were wounded but alive. Miraculously, Woodie lay on the floor of the limousine stunned but otherwise unhurt.

Across Rock Creek Parkway and up the steep hillside of Oak Hill Cemetery stood a marble, pillared gazebo, a refuge for the weary mourner. There, as echoes of the explosion trailed away, a slender, swarthy figure dressed in workman's coveralls and a black watch cap spoke softly into a walkie-talkie. Opposite and below him, two men, similarly dressed, emerged from a slight ravine forty feet to the right of the shattered vehicles. Three more rose from the gully of the creek across the roadway.

Three of the men carried Kalashnikov AK-47 rifles, the assault weapon of revolutionaries around the world. Two others were armed with Czech-made Skorpion VZ-61 machine pistols. The Skorpion, a favored terrorist weapon, could fire 840 rounds per minute.

The five men briskly fanned out and took up positions ten feet from the twisted vehicles. They opened fire, maintaining the fusillade for twenty seconds, each of them pausing only to change his magazine. The two men on the right fired into the security chief's side of the limousine, dispatching the dying security man and the driver. Natalie, screaming, her remaining hand clawing futilely at the window, was silenced in an instant. The three men on the left focused on the rear of the security car. The agents in back, desperately trying to free their pistols, kicked furiously at the jammed rear door. The terrorists poured thirty to forty rounds into each of them.

When every magazine was spent, the assassins swiftly retreated. The last to leave paused momentarily to take a one-pound M-26 fragmentation from his belt. He armed the grenade and carefully tossed it into the yawning front of the security car.

As he started across the parkway to join his colleagues, an elderly woman in an ancient Chevrolet rounded the curve of the highway and slowed, aghast, as her headlights picked out the carnage. The terrorist dropped to one knee, pulled a Makarov pistol from his coveralls, and fired three rapid shots over the top of her car. In panic, she slammed the accelerator and careened wildly down the parkway. Immediately the security car exploded.

Two of the terrorists stopped about thirty yards up the hill across the parkway from the cemetery. They crouched and pointed a bazookalike weapon at the shell of the limousine. The RPG-7 portable rocket launcher fired a warhead powerful enough to penetrate twelve inches of armor at three hundred yards.

The last human sound in the night was the high, thin wail of Woodrow Wilson Harrold III. Then the rocket launcher roared, and the remains of the Secretary of State's limousine and its occupants rose fifteen feet into the air and disintegrated.

Each of the terrorists ritually kissed his weapon and discarded it, without fingerprints and without serial numbers. The three men on the creek side of the parkway clambered quickly up the cemetery hill and joined their leader at the marble gazebo. Two at a time, they disappeared into the night. The two others scrambled up the opposite hill, separated, and were gone.

From the time of the initial explosion to the launching of the rocket grenade, one minute and fifty-two seconds had elapsed.

At approximately fifteen minutes after midnight, the Secretary of State said, "Good night, Mr. President," put down the secure phone, and turned to the three other men in the room. "Thanks for the usual overtime—and for the usual fine work," he said. The men chatted desultorily as they gathered up their papers, ending their long day.

Down the hall, the bells of an Associated Press ticker began the relentless clamor that signaled a bulletin. Peter Hammerschmidt, the Secretary's chief of staff, got up from his desk and went to the machine. His eyes widened in horror. He reached for the paper clacking bulletlike out of the ticker. His hand trembled. "Oh, my God," he said, over and over. "Oh my God."

Saturday, March 21

2   Ordinarily, Cyril Metrinko would not have been sitting in his fifth-story office at 2 Dzerzhinsky Square on a Saturday afternoon. Even KGB colonels need relief from their particular brand of work, and Metrinko, who scorned practically every material acquisition as a sign of capitalist decadence, did permit himself the luxury of weekends at his dacha about twenty-five miles north of Moscow. But today was different. Pleasure could wait until next week. Metrinko knew that today he would receive a message of importance both to him and to the Soviet Union.

He peered out between the dusty slats of the venetian blinds. Snow was starting to fill the gray sky. On the street below men and women in fur hats and bulky coats dipped their heads against the gathering wind.

Metrinko turned away from the room's single narrow window. His office, like the scuffed top of his desk, was barren, a reflection of the personality Metrinko showed to the world. The office was at the back corner of the dun-colored building that had long been the dreaded nerve-center of Soviet intelligence, espionage, and covert operations. Now it had been supplanted by a modern, capitalist-style steel and glass edifice on the outskirts of Moscow. The long, low lines of the KGB's new headquarters were, in fact, inspired by the design of the Americans' Central Intelligence Agency building outside Washington.

Metrinko grimaced at the thought. *We are becoming more like them every day*, he said to himself. He had demanded, successfully, to have counterintelligence remain at 2 Dzerzhinsky Square, a place with memories, with revolutionary principles, with still-active interrogation facilities in the basement. No blood would be spilled in the new building.

A knock on the door ended Metrinko's reverie. "Enter," he said.

The door was opened by Dmitri Natashin, a bright young captain assigned as a military aide to the office of President Leonid Drachinsky. He stood stiffly until Metrinko motioned him to a straight-backed wooden chair in front of the desk.

"I have a message from Washington, Colonel Metrinko."

"To be delivered personally and orally, I assume, Captain Natashin." He sensed Natashin's uneasiness. "Don't worry. My men swept the office just this morning. No one is listening. You may proceed."

"The attack occurred several hours ago. The family of the American Secretary of State was killed. Foreign Minister Suvarov sent an urgent message from our Embassy to President Drachinsky. He said the attack was quite . . . bloody."

"And the Secretary of State?" Metrinko asked. He offered Natashin a cigarette and took one himself. Natashin noticed that the first two fingers of Metrinko's right hand were stained a deep amber.

"Secretary of State Harrold was not harmed, Colonel. He was not with his family in the automobile at the time of the attack."

Metrinko jumped to his feet and slammed his fist on the top of his desk. Those incompetent bastards."

"Colonel," Natashin said cautiously, as if addressing a dangerous animal. "Colonel, is it not possible that fate has been of service?"

Metrinko stared at him. "What do you mean?"

"Is it not possible, Colonel, that we have gone too far this time? While our own Foreign Minister is visiting the United States? There will be implications, consequences, and—"

Metrinko cut him off. "Implications? Consequences? Very unlikely, Captain. The Americans will conclude that we would never jeopardize the peace mission of our *good* Foreign Minister. No, Aleksandr Suvarov might be embarrassed for a very short time, but this will not be a fatal wound to our prince of peace." Metrinko's laugh was without mirth.

"But, Colonel," Natashin persisted in his most diplomatic manner, "we have never before authorized a terrorist attack on American officials in their own country."

"Is it the act or the geography that troubles your moral sensibilities, Dmitri?"

Natashin could not answer Metrinko or meet his eyes. Metrinko, Natashin thought, was an unpleasant-looking man. Not ugly, not disfigured by scars or any such obvious flaws. It was the ophidian narrowness of his head, the deep-set pale-green eyes that seemed to have no lids.

"Well, Dmitri? Would you have only soft academicians at Patrice Lumumba University? Would you want revolution taught and not practiced?"

On the wall behind Metrinko, next to an old black-and-white photograph of Lenin, was a large map of the Soviet Union. "You are interested in geography, Captain? Here is geography." Metrinko's finger darted across the map, stabbing at the places where the university students were sent for terrorist training: "Batum on the Black Sea. Odessa. Baku. Tashkent. Simferopol. The use of explosives, Captain—that is a good course for a revolutionary. How to mine a road, Captain. How to fire a rocket at a moving car. How to kill the people you are sent out to kill."

Metrinko sat down. His face was flushed. "You have no answer to my questions, Captain?"

"This attack was without high authorization, Colonel. If President Drachinsky and members of the Presidium should find out—"

"And who will tell them, Captain?" Metrinko asked, leaning forward. "It is a secret that only a few of us share. All of us have secrets, eh, Dmitri? Even you . . ." He paused, letting the echo of his words hang in the silence. Then: "Secrets are meant to be kept." His voice was savage.

Metrinko rose and walked to the front of his desk, indicating to Natashin that the meeting was at an end. As the captain turned toward the door, Metrinko's arm went around Natashin's tense shoulders in a gesture universally expressive of comfort. The arm felt like a serpent. In that instant Natashin knew that Metrinko would someday destroy him.

"Don't worry, Dmitri. No one will ever find out. No one." Metrinko's lips were smiling, but his face remained as cold as a winter's dawn.

Saturday, March 21

3 In the large, empty house on Foxhall Road, Secretary of State Woodrow Wilson Harrold sat in his darkened study. Here, at nearly ten o'clock in the morning, it was still like night, as if time had stopped at 11:47 P.M. on Friday. The drapes were drawn, and no splash of daylight fell on the dark-blue carpet.

As soon as Peter Hammerschmidt had told him what had happened, Harrold had wanted to go home, to be home, to be in the place where they had been. Gently, Peter had told him, had filtered the details the white-faced Secret Service man relayed to him. *Such a fine man, Peter.* "I . . . I cannot explain it, sir," he had said, as if somewhere Peter, the rational man, could have found an explanation for this horror, this awful horror.

Peter had told him he could not go home right away. The security men kept him in the office until they had checked his house, surrounded it with agents, closed off the street with police barricades. Then they had brought him home. If that was what it could be called now. So quiet, so full of the hushed movement of people assigned to guard his life and help him bury his dead. He had sat here ever since.

The President had come a little after three o'clock in the morning, against the wishes of the Secret Service. He had stayed until dawn. President Arthur Christiansen had wept. Somehow, they had managed to talk, not only as friends sharing grief but also as Commander in Chief and his Secretary of State discussing a crime against their nation. For there was more than private mourning to think about.

Harrold looked across the study at the television console. President Christiansen would be on at noon, speaking from the Oval Office, telling the nation that the assassins would be caught and punished. He would not tell them what he had told Woodrow Harrold: The Commander in Chief had ordered units from the elite Delta Force on alert. The Israeli Mossad had been contacted for assistance in identifying the nationalities of the terrorists. Libya, Iraq, and South Yemen were high on the list of suspects.

Harrold tried to force himself to think like a Secretary of State, but private thoughts intruded. He knew it would always haunt him that he had been the target and others had been hit. Alicia. Little Woodie. Natalie. And those anonymous brave men. He did not even know all their names. The President had ordered the Air Force to fly Woodrow Jr. home from Belgrade. He would soon have his son to share his grief. But no one could share his guilt.

Guilt was a rare feeling for Woodrow Wilson Harrold, who had a reputation for honesty and candor. He was tall and slender, straight as a pine tree. His large, rawboned hands belonged more to a farmer than a statesman, and in fact he had grown up on a farm in Vermont. But ever since his graduation from Yale and the Fletcher School of Diplomacy, he had spent his life trying to cultivate peace in the rocky soil of a dangerous and volatile world.

The Secretary was a reticent man whose language, like his mind, was direct, uncomplicated by the superfluous. *Reserve* was a word always associated with his name. No one could recall seeing him lose his temper, even when outrageously provoked at a congressional hearing.

Now that reserve was broken, and he wept quietly in his study. He had demanded to know every detail of the attack, and his mind kept playing those details over and over. He was consumed with guilt for not having been in that car to die with Alicia and Woodie and Natalie.

But an even deeper guilt gnawed at his mind: He was responsible for the deaths. He was the one who had persuaded a reluctant President Christiansen that Foreign Minister Suvarov's visit could reduce tension, thaw the cold war, avoid the hot one. Now it was all worse than before. Harrold could not believe that the Foreign Minister was directly responsible for the attack, but he suspected that more than coincidence was at work. He had invited Suvarov to Washington. And with Suvarov had come murder.

A soft knock on the study door roused Harrold from his thoughts.

"Yes?" he said, startled by the cracked sound of his own voice.

"Senator Chandler, sir."

"Send him in, Peter," Harrold said, rising from the leather chair, composing himself. He pulled back the drapes to a gray day and switched on a lamp.

Sometimes, through the mysterious chemistry of power, an official Washington acquaintanceship becomes a real friendship. That had happened with Woodrow Harrold and Senator Thomas Bowen Chandler of Connecticut. In a city of many official friendships, theirs was a deep one, forged from trust. Of all the people who had called in the last few hours to offer condolences, Harrold had told Peter he wanted to see only two: President Christiansen and Senator Chandler.

Harrold and Chandler had first met in 1977, at a conference on terrorism held in Bonn following the assassination of West German industrialist Hanns-Martin Schleyer by the German Red Army Faction, an offshoot of the Baader-Meinhof Gang. Harrold was then U.S. ambassador to West Germany; Chandler was the only United States senator invited to address the conference.

Led by Henry Kissinger, David Rockefeller, and Helmut Schmidt, the conference members had urged stringent security measures to curb terrorism. Harrold had been impressed by Chandler's courage in urging that civil rights not fall victim to terrorism as well. The safest position to take at that conference would have been a get-tougher stance, but that was not Chandler's way. Although his impassioned speech had bordered on the naïve at times, the young senator had said something his elders had apparently forgotten: "Democracy must be strong enough to use law, not guns, against the men with the guns."

In that hotel surrounded by armored personnel carriers and police with submachine guns, Woodrow Harrold and Tom Chandler had talked about terrorism, about democratic values. Harrold had come away from their conversations convinced of three things: Chandler was sincere, he was bright, and he was ambitious enough to become a presidential candidate.

The conversations continued down the years, and gradually the relationship of mentor and protégé evolved into a warm friendship of equals.

They talked now of grief and of a need not for revenge but for purpose.

"I thought about that conference, Tom," Harrold said. "It has already come here, as you warned it might. The siege mentality. I don't want Alicia to have died for that—for this beautiful city of hers to become a garrison. You may have something to say about keeping that from happening."

"The Committee?" Chandler asked. His voice was edgy.

"Yes," Harrold said. "I understand there will be a special session on Monday. I hope, Tom, that you will be the voice of reason there, as you were in Bonn."

"Reason? How can you speak of reason, Woodrow?"

"Because it is all I—we—can cling to now. We have to hold the line of reason against terror. That is much harder to do than . . . than what they do."

Harrold asked a few questions to bring himself up to date on the Senate Select Committee on Intelligence. The part of his public mind that could still function was probing as it had so many times in the past, trying to build a bridge between what the executive branch of government wanted to do and what the legislative branch was willing to let the executive branch do.

Chandler fell easily into the briefing role. Talk about the Committee could, at least for a few moments, turn Harrold's mind away from his loss. And Chandler understood why Harrold was asking him about the Committee's interest in terrorism. After the conference in Bonn, Chandler had become a student of terrorism. He knew its weapons, its deeds, its history. He had studied the incident files, from the first Palestinian airliner hijackings in 1968 through the kidnappings and killings of diplomats in the 1970s and into the 1980s, when he saw beyond doubt that the Soviet Union was fostering a rapidly expanding terrorist network. Harrold knew that Chandler, in his position as a member of the Committee, had been trying to get intelligence agencies more deeply involved in the gathering of information about terrorists and their Soviet connections. And so, Chandler realized, Woodrow was turning to him not only as a trusted friend but as a knowledgeable one.

Chandler's intense interest in terrorism, and his concentration on the workings of the Intelligence Committee, had meant that he tended to give less than equal time to his other committee assignments, which ruffled some feathers. And he had to be careful not to step on senatorial toes. The Judiciary Committee, for instance, had a subcommittee on terrorism. Somehow, too, he had to serve his Connecticut constituents and find time to run for reelection. Now there was talk that he was a potential presidential candidate, and he was not doing anything to discourage that talk.

The Secretary had finished his questions. He leaned back in his chair and said, "Tom, I'm not going to be making much foreign policy for a good long while. And then, depending on how I feel, I'll probably be heading back to the university, or maybe into law practice. In the meantime"—the Secretary seemed to be trying to reassure himself as much as Chandler—"Emerson Goldstein has been Undersecretary long enough to take over the reins and continue on with what I've tried to do. And Peter Hammerschmidt, my right hand. He'll be there to be Em's right hand.

"Tom, if Alicia's . . . if what happened to my family"—his voice broke slightly—" if this . . . *horror* can bring about any good at all, you may be the man to see that it does. I'm convinced that what happened to my family, and what was supposed to happen to me, was not a random act. These terrorist acts we are seeing— bombings, killings—seem to be getting more . . . systematic. I guess that's what I'm trying to say. It's what Peter, God bless him, calls 'an explanation.'

"You may have a unique opportunity to prevent what happened to my family from happening to other public officials and their families. You and the Intelligence Committee have the resources to get to the bottom of this thing, to find out what, or who, is causing all this mayhem. In fact, you may be better able to do it than all the police forces and all the bureaucracies in the intelligence services.

"*Explanation*, Tom. There must be a horrible explanation."

Monday, March 23

4 On Saturday and Sunday the media discovered real, bloody terrorism on the streets of Washington. As an issue, terrorism was nothing new in Washington, but the reality of it had been relatively distant. Now it was *here*. The city awoke to *The Washington Post*'s black headlines on Saturday morning, watched the President's speech at noon, and tuned in to television network specials on Saturday and Sunday evenings.

Some senators and congressmen had been located over the weekend—a favorite TV clip showed a grim-faced Senator Chandler waving away microphones outside Secretary Harrold's heavily guarded home. But it was not until Monday that the focus shifted to Congress.

On Monday morning, Capitol Hill resembled an ant colony that had just been kicked open. Network correspondents rushed to interview scurrying congressmen and senators, who raged briefly before the cameras and then hurried on. Beyond the cameras, committee chairmen at hastily convened meetings set up hearings and announced that the intelligence and security agencies would be asked to explain how such an atrocity could have been committed on the streets of the nation's capital.

It all seemed so chaotic—and yet so predictable. The urgency, the posturing, the rush, the rage—it was always the same in the wake of a tragedy. Legislators too small, too timid, too unimaginative to call for action before calamity struck were inspired to do so after the fact. If progress was ever made, it marched on the backs of the buried.

Soon the newspaper reporters and the network camera crews realized that there was a focal point for Capitol Hill's reaction: a little-used and little-known room on the fourth floor of the Capitol building, the room used by the Senate Select Committee on Intelligence. Taken over from the abolished Joint Committee on Atomic Energy, the room had been uniquely prepared for the highly classified military aspects of the atomic energy program—soundproofed, de-bugged, and periodically "swept" by special instruments to prevent technical interception of top-secret committee briefings and deliberations. It was the only place in the Capitol completely secure against the spider's web of electronic devices spun throughout Washington. The room's low false ceiling and its dim, indirect fluorescent lights gave it an almost sepulchral air. Against a curving marble backdrop at the far end, committee members sat behind their traditional horseshoe-shape table, minority to the left, majority to the right, descending by seniority. The witness stand was an ordinary walnut table directly facing the committee members. The congressional reporter, who had special clearance to record and transcribe committee proceedings, was seated at the end of the witness table, almost closing the horseshoe.

The man sitting at the witness table today was a frequent visitor to the room. He was E. W. Trevor, the Director of Central Intelligence. He was buttressed on both sides of the witness table by CIA employees who could easily have been mistaken for middle-aged, slightly paunchy small-town accountants. Behind him sat more staff, clutching black three-ring notebooks filled with documents stamped TOP SECRET in large red block letters. Trevor had been summoned once again to testify before the Senate Select Committee on Intelligence. He was not happy about it. In truth, he resented the very existence of the Committee, which had been established in 1974 to oversee the activities of the CIA.

Trevor was the man responsible for gathering and guarding secrets vital to America's security. He trusted few people in the world with those secrets, and members of Congress were most assuredly not among the few. In his opinion they were voluble impostors, preening political narcissists, generally uninformed on national security matters and incapable of keeping confidential information confidential. While the law required him to report to members of the House and Senate Intelligence Oversight Committees, he never went beyond his two rules for dealing with legislators: If they didn't ask the right question, they wouldn't get the right answer. And if they asked the right question, they would get only half the right answer.

Today, he was even more resentful than usual. The Harrold assassinations had come as a complete surprise. No advance warnings, not even a vague intelligence report, had reached CIA headquarters in Langley, Virginia. He knew that he and the Agency would come under withering attack both here and later in public. The senators would demand answers that he simply did not have.

The chairman of the Intelligence Committee, Charles Walcott, would understand. He was a strong conservative from Oklahoma and, in Trevor's words, a "good soldier." Gordon Nicholson of California would be sympathetic. But Trevor knew that Thomas Chandler of Connecticut, an adversary in many past encounters, would be looking for a chance to nail the Agency once again. Trevor was also aware of Chandler's special relationship with Harrold. This particular act of terrorism had a personal touch, which would give Chandler another motive for calling the Agency to account.

Trevor was disturbed by his inability to understand Chandler or his motives. Trevor believed that motives—especially those of any politician in any country—could be discovered and, when and if necessary, used for the benefit of the Agency. Trevor suspected that Chandler's interest in terrorism was primarily expedient, his use of an issue to further his own, evidently presidential, ambitions. But, Trevor knew, there was more to Chandler than naked ambition.

Looking around at the senators assembled before him, Trevor nodded and smiled automatically, his face doing public duty while his mind squirreled on in private. He was quickly reviewing what he knew about Chandler: The senator from Connecticut was too idealistic, too naïve to suit Trevor. He was always expounding on the need to safeguard the privacy and liberties of the American people. He worked relentlessly to prevent the Agency's carrying out its covert activities, especially those aimed at destabilizing unfriendly regimes. He insisted that Trevor be more forthcoming in his reports to the Committee, and when Trevor refused, Chandler would continue to press for information that Trevor felt he had no right to. Chandler seemed to relish playing prosecutor with him, waiting for Trevor to trip over a misstatement and then pouncing, to send him sprawling in retreat. Sometimes Trevor wondered whose side Chandler was on.

Senator Walcott opened the session, and Trevor began his testimony with a general statement on the nature and extent of terrorist activities in recent months.

"Mr. Chairman," he said, "the Agency has devoted its limited resources in large part to an intensive investigation of the rash of random and reckless terrorist acts of the last two months. Our allies have been entirely cooperative. But no discernible pattern has emerged. The Libyans may have had a hand in the explosion in Cairo. We see the signature of the PLO on several of the bombings in Saudi Arabia. . . ."

Trevor continued to skip through his neatly typed and tightly censored statement. "We certainly are disturbed and concerned about the increased level of violence, which, whatever its origin, appears to be carefully planned and well-financed. . . ."

Before he had finished reading the statement, he was interrupted: "Excuse me, Mr. Chairman," Senator Chandler said, "but I don't need a briefing on what terrorists are doing in Cairo and Riyadh. I want to know what the Agency can tell us about Friday's attack on the Harrold family. Who were the assassins? How many were there? Did we have any advance knowledge that an attempt to murder Secretary Harrold was being planned? If not, why not? With all due respect, Mr. Trevor, I can get more information by reading *The Washington Post*. In fact, the *Post* seems to have greater access to the Agency's activities than the members of this Committee do."

"Well now, hold on just a moment, Senator," said the chairman. Charles Walcott spoke in a cultivated western drawl. "The Director said he was simply giving an overview of the problem and would be happy to respond to specific areas of concern at the conclusion of his presentation." Walcott betrayed not the slightest emotion. Nor was he going to yield to a temptation to lecture Chandler, knowing from experience that a reprimand would only provoke a further, more vigorous response. He was about to urge Trevor to continue when Gordon Nicholson, the junior senator from California, spoke up, his voice steely with indignation.

"Mr. Chairman, the Senator from Connecticut knows that there is an established order for questioning witnesses. Yet he insists on interrupting the proceedings, perhaps to score some illusory point with his colleagues—or perhaps with the Director? There are no members of the press here." Nicholson craned his neck down the line of Committee members to watch his barb sink in.

Walcott pounded his gavel. "Senator Nicholson," he said sharply, "you are not contributing to the regular order of this Committee either. The Chair has already stated that the Director should be allowed to complete his statement. There will be ample time for questions later."

Trevor was surprised at Chandler's outburst. He was usually more subtle, more calculating. This agitation was most interesting. Maybe the pressure of presidential politics was starting to get to Chandler. Worth checking out.

Trevor filed his speculations in the political compartment of his mind and watched the clash between Chandler and Nicholson with detached amusement. His face remained sober, but behind his horn-rimmed glasses appeared the faintest trace of a twinkle. *Thank God*, he thought, *that Nicholson is here to clip Chandler's wings*.

Senator Walcott turned to Trevor: "Mr. Director, you may proceed."

"Thank you, Mr. Chairman," Trevor replied quietly. "I really had just about completed my opening statement. In the interest of time, I'll ask that the full text of my statement be included in the record, and I'll try to answer any questions the Committee may have at this time."

"Without objection, your statement will appear in the record in full." Walcott tapped his gavel. "Now, I have a number of questions that I want to ask, but I'll defer them for the time being, since there seems to be such an urgency on the part of some members to get more details from you. The Chair now recognizes the Senator from Connecticut."

Elaine Dunham, a Committee staff member, was making her way around the table, distributing copies of Trevor's statement. As Walcott began to speak, she handed one to Tom Chandler, who turned to thank her. He noticed Trevor's glance flicker from Chandler's face to Elaine's. Chandler was surprised. It was only natural for any man to appreciate Elaine's dark beauty, but he found it hard to grant Trevor any human impulse. In the same moment, Chandler realized that he had not taken much notice of her himself. She had been a member of the staff for eight months now, but he had met her only a few times at hearings and briefings.

With a slight flourish, Chandler put Trevor's statement aside and beckoned Elaine back. "Let's put some more on his plate," he whispered. He asked her for the file on the head of the United Nations World Health Organization, who had been beaten to death early one morning in front of his apartment building. The New York police had treated it as a routine mugging. "Elaine," Chandler went on, "I think the file's got something on his deputy who was killed a week later in Barcelona. Car bombing. It could have been connected. The *Times* thought so. Anyway, I think we should ask the Director about it, then confront him with the Rangoon bombing. It's been a year and they still haven't—"

Walcott tapped his gavel again. "The Chair recognizes the Senator from Connecticut—that is, if the Senator is still interested in questioning the Director?" His tone made no secret of his impatience.

"Ah, thank you, Mr. Chairman," Chandler began, embarrassed to have been caught off guard. He was third in seniority and ordinarily would not have been called upon for at least thirty minutes.

Turning to Trevor, Chandler said, "Mr. Director, I don't have much in the way of questions—and that's because you don't appear to have much in the way of answers. But I do have a few observations to make. Frankly, I'm disappointed with your testimony. It doesn't tell us anything we don't already know. In fact, it tells us *less* than we know." His voice was rising. "I wonder how long we can continue to maintain the charade that we have a professional intelligence community in this country. At what point will it be possible for the members of this Committee, of the Senate itself, to be able to tell our constituents, the American people, that events are not completely out of control?"

Trevor registered no emotion, but his experienced staff people noted a dark-red flush creeping up the back of his neck.

"Well, Senator Chandler, I can certainly appreciate your frustration," Trevor offered.

"I'm not looking for sympathy, Mr. Director. I'd prefer to have some answers."

"We would like those answers, too, Senator. After all, we have the same goal in mind—the protection of the American people. But we have some problems. We're short on manpower. Our budget has been restricted for several years. And, of course, as you know, the Agency's covert authority has been sharply restricted."

Trevor looked directly at Chandler as he spoke. He could have added that Chandler was one of those who consistently voted to curtail the Agency's authority. But he was too skilled a witness to challenge a senator directly. Such conduct would be unprofessional; whatever moment of personal triumph he might enjoy in pointing out the shallowness of Chandler's moral outrage, Trevor knew the price would be too high. Committees expect total equanimity, if not submissiveness, from their witnesses, even in the face of unfair provocation. No, he would not succeed in embarrassing Chandler. On the contrary, he might even spur the other senators to support their colleague.

If Chandler detected an accusation in the Director's use of the phrase *as you know,* he did not show it. Instead, he almost contemptuously brushed aside the Director's explanation.

"Come now, Mr. Director. Don't try to hang your failures on Congress. The Agency's reporting requirements and restrictions have been practically removed. You don't have an absolute license to kill—but damn near it! What contingency plans do you have to counter terrorist activities?"

"Domestic terrorism is in the FBI's jurisdiction, not the Agency's, Senator Chandler."

Tom Chandler was not about to relent. He looked at Trevor now with open contempt. "Are you telling me that the ghost of J. Edgar Hoover still hovers over Langley? That you don't compare notes with the counterintelligence people downtown? Is that what you're telling us?" Chandler slammed a pad of yellow paper on the hard surface of the committee table. "Should we tell the press that DCI said it's not his problem anymore—once the terrorists enter the United States?"

Before Trevor could respond, a long loud buzz emanating from a clock over the doorway pierced the tense atmosphere. It was the signal that a roll-call vote had just begun. The senators had fifteen minutes to get to the Senate Chamber to cast their votes.

Walcott snatched at the opportunity to break into the confrontation between Trevor and Chandler. "Gentlemen, what is the pleasure of the Committee? We can recess now and then come back to continue the questioning of the Director." He didn't wait for the members to respond. "Why don't we do that and come right back? The Director's a busy man, but I'm sure he's willing to stay a bit longer." Walcott pounded his gavel, signifying that a decision had been reached, however undemocratically.

"I have to meet with the President at noon," Trevor said quickly. "But I'll be happy to come back either tomorrow morning or later in the week if the Committee desires."

Chandler sighed. "Mr. Chairman," he said, "I'd like very much to pursue this matter. But I have to chair meetings tomorrow morning on another committee. Why don't we have the Director back later in the week?"

"All right, gentlemen. The Chair is going to declare this meeting adjourned until further word. I'll see to it that each of your offices is notified as to when we will reconvene. This meeting is now adjourned." Walcott pounded his gavel hard enough to break its stem.

Chandler couldn't tell whether the chairman was angry or not, but it didn't much matter. Chandler was fed up with the game that was being played and replayed. He wanted some answers, even if it made Walcott blow like one of his Oklahoma oil wells.

Trevor left the hearing room, dismissed the elevator as a device for the infirm, and walked briskly down the three flights of stairs he had run up an hour earlier. Brushing through the swarm of reporters, ignoring the outstretched microphones, he got into his waiting limousine and directed the driver to 1600 Pennsylvania Avenue.

Trevor took from his inside coat pocket a single sheet of paper stamped TOP SECRET. The National Security Agency's electronic eavesdroppers had intercepted and deciphered a cable sent from the Soviet Embassy in Havana to the Soviet Embassy in Washington. It read: EAGLE AGAINST THE MOON. Trevor did not know what the message meant, but he was certain it was connected with the attack on the Harrold family.

He was alarmed about the assassination. There had been vague reports that radical groups now in the United States might initiate terrorist attacks against high-ranking American officials. But the information was just the sort of thing that had preceded the bombing of the Marine compound in Beirut—nothing hard, nothing specific, nothing that would warrant extraordinary security for the hundreds of possible targets. Over the weekend he had received some important leads on at least one of the terrorists. Trevor was not about to share that information with the Intelligence Committee if he could possibly avoid it. He would not put it past a politician to leak top secrets for the sake of good press relations.

As the limousine rolled smoothly down Constitution Avenue toward the White House, Trevor sorted through his limited knowledge of the attacks, deciding how much of it could be entrusted to President Christiansen and the National Security Council. "There are a lot of leaks in this town, and they're not all coming from Capitol Hill, not by a damn sight," he muttered.

5 As he wound his way down from the hearing room, Tom Chandler could not shake the acrid aftertaste of Trevor's antiseptic testimony. He pushed open the center doors of the quietly elegant Chamber of the United States Senate, where he must vote for a bill that proclaimed this day—this day after Friday's carnage—Seal Day. He was bitterly angry, and he knew that his colleagues shared his anger. Seal Day.

In front of the tiered marble dais that curved around the elevated chair of the President of the Senate, a few senators were gathered. It was a solemn group, almost sullen.

If anyone could lighten Chandler's venomous mood, it would be his friend Doug Bender, and Tom headed in his direction. The junior senator from Alabama was a spellbinding orator, gifted with an arm-waving, hand-clapping, storytelling style that was an integral part of his southern heritage. But his effectiveness as a senator derived less from his oratorical skill than from his humor. He would come to the Senate every day with at least one new story that might have been heard at a backwoods moonshine still or in a sailors' tavern. Bender would tell it again and again during the course of the day, embellishing it each time, leaving each new audience laughing. And no one laughed harder at Doug Bender's jokes than Doug Bender.

But he wasn't laughing today. Chandler walked by in silence, lightly squeezing Doug's shoulder as he passed in a gesture of friendship.

Chandler cast his vote for Seal Day, mentally cursing the necessity of leaving the Intelligence Committee hearing in order to vote on something so trivial. "What a wonderful sense of priorities we have in the world's greatest deliberative body," he said to the driver of the subway car that carried him back to his office in the new Hart Senate Office Building. The driver cast him an uncertain smile.

A family from Connecticut was waiting in the reception room of his third-floor office suite. Chandler told them that everything that could be done about the terrorist attack was being done. He promised to vote for a reduction in nuclear arms. And he posed for photographs with their two young sons, sitting and grinning sheepishly behind his large oak desk.

Bob Tilley, Chandler's press secretary, insisted that he return three calls from reporters inquiring about the President's cut in the shipbuilding program and what it would mean for Electric Boat in Connecticut. He signed nineteen letters that needed his personal signature rather than the poor imitation scratched out by mechanical autopen, which disposed of more than two thousand letters weekly. He skimmed the draft of a speech he was scheduled to deliver in the Senate the following day. It needed some work.

Shortly after noon, Chandler told his secretary, Margie, that for the next hour he would be lunching in the Senate Dining Room.

He slipped out of the private entrance to his office and into a hallway crowded with staffers heading for lunch and tourists who
seemed bewildered by all the important-looking people engaged in
important-sounding conversation.

When Chandler walked down the corridor, he always drew attention. His height set him literally above the average man. The
graying temples of his dark hair gave him a certain distinction. He
was not a handsome man. His forehead was too prominent, his
nose a bit too long and not quite straight. But his bearing, the way
he walked, identified him as a man in charge. Sometimes the
thought amused him: If only they knew how little in charge he—or
any of the other Washington power players—really was.

The system conferred only the trappings, the illusion of power.
Ironically, the Founding Fathers in their effort to protect the
American people from the dangers of concentrated power had created a system of checks and balances that, in this complex, fast-
moving age, virtually guaranteed paralysis. The House and Senate
checked each other's legislative deliberations and excesses. Together, the two houses of Congress checked the President's executive actions. And the Supreme Court checked both the
President and the Congress. It was a perfect triangle, Euclidean in
symmetry and balance. There could be no rash action, no rush to
judgment, no tyranny of legislative majority, no uncontrolled chief
executive. The difficulty for America in the late twentieth century
was that the diffusion of power that had served it so well in the past
had now cast it adrift.

Chandler reached the end of the corridor and turned left,
toward a bank of elevators marked SENATORS ONLY, a sign that
could be seen everywhere on the west side of the Capitol. Elevators. Subway cars. Parking spaces. Dining rooms. The signs not
only facilitated the movement of senators presumably burdened
with heavy responsibilities; they served also to remind visitors and
employees of a caste system unashamedly promoted and vigorously
protected.

While visitors were usually excited to see a VIP recognizable
from television appearances, they tended also to resent having to
make way for an approaching senator. When Chandler had first
come to the Senate, he had been offended by such flagrant displays
of privilege. He complained about them publicly, expressing his
outrage at the squandering of taxpayers' money. What he gained in

the admiration of his constituents, he lost in the resentment of his colleagues. And though, in the wake of harsh editorials and a barrage of mail from angry citizens, some of the perquisites were pruned away, slowly, almost unnoticeably, they took root and spread again.

Now, eleven years later, Chandler had grown indifferent to the favored status he enjoyed. He rationalized that he was preoccupied with more important issues—the threat of nuclear war, the reformation of the tax code, protection of the environment against toxic wastes. . . . But his constituents noticed the difference, and many of them did not like it.

Senator Thomas Chandler had reached a point in his political career where he needed to do more than he was now doing. He knew that this need had put him on a path marked PRESIDENTIAL AMBITIONS. And in his heart he knew he wanted to stay on this new path, wherever it led.

Chandler stepped into the subway's front car, which was always reserved for senators. Thirty seconds later he was in the Capitol. He got off the elevator at the second floor, turned right and then left, down a corridor at the end of which were the dining rooms. The one on the right was for senators entertaining guests; the one on the left was private—for club members only.

Most days, Chandler would lunch alone at a table in the dining room reserved for senators and their guests. While he ate, he read staff memoranda or the morning papers. Eating in the private room meant he would be socializing with his colleagues.

Today that was exactly what he wanted.

At the long, heavily laden buffet he placed his order, then walked to one of the tables.

Gordon Nicholson was sitting near the window that looked out onto the East Wing steps of the Capitol. His eyebrows rose. "Well, to what do we owe this special treat?" he asked, his voice heavy with sarcasm. "His Highness has deigned to come and break bread with the commoners?"

"Hi, Gordon. Yep. Just thought I'd come slummin' today." Chandler's smile was blindingly sincere. He was tempted to address Nicholson by his last name, but decided it would annoy Nicholson more to presume a friendly intimacy where none in fact existed. Chandler and Nicholson differed considerably in political matters, but in congressional friendships, such differences were relatively unimportant. Chandler disliked Nicholson because Gordon Nicholson was a hater, a politician who lacked the ability to distinguish between politics and character.

Chandler moved deliberately away from Nicholson and slipped into a chair beside Charles Walcott. The two men had little in common philosophically, and yet for years Walcott had treated Tom almost as a younger brother. Chandler could not share Walcott's hidebound conservatism, but he profoundly respected the older man's intellectual honesty. Theirs was a relationship that confounded most members of the Senate. "Mind if I join you, Mr. Chairman?"

"Come on in. The water's fine," Walcott replied. "Better than the food, I might add. Man, stick with the steak. It's the one thing they haven't discovered how to screw up in the kitchen."

"You're being transparent again, Charlie. You've got to stop promoting Oklahoma beef. It gives people cancer of the rectum."

"Spoken like a damn Yankee, Chandler. But I've always known you were an expert when it came to assholes."

Both men laughed and then, as if by inner signal, stopped. This was no day for bantering.

To those who did not know him, Charles Walcott looked like a stern man. He could be stern, as Chandler well knew. Tall and lanky, Walcott sat so straight that he seemed always to be at attention. He also seemed always quietly in command. Chandler had once asked him about his habitual frown. "Looking mean," Walcott had said, "is half the battle."

A waiter brought Chandler a bowl of minestrone.

"You were pretty tough on the Director this morning, Tom," Walcott said softly, but without a frown.

"I know. I was out of line. But damn it, Charlie, we get the same crap every time. They've got their testimony down to a goddam science. Chew up twenty minutes with an opening statement that we can read in five. Then give long, convoluted answers to questions we ask, consuming our ten-minute allotment. We usually get one shot at them and either the bell rings for a vote or we're off to another committee hearing. They know that time is always on their side. And the Director—he's the best. Or should I say the worst?"

"That's all true enough, Tom. But you know you're never going to pry anything out of him by coming at him head-on that way.

You have to get your ducks in line and then hit him from the side, with questions he hasn't anticipated. That's supposed to be your specialty."

"I know. I just couldn't resist this morning. We play so many games in this place—I just wanted to stop being clever and coy and give him a verbal punch in the nose."

"Didn't help. You didn't get any answers and you looked bad in the process."

Chandler took no offense. In fact, he regarded Walcott's candor as a singular mark of redemption in an institution where false flattery was rife. He nodded his head in agreement. "You're right, Charlie. It's just that this thing hit pretty close to home. You know that Woodrow Harrold is one of my closest friends, and Alicia is—was—such a lovely woman. I never knew Natalie very well, but Woodie . . . I'd promised to take him to the zoo next weekend. . . ." Chandler's voice cracked and he sought refuge in his coffee cup. The brew tasted bitter. He winced as he swallowed it, and downed his memories. "What's going to happen when a few more bombs start going off in our streets? Everyone will start calling for action—'let's get tough' and never mind whose freedoms get trampled in the process. Charlie, this country is not prepared for what's coming."

"I don't disagree with you, Tom. But you're going to have to handle it more intelligently than you did this morning. Do you think you can approach this business with your head coming first, not your heart? Because if you can, there's something I want to talk to you about."

Chandler nodded, saying nothing but raising his brows inquiringly.

Walcott's gaze was intent on Chandler's face. Whatever he saw there evidently satisfied him. Leaning back, he pulled a thin gold case from an inside pocket, withdrew a cigarette, and tapped it on the case. He lit the cigarette with a monogrammed lighter and slowly exhaled the smoke. At last he spoke. "This morning, after the meeting broke up, I gave some thought to creating a special task force to investigate the subject of terrorism.

"I'm going to recommend that you serve as chairman of the task force."

Chandler's face expressed his astonishment, and his gratitude. "Charlie, I really appreciate it. I really do. Thank you."

"Don't be *too* thankful," Walcott said. "I assure you it's not a gesture of charity. I'm going to need your help with some of your friends when the vote is taken on that new laser system we've been working on. It's far more sophisticated than anything the Russians have, and you know what the press and those so-called moderates of yours are going to say—it's escalating the arms race or it's destabilizing the balance of power."

"I should have known. There's not an ounce of charity in all of Oklahoma," Chandler said lightly. "And by the way, I haven't made up my own mind on the laser system."

"Well, I'm just helping to persuade you." Walcott got up from the table, slapped Chandler on the back, and said, "Happy hunting . . . Mr. Chairman."

Back at his office, Chandler lifted the top of the Mexican humidor on his desk. He picked out a thin, dark-colored Jamaican panatela and unwrapped the protective plastic. He never smoked in public. At forty-eight, he still considered himself a young man, and cigars in the mouths of young men, he thought, made them look pretentious. He lit up and lowered his long frame into the Eames lounge chair that sat in front of the floor-to-ceiling bookcase. The rosewood and leather chair was his favorite, a striking contrast to the lumpishness of standard government-issue furniture. He had added a deep-ruby-toned Oriental rug to the light-blue wall-to-wall carpeting and hung two abstract paintings over his couch. In furnishings as in politics, Chandler favored a blend of the traditional and the contemporary.

His shelves were crammed with books ranging from Shakespeare and Tennyson to biographies of Lord Macaulay, Dag Hammarskjöld, Churchill, Roosevelt, Margaret Thatcher. There were two thick memoirs by Henry Kissinger of his White House years. Next to volumes by and about him, a bust of John F. Kennedy broke the ranks of books on the third shelf. It was a replica of Robert Berks's giant one in the Kennedy Center. Jack Kennedy was a hero to Chandler, not because Tom totally accepted what Kennedy stood for or even because of his qualities of leadership. Kennedy had moved people with his intelligence and wit.

And Kennedy had died, like the Harrolds, a victim of assassination. Chandler's contemplative reverie was over. He stubbed out his cigar and set his mind to the job that lay ahead of him. *Why* did

Trevor have so little information on the assassination of the Harrold family? Terrorism seemed to be eluding the Agency. Now, with the new task force, the subject was being taken up by the Senate. By him.

Chandler found himself inevitably examining the political consequences of running the task force. Investigations of this importance came along seldom in a politician's life. It would mean more staff, more media interviews—national exposure. And if he did a competent job, it just might give him a head start on his Senate colleagues who were already jockeying for inside position in the presidential race that was still several years away.

Through Chandler's mind passed a swift series of names and images: Senator Harry Truman with his war profiteering investigation, Estes Kefauver's crime investigation in the fifties, Richard Nixon and his anti-communist probes, George McGovern's poverty hearings. The Senate had put them all on the presidential path.

Thomas Bowen Chandler was on that path now. In recent months there had been articles about him in newsmagazines and out-of-state papers. Several had suggested it was time for him to start exercising leadership on national issues. "The jury is still out on him," one of the political savants had written. "Either he has failed to measure up to our expectations or our expectations were raised to false heights by his public relations experts. Chandler will have to start moving soon if he intends to occupy the White House."

Chandler had laughed at the reference to his public relations experts. He was his own expert, if that was the word. He sometimes felt more like an amateur who had come late to professionalism. He felt there was still a part of him that was too naïve, perhaps even too patriotic.

Yet, within these past terrible days, two men he respected had shown their respect for him. Woodrow Harrold saying that the Committee might be able to do what no one else in government could do, and now Charlie Walcott. For a moment, Chandler wondered whether Walcott had discussed the task force and its proposed chairman with Harrold. He would probably never know. Washington was a place alive with uncertainties.

As the afternoon wore on, Chandler found it difficult to concentrate on the work in front of him. He signed letters to several members of the President's Cabinet, answered phone calls, reviewed reports and staff memos, but his mind kept drifting elsewhere and a headache was starting to nag behind his eyes. At five o'clock he decided to cancel the rest of his schedule for the day. He needed to be with friends right now. He needed warmth and shared memories and laughter. Arranging for two staff members to go in his place to a cocktail reception he had agreed to attend, Chandler packed his briefcase with files for late-evening study. He placed a call to Doug Bender's office and found that Doug had just left. Another call to Kathy Bender, Doug's wife, won him the hoped-for invitation, and a few minutes later he drove out of the Hart Building in his vintage blue Mercedes sedan, up Pennsylvania Avenue toward the Benders' Georgetown home.

He had known Doug for thirty years and Kathy almost as long. He and Doug had met as classmates at Yale, where Doug's Alabama humor and openness, his talent for making other people happy, his—*yes*, Tom thought, *his gift for life*—had brought a refreshing warmth to the New England climate. Tom and Doug had stood up for each other at their respective weddings, and Tom flew to Fairhope to be godfather to the Benders' firstborn daughter. Doug had gone into politics first, but it was Tom, an old hand of four years' experience, who was able to welcome Doug to the Senate.

Since Tom and Danielle had been divorced three years ago, he had spent too little time with the Benders, though of course he and Doug saw each other almost daily at the Senate. But even there, their offices were in different buildings, they served on different committees. . . . *Damn it, just because Danielle's gone doesn't mean I can't still see my friends. Am I turning into a goddam hermit?*

As Chandler pulled up in front of the Benders' narrow rose-brick town house, Doug was just putting his key in the front door lock. He turned in answer to Tom's call, and a welcoming grin lit his ruddy face. "Hey, stranger," said Doug. "You haven't brightened our doorstep for many a long day."

"Kathy told me you weren't home, and I was hoping to catch my favorite redhead alone."

Kathy kissed them both hello and led the way into the kitchen. "I've got dinner in progress, and I don't want you guys off in the living room while I'm stuck in here wondering what you're talking about. Besides," she added, with a wink at Tom, "I've been starved for a glimpse of your handsome face."

Chandler settled himself on a tall stool and leaned a weary elbow on the butcher-block counter while Doug coped with a recalcitrant ice tray in the freezer. "Just one drink and no more," Chandler said. "I've got a briefcase full of work waiting in the car."

Kathy looked up from the sauce she was stirring. "Aren't you staying for dinner?" She sounded genuinely disappointed. "None of the kids are home and I'm making lasagna. Two kinds of sausage and three kinds of cheese?" she coaxed.

Chandler shook his head regretfully.

"And pineapple *sorbet* for dessert—from scratch! I'm practicing up for a big-deal, everybody-bring-something gourmet dinner next week. It's in honor of some *pompier visitant* from Paris—that's 'visiting fireman' in French. I'm practicing up on my French too." Doug gave her a glass of white wine and an affectionate kiss on her neck. "I have to keep taking this pineapple stuff out of the freezer and whipping it some more and putting it back. It seems like an awful lot of trouble, but Doug says I can't just sneak in some plain old sherbet from the ice-cream store. *Les français savait la différence*, he says."

She looked so delighted at having managed a whole French sentence that Chandler laughed with her. "Ah, it feels good to laugh," he said, accepting a scotch on the rocks from Doug. "That's a commodity in short supply these last few days."

Immediately all three were sobered. "Oh God," said Kathy. "I was forgetting the Harrolds. How is he, Tom? Have you seen him?" There were sudden tears in her deep blue eyes.

For a few minutes they talked about Woodrow Harrold, and shared reminiscences of Alicia. Then, inevitably, the talk came around to the subject of terrorism. Chandler told them of his selection as chairman of the Intelligence Committee task force, and it was in a flurry of congratulations that he took his reluctant leave of them.

When Chandler finally reached his home in Spring Valley, his head felt as if it were about to burst. His headaches were recurring more often lately. He vaguely wondered if they were psychosomatic.

He took off his jacket and tie and went to the kitchen. Barbara, his daily help, had left his dinner in the oven, and, as was his recent habit, he poured himself a scotch to have with it. This was the lonely time of day, and, looking about him at the sterile tile walls, he felt a pang of nostalgic envy for the Benders' merry kitchen. He took his plate and glass into the living room, propped a report from his briefcase on the coffee table in front of him, and tried to concentrate on it as he ate desultorily.

Later that night, as he tossed in bed, too tired to sleep, he watched the shadows of trees shift across the moon-washed ceiling in a ghostly dance, and he wondered what had happened to him since he first came to the Senate. There was a time when he thought he could resist the lure of power. Now power was threatening to possess him.

It seemed that he lived in motion. Any place was more comfortable than this house that was no longer a home. Life was the act of going somewhere on an airplane, heading for Connecticut, California, Munich, Tokyo. In a week, he might visit six countries, cross three time zones, and return to Washington thinking now he could stay put for a while. But in a day or two he was restless, ready to go again. He was running harder every day, for something or from something. It didn't quite matter, just as long as he was running. Days had become a blur. He could not tell where he had been yesterday or whom he had met the night before. He began to see everything, everyone, in silhouette, without color or definition.

There were moments when the futility of his life would nearly overwhelm him. The black floodwaters would recede, but the futility remained, a faint imprint like a fossil on the tissue of his mind. And then he would be off again on another airplane, heading somewhere, anywhere, on some mission of imagined importance.

He had tried to discuss it with Danielle—the way politics was taking control of his life. But somehow, as their marriage began to fray, and then to unravel, they had not been able to talk about anything except the marriage. The talk had gotten them nowhere. It had been his fault that she left. *No, it was no one's fault. That was what the lawyer said. No fault.*

Chandler knew what was happening to him, but he could not change. He could no more resist reaching for the shining sword than an alcoholic could resist a drink or a compulsive gambler a poker game. It would always be one last drink, one more hand.

At last he began to drift off to sleep. He seemed to be floating along a dark river that had no beginning and no end. It simply ran, and it carried him remorselessly in its current.

43

6 Three days after Charles Walcott told Chandler he would be chairman of the task force, the *Today* show broke the story in an interview with Walcott. A correspondent asked Gordon Nicholson for a reaction. "Amazing choice," he said. "Or perhaps I should say remarkable."

That morning, as soon as Chandler entered his office, he called in Kevin O'Brien, his staff member in charge of keeping track of information on intelligence and terrorism. O'Brien, a stocky, balding man in his mid-forties, was carrying his customary thick notebook neatly divided by lettered thumb tabs. O'Brien's bible, the staff called it. He had a reputation for knowing practically everything there was to know about whatever subject he had been told to study.

Through several years of intelligence work at the Pentagon, O'Brien had acquired a thorough understanding of the bureaucratic structure and methodology of intelligence operations. To Chandler, the CIA was a chameleon, blending in with any change of habitat to protect itself from the public, the press, and especially the Congress. But O'Brien knew how the Agency budget planners could conceal undesirable, even illegal activities within some innocuous-sounding research-and-development program so that even expert eyes reading a general request for appropriations could not detect them. O'Brien knew the location of the unmarked graves where they buried their secrets. He focused on minutiae. Nothing was too trivial to examine in the daily newspapers or the National Intelligence Estimates from the CIA.

O'Brien displayed no trace of the fabled Celtic humor—or melancholy. His eyes held no hint of an Irish smile. They were ice-blue. Ice-cold.

"Kevin," Chandler said to those eyes, "I want you to organize a meeting of the task force staff as soon as possible. We're going to get a reasonably good budget and staff. Walcott has given us three people from the Intelligence Committee. The co-chairman will be Senator Feldsdaver, and he'll have another three staffers. Walcott has said we can have as many Committee staff as we need for backup, but we want to keep the core group relatively small or we'll have too many cooks.

"Also, begin to think about how to lay this investigation out. Talk to some of the people still left around from Frank Church's committee. And keep in mind that we're going to have an even greater mandate to investigate than they had."

At four o'clock Senator Chandler was meeting with his task force staff. "There are three things I'm going to insist on in this investigation," he began. "Secrecy, secrecy, and secrecy."

Chandler hiked his leg over the arm of his desk chair. "If *any* information we gather, or any interpretation of what we've learned or speculation about our conclusions appears in the press, I'll ask each of you if he or she is the source. And if I don't get a confession, I'll let you *all* go."

Chandler was uncharacteristically harsh. But he had managed to get the full attention of the six staff members gathered in his Senate office and he intended to keep it. Elaine Dunham sat primly, legs crossed, in the corner of the couch. Her long dark hair was twisted into a French knot at the back of her head, and she held a Styrofoam cup of coffee rather stiffly. In her chic gray business suit she might have been posing for a fashion advertisement. Kevin O'Brien slouched coatless, tie loosened, in a large corner chair. He sipped coffee from a mug with a Washington Redskins emblem on it. The investigative staff was rounded out by two crisp new Ph.D.'s—one from Stanford and one from Berkeley—and by Maude Duberstein and Clarissa Logan. Recent graduates of Fordham Law School, they lived together and quarreled incessantly. Both were brilliant and indefatigable researchers.

Everyone was there except Senator Everett Feldsdaver. Earlier this afternoon he had been admitted to Bethesda Naval Hospital for emergency hip surgery. One of the steel rods inserted more than eight years ago had bent when he tripped coming down the Capitol steps. Feldsdaver was the liberals' favorite conservative. Proud and principled, he was solid as a piece of hickory.

Feldsdaver's departure had created a problem for Walcott. Ordinarily he would have appointed another senator to fill the vacancy. Walcott knew that Gordon Nicholson would push hard to be the replacement. He also suspected that Nicholson could turn the investigation into a partisan sideshow. So Walcott had appointed himself to serve as co-chairman of the task force.

It was a stroke of genius, as far as Chandler was concerned. To the press, the task force would assume an even higher visibility. At the same time, it made it impossible for Nicholson to complain that he had been passed over. Chandler knew that Walcott would delegate the responsibility for conducting the investigation to him, particularly since the chairman had not assigned Craig Delvin, the Intelligence Committee's chief of staff, to the task force itself. This was another bonus: Delvin shared Nicholson's ultraconservative philosophy and barely managed to mask his dislike for Chandler.

Chandler was aware that he would be out front on this one—the biggest challenge and the best opportunity of his career. He swung his leg back to the floor, stood up, and removed his coat. "I know I don't have to read you any lectures," he continued. "You're professionals or you wouldn't be involved in this investigation. However, there is just too much riding on this to let a press leak spoil it all. One story and the Committee will close us down like that." He snapped his fingers.

"Enough about security. I trust you all. That's why you were picked. And I don't intend to raise the subject again. Just let me know if you are approached by *anyone* trying to find out what we are up to.

"I do want to emphasize this: We don't have much time. My best guess would be six months at the outside. We have plenty of the Committee's resources to draw on, but I want you, as the inner circle, to organize and shape the investigation. If we get too many people involved, it'll turn into a monumental mess.

"Because of the shortness of time, we have to get moving." He turned abruptly to O'Brien. "Kevin, before the close of business on Friday, I'd like you to draw up a chronological plan for the investigation, with sufficient time built in for preparation of a preliminary report and a final report to the Committee. Also notify the Government Printing Office of our production schedule so we can get into their printing calendar.

"Elaine, with the same deadline, I want you to outline topics for investigation. That should include specific significant acts of terrorism and assassination, briefings by appropriate government agencies—including the CIA, the FBI, and the Drug Enforcement people—and relationships among varous international terrorist organizations. Think big here. The sky's the limit. Also, develop a plan of research for Clarissa and Maude so they can get started."

O'Brien raised his hand. "Senator, do you plan any international travel?"

"I don't know yet," Chandler said. "Probably. We'll wait to see what turns up. Unquestionably we're going to need information from the various international law-enforcement agencies. Which reminds me: Kevin, contact the Committee staff director and set up a budget for the investigation and an accounting system separate from the full Committee."

"Senator." Elaine's low, cool voice broke in. "I have a question." He nodded, and she asked, "Do you assume there's a connection between the Harrold assassinations and other recent terrorist acts?"

"I don't know. The Committee thinks there's enough evidence—or maybe a better term is *appearance* of evidence—to justify looking into it. That's why they created this task force." Chandler found himself distracted by the green of her eyes. He pulled himself back to the subject at hand. "Personally, I'm not a conspiracist. Lord knows there are plenty of those around these days. Let's just say I'm an agnostic on the subject until we find out a little more."

"What kind of cooperation do you expect from the intelligence community on this?" Kevin asked. "Do you believe they have anything to hide in this area?"

"You know how the CIA works," Tom replied. "I suspect they'll let us know about as much as they want us to. I'm not sure *they* really know what's going on, either. We've got to try to convince the intelligence community that it's in their best interests to share with us whatever information they have."

Even as he talked and, he hoped, fired up his small staff, Chandler reflected on the risks he was taking with this investigation. *Good God,* he thought. *Two bickering researchers. A couple of computer-carrying technocrats. A somber Irishman. And a gorgeous iceberg.* Out to conquer, in six months, what he was already imagining to be an international brotherhood of assassins.

"This is not a political effort to get headlines," he said. "Neither is it a witch hunt or an ideological platform. And it's certainly not a dragnet license to look into anything that interests us. We all have to remember we are responsible to the Committee and can act only within the scope of the mandate given us. That is to document, dispassionately and in detail, any specific pattern we may find in this epidemic of terrrorist activities."

Timidly, Maude raised a finger. Chandler nodded to her. "Yes?"

"Senator, aren't there a lot of terrorist groups around? How many are we going to be looking at?"

"That's a good question," Chandler said. "Obviously, because of our limited resources, we'll have to confine ourselves to the better-known groups. We know more about them, for one thing. Also, they seem to be the people most willing to claim the 'credit' for this new bloodshed. Kevin drew up a list for me: the IRA Provos in Ireland, the Red Brigades in Italy, the Japanese Red Army, the German Red Army Faction and what's left of the Baader-Meinhof gang, the PLO, the Islamic Jihad, the Puerto Rican FALN, the ETA—that Basque group in Spain—and there may be one or two more that are less well-known."

O'Brien roused himself. "Senator, I'm not even sure what questions to ask. What *specifically* are we trying to find out? If Baader or Meinhof or Yasir Arafat walked through that door, I'm not sure I'd know what to ask them."

Chandler got down to cases: "First, I want a briefing on the major terrorist acts of the past four months. Clearly, since the first of the year there's been a major increase in the number and viciousness of the attacks. Let's find out from our intelligence people who was involved in each case—were there any similarities among the victims? Any correlation among the incidents?

"Finally, if there is some kind of reign of terror going on, we have to find out why. Right now, it makes no sense. A car bombing here, a hijacking there, a kamikaze raid somewhere else. If there *is* no scheme behind all this, if it's all just random and senseless, we need to know that too.

"I said earlier that I'm no conspiracist. So don't take what I'm saying to you now as gospel. I'm presupposing nothing"—he looked directly into O'Brien's eyes—"but I *am* bothered by something: These incidents, as a kind of byproduct, always seem to increase tensions between us and the Soviets. Some writers are claiming that the Russians are behind all the terrorists—that we've entered a new phase of Russian expansionism: communization by terror. And the Soviets are saying that the CIA is instigating attacks on Third World leaders, that we're reviving the technique of assassination that began in the fifties. The net result is propaganda and tension, the kind of situation we had at the end of World War Two.

"Okay. End of speechmaking." He turned to O'Brien, whose face wore a familiarly cynical look. "Kevin? Any particular thing on your mind?"

"I think I've got an idea of what you want, Senator," O'Brien said.

"Fine. If there are no other questions, let's get started." Chandler's smile took in the whole group. Maude and Clarissa blushed. "Go get 'em. And remember, get a friend to start your car and taste your food—just not too good a friend."

Even Elaine smiled at that.

Tuesday, March 31

7 Five days after the staff meeting, Chandler received a call from Peter Hammerschmidt. Woodrow Harrold wanted to see him as soon as possible. Less than an hour later Chandler was at Harrold's house.

Hammerschmidt showed Chandler into a room full of morning light. But Harrold, slouched in his leather chair, still seemed submerged in an inner midnight. He looked as haggard as he had on that Saturday morning when the two men had sat in the darkness of this room. Harrold rose when Chandler entered. His handshake was as firm as ever, but when he looked up at Tom, his eyes seemed to focus on something beyond.

Hammerschmidt hesitated in the doorway. "You can leave us alone, Peter. Perhaps you can find some coffee?" As Hammerschmidt started out, Harrold added, "And, Peter, I'll want to give Tom a copy of the transcript."

Harrold sank into the couch next to his desk and motioned for Chandler to sit beside him. "Thanks for coming so quickly, Tom. I guess you know Peter well enough to know that when he says 'as soon as possible' he isn't trying to sound dramatic."

"I assumed it was something about the . . . attack," Chandler said. "But you could get Peter or someone to—"

"No. I couldn't have delegated this, Tom. I wanted you to hear it from me." Harrold drew a breath and began, speaking more rapidly than was his custom, wanting to get through it, be rid of it.

"Late last night—at eleven fifty-seven to be exact—a call came to the White House switchboard. The caller said he had to talk directly to me. The operator put him through to a security man here in the house. They've set up a headquarters downstairs, in the . . . in the room where Alicia and I played Ping-Pong."

He paused as the door opened and Hammerschmidt maneuvered awkwardly through. A file folder was tucked under his right arm, and he balanced a tray with two large gray mugs and a battered aluminum coffee pot. *A house without women*, Chandler thought. Lowering the tray onto the table in front of the couch, Hammerschmidt handed the folder to Chandler. He poured the coffee, strong and black, bowed slightly in acknowledgment of their thanks, and left.

Harrold resumed his story: "I was still here—staring into the dark, I must admit—when a security man knocked on the door. He told me about the White House call, and said that the man was on the line with some information he wouldn't give to anyone but me. The security man thought I should take the call. Of course it was being recorded—and traced.

"Tom, rather than have me repeat the conversation, why don't you read the transcript, and then we'll talk."

Chandler flipped to the second page, where the call was transferred to Secretary Harrold, referred to in the transcript as SEC STATE. The other speaker was called VOICE.

VOICE: Mr. Secretary?

SEC STATE: Yes. This is Woodrow Harrold. You have information for me?

VOICE: Yes. Listen closely. I don't have much time.

SEC STATE: I'm listening. Please go on.

VOICE: The Miami police have arrested a man for traveling on an illegal passport. They don't know who he is yet. I do. His name is Ahmad Rashish [apparent spelling]. This man was one of the assassins of your family.

SEC STATE: Are you certain, Mr. —?

VOICE: Never mind who I am. I am certain. I'm also certain of something else. By the time the police find out who he is, he will be dead. You must act fast. But there is more. A week ago—also in Miami—an old Mafia man was killed. A man named Sam Fabricante [apparent spelling]. Now listen, Mr. Secretary. Have someone you trust look into this, and do it very carefully. Do you hear me? Very, very carefully. The death of this man—this Sam Fabricante—was related to the deaths in your family.

"And that was it," Harrold said as Chandler reached the end of the transcript and looked up. "The line went dead."

"What was the voice like?"

"Accented. Hispanic, I think. Perhaps Portuguese or Spanish, but I'd bet on Latin American."

"What about the tracer? Did they find out where the call came from?"

"Unfortunately not. He didn't stay on the line long enough. All they know is that the call was local—from somewhere within this area code."

"What about the man named"—Chandler referred to the transcript—"Rashish? Anyone check to—"

"Peter and the security boys checked with the Miami police immediately. A man carrying a very slick illegal Panamanian passport was arrested about ten o'clock last night in Miami. He was stopped as he was about to get on a plane for Panama. The name on the passport was Fernandez, not Rashish. But he was described as looking like an Arab."

"My God! They've found one of them."

"Maybe, Tom. Maybe. And another thing. Peter says that the business about the old Mafia fellow is true."

"It sounds like a strange connection, Woodrow. The Mafia involved in terrorism?"

"I know. So far, Peter tells me, no one can make anything out of it. Maybe you can."

"But surely the FBI, the CIA—everything the government has—is being put into this, Woodrow. What can I do?"

Harrold stood up and walked to the window. He took a sip of coffee, then put the mug down on his desk. Leaning on his hands, he looked across at Chandler, and now his eyes were hard. "I trust you, Tom. It's that simple. We've both been around this town long enough to know that agencies and departments and bureaus sometimes have hidden agendas. And they don't have feelings. I want you to look into this because I know that no one will be tying your hands. I know you will be looking for the truth."

Back in his office, Chandler called in O'Brien and showed him the transcript of Harrold's phone call. "I want to go to Miami as soon as possible, Kevin."

"I can understand why you want to go, Senator, given your friendship with Secretary Harrold. But why go rushing off to follow up on an anonymous tip that hasn't even been evaluated yet?"

"Part of it's already checked out. A guy was picked up in Miami last night."

"How many guys do you think they pick up down there on an average night?"

"I don't care how many guys they pick up on an average goddam night, Kevin," Chandler said, his voice sharp. "I want you to get the Miami police on the phone for me. And the Immigration and Naturalization Service. I want confirmation that they are holding an Arab type, picked up last night on a phony passport charge. Tell them you are calling for me, that we are investigating the Harrold attack as part of a wider Senate investigation on terrorism, and that we will be down in the next few days to talk to this guy Fernandez, or Ahmad Rashish—I'm not sure of the spelling.

"And tell them that in the meantime they better look after this character, because he just might be in some danger."

"Right, Senator."

"And I want to find out about this Mafioso named Fabricante."

"I read about that," O'Brien said, knowledgeable as usual. "They fished him out of Miami Bay. He was stuffed in a barrel."

"Spare me the details. He was an old man, wasn't he?"

"Right. Retired."

"Then why was he killed—and killed that way?"

"The heart has its reasons and so does the Mafia—if there is a Mafia," O'Brien said, allowing weariness to enter his voice. "I don't see what it has to do with what we're supposed to be doing."

"Maybe it does. Maybe there's a Cuban connection to the Harrold murders." Chandler paused, struck by the word *Cuban*. "And get me a copy of the Church Committee's summary on the Kennedy assassination."

"May I ask why? Senator Church's investigation was a long time ago—and they were looking at an old assassination, not current terrorism."

"Mine always to reason why for you—right, Kevin? The reason is I knew Frank Church, and one time when he was talking to me about his investigation, I think he said something about Fabricante. I can't quite remember what, and I can't ask Frank. Unfortunately, he's dead. So I thought it might be in the Church Committee report. Satisfied?"

O'Brien, obviously unsatisfied, disappeared.

Good old Kevin, Chandler thought. *Reliable and efficient—if difficult*. He pulled a legal pad from a desk drawer and started making rapid notes, his adrenaline running. He had filled a page and a half when the door burst open.

O'Brien stood there, his face flushed and his eyes wide. Chandler had never seen him excited before.

"Senator, I hate to tell you this . . . but that guy?—Rashish or Fernandez or whatever it is? He just killed himself!"

8
Friday, April 3

Tom Chandler drove along the George Washington Parkway in the eerie light of dawn. The gray fog that had lain like a sheet of insulation over the Potomac was beginning to lift. The river was dark and still, except for a solitary scull sliding along its surface like an oversize water bug. Chandler realized, startled, that the sculler was probably E. W. Trevor. He had heard that the CIA Director took his scull onto the river every morning. In the lifting fog Trevor was almost an apparition. And that was how Chandler viewed him—as almost ethereal, without substance, not someone you could reach across a table and touch.

Not for the first time Chandler wondered what made Trevor tick, why he had to reduce life to black and white, an antagonism of absolutes, why he was so unyielding, so rigid. As the scull disappeared in a stubborn patch of fog, Chandler concluded that Trevor had long ago abandoned any interest in moral niceties. Winning was his only moral code. The means were irrelevant

Well, screw him. Chandler smiled to himself. *And his lackey Gordon Nicholson—another great inquiring mind! As long as Trevor creates a covert action against some emaciated tribe in East Angola, Nicholson will be the first to cry national security. To hell with both of them.* Chandler had his own covert action program to get on with, beginning now.

The sun was just starting to rise above the Jefferson Memorial, splashing it with a red glow that would turn a blinding white by noon.

Chandler pulled into the special parking lot at National Airport reserved for congressmen and diplomats. There was no charge. If he left his car there for weeks, it would cost him nothing. It was one of the symbols of rank that irritated others who had come to Washington to feed at the federal trough. They grumbled, wrote letters to the editors of *The Washington Post*, but the privilege remained permanent.

The Eastern Airlines jet climbed high over the 14th Street Bridge, then dipped to the right, heading south. The sun was up now. Washington no longer resembled a dream city wrapped in a sheet of gauze. It was alive with motion. An army of government employees moved evenly, like plasma through tubes, into little individual cells of authority. Viewed from the air, the gleaming monuments, the clusters of gardens, the dogwoods just coming into bloom impressed themselves on the mind.

Chandler had an aisle seat. Across from him, O'Brien's balding head was bowed intently over his looseleaf bible. Next to him sat Elaine Dunham, whose fluent Spanish might come in handy in Miami's "little Havana." If there *was* any Cuban connection to the latest outbreak of terrorism.

"What do you think we'll find down there, Kevin?" Chandler asked. He had requested a reluctant O'Brien to set up meetings with the Miami police and the local FBI office. A briefing on the increased drug traffic coming through south Florida might confirm his hunch that something about the Harrold attacks could be picked up on the drug grapevine.

"I don't think you'll be finding much, Senator," O'Brien replied. "Usual story from the FBI—they're understaffed and overworked. They've got a unique set of problems. The Cubans have just about taken over the city. Some anti-Castro groups are working closely with organized crime. There's a large narcotics network operating almost in the open, sort of thumbing their noses at the cops.

And, of course, the Agency uses both groups whenever it fits into their own plans." He spoke matter-of-factly, as if there were no room for doubt about anything he said.

"Come on, Kevin," Chandler said. "The Agency may have had contacts with the Mafia and the Cubans, but that was in the sixties. I doubt if they're maintaining any connections now—especially after all the congressional investigations into CIA activities . . . Senator Church's committee—"

"Senator," O'Brien interrupted in his most professional tone—which sounded to Chandler more like a reproach than an expression of respect. "The record is clear: The Agency used the mob when it tried to murder Castro. Why would you think that things are any different now?"

Chandler decided to drop the subject. While he was not exactly a novice on the Intelligence Committee, he didn't want to debate the matter of the records—which O'Brien knew a lot better than he did. Particularly not with Elaine across the aisle in the seat next to Kevin. Chandler was amused to recognize that he didn't want anyone to outshine him in Elaine's eyes—*those astonishing green eyes* . . .

He was finding Elaine's proximity increasingly disturbing, though she gave him no reason to think she looked upon him differently from any other man. She was always completely professional. She never gazed directly at him or engaged in any eye codes—a bit of flirtation that some senators had come to expect in the women who worked for them.

Chandler looked at her now. She was immersed in a report, her face serious in concentration. Her skin had a light, butternut tone. Her cheekbones and jaw line met cleanly, forming a triangle softened by dark hair that fell smoothly to her shoulders. Her eyes needed little makeup to magnify their emerald brightness. Tom had never known a woman who took her own beauty so casually, made so little of it. Or at least seemed to. *God knows Danielle didn't.*

He found himself wondering who Elaine really was, what she was like behind that cool exterior. Where, given that Yankee name, did she acquire such an exotic Spanish gorgeousness? *Elena* . . .

Chandler caught himself up sharply. He was too busy, he told himself, to be distracted by any woman right now, no matter how intriguing. He served on three other committees, traveled constantly—he had no time for escapades. Besides, he made it a rule never to become emotionally involved with staff.

He took a sip of the hot coffee he hoped would wake him from his reverie and then, inconsistently, leaned his head back against the seat, closed his eyes, and imagined himself a silver hawk soaring, circling, a tiny Elaine thirty thousand feet below.

To avoid any reporters who might be lingering outside the FBI offices, Tom, Kevin, and Elaine took the service elevator to the seventh floor of the Federal Building, got off in the middle of the Agriculture Department's regional office, then climbed the utility stairway to the ninth floor. Emerging in the back hallway of the FBI offices, they were immediately ushered into a small, drab conference room.

Vincent McNally, the Special Agent in Charge, greeted them: "We're honored to have you here, Senator Chandler, and stand ready to help you in any way we can." He acknowledged Chandler's introductions of Kevin O'Brien and Elaine Dunham, and listened intently as Chandler said, "I want to know three things: What's going on with this enormous increase in drug trade down here? What do you—or the Miami Police—know about Ahmad Rashish's death? And Sam Fabricante's? We'll listen as long as you have something to tell us."

Chandler hated most briefings. They usually consisted of junior personnel standing ramrod-stiff before a slide projector reciting elementary facts as dry as old bread crusts. Those who gave the briefings generally hated them, too, regarding politicians as pompous dilettantes or pretentious fools, a nuisance that had to be suffered.

But today was different. Chandler had come to learn. It was not coincidental that McNally treated him less as an intrusion than as a guest.

"The state of Florida is under siege." McNally began the briefing on that note of alarm. Things were out of control and he had decided there was not much to be gained by trying to protect the reputation of the FBI. "Drugs have become the biggest retail business in Florida. We estimate the gross value of the marijuana and cocaine traffic last year at over ten billion dollars. And that doesn't even take into account the sale of heroin."

He moved to a large map on the wall, took up a two-foot pointer, and placing its tip on the state of Florida, swung the base of the pointer down to South America. "Point to point, Miami is less than twelve hundred miles from Barranquilla, Colombia. That's where a major part of the drugs are coming from. Florida has a shoreline of more than eight thousand miles. There are more than two hundred thousand private pleasure boats in Florida that can offload contraband without fear of detection. There are more than ten thousand privately owned aircraft in Florida and more than twenty-five hundred registered airports. Most cargo aircraft and commercial fishing vessels can make it nonstop from Colombia. The private boats and planes can refuel in the islands and make it easily on the second hop. For every pound we seize, at least ten pounds get through. It's a smuggler's paradise.

"And, Senator, when you have that kind of access and that kind of money, you can be sure that corruption and violence aren't too far behind. There were more than *thirteen hundred* murders in Florida last year, most of them drug-related. These people are vicious. They blow up houses and cars by remote control. They tote automatic machine guns as routinely as if they were just going out to the rifle range for target practice."

McNally pulled a white screen down over the map of the Western Hemisphere, turned on a large slide projector, and flipped off the overhead lights. They were looking at a skeletal organization chart that was at once clean, simple, and comprehensive. It was divided into segments indicating operational responsibilities, from financing to production, distribution, and transportation. In turn, transportation was divided into subcategories of land, air, and marine. A separate category was reserved for "specialization," listing pilots, forgers, bankers, attorneys, craftsmen, vessel captains, crew, electronics, and drug and money couriers.

"How many 'families' of organized crime are there in Florida?" Chandler asked.

"We don't know for sure. It gets a little complicated. There are the traditional organized-crime families like the Cosa Nostra. But there are groups known as the Black Mafia, the Jewish Mafia, and the Dixie Mafia. Then you have the Latin American groups dominated by the Colombians and Cubans."

McNally went on to explain that the traditional families were the best organized. The most recent groups, such as the Colombians, were less so, but they were getting more sophisticated in their organization and operations every day. A recent phenomenon, he said, was the emergence of the Cocaine Cowboys.

"When the Colombians decided to become dealers and distributors instead of just suppliers, they ran smack into the Cubans, who controlled most of the traffic in southern Florida. The Colombians and the Cubans converged at the same time the American dealers were trying to eliminate all middlemen and buy directly from international suppliers. As a result, Miami resembles an O.K. Corral shootout between killers who will execute a trafficker of *any* nationality at the drop of a coca leaf."

"I notice that you didn't make any reference to an Arab connection in any of these groups," Chandler said.

McNally looked puzzled. "We're not aware that there is one, Senator. Not in Florida at least."

"What about Ahmad Rashish? What were you able to find about him?"

"Not much. He was a professional assassin with a lot of aliases. Palestinian. Got most of his training from Cubans in South Yemen. Italy has had a warrant out for his arrest for three years—he killed an Israeli diplomat in Rome. Walked up to Shimon Yadin's front door, rang the bell, and when Yadin looked through the peephole, fired a shotgun point-blank through the door. The French were after him too. Remember that bomb that exploded in Paris? Killed fourteen and wounded forty-six?"

Chandler nodded grimly.

"He was well financed. Traveled extensively between Europe and the Middle East." McNally turned off the projector, switched on the lights, and returned to the chair behind his desk. He quickly looked through some papers clipped to a manila folder. "We have no record of his ever being in the United States before. And if he *was* involved in the attack on Secretary Harrold's family, it would be a departure for him."

"How so?"

"Rashish was a loner. He didn't work under anyone and he didn't have anyone working under him. He always acted solo."

"And died that way. Are you satisfied he killed himself?"

"Officially, I have to say that the Immigration and Naturalization Service is satisfied that he killed himself while in their custody. You realize, Senator, that he was never in *our* custody."

"You said 'officially.' What do you think personally?"

"Off the record?" McNally said, his gaze taking in Kevin and Elaine.

"Yes," said Chandler. "You can talk freely. All I'm looking for is the truth."

"I don't like the smell of it, Senator. The INS says he asked for a lawyer—he could speak that much English, I guess—and *someone* visited him in a holding cell that was not being surveilled. They have no record of the visitor's name. You see, Senator, they are used to dealing with, well, only immigration matters, not major-crime matters. Anyway, a half hour after that guy saw him, Rashish was dead. Hanging from his shirt tied high up on the cell door. Personally, I think it stinks."

"Thank you, Mr. McNally. I appreciate your candor."

McNally grinned. His frankness was not popular with most officials.

"What about Fabricante's death?" O'Brien put in. "Do you think Rashish had anything to do with it?"

McNally shook his head. "We don't know. Fabricante was an old Mafia don who was being pushed out by the younger family members. We can't make any connection between him and Rashish. Besides, the way Fabricante died . . . well, that just doesn't appear to be Rashish's style."

"Secretary Harrold seemed to think Rashish was involved," Chandler said. "But you don't?" Chandler was aware of O'Brien's rather theatrical sigh.

McNally cast a glance in O'Brien's direction. "Well, Senator, there isn't much to go on. We received an anonymous phone call. A man. He said Rashish had arranged for Fabricante to be hacked up. But we weren't able to follow up on it in time. By the time we got someone down to the INS holding tank, Rashish was dead."

"Do you think there was anything to the call?"

"We don't know. It could have been a nut. We get a lot of calls. Personally, I think it was more likely that Fabricante got caught in a territorial dispute, and somebody wanted to send a message."

"Can we talk to the Miami police about Fabricante?"

"Sure. I've made arrangements for us to go there today." McNally hesitated a moment. "The Fabricante murder was pretty gruesome and some of the evidence isn't particularly pleasant to look at. If you've got a weak stomach, I'd recommend you skip that part. Frankly, I don't think your aides should see it."

Chandler glanced quickly at Elaine. McNally had said "aides," but his warning was obviously directed at her. She stared back coolly.

*   *   *

The FBI brief on the drug epidemic had taken just over two hours. McNally led Tom, Elaine, and Kevin into the hall, down the stairs, and then out of the basement parking garage in a vintage Chevrolet.

As the car moved in and out of traffic along Biscayne Boulevard, Chandler wondered why he had insisted on pursuing the grisly details of Fabricante's murder. He remembered his term as a prosecuting attorney for the State of Connecticut. He had seen every kind of brutality: babies strangled by unstrung mothers or their inflamed lovers, young victims of homosexual rape and murder, old people beaten to death by hoodlums. Chandler believed he had seen it all. *But Elaine . . .*

As they proceeded through downtown Miami toward an anonymous house near the police headquarters, McNally briefed them. "You will meet a Miami detective who has worked on the Fabricante case and on a lot of the Cuban terrorist cases. Fabricante's base is—was—in Cleveland, but he kept a home down here and did a lot of business in Miami. Anyway, about two weeks ago his car was found at the Miami airport and he failed to turn up at home. After a couple of days his daughter notified the police. They called us, but we didn't have clear jurisdiction. So we've watched from the sidelines, but stayed close."

McNally wheeled around a corner on a yellow light, and continued: "An incoming tourist fishing boat spotted a barrel in Biscayne Bay, out about two to three miles. Harbor Patrol checked it out—and brought in the barrel. It smelled like . . . it smelled pretty putrid." McNally steered the Chevy down an alley and into a garage attached to a cottage. The garage door closed almost on the Chevy's trunk, and he led them through an enclosed breezeway into the kitchen. "Senator, meet Detective Harley Waldron. Harley helped pull the barrel out of the bay. Harley, this is Senator Tom Chandler, who's down here from Washington. And Miss Elaine Dunham, Mr. Kevin O'Brien."

McNally repeated his caution to Elaine. She dismissed it with an impatient wave of her hand, and Waldron spread a dozen full-color pictures on the kitchen table. Elaine's eyes widened and the color drained from her face. Kevin remained silent. Chandler gritted his teeth.

The corpse's face at the top of the barrel was twisted into a grimace that seemed to scream at the camera. A garrote loop had partly severed the head, which was set in a bizarre cluster of hands and feet. Only one conclusion was possible. To fit the body into the fifty-five-gallon drum, the arms and legs had been crudely severed and then stuffed in with the torso.

"Here is what the coroner says. . . ." Waldron's clinical description of the corpse was interrupted by the ringing of a telephone. Waldron answered and handed the phone to Chandler.

Chandler listened for a moment, then covered the mouthpiece with his hand. "It's Ned Dempsey," he said to O'Brien. "Someone fired a small heat-seeking missile at Vice-President Jaworski's plane at Andrews Air Force Base."

"And?" O'Brien's voice was barely audible.

"It missed."

Chandler was not surprised that Ned Dempsey, his administrative assistant, had tracked him down. Working the phones, as Dempsey called it, was one of his specialties. He not only seemed always to know where Chandler was, he also knew where to find anybody Chandler wanted to talk to.

Now in the calm, deliberate voice he used in crises, Dempsey quickly filled Chandler in on the attempt to kill the Vice-President. Investigators had located the spot from which the missile was fired. "They have bloodhounds there now. There's no hard evidence about who's involved. Obviously they suspect a connection to the group that tried to kill Harrold. I've got calls in to the White House, the Defense Department, and the CIA. What I don't understand, Tom, is how they could get so close to Andrews and then disappear without a trace. It's either incompetence out there or they had help from the inside."

"Ned, as soon as you get more information, call me at The Barriers. We'll be there in a couple of hours." Chandler hung up. He tried to appear calm but his eyes gave him away. His stomach was churning. *How many more public officials are on the terrorists' hit list?*

And for the first time a dark thought entered his mind. Would he become one of their targets?

9

The Barriers was a very private club, a playground for America's multimillionaires and jet setters who wanted to unwind in the Miami sun, sip piña coladas, and play cards at a thousand dollars a hand.

O'Brien was the first to arrive at the table he had reserved for eight o'clock. He was scowling. He didn't like the idea of being here. He didn't like the luxury, the decadence. The men were too tanned, their wives too pampered. Everybody wore too much gold. Chains, bracelets, watches, rings. They were vulgar and arrogant. They were crude. And cruel.

O'Brien wondered how many of them were "legitimate" businessmen engaged in the illegal drug traffic. McNally had said many were profiteering: charging exorbitant rates for private aircraft and high-powered speedboats, pretending not to know they were used for smuggling; inflating prices for real estate; making their seafood and fishing businesses—with direct access to docking facilities—available to the scum who were destroying the young people of the country. Take the cash and run.

No, O'Brien was not happy to be here. His original plan had been for the three of them to stay under assumed names in a small hotel, where the guests would be unlikely to recognize Senator Thomas Chandler. He wanted Chandler to slip in and out of Miami without inquiries from the local press.

But Chandler had insisted on staying at The Barriers, where a wealthy friend from Fairfield County owned a penthouse suite in the new high-rise condominium. Since it was not at all unusual for congressmen and senators to be seen there, the residents were unimpressed by politicians, whom they regarded as merchandise to be bought with campaign contributions. Otherwise they left politicians alone—and demanded the same treatment in return.

Well, O'Brien thought grudgingly, *maybe Chandler was right.* When you have a high profile, maybe it's better to be obvious—the

"Purloined Letter" technique—instead of slinking around some fleabag hotel looking conspicuously out of place. Not a head turned now as Chandler approached the table, followed closely by a waiter who looked disdainful when Tom ordered "the same kind of beer my friend is having."

While they waited for Elaine, who had gone back with McNally to his office to collect every last detail the FBI had on Rashish and Fabricante, Tom and Kevin filled each other in on their late afternoon activities. Both had gone directly to The Barriers. Chandler had asked O'Brien to call Ned Dempsey and get from him any updates on the Jaworski attempt. "And see what else you can find with some discreet calls."

As soon as Chandler reached his suite, he began making some calls of his own. The first was to Woodrow Harrold.

"Tom, I'm glad to hear your voice," Harrold said on an outrush of breath. When I got the news just now, I thought of you. What you're trying to do. I had an idea this might be a warning. When your office said you were out of town, I . . . I was worried about you."

Chandler was genuinely touched. "Thanks, Woodrow. It's been a long time since anyone worried about me." Tom tried to keep his voice light, but it was husky with emotion. "What do you mean by 'warning'? For me?"

"I couldn't help wondering, Tom. Why the miss? Did they *want* to miss? Did they want to say, 'This time we miss. This is a warning'? Perhaps not to you personally—not yet—but to the whole idea. To *any* attempt to fit all the different pieces together— to find out what this is all about."

Chandler's second call was to Edwin Schumacher, director of the FBI. As he listened, Chandler pictured him puffing on his pipe and reading from the latest half-page memo prepared by one of his assistants. Yes, there were several promising leads. No, he could not discuss them over an open phone. Yes, of course he understood the task force's need for information and cooperation from the FBI. No, he saw no significance in the fact that the Harrold attack and this one were both on Fridays; still, one never did know, did one? Yes, he certainly would meet with Senator Chandler as soon as their offices could work it out. Yes, he was penciling in a date.

Next, Chandler tried to reach Trevor but was told that the Director was on his way back from Honduras. The Deputy Director, expressing surprise that Chandler would call, said that the attack "could have been carried out by any one of a hundred terrorist groups." As he started ticking them off, Chandler angrily interrupted him.

"I don't need to hear the names. I know them. You just take a message for Mr. Trevor. You tell him that I think Honduras is a hell of a place for him to be when someone is trying to kill off our leadership."

It was almost 8:15 when Elaine came into the dining room. Chandler's arrival might have gone unnoticed, but heads certainly turned for her, O'Brien observed. She had changed into a softly tailored white dress that accentuated her dark hair and burnished complexion. She took a seat to Kevin's left, directly across from Tom, ordered a glass of white wine, and began to study the menu.

"No one we've talked to in Washington seems to know anything at this point," Chandler said, in what amounted to a quick summary for Elaine's benefit. "How did McNally treat you?"

Elaine closed the menu. "He gave me copies of their reports. Basically they say what he said in the briefing. Nothing more, nothing less. And he said he had nothing at all on the attack today."

"Okay," Chandler said. "Then we are left to our own theories at this point." He became aware that his gaze was lingering too long on Elaine's lovely face and turned toward O'Brien. "What's your most far-out theory, Kevin?"

O'Brien took a long pull at his beer and then answered, "Carlos."

Chandler was startled. "I haven't heard anything about him for a long time."

"Well, he's still around, I understand," O'Brien said.

"Carlos is one of Kevin's many specialties," Chandler said to Elaine. "Know much about him?"

"Not much," Elaine said. "He's not one of my specialties."

So cool, Tom thought. *So very cool.* He turned again to O'Brien. "How about an update on Carlos, Kevin?"

"Carlos is short for Ilyich Ramirez Sanchez," O'Brien began, leaning back in his chair and gazing up, as if a dossier were printed on the ceiling. "Venezuelan. He was known for going around pumping bullets into the eyes of his victims or dropping hand grenades into French drugstores. He was trained at Matanzas, the

KGB training camp in Cuba, and was sent to Patrice Lumumba University in Moscow. He was quite a cutup there, but the Russians liked his style, I guess. They put him on the KGB payroll.

"As to my theory—well, there's an interesting similarity between the Jaworski attack and some of Carlos's jobs. He hooked up with some Palestinians in Rome in 1973 and rented an apartment near the airport. They had a couple of heat-seeking ground-to-air Soviet rockets. They were planning to shoot down an El Al plane. The Israelis tipped off the Rome police. Carlos was not picked up, but the others were. Two years later, in Paris, his gang twice tried to shoot down El Al planes with rockets. They screwed up both times."

The disdainful waiter reappeared and took their orders, which he seemed to find somehow wanting in taste or discrimination. Chandler was amused.

O'Brien resumed: "So Carlos has had some experience—unsuccessful, but experience—in trying to shoot down planes."

"How much help would he need?" Elaine asked. "To get into Andrews, for instance?"

"He wouldn't need to get into Andrews. All he'd need is an apartment in Prince George's County, on a sight line with most takeoffs and landings. In Rome he had five people for the job— logistics, lookouts, whatever. Maybe the same number in Paris. Figure he needs five."

"He's not very good, though, is he?" Chandler remarked. "He always seems to miss."

"Maybe they don't care if they miss," Elaine said. "'The purpose of terrorism is to terrorize,' if I remember my Lenin correctly."

Chandler raised an eyebrow. "Interesting possibility, Elaine." Turning to O'Brien, he asked, "Do you actually think Carlos is in the United States?"

"No. I'm really talking about his signature. He could have pulled this off without being here. No one knows where he is, but the last I heard, he was in the Soviet Union."

"What would he do there?"

"Stay alive. There are an awful lot of gendarmes looking for him. Russia is the one place where no one is likely to be able to kill him."

*　　*　　*

Over coffee, Chandler shifted the conversation to Fabricante's career—and then his death. "What did he do to get that kind of treatment? A bullet in the back of the head would have killed him just as dead. It looks to me as if whoever did it wanted to send a message. Did your conversation with McNally give you any ideas along that line, Elaine?"

"Nothing concrete," she said, "but maybe a hunch. You say Fabricante was involved in the attempt to kill Castro twenty years ago. Maybe there's a connection there—in Cuba. Maybe Ahmad Rashish was planning to get to Cuba from Panama. Maybe he was sent to kill Secretary Harrold and then Fabricante on the same mission. But then again, Fabricante may still have been involved in drug traffic in the Miami area. Maybe he just crossed a competitor."

"For connections," Chandler said, "why not a Soviet Union–drug connection?"

"Sometimes I think we give the Soviets too much credit," O'Brien said. "When they see a weakness, they exploit it, ruthlessly. But I think we're overdoing it if we start believing that those old dinosaurs in the Politburo sit around a table engineering international drug-smuggling operations into the United States."

Chandler thought O'Brien was probably right, but he decided to play out the question. "Wouldn't you say that drug addiction is a 'weakness'?"

"Sure," O'Brien said. "But the Soviets are just letting human nature—basic greed—take its course. They know that, historically, democracies don't survive—that they lose the capacity for discipline. Just a question of time." O'Brien's tone was matter-of-fact, without alarm or apparent concern about the future. It was as if he had simply drawn a window shade down over tomorrow.

"You don't offer much hope," Chandler said.

"Maybe not, but I'm a realist." O'Brien spoke with the finality of a convict who has come to terms with his death sentence. "Take the American farmer, for example. Not a more loyal patriot can be found in the world. God-fearing, Bible-quoting—hates communism. But just let a President embargo a sale of grain to the Soviet Union and the farmers are ready to roll their tractors all over the Rose Garden. Same with the *wunderkinds* out in Silicon Valley who make those little computer chips.

"And the Soviets know the same rules apply to the drug dealers of the world. The Politburo doesn't have to manipulate the farm policies of Colombia or Pakistan or Turkey. They can just sit back and wait for the walls to crumble. They won't need tanks. There won't *be* any will to resist."

"No wonder you don't smile much," Chandler said.

"No, Senator," O'Brien said. "I've read too much and seen too much to believe it's going to be any different this time. Humpty Dumpty has fallen off the wall and shattered into a million pieces. And I don't know anyone who can put him back together again."

"It's funny," Chandler said, staring bleakly into his coffee cup. Elaine and Kevin looked at him, unable to anticipate what he would say. "How everything keeps going back to the sixties—to Kennedy, I mean."

O'Brien looked puzzled. "Why to Kennedy? How did you suddenly get to Kennedy?"

"Something was going on then that has never been resolved. There was something in Miami then. There's something now. Fabricante was a hit man for the CIA. Now *he's* been hit. The Agency was running loose then to get at Castro. Some of the same anti-Castro Cubans have been implicated in running drugs into this country. Some of the old Bay of Pigs CIA case officers are in Libya training terrorists. Almost the same cast of characters. Only Kennedy is gone. . . .

"You know, I think something really happened to this country that day in Dallas. I think it changed the way Americans perceive themselves—our sense of our mortality. When we lost Jack Kennedy, it was just the beginning of a whole string of defeats. Somehow, I can't think it was an accident, the solitary act of a lunatic."

"Senator, I understand the way you feel about Kennedy," O'Brien said consolingly. "I admired him too. Hell, I'm Irish. But a lot of people didn't like him at all, and a lot of people had reason to kill him." He ticked them off on his fingers. "Castro, because the CIA was trying to kill *him*. The Mafia, for what Bobby was doing to Hoffa. The anti-Castro nuts, for Kennedy's screw-up in the Bay of Pigs. Maybe even the Soviets, for what he did to their self-esteem during the missile crisis. The list is longer than your campaign contributors. But the finger that pulled that trigger in Dallas"—O'Brien aimed his hand, pistol-fashion, at Chandler—"belonged to a nut. A screwball who wanted his name in the history books.

"By the way, I thought you said you weren't a conspiracist."

"I'm not," Chandler said. "But there are just too many unexplained coincidences. Oswald defects to the Soviet Union. He works at a U-2 base in Japan, and is in Russia when Gary Powers is shot down in his U-2. May have been just a coincidence, but it's an interesting one. Then Oswald marries a Russian woman and re-defects to the United States. No questions asked by the CIA or the FBI. He joins anti-Castro groups in Miami, distributes pro-Castro literature in New Orleans, assassinates Kennedy, and then is killed by a thug who claims to be suffering from post-traumatic epilepsy."

"That's old turf, Senator. The Warren Commission, the House Committee, the Senate Committee—they've all covered it nine different ways."

"I know, but what if—what if Oswald was, in fact, working for the Agency at the time he defected? You know, in one of those phony defector programs we were running at the time? And somehow he got turned around or went crazy or whatever, and came back to take out our President? What if the Agency threw out a boomerang and it came back and decapitated Jack Kennedy?"

"It would be sensational, no doubt. Problem is I don't think anyone would believe it if it *was* true. By the way, at the risk of sounding impertinent, what's all this got to do with the terrorist investigation?"

"Just something that keeps gnawing at me. A riddle that I'd like to know the answer to. I got to thinking about it during the briefing today. It occurred to me that there is some link, some connection: the anti-Castro groups, organized crime, terrorism. I think it's more complicated than drug dealing and general lawlessness."

"Sometimes," O'Brien said, "the most obvious answer *is* the answer. Well, here's hoping you find the key that will unlock the secret." He raised his glass in a mocking toast. "As they say in Peking, *ganbei, ganbei.*" He drank, then set the glass down on the table with a thump. "Listen, I've got some work to do yet. We've got an early flight tomorrow so I'm going to run. I've arranged for a cab to pick us up at six-thirty. See you in the lobby."

Watching O'Brien make his way out through the tables surrounding the small dance floor, Chandler began to feel oddly uncomfortable. He was conscious of a slight embarrassment at being alone with Elaine in the subdued light of the candles, away from the formality imposed by a professional setting. He wanted to appear casual, but he felt the heat of an uncharacteristic blush in his cheeks, and as he looked across the table at the candleshine reflected in her green eyes, he felt the growing strength of his desire for her.

"You were pretty quiet tonight, Elaine."

"I didn't want to interrupt. Kevin isn't usually so talkative. He keeps his opinions to himself most of the time. Besides, I don't know that much about the subject and I can learn more by listening than I can talking. As my father used to say, that's the reason I've got two ears and one tongue." Elaine felt the warmth of Tom's eyes on her now. For the first time in his presence she felt—she groped for the right word—not relaxed; there was too much electricity in the air tonight for that. But, almost . . . *happy*. She smiled.

Chandler felt the temperature rising. He searched his uncooperative brain for a safe topic of conversation, something to bring them back to a professional footing. At last: "How are you liking the job, Elaine?" He felt like a fool. *Now there's a clever conversational gambit*. But it served to bring matters back to the impersonal.

"It gets tedious at times, of course," she said. "Some of the Committee's work is routine. But I can't think of another job that would be as interesting, especially now, with the task force. Working as an analyst for an investment firm, with a company picnic once a year, didn't exactly give me a lot of exciting entries for my diary."

Chandler was surprised. For Elaine even to suggest that she might be keeping a private record of her observations as a Committee staff member could lead to her exclusion from sensitive meetings and, ultimately to separation from her job.

"Do you keep a diary?" he asked warily.

Elaine laughed. "Not since I turned ten. But I must confess, there are times when I wish I still had that innocence—thinking that my experiences would somehow matter to posterity. I gave up that fantasy a very long time ago."

"Ten seems like an awfully early age to have your dreams die." Tom looked directly into Elaine's eyes. Her face was perfectly framed by the white candles. The scent of her perfume seemed to settle in every crevice of his brain. He wanted to reach across the table and take her hand, invite her to spend the night with him.

His hand touched hers—but all he said was, "It's getting late. We ought to be going." He found himself running on: "We're on the first flight back to D.C. in the morning and I've got a speech to work on. There's a delegation coming from the Tulsa Chamber of Commerce at noon and I promised Charlie Walcott that I'd help entertain his constituents. I don't have the slightest idea of what to say."

Elaine took her cue from him. "You're right, Senator. It is late. And I have to put those notes of mine into some sort of readable form for my report."

Chandler signed the check, then shepherded Elaine through the maze of tables and out past the bar, around which the seduction game was being overtly played. Outside, they skirted the swimming pool, which glowed like a tourmaline in the velvet night.

Elaine was quartered in one of the bungalows reserved for guests of the club's members. Her room adjoined O'Brien's. *He'll hear Elaine come in*, Chandler thought, *and make a note of how long she stayed behind.*

As they reached the pathway at the end of the pool, Chandler paused. He felt schoolboyishly awkward. A handshake seemed preposterous, too businesslike. But a kiss, even a light one on her cheek, would presume an intimacy that didn't exist. *Not yet.* He caught himself. It was time to put his mask back on. *Nice smile. Self-assurance recaptured. Senator in control.*

"After the kind of day we had, I certainly enjoyed the dinner, Elaine. Thanks for the company and the conversation. See you in the morning."

"Good night, Senator. I enjoyed it too." Elaine seemed never to be out of control. "Don't spend too much time on your speech. You're much better when you're not too formal."

Chandler couldn't decide if the ambiguity was intended. He let it pass. "Thanks," he said. "I think you may be right. Good night."

Chandler watched her enter her bungalow, then headed for the high-rise. Preoccupied with thoughts of Elaine, he failed to notice the man who stepped off the elevator just as he got on. He was an inconspicuous sort of man, but still there was something unusual about him in this place. He did not look the part of a guest. His eyes were too alert, too intense, and he moved with the ease of someone trained to fade into shadows.

A few minutes later, Chandler tossed his suit jacket onto a couch in the living room of his penthouse suite and stared out at a night filled with stars. He lit a cigar and blew out the smoke with a deep sigh. Impulsively, he picked up the phone and dialed the club's operator.

"Would you please connect me with Miss Dunham's room?"

"One moment, sir." The phone rang three times. *Damn it, she's probably halfway into the bathtub—and Kevin's going to wonder who's calling her at this hour.* He was tempted to hang up. Finally, he heard her pick up the receiver.

"Hello?"

He tried to sound perfectly composed. "Hello, Elaine? Sorry to bother you." He wanted to invite her up to his room for a drink. But on the instant, he was afraid she might reject the offer. He stammered. "Oh. I—uh—forgot to ask. What is the name of that perfume you wear?"

"It's Flora Danica. Why?"

"Oh, just wondering. It's very subtle. Elegant."

"Thank you, Senator."

"See you in the morning. Good night."

Chandler felt foolish as he hung up the phone. He was behaving like an adolescent. He untied the knot in his tie and unbuttoned his shirt. He went to the bathroom and switched on the light.

His eyes were drawn immediately to the mirror directly over the sink. A small piece of paper was taped to the glass. A message was neatly typed on it.

> Senator Chandler. You are on the
> right
> track. I have information important to
> your investigation. Meet me at the bar
> next to the pool at 12:45.

Chandler shook his head. *What the hell is this?* How did anyone know he was in Miami today on an investigation? How did they know what he was investigating? How did they know where he was staying? How did they get into his room?

His instincts warned him to ignore the note. But curiosity prevailed. He glanced at his watch. It was 12:32 A.M. The poolside bar had been closed for more than an hour. He would dress and go down, to stand in the darkness. And wait.

10

Dmitri Natashin, driving north out of Moscow, listened attentively to the throb of his engine. His position in President Drachinsky's office had got him to the top of the list for a very used and somewhat undependable black Zaporozhets, a minicar that used little petrol but demanded constant care. So far, the engine was turning over well today. Colonel Metrinko would be in a rage even if Natashin was on time; being late would make him even worse.

Thirty minutes after leaving the Kremlin, just outside the village of Zhukovo, Natashin turned off the highway into a narrow dirt road. About half a mile up the road he parked under a tall pine tree near the end of a path that disappeared into a pine forest.

Metrinko emerged from the forest, beckoned silently to Natashin, turned, and vanished. Natashin got out of the car and hurried to catch up. Around a bend in the path, where he could see but not be seen, Metrinko waited. When he was satisfied that Natashin had not been followed, Metrinko beckoned again, and the two men continued up the path in silence. Natashin was pleased that the colonel seemed now to trust him enough not to frisk him for recording devices.

At the end of the path a large log cabin stood in a clearing. As they neared the cabin, its bright-blue wooden door opened and an old man in a wrinkled army uniform bowed slightly and ushered them into a dark hallway. They handed him their greatcoats and climbed the stairway to the second floor. At the head of the stairs a door stood open into a small room.

The whitewashed walls of the room were bare below the steep pitch of the ceiling. The only furnishings were a long wooden table with a squat brass lamp, two wooden chairs, and a low bookcase holding a few books and a clock with black roman numerals against a white face. It was a few minutes after eleven on Saturday morning.

Metrinko sat down behind the table and muttered something that Natashin took to be an order to sit down on the other chair. Metrinko wrote a few lines in a brown-covered notebook, which Natashin recognized as the kind his children used for their school-work. The green ballpoint pen was cheap, the kind a hotel waiter might use. Natashin sighed. The morning was gray in the uncur-tained window. Cyril Metrinko, Natashin mused, would never think of anything as ostentatious as curtains. He could not, of course, refuse the state dacha. One did not turn down this symbol of rank and privilege. But there would be no luxuries, no sign that he was succumbing to what he called corruption.

Metrinko looked up. The ophidian eyes blinked again, then stared directly across the table. The clock ticked softly. There was no other sound in the room.

"Bad news, Comrade. You bring bad news."

"You have heard? But I—"

"No. Not heard. *Sensed*. I *sensed* your message, Captain Natashin."

"President Drachinsky is angry and suspicious," Natashin be-gan, "but he said nothing that would indicate that he suspects you are in any way connected with those events of the last two weeks. He wants answers. He is calling for an investigation, Colonel. He thinks whoever is responsible must be mad. Insane . . ."

"And you, Dmitri?" Metrinko said, leaning forward with a smile that was the barest upward movement of his lips. "Do you think I am mad? Insane enough to try to kill the Vice-President of the United States?"

Natashin hesitated, wondering what answer would best serve him. "I . . . Yes. Yes, Colonel. I do believe you are not surprised by the incident—or by the failure."

Metrinko's fist came down on the desk and he exploded in laughter. "So you see the joke! You are an apt pupil, Dmitri, a very apt pupil."

Natashin smiled weakly. "Thank you, Colonel," he said.

"Yes, a very apt pupil. First, as you know, it is very difficult to hit a well-equipped plane. Ask Carlos." Metrinko laughed again. "But it is not difficult to make it *appear* that an attempt was made. And the result, Dmitri, is that you have produced terror but you have not produced an incident that could have unexpected con-sequences.

"The others did fail. Rashish was fairly paid for his failure. But these others. They did well. Do you understand?"

For years Natashin had been risking his entire career on understanding Metrinko, understanding how he learned things, did things. "No, Colonel. I do not understand."

"You must begin with an understanding of the United States. Killing a Secretary of State or a general or an ambassador is merely killing a worker, a hired person. A Vice-President is not hired. The people select her—think they select her. She is not important in herself, Dmitri. But she is a symbol, and her death becomes a symbol. You, of course, are too young to remember John Kennedy. He became a symbol. We do not want symbols, Dmitri."

They know so little, these bureaucrats, Metrinko thought. Even the rare bright one like Natashin knew so little.

He called to the old man and ordered tea. Then he took up his notebook again, ignoring Natashin until the tea tray was brought in. Handing a glass to Natashin, he said, "There is another matter I wish to discuss, Dmitri. It concerns Comrade Tupolev."

Natashin had been expecting this for several weeks now. Georgi Tupolev was KGB station chief at the Soviet Embassy in Washington. But someone else there was Metrinko's man; communications between them were relayed via the Soviet Embassy in Havana. Metrinko called it his private channel. Natashin knew about the private channel but had never seen the traffic. From hints that Metrinko had been dropping, however, Tupolev had been the subject of many recent messages.

Metrinko asked Natashin for everything he knew about Tupolev's relationships with President Drachinsky and others in the Politburo. Natashin realized from the probing questions that he knew far less about the Politburo than Metrinko did. But he also knew that Metrinko was by reputation a cautious man. And, precisely because of that reputation, his boldness went unsuspected.

After dismissing Natashin, Metrinko turned his thoughts to his country's leadership. One by one he passed their names through his mind. Only in name were they different. Their policies never changed. Drachinsky had inherited the stalemate in Afghanistan and had accepted stalemate; he had resisted suggestions to harden the military there, to use all means to wipe out the rebels. He had made Poland something for the Poles to deal with, and he seemed to give little care to events in Ethiopia and South America.

We need to put another 100,000, possibly 200,000 more men into Afghanistan—to wipe out their population, if need be. Every day of delay only makes them bolder. We will be there for years, until our people start to rebel when their sons do not come home. . . .

We continue to negotiate with China—what stupidity. They have nothing to offer but people. And we should strike now before they get too many bombs. We have given millions to the Syrians. They take our missiles and money and insist they are sovereign Arabs.

Metrinko rarely discussed anything political with a colleague. But once, when an agent long in America had told him that the Americans did not understand the Soviets, Metrinko had said, "Some of them do." He had taken from a drawer in his desk a translation of a column by an American conservative journalist, who had written: "There is no established 'peace party' or 'war party,' liberal wing or conservative wing, in the Soviet leadership. There are only the ins and outs." The last sentence translated well.

Now, Metrinko realized that he himself was not concerned merely with the drift of Soviet foreign policy. Cyril Metrinko wanted to be one of the *ins*, one of the very big *ins*.

He lit a loosely packed Russian cigarette—he did not profess to enjoy weak Western tobacco, as some of his subordinates did—and thought about himself. He was a student of the history of conflict. He marveled at his own genius in discovering years ago the possibility of using terrorism to restructure the superpower balance. He hoped he had not erred in making two moves so closely spaced, and so near the top of the American government. But the assets had been in place, and they were inclined to take the chance themselves. Metrinko, behind the scenes, had provided the final incentive, the escape routes, and the hiding places.

Now he would await the repercussions. And he would strike again. The network, after years of preparation, was finally in place. The time for action had arrived. He had terrorized a giant nation, had made it feel vulnerable, had frightened its leaders.

Now his plans could begin to be realized. The links to the principal terrorist assets had been forged. Although their leaders knew nothing of Metrinko, they had come to rely on him for money, weapons, passports, communications. He had become, over a period of time, indispensable to almost all of them. They needed him, and now he could use them for his own purposes.

A pattern of terror was emerging. The anarchist forces stirring in the West must be encouraged, financed, organized. Terrorist acts everywhere had to be better timed and better coordinated. Targets had to be more carefully selected for their political effects. Most of all, terrorism had to be seen as a political weapon.

War was no longer an acceptable extension of foreign policy. Invasions, military adventures, border clashes, all were made more dangerous by the reality of nuclear arms—and thus less viable to diplomats and political leaders. More and more the superpowers found their options limited, their hands tied. Only one man, Colonel Qaddafi, had been quick to recognize that terrorism could be an effective instrument of foreign policy.

Metrinko recognized it, but he had not confided his plans to the weak men who were his superiors. He had begun, for now, a private war. His position of near-autonomy inside the KGB gave him a perfect cover for his operations. As chief of counterintelligence, he could investigate anyone in the Soviet Union. To Metrinko, that meant *anyone*, including the premier or the head of the Party. Metrinko's power was feared throughout the Soviet government. His rigid Leninist orthodoxy made him incorruptible. He was unrivaled in his dedication to the state and he had a drawerful of medals as evidence.

Through years of patient effort, he had managed to establish at the very highest levels of the government of the United States his own personal source, known as Eagle. That effort had recently begun to pay off in the form of a steady stream of vitally important, highly classified military and intelligence secrets. Through Eagle, Metrinko was now providing the Soviet hierarchy with some of the most important intelligence information obtained since the end of World War II. The gratitude showered on the KGB by the Politburo further enhanced Metrinko's prestige with his superiors.

Cyril Metrinko's position was unassailable, his authority unquestioned. His plan was beginning to unfold.

11

Ned Dempsey was meticulous about everything. The time he arrived at Senator Chandler's office (seven forty-five). The way he packed his briefcase (two packs of cigarettes, pencils neatly holstered, a small memorandum pad, a Lanier dictaphone). He had his own unswerving system for organizing his desk and stacking his phone messages. He had a compulsion for neatness and order—except for his cigarettes, which he chain-smoked and stubbed out in ashtrays scattered throughout Chandler's spacious office suite in the Hart Senate Office Building.

Dempsey was Chandler's Administrative Assistant—his AA—a title, he told himself, that would be carved on his headstone if he didn't get out soon. He had stayed too long and was going stale. Loyalty to Tom Chandler kept him on, but even that was growing thin. The idea of his own public relations firm was looking better to him every day. Better money, maybe a Mercedes instead of a broken-down Honda . . .

Most of all he was tired of playing shrink for the forty-three employees who worked in Chandler's office. In fact, you couldn't really call it Chandler's office. It was Ned Dempsey who screened the hundreds of job applicants and made the hiring decisions. He listened to the personal problems and frustrations of all the staff. He knew about their family stresses, their infidelities. He was aware of who was using alcohol or popping pills. He stroked them or scolded them as the situation demanded. He organized their duties and secured their pay raises. He rotated them periodically to ensure freshness and stimulation. He was their Father Confessor. They were his parishioners.

The staff was Dempsey's, not Chandler's, and Tom knew it. To his staff members Chandler was "The Senator," the man with the title, who took credit for their labors. It wasn't that they resented him. They simply felt he didn't fully appreciate them. He drew them around him like a circle of wagons to protect him from interruptions, from lobbyists, from importuning constituents.

On this rainy spring morning, Dempsey scanned Chandler's schedule. The breakfast meeting with Ron Barber of the *Post* had been rescheduled. Intelligence Committee at nine o'clock. Chandler would just make it. John Irby from Darien at ten-thirty to talk about the Highway Trust Fund. No, he thought, let Sandra Feeney meet with Irby. No need to tell anyone that Chandler's desk was piled high this Monday morning because of the Miami trip. Lunch with Saul Bernstein, the former staff director of the Senate Intelligence Committee.

Ned heard Bob Tilley coughing in the back room. He walked through the reception room, pausing in mid-stride to realign one of the paintings of Connecticut scenes that adorned the walls. Passing through the office supply room, he headed for an L-shaped cove, where Tilley, Chandler's press secretary, sat surrounded by bookcases filled with dreary green-covered government reports. Judging from the Styrofoam evidence, Tilley had already consumed two cups of coffee and was well into a third.

"In a little early this morning, aren't you, Bob?" Dempsey asked the question with honest concern, and just the slightest hint of approval.

"Woke up a little earlier than usual, I guess," Tilley answered, not quite finished coughing. "Actually, I wanted to check in with some friends at the Pentagon about the attack on the Vice-President's plane."

"Any progress on who did it?"

"No. But they found the missile launcher less than half a mile away from where it was fired. It was a Soviet-made SA-7, called a Grail. Has a range of about three kilometers. All it's got is a tail-chase capability. Same type the Syrians used to knock out the Israeli Phantom jet over the Bekáa Valley last year. You can find them anywhere from Vietnam to Libya. Can't compare to our Stinger."

"I suppose it's easy to smuggle into the country?"

"Easier than sending your golf clubs by commercial air. Looks like an ordinary four-foot piece of steel tubing. Weighs about twenty-three pounds."

"Jesus. The guys that fired that thing must be crazy. They could start a goddam war!"

"Who would we retaliate against, Ned? Chances are we won't take any of them alive, if we ever do find them. We'll probably never know whether they're on their own or working for some crazy Third World dictator." Tilley started to cough again.

"I can hardly speak from a position of moral authority, Bob, but have you thought of quitting? Cigarettes, I mean?"

Tilley's cough ended in a laugh. "Ned," he said, "how long have you worked for Chandler?"

"From the time he was Governor. Why?"

"Do you know who he is? I mean . . ." Tilley groped for the right words. "I mean, do you know *why* he's a senator? Does *he* know why he's a senator? Does he give a damn about any of the issues? For instance, why did he take the task force job? Christ, Margie tells me he has an Appropriations Committee report that isn't half done. It needs his attention."

"Come on, Bob. Ease up. A friend of his—a *real* friend—had his family wiped out. Besides, no one on the Intelligence Committee has followed the terrorism issue more than Tom. What's really bugging you?"

"He doesn't finish what he starts. He drops the load on somebody else's desk and takes off on another project. We all crank out these goddam memos he's always demanding, and they've got to be fast and first-rate—and you know something, Ned? I don't know if he ever reads them."

"Bob. Let me ask you. Has he ever embarrassed us at a hearing? Has he ever asked a dumb question or looked unprepared? Does he mumble 'No comment' every time a reporter asks him something, so that it would immediately reflect on you? You know, so that your buddies would say that you, Bob Tilley, screwed up in briefing your boss?"

"No," Tilley admitted.

"He reads your memos, believe me, and he doesn't move his lips when he reads. There are some who do, you know." Dempsey smiled, trying to lift the frown from Tilley's forehead. Something in the tone of his voice, however, told Tilley it was time to stop complaining.

But he wasn't quite ready to let go. "I still don't understand why he had to rush off to Miami. I had to cancel an interview with the *Hartford Courant* on Friday, and now this morning's breakfast with the *Post*. These reporters get antsy when you keep putting them off."

"I know, I know," Dempsey said, letting his exasperation with Tilley start to show. "But this is a big step up for him, chairing a task force on terrorism. If he does it right, it could help him reach the Oval Office."

"What if he doesn't?"

"If he screws up, he'll fall on his face. Somebody else will go for the brass ring and maybe he'll go back to being a senator."

Tilley shook his head and sighed. "Okay. I guess we don't have much to say about that anyway. But you might tell him, while he's out jetting around with his committee staff, not to forget us back here in the office."

"I understand, Bob. I'll pass the message along."

One of these days, Dempsey vowed, he was going to get out of the middleman business. Trying to make everybody understand everybody else's problems left him precious little time for his own.

Dempsey revealed to no one that he was worried about Chandler. He was running out of excuses for him. Dempsey used to tell everyone that Chandler was chiefly occupied with big issues, that he had a low threshold for the inconsequential. But he knew what the real problem was: Chandler was simply not interested enough in being a legislator. He felt superior—hell, he *was* superior—and it looked to Dempsey as if Chandler wanted—more than anything else—to be President. Trouble was, Dempsey mused, Chandler didn't understand that sometimes the best way to get something you really wanted was not to want it too much.

And there was something else that worried Dempsey. He didn't like the idea of Chandler's traveling around the country with Elaine Dunham. All some gossip columnist needed was one good look at Elaine. Dempsey didn't care if she had a 150 IQ. She was a knockout and no one in the press was going to talk about her brains. Something told him she was going to be trouble for Chandler. Real trouble.

Monday, April 6

12 By working through the weekend and all day Monday, Elaine was able to put her Miami report on Chandler's desk at 6:30. She was relieved to find he had left for the day. She didn't want to be late for her appointment.

She drove from Capitol Hill to Georgetown, parked her car on Volta Place, and then, merging with the pedestrian traffic, she crossed Wisconsin Avenue and went into one of Georgetown's busier shops. Ignoring the ladies' room to which the salesclerk had directed her, she quietly left the store by the back entrance—as her instructions had specified.

Dusk was just giving way to darkness when she arrived at the servants' entrance of an elegant N Street town house. Using the cover name she had been given, she introduced herself to the maid and was promptly led up the back stairs to a rear study. Beyond the small pool of light cast by the green-shaded desk lamp, she saw heavy drapes drawn close across a windowed wall in a room clearly intended as a homeowner's retreat.

Elaine settled into a deep leather chair in the darkest corner. He would enter in about fifteen minutes, she figured—fifteen long minutes. He always let her wait. *He knows it makes me edgy,* she thought. *Maybe he wants me that way. Edgy.*

It had been a long and crooked trail to that room in Georgetown, beginning at the Agency. There Elaine had worked for four years, advancing rapidly. Her job was analyzing the Soviet Union's foreign policy objectives in Latin America. She was very good at it. She enjoyed the work and the faintly glamorous aura of mystery that clung to the letters *CIA*. She had even felt she was performing a patriotic service.

But when she heard that she could earn almost double her salary as an analyst at the Washington office of a major investment house, she could not resist. She did well there, too, and was on the brink of promotion.

Then one day about nine months ago, she had received a phone call at her Reston, Virginia, home. She was told that a car would pick her up at nine o'clock the following morning, a Saturday, and take her to Langley, Virginia, to the headquarters of the CIA.

She was whisked through the labyrinth of security, into an elevator, and past double doors to the office of the Assistant Director. Checking her face against a photograph in a folder on his desk, he had handed her a plain white sealed envelope. His shrug and slight smile indicated his ignorance of what was inside it. The only words he spoke were: "You will be taken home. Read this when you get there and destroy it." He motioned, and the security man who had ushered her into the office took her back through the maze.

Inside the envelope, a single typewritten sheet directed her to drive on Sunday to a secluded inn about thirty miles outside Philadelphia. She had waited in a private dining room, as instructed, for more than an hour.

"Good evening, Miss Dunham," he had said. "Thank you for joining me."

She had never met the Director of Central Intelligence before. But fleeting hallway glimpses had been enough to assure her that, indeed, this was he.

After dinner had been served and the dining room door closed by a silent, discreet waiter, Trevor had begun.

"Miss Dunham, I have heard there were many tales of Camelot that never made their way into the official chronicles of King Arthur and his Court. Let me tell you one tonight. You see, King Arthur had great faith in Merlin, and because of his need to know all that happened in the realm, he tasked Merlin with the duty to listen and report back to him from time to time whatever he might hear."

Elaine's bewilderment at finding herself in this remote place with the Director of Central Intelligence had begun then to give way to bemusement. *King Arthur? Merlin?*

Trevor continued his story: how Merlin came into conflict with the Knights of the Round Table, who resented his power over King Arthur and decided to inquire into his authority and activity. "Obviously aware of this inquiry, the clever Merlin foresaw the possibility that his enemies at the Round Table—and there were many—might use this opportunity to reduce his stature in King Arthur's eyes, or even falsely accuse him of disloyalty."

Elaine was by then fully alert. Trevor poured them both another cup of coffee.

"Now, you see," he said, "what was Merlin to do? He warned poor foolish King Arthur of the dangers. But to protect himself fully, he needed to know what the Knights were saying among themselves—behind their closed doors."

Trevor paused. "It so happened that a few ladies of the Court were retained to serve the Knights as they conferred about the Round Table. And one of these was Queen Guinevere's cleverest handmaiden."

Elaine's heart began to pound.

"This maiden was well known to Merlin and highly regarded by him—and he by her. So when Merlin discussed his need, this young woman readily agreed to serve his interests. For, you see, she not only respected Merlin but also valued the role he played."

Trevor paused again, looking into the dimming fireplace, then directly at Elaine. "Yes, she loved Camelot," he said. He sat back and was silent, staring at her intently. She knew he was letting the myth sink in before he gave her the reality.

He raised his voice slightly and changed the tone, speaking in a clipped, businesslike way. There was an opening on the staff of the Senate's Select Committee on Intelligence. He had been advised that someone with intelligence experience was what was needed. She knew then that the way had been prepared, just as she was certain at that moment that her job in the investment house had been arranged. She remembered something an older analyst had told her at her farewell lunch in a small Chinese restaurant near the Agency. "You'll be gone," he had said, "but not forgotten. They never forget, and you never really go."

The Director, in the end (and in terms designed to protect his "deniability"), had made it sound a patriotic duty to penetrate the Senate of the United States. But why her? She could not understand why he was asking her, making her feel that she somehow had to cooperate, that she had no choice. Why her?

Now she was in a Georgetown study, waiting to deliver her fourth report as a high-level CIA spy in the Senate. Twice she had met with the Director to report on the Committee's consideration of the Agency's request for approval of covert operations. The third time, she had informed him of the Committee's investigations into the sale of sensitive documents by an Air Force captain to a Polish spy.

Since that first meeting, Trevor had mercifully dropped his references to Camelot, but Elaine was still not happy with her role. And she hated the code name Trevor had given her: "Janus." It made her feel two-faced, dishonest. But, of course, she *was* dishonest. Dishonest in the name of country, but dishonest nevertheless. She had often wondered whether the Director had selected the name out of sheer perversity, to remind her of his power—or of her own commitment to help the Agency even though she was no longer officially employed there.

Trevor closed the door quietly behind him and settled himself in a leather chair facing Elaine's. She wondered how he could seem at once so fatherly and so sinister. Despite all his avuncular, practiced geniality, Elaine knew she would always fear him.

"Take your time, Miss Dunham," he said reassuringly. "Our host is one of my oldest and closest friends and he lets me use this lovely room for personal meetings whenever I wish. As I was coming here for dinner tonight in any case, it provided an excellent opportunity to catch up on the progress you've made in your . . . 'mission.'"

Elaine wondered if Trevor's other "personal meetings" had been with his spies from the White House and the Supreme Court.

"Mr. Trevor, I'll get right to the point, if I may. As I'm sure you already know, Senator Chandler spent Friday in Miami. He took another staff member with him, and me. We were briefed by the Miami FBI office and detectives from the Miami Police Department. . . ."

Elaine's presentation was precise, factual, and bloodless. Clearly she was hurrying to get through with it. Trevor interrupted, in an effort to penetrate her detached professionalism. He was not finding out what he really wanted to know.

"Miss Dunham, before you proceed," he said, "I'd be interested in your impressions of Senator Chandler—how you see him approaching this investigation, what he's after, and so forth."

"Mr. Director . . ." Elaine paused. She no longer was an Agency employee. "Mr. Trevor, I think you can tell I'm extremely uncomfortable in this role. It will be easier the less I have to deal in personalities, particularly senatorial personalities."

"That's understandable," Trevor said quickly. "But, on the

other hand, I must be able to appreciate Chandler's motives and attitudes if I am going to be prepared to protect the, ah, the Agency, and its, ah, assets."

Elaine peered through the gloom, trying to make out the expression, if any, on the heavily shadowed face. Light from the single dim lamp reflected off the flat lenses of his glasses. She could see nothing through them. But she noted the unease with which this otherwise smooth, self-contained man explained his reasons for spying on this Senate operation.

"At this point," she said, "I don't think he has a particular motive or attitude. He was shocked by the assassination of Secretary Harrold's family, of course. He's commented on it several times. But so have a lot of others. Clearly it made this investigation more of a cause than it otherwise might have been. Certainly more than just a political circus or a self-promotion scheme. Chandler's a shrewd enough politician to know you can't take an issue as sensitive as terrorism—and an issue that's becoming more and more a domestic problem—and blatantly turn it into a platform for national office."

Elaine could not know she had activated the note-taking device in Trevor's mind for the first time. "I would only say that he's taking this whole thing much more seriously than he seemed to in Committee hearings before the bombing. And it looks as if he intends to stay with it. All of us are beginning to believe there's more to this than isolated acts of terrorism."

"What do you mean by 'more to this'?" Trevor's voice was as even and detached as usual, but Elaine thought she detected a faintly keener sense of interest.

"Well, I don't know, Mr. Trevor. We certainly turned up no hard evidence in Miami. But of course the law enforcement people are intrigued by the parallels: more drugs coming, more terrorist attacks. They don't seem to think the answer is necessarily here, in this country.

"But the Fabricante murder has them puzzled. He was old. He was out of action. He wasn't involved in mob-family activities anymore, except for an occasional card game with his old cronies. Surveillance turned up no evidence that he'd participated in any recent meetings. It's all very strange. Chandler asked a lot of questions in Miami about Fabricante's activities in the early sixties—especially about Mafia involvement in the plots to kill Castro."

Elaine thought Trevor straightened a fraction in his chair. "He asked the other staff member, Kevin O'Brien, to order up the complete FBI file on Fabricante—particularly for the period from 1958 to 1963. And he asked for the Church Committee's records on Fabricante's testimony in 1975 on the Castro murder plots. He said he might want me to do some work on Fabricante's connections with the Agency in the early sixties, and he said he might want to come out and talk to you about that period."

"How interesting." Trevor's glasses reflected dull light from the lamp. "Fabricante was certainly one of the three key Mafia figures our government"—Elaine noted he did not say *Agency*—"had dealings with at that time. But that was twenty years ago and seems hardly to bear on current events. Although of course I know nothing more than what I read about this, it would seem to me only a matter of logic that the old fellow was simply the victim of one of those ancient gangland grudges that keep popping up." Trevor gave the impression of arguing a case—subtly, perhaps, but arguing all the same. He seemed to be saying, *There's less here than meets the eye.*

Elaine sensed that Trevor was worried. "On the other hand," she said, "Senator Chandler believes—and I tend to agree with him—that there are some interesting coincidences in this Fabricante business and they're worth pursuing. In the police pictures the old man looked as if he had been put through hell *before* he was killed. Those pictures are the worst thing I ever saw in my life. Or hope to see. And what they did with his body"—she shuddered. "You don't do that if you just want someone out of the way. As Tom said—" She stopped short and flushed. "As Senator Chandler said, whoever did this was sending a message: *Don't talk about Mafia operations, even if they involve the federal government.* Maybe, specifically, *don't talk about the early sixties and the Castro plots.*

"Anyway, I think he'll continue to follow it up, just to see where it leads."

Trevor casually shifted the ground. "From the news accounts, I gather that Chandler intends to take four to six months on this investigation. It seems to me he's going to have trouble getting it done in that time if he gets into a fishing expedition with every crime committed in this country. It's certainly in the interest of the Agency and its long-term stability to get this thing over and done with."

"Mr. Trevor." Elaine took her courage in both hands and interrupted boldly. "You asked me to report to you on the progress of the investigation. You didn't say anything about altering its course or getting it finished or tampering with its conclusions. Whatever sense of patriotic duty you've managed to tap in me, it doesn't extend to that. I want our understanding clear on this. On the limits of my obligation."

"Of course, Miss Dunham," Trevor said soothingly. *Humoring me*, Elaine thought savagely. He continued, "As I told you when we first discussed this, I simply need to know what the Senate's up to, so that I can protect the Agency. I certainly don't intend to *tamper*—in any way." He paused, looked around the dim room, then directly back at Elaine.

"Did anything else happen in Miami?"

Elaine was startled, her composure further unsettled. Had Trevor had them watched? Had one of his agents seen them together in the dining room? Were their phones tapped? Did Trevor know about Tom's late-night call?

"Nothing else of any consequence," she said quickly. Then she hesitated. A recollection troubled her. She had dressed and gone to the small pharmacy at The Barriers sometime after midnight for the toothpaste she had forgotten to pack. She had seen a tall man quickly slip out of the side door of the condominium lobby leading to the swimming pool. Despite the distance across the length of the spacious lobby, and her glimpse only of his back, she could have sworn it was Tom Chandler. Curiosity aroused, she had walked completely around the high-rise from the front door and approached the pool from the far side. The cabana and poolside bar area were darkened, except for small built-in lights around the rim of the pool to protect late, possibly tipsy diners returning to their rooms.

At the far end of the pool, just at the edge of some short palm trees, she had seen the dim outline of two men standing side by side in the darkness, their backs to her. She had been tempted to giggle, reminded of boys in her high school class who had gone into the trees near the football field to urinate after practice. Then she realized the men were engaged in a hurried, furtive discussion. Except it wasn't a discussion. The shorter man, in a hat with a broad downturned brim, seemed to be doing all the talking, the taller man listening attentively. The conversation had lasted no more than a few minutes and concluded with the passing of what seemed to be a small piece of paper between them.

The shorter man had then seemed almost literally to disappear.

She had slipped quickly behind a palm tree as the tall man looked around. He reentered the condominium through the side door. The lobby lights had briefly illuminated the face of Thomas Chandler.

"There was nothing else, Mr. Trevor. Just the briefings and Chandler's interest in Fabricante."

"Well, thank you, Miss Dunham." He smiled, professionally, and she could tell he wasn't entirely convinced she had told him everything. "You've done well in this uncomfortable assignment. I want you to know, again, how very important all this is to the Agency. Even if nothing directly affecting our interests ever turns up—and I see no good reason it should—just being on top of things is a great help in preparing for any eventuality. If in no other way, your service will be rewarded by your sense of satisfaction at having served your country and its eyes and ears—without, of course, in any way violating its principles."

Elaine hesitated, puzzled by Trevor's raising of the issue of reward. She had long since decided that Trevor never said anything without purpose. She moved to the edge of her chair, increasingly eager to return to the clear night air. "I guess I will have to be the final judge of whether I am violating any principles, won't I, Mr. Trevor?"

Suddenly Trevor was on his feet, thoroughly in control. "On the subject of reward, Miss Dunham: I know how much more you could be making in the investment business. Indeed, I know you took a salary cut with the Senate job. You should not have to make a financial sacrifice." He had never discussed the subject of money with her before. "I'm going to insist that you be compensated for any costs you incur in carrying out this assignment."

Seeing that she was about to interrupt, he hurried on. "Now don't deny it. There are costs involved. And there will be more. This is business, pure and simple. And you mustn't be troubled by it. You'll have long-distance phone calls, transportation costs. You may even have to buy some additional clothes. This mission apparently is going to require that you do a good deal of traveling in a fairly short period of time.

So. I won't have it any other way. There will simply be a cash deposit to your bank account each month to cover these extraordinary expenses. No questions asked. I simply insist."

The man positively oozed fatherliness, Elaine thought. *This man would have been—is—a magnificent actor. It must go with the territory.*

She did not know what would be the appropriate response. She hadn't thought about the idea of being paid to spy. It cheapened the Camelot web Trevor had so craftily woven. Would this make her an agent, bought and paid for? Or, worse, a mercenary? Or, worst of all, a prostitute? The job *was* costing her money, money she didn't have. He had that much right. But she hadn't taken the job for money and she wasn't going to finish it for money. But no protest would work with Trevor once he'd made up his mind. She'd have to figure out a way to return the "reward" once the investigation was over. Right now, her thoughts were jumbled and pressured. And she desperately wanted to escape.

"Whatever you say, Mr. Trevor," she said as she crossed the shadowed room to the door. "Whatever you say."

13

Saturday, April 18

The chimes in the Robert A. Taft Memorial across the street from the Capitol toned eleven-thirty. Except for an occasional patrolling Capitol policeman, the darkened grounds were deserted. Chandler had parked his car on the short curving drive that bisected the northwest corner of the grounds. He had walked slowly toward the small, vine-covered brick pavilion located at the bottom of the Capitol slope. Now he checked his watch to confirm the hour, feeling like someone in a spy novel as he slowly circled the pavilion.

He was beginning to believe he'd been the victim of a practical joke when a voice from within the small structure softly called his name. Chandler peered into the inky interior but could see nothing. The lightly accented voice again said, "Chandler," and the wrought-iron gate to the pavilion swung slowly inward with a small, grating squeak.

"Who is it?" Chandler whispered.

"It is all right," the soft voice said. "It is your friend from Miami. Please come in quickly before you are seen."

A hand at his elbow guided Chandler down a shallow step onto the slate floor of the pavilion. The hand opened the gate, closed it, and refastened the padlock that had been hanging open. "Wait!" Chandler said. "How do we get out of here?" His nerves were on edge, and he felt he'd been stupid to get himself into this potentially dangerous situation. In the tight security surrounding the Capitol it would be ridiculous—and ironic—if he were to be picked up as a terrorist by Capitol Hill police. Or, he suddenly thought, if it turned out he was dealing with a terrorist.

Chandler was still uncertain about his meeting with this man in Miami, the man he had mentally dubbed "Memory." The man had stayed in the darkness, away from the lights of the pool. His hat had almost completely shadowed his face. He had spoken in a low voice, as if his life depended on not being overheard. And Chandler still could make no sense of what the man had said: "Don't forget November twenty-second. Look for the rifle."

What did he mean, *Look for the rifle?*

A hand again was guiding him, across the interior of the pavilion, around a stone fountain in the center, to a low stone bench ten feet away. Feeling the surface of the bench with his hands, Chandler seated himself in the pitch darkness. He felt Memory's bulk beside him.

"Senator, do not mind the lock. It is very easy for me to open. The guard comes by every half hour. Sometimes he checks the lock, but he never looks inside. We can hear him approach. We have only to keep our voices down. This spot is a perfectly secure place to talk. We can use it whenever it is necessary."

"You told me in Miami that I was on the right track," Chandler whispered. His voice rose with urgency, but he kept it low. "I contacted you through the newspaper ad, the way you told me to do, because I needed your help. None of this is making any sense. It's been two weeks since I was in Miami. In the meantime, we've been following the drug lead. Clearly, a lot more drugs have been coming into the States in the last six months than ever before. Our drug enforcement people don't know exactly where they're coming from yet, but they've narrowed it down to Caracas, Frankfurt, and Amsterdam. That's where the big deals are being made."

Chandler's eyes were now sufficiently accustomed to the dark that he could distinguish the outline of shapes within the pavilion. But the features of his companion remained hidden.

Chandler resumed speaking, his words coming faster. "I have a hunch—I guess because of the coincidence of timing—that something connects the increase in drug traffic and the outbreak of terrorism, particularly in this country."

"Follow that," Memory said.

"Follow that? Follow what? An . . . I'm not sure how to do that—how to follow that connection."

"Just ask questions. Ask a lot of questions," the man said.

"Right," Chandler said. "Let's begin right here. Who killed Fabricante, and why was he killed—slaughtered—the way he was?"

"Well you might ask," said the man. "Good question."

Chandler detected a note of mockery. "Wait a minute. First you say, 'Ask questions.' Then you say, 'Good question.' What am I doing here, playing Sherlock Holmes at midnight with someone I don't even know? I asked you to meet me because I thought you had some answers."

"I do, Senator Chandler," the voice said softly. "I have many answers. But I cannot simply give them to you. Unfortunately for you, you must find them out for yourself. For me to do otherwise would be distinctly unhealthy. Unhealthy for *me*."

"Great!" Chandler groaned. "So I'm supposed to ask questions and you'll tell me whether they're good questions or not."

"Something like that, Senator. Would you rather spend your time asking the wrong questions?"

Chandler was silent. He could faintly hear the other man breathing. It didn't take him long to decide he had very little choice in the matter.

"All right, let's begin with Miami. You said I was on the right track. I went down there primarily because the FBI picked up this Ahmad Rashish in the Harrold assassination case. Also because Fabricante, an old Mafia don, was chopped up. Also because of my suspicions about the connection between drugs and terrorism. Now, how do I know which of those tracks is the right track?"

Chandler felt the man's hand on his knee and involuntarily jerked his leg away. Then he heard the footsteps of the Capitol policeman strolling down the sidewalk not ten yards away. The two men sat motionless. The footsteps paused briefly at the gate, there was a small metallic sound, and then the footsteps resumed, dying away into the night.

Chandler discovered he'd been holding his breath. He let it out on a sigh. After a minute, the voice from the dark said, "Could it be possible that all those trains are headed down the same track?" There was a pause. "When too many trains get on the same track, even when they are headed the same way, often there is a collision."

"So, there's a connection between an Arab suspect in an assassination case who killed himself or got killed—that's one train. And a Mafioso who got dismembered—that's two. And a big surge of drugs. Three." Chandler softly repeated the thought in his mind: "Find the connection."

Suddenly he turned toward his companion in the darkness. "Wait a minute. That night in Miami you said, 'Look for the rifle.' There *are* no rifles. No rifles for Rashish, no rifles for Fabricante, no rifles for the Harrolds. But wait—you said November twenty-second. You were talking about Kennedy—the Kennedy rifle. That's it!"

The triumph left his voice. "If you're talking about me going back over the rifle in the Kennedy assassination, forget it." He stood up. "If you think you can get me to turn this investigation into some platform for a conspiracy circus, forget it!"

"Z-R-rifle," the man said.

Chandler sat down. "Z-R-rifle. ZRRIFLE . . . is the CIA code name for . . . for the assassination capability. For what they called—what was it?—'executive action.'" He paused. "Is that it? Is that the connection?"

Memory said, "Good question."

"Goddammit!" Chandler exploded. "Don't play games with me! This is too important!"

"Shhhh!" the man warned. He got up and looked outside. "Shhhh," he repeated and sat down again. "I *cannot* be found talking to you. Do you understand? I *cannot*! If you burst out like that again, I will have to leave. For good." He paused. "I am not playing games with you. I want you to succeed. It may be the only hope. But I *cannot* give you the answers. I can only try to point you in the right direction."

Chandler was quiet. "All right. I'm sorry. I can't be caught here either, or it will be all over Capitol Hill tomorrow and I'll have a gay charge or something to face." He thought briefly. "ZRRIFLE. I'll find out everything I can about it."

"Also find out everyone who knew about it," Memory whispered. "There were very few. And even fewer are around today. None of them talked—not even under oath to Senator Church's Committee in 1975. To risk perjury before Congress, you must be afraid of more than embarrassment. Also find out who the rifle was. What were the rifle's assets? Sooner or later you must find the rifle. You must find the rifle yourself . . . but you will need my help."

Chandler waited, but Memory was silent. "That can't be all of it. 'Find the rifle?' This whole thing is more complicated than that."

"You are once again right, Senator. Trust your instincts. The rifle is only a piece—a very important piece, perhaps a necessary piece—but only a piece." His hand gripped Chandler's arm. Finally he said, "There is a snake in the tower. Never forget this. I cannot tell you more. But never forget this."

Chandler thought to himself, *This is surreal. Find the rifle. There is a snake in the tower. I cannot tell you more. What in God's name have I gotten myself into? This man might be crazy as hell. But somehow I don't think so. He is too sure of himself. He doesn't seem to have an angle. He wants some kind of buried truth to come out. And he sees my investigation as the way to do it.*

"Okay. Let's sum up: I'm supposed to ask the right questions. But you can't tell me what they are. Based on what I *assume* are your directions, here are the questions I'm going to ask. You tell me if they're wrong. One, what is the connection between terrorism and drugs? Two, what are the connections between Rashish and the Harrold assassinations, Fabricante's death, and the drug market in Miami? Three, what can I find out about ZRRIFLE, the people involved in it, and why it's important today? Four, who or what is 'the snake in the tower'? That's my agenda. Now you tell me if it's wrong."

The pavilion was silent as a tomb.

Silence means assent, Chandler thought with a sudden rush of elation. *I'm on my way.* For the first time since he had undertaken the investigation, he had a compass to guide his instincts, and he had a source that, for whatever reasons, did not want him to lose direction.

Damn, Chandler thought, *this could get very interesting.*

Memory stood up and moved to the wrought-iron gate. The patrolman would be circling back soon. He inserted a small piece of wire into the rusty padlock, and it snapped open. He took it off the catch and swung the gate half open. Chandler could just see him beckon in the dark. "I will go first. Wait two minutes. Then close and lock the gate."

The man started to go. Then he turned back. "If you need to

talk to me, put the ad in the paper—same as last time. And, Senator Chandler . . . never forget you are involved in a *very* dangerous undertaking here. Some very important individuals do not want you to succeed. They will do what they can to see that you fail. Always remember what I said about the snake."

And he was gone.

Chandler waited for one of the two minutes. Then, reconnoitering first, he stepped outside, closed the gate, and snapped the padlock shut. He walked directly to his car without looking around. As he got in, he heard the Taft chimes begin their midnight strokes and saw the Capitol patrolman start down the long sidewalk leading from the East Front.

Chandler started his car, shivered briefly in the chill, and let out a short ironic laugh. *I still don't know what he looks like,* he thought.

14

As he closed his suitcases in his Washington apartment in preparation for his return to Moscow, Georgi Tupolev was a troubled man. For the first time in his life he was truly frightened. He believed there was an Intruder in the Soviet intelligence service, and that only he and the Intruder were aware of his existence.

Tupolev had been planning to return home on the first of June. It was to have been his journey into retirement. After more than three decades of service to his country, he was tired of intrigue. He had proved to be one of the Soviet Union's best players in the game of intelligence. But after all those years, all those agents, all those supposedly critical secrets, the game had begun to bore him.

Then, a month ago, his instincts had warned him of serious trouble. The assassination of the Harrold family, the attempt made on the Vice-President's plane—these were not isolated events. They were organized, if crudely, and well funded. Carlos. KGB. These events had the signature of someone he knew, and feared.

Something else was in the air. The Western services were talking of "moles"—agents from the other side who penetrated their organizations. The Soviet services talked secretly of something worse, some poison that could move throughout the intelligence community and destroy it. Someone was trying to drive the United States and the Soviet Union into a direct confrontation through terrorist acts.

Viktor Tupolev was frightened because he had come to believe that more than his own paranoia was involved. There was a sinister force at large in Soviet intelligence. He thought he knew and could prove who it was. And that was knowledge he did not want to possess at this point in his life. It was very dangerous knowledge to have.

And now he had been summoned home. Six weeks before the scheduled time for his retirement. No explanation had been offered for the peremptory recall. Indeed, he would have expected none. But alarm bells were ringing in his mind.

His fear was somewhat tempered by his relief at leaving Washington. Not that he had not found some enjoyment in his final tour of duty as KGB station chief here. From his first tour of duty in Washington in the early 1960s, his background as an expert in American civilization had made him feel right at home. He knew the language, the ways of Americans, their weaknesses. He had been taught how to spot potential recruits and how to develop them into agents. And he had been taught well. On his first tour he had managed to recruit several Americans. Adept in the role of model diplomat, he had been no more than routinely suspected by the American counterintelligence people. He had performed so well that when he finished his first tour, he had been called home for special advanced intelligence training.

Ordered back to Washington for a second tour of duty, he had returned on the Ambassador's plane, and it was the Ambassador himself who told him he was to be doubled. He knew of the practice—an agent allowed himself to be approached by the opposition, allowed himself to be recruited as a double agent, and all the while he remained under the control of his own superiors. "A very tricky game," Tupolev had said then to the Ambassador, in English, as the plane began its approach to Washington. The Ambassador had replied, also in English: "Much of it is a game, Georgi. But what you must do is no game. It is dangerous work. Very dangerous." Then, in Russian, "And you can have no friends, Georgi. No honest friends."

That had been the most difficult part. No honest friends.

For twenty years he had lived an emotionally exhausting double life, first as deputy chief and then as senior political officer of the KGB station, and as a mole in the American intelligence garden. As an ostensible spy for the FBI, he had passed on a great deal of disinformation to his American counterparts. But his most vital task as a mole had been to authenticate even more important disinformation provided by Soviet "defectors." Over the years, Soviet intelligence had planted a considerable body of incorrect data in the Western intelligence mill by means of a half-dozen key agents whose job it had been to appear to defect.

The most significant of these had been Yuri Nosenko, who had been sent over within weeks of John Kennedy's assassination to satisfy the members of the Warren Commission that Lee Harvey Oswald had had absolutely no contact with Soviet intelligence. Under the code name "Fedora," given him by his American handlers, Georgi Tupolev had dutifully confirmed Nosenko's bona fides and helped to quiet the continuing debate within the CIA and the FBI over Nosenko's credibility—and over the possibility of Soviet involvement, official or otherwise, in Kennedy's death.

For his success as a double agent, Georgi Tupolev had paid a high price: his own well-being. It was a severe strain for a man his age to keep the lies, double lies, and triple lies straight. The contradictions were starting to confuse him. Lies had the scent of truths, and truths stank of falsehood. It was difficult to distinguish between noxious and wholesome plants in that treacherous garden. One slip and the whole game would be over. He was tired to the very bone, and a few months ago he had requested early retirement. His wife waited for him in her native Georgia, and he wanted to become reacquainted with his children and grandchildren.

It was then, just when he anticipated release from his burden of duplicity, that the new spiral began. At first there was no palpable evidence of the Intruder, as Tupolev thought of him. Like a seasoned hunter, Tupolev simply sensed the presence of a predatory force. But certain signs began to appear. Subtle conflicts. Actions at cross-purposes. An increase in deep-ciphered cable traffic through the Soviet Embassy in Havana. Contradictory orders. It took a seasoned hunter to follow the spoor. Hints from lifelong reliable sources. Odd pieces of information from old friends in the service. Soon the shape and color of the danger began to emerge.

It frightened Georgi Tupolev. It frightened him to think—even to suspect—that the Intruder was one of his closest associates.

The two of them had entered the service in the same class, but, Tupolev remembered, they had been very different. All his life, Georgi Tupolev had been friendly, outgoing, interested in the world beyond Soviet borders. That interest was what had led him into the world of intelligence. Where better to find out about the world and serve his country at the same time? But his associate was different—suspicious, hostile to all things not rigidly Leninist, mysteriously private, ascetic. Georgi Tupolev spied to learn. The other spied to destroy.

Now Georgi Tupolev, sixty-three years old, had been ordered home ahead of schedule. Whatever that ominous summons meant, he was determined to appear before his superiors, to present his suspicions about one of the most dreaded figures in the KGB. If Tupolev had indeed discovered the secret, then surely his life was in gravest danger. For the man he believed to be the Intruder, if he knew, would never let Tupolev live.

A KGB limousine bore Tupolev directly from Sheremetyevo Airport to the old dun-colored building at 2 Dzerzhinsky Square. A young man he did not recognize—there were so many young men he did not recognize—sat in the seat next to him. They did not speak during the twenty-five-minute ride. Tupolev had wanted to ask why they were not driving to the new KGB building on the circumferential highway, but he sensed that he was not to speak.

Long ago he had learned never to show fear. It must be kept locked in the gut, like the Spartan boy's fox in the fable, eating away under his bloody tunic while his face betrayed neither pain nor emotion. But he was afraid. Something was wrong. Somehow they knew of his suspicions about the Intruder. *There will be an interrogation. Tonight, without any rest.*

But Tupolev's prediction was mistaken. He was taken to an apartment at the old headquarters. *A Spartan room.* He smiled to himself. He was brought vodka, caviar, *shashlyk* in the Georgian style he loved, and a bottle of good Georgian wine. Tupolev had long since decided that vodka was not his drink. He did not take a sip, although he did drink half the wine before he got ready for bed. He slept deeply without remembered dreams, a faculty he had always supposed to be part of his subconscious apparatus for remaining sane. For, if he dreamed, who would he be in the dream? Which lie would he live in the dream?

The young man from the limousine awakened him at seven o'clock. He had a breakfast of tea and dark bread, and at eight-thirty he was ushered into a large office. Four men in dark suits sat behind a long table. One was his direct superior. The other three were men he recognized from the First Chief Directorate, the KGB section for foreign operations. Two of them were career bureaucrats. The third was Colonel Cyril Metrinko, the chief of counterintelligence.

Tupolev tried to convince himself that this was routine. At first, it seemed so. He had done the paperwork: his final report as Washington station chief, his formal request for retirement. They probably wanted a verbal report. He waited for their questions. There were none. For long minutes the four men looked across the table at him. He sat in a wooden chair without arms. The chair was just far enough from the table so that he could not lean on it.

Finally, Metrinko said, "You state in your report that you have a matter you wish to"—he looked down at a paper in front of him—"discuss verbally with your direct superior."

"That is correct," Tupolev said. His voice sounded firm. The fear had not escaped his gut.

"You may do so now," said Tupolev's direct superior.

"I had expected to talk to you in private."

"This is as private as our talk will be, Comrade Tupolev. You may proceed."

His prediction had not been mistaken, only delayed. Something was wrong. Terribly wrong.

He told them what he suspected about the Intruder. Then, looking directly at his superior rather than Metrinko, Tupolev said, "I will give the name of the man I suspect only to President Drachinsky." He turned toward Metrinko. "And only in private."

There was silence again, and then, abruptly, Metrinko began asking questions. Tupolev knew the tone and the technique. An inquisition had begun.

The questions began with Tupolev's early career.

"During your first tour in Washington, from 1960 to 1963, did you run agents in the Cuban exile community in Miami for Castro and the Soviet Government?"

"Certainly. That was in my reports."

"Through those agents did you become aware of the plots to assassinate Fidel Castro?"

"Indeed. That also was in my reports."

"Was that information passed on to Castro through the Soviet Government?"

"Naturally. But Castro had his own agents in the exile community as well."

"After efforts to overthrow Castro were called off by Kennedy, did you not maintain contact with a highly placed Cuban exile who was very close to the CIA assassination planning unit, codenamed ZRRIFLE?"

"Yes."

"Did that Cuban émigré inform you in the spring of 1963 that a plan was under way to assassinate President Kennedy?"

Tupolev hesitated. How did the inquisitors know that?

"Yes," he said finally.

"Did you, on your own authority, communicate that intelligence to a CIA officer now very high up in the Agency?"

Georgi Tupolev was dumbfounded. No one else in the world knew that.

"Yes," he said.

Metrinko drew himself up. "Georgi Tupolev," he said, "have you, throughout your career in the KGB, continued to pass valuable state secrets to that same individual in violation of your solemn oath of loyalty to the Union of Soviet Socialist Republics and to the detriment of the security of the state?"

"No! No! No! No!" shouted Tupolev. He sucked in his breath. *Calm*, he told himself, *calm*. "I have operated as a double agent, spreading disinformation only in accordance with the instructions of my superiors. I communicated that one fact, and that one alone, because it was not our policy then, nor is it now, to aid would-be assassins of the President of the United States. I have done nothing wrong."

"Nothing wrong, Comrade Tupolev?" Metrinko repeated, looking first at Tupolev and then at the other men at the table. "Do you call what you have been doing *nothing wrong*?

"Let us correct some of *your* disinformation, Tupolev. Yes, you did tell your control in the CIA that there was to be an assassination—and when the assassination did happen, you told your CIA control that the Soviet Union was implicated."

"No! No!" Tupolev shouted, panic rising for the first time in memory. "That is a lie!"

"Your treachery forced your country to expend considerable resources to discredit theories connecting Oswald to the Soviet Union."

"No! No!" Tupolev shouted again. "I confirmed Nosenko's credentials. You *know* this, Colonel. I have commendations. The record—"

"There are *two* records, Tupolev. One that you could show your CIA friends who were here in Moscow"—Metrinko swept his arm about the room—"and in Langley. There was another record, Tupolev. A record of treachery. Clever treachery, but I have managed to uncover it."

"Comrade Colonel," Tupolev's superior cut in. "A moment, please. We are talking history here, Comrade. Treachery, as you call it, long undiscovered, even by you, Comrade. History."

Metrinko turned toward the man and, with a cold smile, said, "It is not history I talk about, Comrade. Counterintelligence is like one of your fine Georgian onions. You peel away, Comrade, until you get to the heart. Not until then do you know that the heart is rotten." He paused, opened his dogeared notebook, glanced at a page, and looked up.

"The innermost layers are recent events. It should be recalled, for example, how weak and ineffective were Tupolev's efforts to persuade the Western media that the United States had deliberately arranged for that Korean airliner to fly over Soviet air space, knowing that it would be shot down. Who could forget or forgive that great slander the Soviet Union had to suffer because Tupolev treacherously turned disinformation against his homeland?

"And there is this." Metrinko held up a document. "A very recent report from a loyal man at the Soviet Embassy in Washington. Tupolev alone knew that documents vital to the Soviet Union had been placed in a dead drop in Washington. The documents were intercepted by the FBI. Only one man could have known, could have blatantly informed his keepers."

"That is a lie," Tupolev said. "I knew nothing of that dead drop. *You*, you and your 'loyal man,' whoever he is. You arranged for the drop to be known to the FBI. You, *you* are the Intruder."

Tupolev's superior paled. The other men looked toward Metrinko. He smiled and shook his head. He stood and walked out of the council room. The others followed.

*   *   *

Minutes later, the inner chamber door opened to admit the head of the First Chief Directorate, who wordlessly approached the table. The officer was in full uniform. Tupolev still sat numbly in his chair. Without lifting his eyes to Tupolev's face, he placed on the table a pistol and, next to it, a single bullet. In his thirty years of service Tupolev had never touched a gun except in training. He did not even know what kind of gun he was now staring at. But he knew he was expected to put that bullet in the gun, aim at his temple, and fire the bullet into his brain. It was, he knew, a special kind of bullet, one that would explode in his brain. He would die quickly.

After several minutes Tupolev picked up the pistol and bullet, examined them, and carefully set them down again. If he did not use the pistol, he would face a far more painful death in the cellars of Number 2 Dzerzhinsky Square. And what might be done to his widow? To his children?

Georgi Tupolev took a pen and a note pad from his pocket and wrote a last, loving letter to his wife of thirty-eight years. He inserted the bullet into the pistol, and rose to take one final look at the world beyond the room that held him.

As he looked down, in the courtyard below he saw a familiar figure. Gazing up at his window, a faint smile on his narrow face, stood Colonel Cyril Metrinko.

PART TWO

Why did the watchdog never bark?
Why did the footsteps leave no mark?
Where were the servants at that hour?
How did a snake get in the tower?

15

IT WAS 6:00 A.M., and Gordon Nicholson seemed angry even at that hour. Maybe it was because he lived with fools, knaves, and foreboding. Or maybe it was last night's prodding call from Trevor. It had been two weeks since Trevor had told him that Chandler's task force was resurrecting the Kennedy assassination. Nicholson still hadn't found out why. *And why*, Nicholson thought, *is Trevor so concerned?*

Nicholson was in the shower, letting the hot water beat down on his shoulders, easing his constant tension. He stayed in the shower for at least ten minutes every morning, thinking about to-day's schedule or tomorrow's meetings, working out a letter to be dictated later or a line of examination for an evasive witness. He took politics very seriously. And he was taken that way by his colleagues.

On the phone last night, Trevor had almost rambled. Very unusual for him. But these were unusual times. In the month since the creation of the task force, violence had spilled onto the streets of the world. A homemade bomb had exploded in a London department store; thirty people were wounded, four critically, and six people, including a baby, were killed by the nails, bolts, and nuts that blew into their heads and ripped away their limbs. In Rome, American diplomat Russell Kraemer was all but cut in half by a hail of machine-gun bullets fired by three men wearing black ski masks. Kraemer had just kissed his wife good-bye and was walking down the front steps of his home when the attack came. It took less than ten seconds. In Amsterdam, the Secretary of the Dutch Cabinet was stabbed to death in his bed.

Just a few months ago, people in America had been concerned, but not really alarmed, about the increase in violence. The savagery seemed to be at large only in Europe. The Atlantic was a wide blue buffer. Then the madness had struck at home, and the terror had become real.

Trevor's conversation had implied that if terrorism became a political issue—especially a political issue for Chandler—"the intelligence community" (make that CIA) would find it impossible to grapple with this menace. Terrorism lived in darkness and had to be fought and killed in darkness. All this had been preamble to what Trevor really wanted, without specifically asking for it: If Nicholson could not discover the reasons for Chandler's interest in long-dead history, how about a leak that would hurt Chandler?

Nicholson stepped out of the shower into the steam-filled bathroom and toweled his muscular body. His hair was so blond that his eyebrows seemed invisible. His skin was the kind that never seemed to tan. When he returned from a weekend of California sun, the redness of his face made his hair look white. Some root in his family must have been deep in Scandinavian soil. His eyes were so pale a blue that they were almost without color; they had been likened to the eerie eyes of a Siberian-bred husky.

He was not tall, but he was powerfully built. And he used his 205-pound frame to intimidate. If, in his opinion, a witness was unforthcoming, Nicholson would back him into a corner with a menacing glower, apparently ready to maul him. It was an effective technique, especially with a timid or unseasoned victim. There was nothing subtle about Nicholson; he came at you like a battering ram.

After he shaved, he put on a blue pin-striped suit with a white shirt and regimental-striped tie. His black shoes were always polished to a high gloss. Everything about him—his clothes, his step, his manner—told the world that he was conservative, and proud to be so.

Nicholson had once worked for ZTS, a company that did high-level research and development work for the Pentagon. That was before he had been encouraged to resign from his job. Information concerning one of the major satellite systems then under development had been compromised by two employees who had worked in Nicholson's department. They had sold photographs of critical sections of the satellite's blueprints to a Soviet agent masquerading as a West German business executive.

An internal investigation had been conducted by Morris Tucker, one of ZTS's senior vice-presidents. Tucker was shocked by the utter laxity in security he found in ZTS's Crystal Vault operations. Drugs, parties, sex—carried on during working hours in the most highly classified department of the company's business. He concluded that Nicholson had to be held responsible for gross supervisory negligence, if not worse.

But Tucker's report was never filed—or found. The night before he was to meet with ZTS's board of directors, Tucker was driving home from a late night at the office when his car suddenly swerved off the road and struck the concrete abutment of a highway overpass. The coroner said Tucker had died instantaneously. The police concluded he had fallen asleep at the wheel. The death was ruled accidental.

ZTS's management had decided to minimize the implications of Tucker's death. The officers feared that any disclosure of further wrongdoing within the company might raise questions in the Pentagon about the company's reliability. Billions of dollars were at stake.

A statement was prepared that put the best possible light on the breach in security and the transfer of the documents. New security procedures were instituted. Employees were forbidden to enter or work in the Crystal Vault alone. No briefcases, parcels, food, or beverages could be brought in. Smoking was prohibited. A closed-circuit television system was set up to monitor the vault around the clock. Employees faced periodic interviews about their personal habits and associations, with lie detector tests scheduled every six months and random tests conducted at the discretion of the division manager. The Pentagon seemed satisfied.

But when it came time for promotions two months later, Gordon Nicholson was passed over. In a moment of anger Nicholson tendered his resignation. It was accepted.

The stain in his professional portfolio made him a less than marketable product. He moved into the private consulting business, and almost immediately became active in local party politics, building a base of clients and a constituency for his right-wing philosophy. In Southern California he needed no converts, only exposure. It did not take long. After two terms in the House of Representatives, Nicholson ran for the Senate seat left vacant when California's senior senator died in the crash of a chartered airplane.

Nicholson preached a hard line—back to basics, anti-abortion, pro-prayer, and capital punishment—in a well-organized and heavily financed campaign against a former lieutenant governor. He won with surprising ease. Surprising because the voting record of the popular senator he replaced reflected values quite opposite from his. "Only in California" was the conclusion reached by political commentators. But his success at the polls did not erase the bitterness he kept locked inside.

Nicholson did not like Thomas Chandler. Though others characterized the Connecticut senator as a moderate, Nicholson considered him a dangerous liberal. And he resented the way the press lionized Chandler, always inviting him to appear on *Face the Nation* and *Meet the Press*, as if he represented the enlightened view—the Thinking Man's Senator. Chandler had been in favor of SALT II and against building the B-1 bomber and C-17 transport plane. He opposed the draft and continued to speak of voluntarism as "the American way." He did favor a stronger shipbuilding program, Nicholson conceded, but that was political expediency, not philosophical conviction. The shipyard in Groton was an important part of his constituency.

Nicholson finished a quick breakfast and slid into his Buick station wagon. He lived with his wife, Carolyn, and two children near Gallows Road in Fairfax County, Virginia. It was a twenty-minute drive to his office if he left by seven, before rush-hour traffic began in earnest. His schedule today called for him to be at the Pentagon by seven-thirty for a briefing with the Secretary of the Army. The Intelligence Committee was meeting at nine. And then at noon, he was to have lunch with Clinton Atwood, a nationally syndicated conservative columnist who believed that the sun was setting on American glory. *Did Trevor know about the date? Was that why the phone call?* Nicholson could only wonder.

Atwood was something of a clown in Nicholson's view, but he could be manipulated easily. He was certainly the right man for a leak about Chandler's more recent activities. Just alert Atwood to a few things—on background, of course.

Carolyn Nicholson heard the front door click shut and, moments later, the roar of the car engine. She was disappointed that her husband had left without waking her. She had wanted to have coffee with him and perhaps a chat before he left for work. There seemed to be so little time for talk lately. *Nothing heavy,* she thought, as she slipped out of bed and into her robe. Just personal things, maybe about how their daughters were doing in school.

A photograph of the family rested on the small desk in the bedroom. Contemplating it, she smiled. The girls had the Nordic look of their father. She wondered what Gordon had been like when he was a boy. She guessed that his childhood must have been a bad experience for him. He never spoke of it. He didn't seem to want to remember.

Lately, Gordon seemed to be in a perpetual hurry. He was off speaking to a group somewhere at least once a week. He always left a number where he could be reached in an emergency, and one night, feeling lonely, she tried to call him. The hotel clerk said no Gordon Nicholson was registered there. She never called again. Carolyn decided she didn't really want to know where he was.

16

Tuesday, April 21

Precisely at ten minutes before eleven on the day Gordon Nicholson would lunch with Clinton Atwood, a dark-blue Ford LTD with District of Columbia license plates pulled into the curved driveway of the Hart Senate Office Building. There were two men in the front seat. One of them got out and walked briskly to the first of two sets of glass doors, went through them, and stepped around the large white concrete tubs scattered about in the space between the sets of doors. The tubs were filled with long-leaved spiky plants, an aesthetic compensation for this clutter designed to prevent terrorists from driving a car-bomb into the building.

He opened an inner lobby door, nodded to one of the uniformed guards, crossed the spacious, marble-floored atrium, and took an elevator to the third floor. Entering the outer office of Senator Thomas Chandler, he told the receptionist he had an appointment.

The visitor was an armed man, and he had been waved through the public entrance of the Hart Senate Office Building by a guard who did not know that he was an FBI agent. While he waited for Senator Chandler, the visitor pulled out a small black notebook and began drafting a sternly worded memo about lax security.

The agent escorted Chandler to the car and sat next to him in the back seat. He mentioned Washington's balmy spring weather, and Chandler asked him about the Armed Resistance Unit. The agent winced. "Nothing new on that, Senator." The Armed Resistance Unit was a terrorist group particularly bothersome to the FBI. The group had claimed responsibility for a midnight bomb that had blown up a room adjacent to the Senate chamber. No one had ever been arrested for the bombing, but it had been one of the incidents that had led to the tightening of security on Capitol Hill.

"The investigation is still being conducted by the Washington Field Office, Senator," the agent hastily added. "The Director would not necessarily have day-to-day knowledge of the case. But of course he remains on top of it."

"Of course," Chandler said. The agent thought of mentioning the security in the senator's own office building but discreetly decided against it.

The car headed down Constitution Avenue and turned onto Pennsylvania Avenue, then turned again and stopped at a gate behind the immense sand-colored box officially named the J. Edgar Hoover Building and popularly called the FBI Building. Lines of tourists were filing into one of the ground-floor public entrances as the car dipped down an incline into an underground garage. Chandler and his escort were deposited at an elevator that took them up seven floors to the office suite of the Director of the Federal Bureau of Investigation.

Below that office were two FBI enterprises: the headquarters, where the real labor of the Bureau went on, and, along the lower floors of the building, sealed off by tight security procedures, the FBI Tour. There were glass-walled "crime laboratories" and real-life firing of weapons at a target range in an amphitheater. The show made this tour one of the most popular tourist attractions in Washington. Groups of awed tourists followed FBI staff people in blue blazers as they wound their way around a series of exhibits rich in history: gangsters of the 1930s, Nazi saboteurs of the 1940s, atomic spies of the 1950s, Most Wanted Criminals of every decade.

Like every other senator and representative, Chandler had filled countless requests for tickets to the tour. Now, he mused, he was about to get his own tour from Edwin Schumacher himself.

The Director met him at the private elevator and ushered him into a room that rivaled the Oval Office in size. Directly under a reproduction of an FBI agent's badge, enlarged to the dimensions of a knight's shield, was a red leather couch. Schumacher waved Chandler to the seat of honor and assumed his chair behind a large desk, whose gleaming surface held a communications console, also of Oval Office size, a separate telephone that did not need to be labeled WHITE HOUSE, and a blue leather folder emblazoned with the FBI badge. Chandler recognized it as Schumacher's briefing folder, which he brought along when he testified before congressional committees.

Judge Edwin Schumacher was tall and slim with close-cropped white hair. Even on this warm spring day he wore one of his many tweed suits. He had the air of a professor, which he once had been at the University of Wisconsin. He had also been a distinguished federal judge, and his acceptance of the directorship of the FBI had inspired the Washington theory that it was an interim appointment until the next vacancy on the Supreme Court.

The theory passed through Chandler's mind as he looked at Schumacher. *He's in for the long haul*, Chandler thought. *He never wants to go back to Wisconsin.*

Schumacher lit his pipe, shook out the wooden match, and placed it carefully in a glass ashtray on a stand next to his desk. Chandler remembered a scene from his boyhood. His father, a cigarette smoker, had said, "When you grow up, Tommy, smoke a pipe. You'll get somewhere. When someone asks you a hard question, you can go through a lot of motions while you're thinking, see? And it won't look like you're stalling. It'll just look like you're lighting up your pipe."

After the usual exchange of Washington discussion-opening pleasantries, Chandler said, "Judge Schumacher, I'm sure you're briefed on my subject. I'm ready first for numbers and then maybe for some talking that's not numbers."

"That's fine with me, Senator." Schumacher glanced down at the briefing book, closed it, and looked up, very much in his testifying posture. "Let's start with terrorism aimed at diplomats— American diplomats. As you know, the *sites* of these particular cases are outside the FBI's jurisdiction, but we monitor groups that are transnational or international. And we gather information that enables us to determine trends—is terrorism going up or coming down?"

He paused, as if expecting Chandler to ask which way the trend was going. As Chandler said nothing, Schumacher cleared his throat and went on: "The answer is up, sharply up. In 1981, two U.S. diplomats were killed and seven were injured. In that same year, there were twenty-four attacks on U.S. embassies and other overseas installations. In 1982, there were four diplomats killed and two injured, and twenty-six attacks on our overseas installations.

"Things began to change in 1983. To change drastically. There were *sixty-five* U.S. diplomatic personnel killed that year and one hundred and forty-two injured. The number of attacks on embassies did not change much—twenty-nine. But the level of violence had suddenly risen, and—"

"Excuse me, Judge," Chandler interrupted, "but I must say that the Senate bombing made 1983 a memorable year for me and every other senator." The look he cast Schumacher was pointed. "Have anything on the Armed Resistance Unit?"

Schumacher knocked his pipe against the ashtray, pulled a red plaid pouch from his coat pocket, and began the ritual of filling and relighting his pipe. Chandler smothered a reminiscent chuckle. At last, Schumacher exhaled a cloud of smoke and said, "The Washington Field Office still has nothing on that, Senator. But let me say something in general about cases like that. We work under handicaps worse than any faced by comparable agencies in other democracies. Great Britain, for example, has for some time had the Prevention of Terrorism Law, which allows police, under certain conditions, to arrest and hold suspects without charge. West German police have similar emergency powers. The use of wiretaps by other democratic countries, for example—"

"Excuse me again, Judge, but we are talking about this country. *Now.* As I said, I don't just want numbers. I want a feel for the texture of your investigations. This is not testimony, Judge. I'm here only for background."

"I know that what I've been saying does sound defensive, Tom." Schumacher had never before addressed Chandler by his first name. "But the frightening facts are that we haven't much *but* numbers on terrorist organizations. And the restrictions I'm talking about are very, very real. In 1974, the FBI was working on—more or less just keeping an eye on—about fifty-five thousand domestic-security situations. By 1977, we were down to seventeen organizations and about a hundred and thirty individuals. In a country this size that is not excessive, in my opinion. And yet the civil-liberties liberals and their friends in the Congress, Senator, put such pressure on the FBI that lots of cases had to be closed. Now we have active investigations into four organizations and ten individuals. *Ten.*

"We don't even know how many Iranians there are in this country—just to name one potential recruitment group. Perhaps three hundred thousand."

Schumacher came around from behind his desk, sat down on a leather chair next to the red couch, and placed the briefing folder on a low table between them. "I'd rather this didn't get out of the office, Tom. God help us if some pressure groups got hold of this information. I'd be up to my waist in discrimination suits. But I wanted you to see it."

Schumacher opened the folder and extracted a paper that listed nineteen U.S.-based groups suspected of terrorism. The groups included the Armenian Secret Army for the Liberation of Armenia, the Croatian Freedom Fighters, the Jewish Defense League, the Japanese Red Army, and the Omega Seven, a pro-Castro Cuban group.

"You understand, Tom, when I say 'suspected,' it doesn't mean that these groups are under active investigation. It just means we have good information that all of them have operations going in this country."

Chandler scanned a secret report showing that the United States was the target of more than 40 percent of all terrorist activity throughout the world. The United States was especially vulnerable to terrorism, the report said, because of "constitutional guarantees" and a wide-open border. Another paper listed incidents by category. There had been more than two hundred terrorist attacks against electrical power installations alone.

"We try not to give 'em any publicity on episodes like these," Schumacher said. "Power company security people are good at keeping the lid on. Anyway, our experts tell me it's all theater—or mostly all. Guerrilla theater."

"Murder isn't theater, Ed," Chandler said, trying the first-name ploy himself. "I'm not sure if the old theories about terrorism are holding up."

"It's not murder that we're expecting," Schumacher said. "It's theater. Hostage theater."

He spoke of the formation of the FBI's fifty-member Hostage Rescue Team. Chandler decided, politely, to say nothing about FBI theater. He didn't mention that he had seen a classified film on the team. In the film, several burly FBI agents, wearing baseball caps and coveralls that shimmered under studio lights, saved three lovely young bank tellers who were bound and gagged like characters on the cover of a vintage detective magazine. Chandler had wondered about the worth of the team when he saw the film. Now, wiser in the ways of terrorism, he wondered even more.

"I'd like to get specific, Ed." Chandler allowed the slightest note of exasperation to creep into his voice. "I want to know what the FBI feels about, one, any connection between drugs and terrorism, and two, any connection between the Soviet Union and the international traffic in drugs."

Schumacher picked up the papers, returned them to the folder, and went back to the chair behind his desk. When the pipe ritual began anew, Chandler was forced to turn his laugh into a cough.

"You raise interesting possibilities, Tom." Schumacher said. "But I'm afraid that's all they are. Possibilities."

"What about the fact that Cuba is allowing drug runners to use Cuban waters to hide out from Coast Guard drug-patrol ships? What about the fact that Colombian drug smugglers even refuel in Cuba and pay port fees?"

"Have you talked to the Coast Guard about that?"

"No, Ed, I talked to your very hardworking agents in Miami."

"The FBI is a very big organization, Senator. As Director, I try to stay on top of things. But I can't keep my eye on every case."

"These are not 'cases,' Judge. These are facts that are so well-known I can read about them in *The Wall Street Journal*."

"No one knows your frustration more than I do, Senator. We have every available agent on the Harrold tragedy."

"And the Vice-President's near-miss?"

"Same thing, Tom. A lot of my people are working seven-day weeks, fourteen-hour days."

Chandler soon found himself engaging in Washington farewell pleasantries, including the inevitable suggestion for lunch someday and the inevitable appearance of the official FBI photographer to take a picture of the two men standing before the FBI badge on the wall. The photograph would join the dozens of similar ones arrayed in prim black frames along a wall outside the Director's private office.

Chandler was driven back to his office, where, as he ate a tunafish sandwich and an apple at his desk, he reflected on the morning's meeting. Schumacher had given every appearance of full cooperation, but, like Trevor, he had revealed little.

17

Tuesday, April 21

Columnist Clinton Atwood was well-known, if not notorious, in Washington. He was stocky, with a soft face, and what remained of his hair was red. His skin was the color of flour. He had a habit of licking his lips. He looked like a lizard when he did it. He was not an attractive man. Although a Texas Democrat by family tradition, there were few Democrats he admired—or ever voted for. Harry Truman had been one of them. The others were either too liberal or too weak.

Atwood had started as a reporter on Capitol Hill for the Philadelphia *Inquirer*. He gained a reputation for being a tough, persevering investigator who never relied on single sources. He checked, double-checked, cross-checked, and then checked again. *Newsweek* magazine hired him as Capitol Hill correspondent, and in its pages he gained a national readership. But over the years his columns began to acquire an ideological stridency. His use of language, once straightforward and crisp, became rhetorical and convoluted. His preoccupation with style began to overshadow his reputation for substance. *Newsweek* and he parted company in 1968. Atwood said it was a "mutual decision," but word in the trade was that his drift toward the right had angered the publisher.

By then, Atwood had a following, and a national syndicate was quick to offer him a biweekly column. He dedicated himself to alerting the American people to the ominous arms buildup in the Soviet Union. He warned them against signing the SALT I Treaty. He denounced the evils of Henry Kissinger's internationalism and pursuit of détente. Jimmy Carter, as a former member of the Trilateral Commission, was a hazard to the nation's health. The Trilateralists, under the leadership (how he sniffed at the word) of David Rockefeller, were undermining the national integrity of the United States. He labored to defeat Senate ratification of SALT II. "A runner," he wrote, "does not yield his lead to a second-rate athlete and walk across the finish line in the name of equality."

Now the West Europeans were demanding that the United States endorse a Law of Space Treaty that would restrict the use of space and limit the number of satellites that could be launched or space stations established. He found the demand preposterous. But, most preposterous of all, the United States would be required to share the information it had obtained from its own space program with other members of the United Nations—"as if the vast reaches of space were the common heritage of mankind to be shared equally with Third and Fourth World countries and the groveling and hypocritical puppets of the Soviet Union."

Atwood entered the Jockey Club, where he lunched every day, precisely at noon. The maître d' always reserved for him the corner table in the rear of the club, which was not really a club at all but a restaurant.

"Good morning, Mr. Atwood," the hostess greeted him.

"Good morning, Miss Hunt," Atwood replied, pronouncing "Miss" so precisely that his meaning could not be mistaken. He didn't know whether she preferred "Ms." to "Miss"—although he thought she probably did—but he wanted no part of the new feminism. Atwood had never married. Some said he was gay, others that he was just too mean-spirited to love anyone, male or female.

The tables were starting to fill with sub-Cabinet-level officials, a few diplomats, many lawyers. Atwood spotted his least favorite Washington lobbyist greeting the chairman of the House Ways and Means Committee. A reporter from the *Post* was lunching with Ed Colman, the Assistant Attorney General in charge of the civil rights division. Atwood wondered what conspiracy was being hatched to foist some new level of guilt onto the white Anglo-Saxons of America.

He slipped into his favorite chair, back against the wall, so he could peer over his half-moon glasses at anyone entering the room. His waiter handed him a menu. He ran down the left-hand column quickly, then the right. It was unnecessary for him to do so; he knew it by heart. But he enjoyed the ritual. Besides, he did occasionally break from his established pattern and order one of the specials of the day.

He took his watch from his fob pocket. Three minutes past noon. Senator Nicholson was late, uncharacteristically so. Punctuality was what Atwood liked in a legislator. It showed a healthy regard for the value of time And it said something more. A person who would not waste time—especially someone else's—was not likely to waste money either. And Clinton Atwood hated the shocking waste of other people's money.

More than Nicholson's punctuality, Atwood liked his philosophy, his world view that the Soviet Union was an enemy to be kept constantly in the cross-hairs of a gunsight. Nicholson was one of the few people on Capitol Hill who hated the Soviets as much as Atwood did.

And here he was now. "Hello, Clinton. Sorry I'm late. Got caught in a traffic snarl around Dupont Circle."

"No problem at all, Senator," Atwood said. The merest hint of reproach in his tone suggested Nicholson should have anticipated the noonday traffic. "We'll just make up for the lost time." Nicholson glanced at his watch. It was six minutes past noon.

The waiter hovered.

"What will you have, Senator, to slake your thirst?" Atwood asked.

"Vodka martini on the rocks. Very dry. With a twist."

Any momentary annoyance that Atwood had felt soon evaporated. He liked Nicholson. Actually, he liked him for what he was not. He was not a lawyer, and there were too many lawyers in Congress to suit Atwood. Their training and catechism always spelled compromise. They dulled the edges of issues with sophistries. They always managed to elevate cowardice to principle. Nicholson was a businessman. Atwood liked that.

"How's the President doing with you fellows on the Hill?" Atwood asked, sipping delicately from his wineglass.

"The President's doing fine," Nicholson responded. "I'm not sure his program is doing as well." He spoke with a note of calculated sorrow.

Atwood arched his eyebrow. "Oh? How so?" There was a hint of irony in his voice. Nicholson was a man who never indulged in subtleties. It was one of the few traits Atwood did not admire in him.

"Nothing serious, just yet. But I don't think his legislation on strengthening the Agency is moving very quickly. The *Times* editorial—the one that was probably written by Toby Segal—it hurt.

Everybody on the Hill has been talking about the lessons of the past that we're in danger of forgetting."

Nicholson paused to accept his martini from a waiter who disappeared as quickly as he had appeared.

"Segal!" Atwood practically spat. "He's been writing that same drivel since he graduated from Harvard. He's so concerned about the skullduggery in our government that he's forgotten who the enemy is. He's done more to injure the morale of the Agency than any journalist in the country. . . ."

Atwood continued the recitation of his familiar litany, Nicholson nodding sympathetically in ritual tribute to the denunciations that could be found in almost any of Atwood's columns.

"And, Senator," Atwood said, shifting to a new target, "there's not much backbone up there on the Hill. What your cohorts lack in spine, they seem to make up in olfactory skill. They gather in the faintest whiff of 'popular opinion' and go racing around claiming they are the new leaders of America, hoping *Time* or *Newsweek* will carry a photograph of them in a pose of stern moralism or dewy-eyed idealism. It's downright despicable."

Atwood lifted his wineglass to eye level as if to propose a toast. "But there are exceptions to that unfortunate rule up there and I consider you to be one of them."

Nicholson lifted his glass to express his appreciation, and Atwood nodded in return.

"Frankly," Nicholson said, "I expect that sort of conduct from the liberals, but it's discouraging to see some of the so-called moderates pick up that line."

"Anyone in particular?"

"Well, there are several. But only one who really concerns me."

"Let me guess," Atwood said. His tongue flicked across his upper lip. "Chandler?"

"Yes." Nicholson regretted that he had been so obvious. "The national press has been grooming him for bigger things."

"True, and all rather shameless, but what makes him any more of a concern now?"

Before Nicholson could answer, their waiter approached carrying their lunch. "Excuse me, gentlemen." His white-gloved hands moved the plates to the table with the precise movements of a jewel thief. Nicholson had learned not to talk around Washington waiters. Quick and professional as they might be, expressionless as automatons, their ears were as sensitive as audioscopes. Washington thrived on gossip, and waiters were prime sources for fragments of conversation that might later become items in a gossip column.

When the waiter had gone, Nicholson spoke. "I have no idea why Walcott named Chandler chairman of the task force on terrorism."

"Sounds like a pretty good idea," Atwood said, swallowing a morsel of lamb. "The task force, I mean. Long overdue."

"It is. But I'm not sure Chandler's the right man to be in charge of it."

"Well, he's not my kind of senator, to be sure. But he's a bit smarter than most. . . ." Atwood adopted a deliberate nonchalance as he continued to cut up his meal into small, almost perfectly proportioned chunks. He ate with his fork in his left hand in the European style widely favored in Washington. Nicholson, Atwood noticed, always held his fork in his right, and ate in a rough and ready way. Food was merely fuel for his furnace. There was no art or taste involved.

It was the one thing for which Atwood faulted some of the *new* conservatives today. They seemed so uncultured. They spent all of their time talking about balance sheets and welfare cheats. They had no time for the finer things in life. Art. Gourmet food. Fine wines. A love for language. Unfortunately, the liberals were the ones who indulged in these pleasures now. But by rights they were conservative pleasures—the sense of history and heritage!

". . . Smarter *and* more ambitious than most," Atwood continued, picking up the thread. "I'm afraid he might use it as a launching pad for a presidential rocket. That certainly would set no precedents for the Senate. It's been the breeding ground—some have said hatching ground—for would-be Presidents for decades." Atwood was enjoying the role of disinterested pedagogue now. After all, he was not some rumormonger who took tips over the telephone. That's not why he had invited Gordon Nicholson to lunch. He wanted to rub philosophical shoulders with Nicholson for a while, not just serve as a vessel for his jeremiads and jealousies.

Nicholson willingly obliged. "I know. I happen to think it's a bad tradition, myself, but that's not my concern. What *is* my concern is that Chandler seems to be going off track with his investigation. I'm told he's decided that it's within the scope of his mandate to reopen the Kennedy assassination."

"What?" Atwood responded in a rising exclamation. "You don't mean it." He peered intently now over his glasses, challenging Nicholson.

"Unbelievable, but true."

"My God, how many times does that particular can of peas have to be opened up?" Atwood set down his fork, almost flinging it onto his plate. "The man is dead. Let him rest in peace. On what basis does Chandler think he's doing the country any service with this?"

"I'm not certain he's doing anything just yet. He's been fairly discreet so far. You might even say surreptitious. But I'm told that he's reviving the old suspicions about a connection between the Kennedy assassination and the CIA—this time with a new twist. Somehow there's supposed to be a modern drug connection."

"What kind of connection?" Atwood asked. His voice was more controlled, but clearly angry.

"I don't know. I don't think *he* knows. But I'm told he thinks there's some thread of cause and effect between illegal drugs, organized crime, some anti-Castro Cubans . . ."

"Even so. What's that got to do with the Agency?"

"Some suspicion on his part, I guess, that the Agency has been too close to these groups over the years, particularly at the time of Kennedy's death."

"That's a lot of hogwash. But what does it have to do with terrorism in any case?"

"Clinton, I don't know. I don't even know if what I've been told is accurate. But . . ."

"But if it is, Chandler is going to inflict a blow on the Agency at the very moment it is starting to regain its credibility and effectiveness."

The waiter returned. "Gentlemen, can I interest you in dessert? We have chocolate mousse—"

"No, thank you," Atwood interrupted. "None for me. Perhaps coffee. Senator, how about you?"

"Just coffee for me, too. Black, please."

By the time the coffee had come, Atwood's passion for a leisurely lunch had vanished. He became edgy, almost irascible. It was obvious that he no longer had any interest in Nicholson. He had to get back to the office and make some calls. He had friends in the Agency. He needed to find out what they were saying in those cold, stark cubicles behind those gray nameless doors.

Were they concerned that an ambitious senator would give them a black eye while elbowing his way into the headlines? Was Chandler on to anything? Any skeletons that had not already come crashing out of the closet onto a Senate committee floor?

Atwood glanced at his watch. "I've got someone waiting for me at the office," he said rather awkwardly.

Every experienced politician knows that journalists never have anyone waiting at their offices. They talk over the phone or arrange meetings in the coffee shops or dining rooms of hotels. But Nicholson appeared oblivious to the falseness of the excuse. He was satisfied that his mission had been accomplished.

18

Wednesday, April 22

Elaine Dunham was running late for work. Her alarm clock had failed to ring at its customary hour of six-thirty and she might still have been asleep if her cat, Greyfur, hadn't awakened her by standing on her chest and meowing into her ear. Hurrying to get her breakfast, she had dropped a glass of orange juice on the kitchen floor and cut her finger on a vagrant sliver in the mop-up operation; then she'd gotten a smear of lipstick on her favorite ivory silk blouse and she'd had to change.

As she opened the front door, wondering what else could go wrong this star-crossed morning, Greyfur seized a golden opportunity and shot out the door.

"Greyfur!" she called. "Come back here this minute!" But he was gone, and from past experience she knew he would probably turn up two days later, hungry, tiger-striped coat unkempt, but with a smile of feline contentment on his furry face. "Damn!" she said.

She stepped back inside to collect her briefcase, and her heel brushed something from the doormat. A white envelope, addressed to her. There was no postmark and no return address. *Trevor?* Unlikely.

She picked up the envelope, took it into her small living room, and sat down on the sofa. A glance at the clock told her that a delay of even two minutes more would land her smack in the middle of rush-hour traffic, but she was too curious to wait. She opened the envelope and took out a snapshot and a single typewritten sheet. She set the photograph aside.

As she skimmed the letter, her hands began to shake. She read it again slowly, hearing every word in her mind.

Querida Elena,

There is no way to apologize for the past. And no way I can tell you in this letter how much pain I have known in my heart for you and for your mother. I had to leave. My life was—is—in danger. They might have killed you too.

Who might have killed us?

I cannot tell you where I live or even how I have lived for all these years. I have lost myself as well as you. We were all dead. Dead to each other—your mother finally in a nursing home, me in another kind of prison.

I recently learned, never mind how, that you are on the staff of Senator Chandler's task force. And I thought this could be a gift from God—a chance to help me clear my name so I can safely see you and perhaps come back to life again.

I pray you will forgive me. . . . I will contact you again. Soon.

Then one last line:

Trevor is not to be trusted. I repeat. Do not trust him.

Trevor? What did this ghost from the past know of Trevor? How could he know she was secretly working for him?

Then Trevor was forgotten as she picked up the snapshot and a wave of half-forgotten images from her childhood came rushing at her, washing through her unbelieving mind. She *had* to believe. The photograph showed a dark-haired man of medium height holding a little girl. She was wearing a yellow sunsuit with white ruffles. The man was dressed in khaki pants and a blue shirt, sleeves rolled up above his elbows. There were epaulets on the shoulders. She stared at them. *Like a uniform. Not a uniform.* The man's face was faintly familiar, like something known only in dreams. The little girl's face she had seen many times before.

The letter was signed *Your father.*

Elaine's throat was tight with unshed tears. For a few minutes she fought for control—*Cool Elaine. Clever Elaine. Don't feel, Elaine. Just think.* Then she went to the telephone and called the Intelligence Committee office. She would not be in today. She was coming down with a cold.

As she hung up the receiver, the constriction in her throat gave way. She was three years old again, and she sobbed for the little girl in the yellow sunsuit and for all the years between.

19

This morning Chandler was scheduled to attend an Appropriations Committee meeting at ten o'clock. He decided to skip it, and went instead to his hideaway office in the Capitol to catch up on some important reading.

Each of the most senior senators had a hideaway like this, tucked away on the Senate side of the Capitol and varying from palatial for the highest-ranking senators to modest for the lowest-ranking. Tom Chandler, who was thirtieth in seniority, had a hideaway that was small but historic. The fabled Senator Everett McKinley Dirksen, before he became Minority Leader, had used it mostly as a very private club for senators who felt like some good talk over a glass of bourbon and branchwater.

The office was also convenient. Chandler could reach the Senate floor within two or three minutes from the time a roll-call vote began. He often needed that speed because he hated to give up a minute of his cherished privacy in his hideaway. Only Ned Dempsey and Margie knew how to reach him there by phone, and called him only on those occasions when they judged that his annoyance at being disturbed would exactly equal his later anger if he found out they had failed to relay an urgent message.

Chandler had been reading for more than two hours now, from a batch of documents whose red-and-white cover sheet was stamped TOP SECRET. His eyes hurt and the words were starting to blur out of focus, but he vowed to finish the final twenty pages.

> . . . New sensor materials, cryogenic super cooling, bubble data stage, advance sensor processes, and other advanced technologies could result in a broad-based electromagnetic sensor capable of detecting radio broadcasts, radars, heat and light, and even radiation. Such a sensor mounted in space could, for example, examine an area for heat from vehicle engines, radiation from stored nuclear weapons, and radio broadcasts. Thus an encrypted radio broadcast on a moving object over the Arctic with a small radiation signature could activate an optical mode which would see that this was a Soviet Backfire bomber launching a cruise missile against the U.S. We are on the verge of developing such a capability. . . .

The sound of a bell, alerting him to a vote, rescued him. He turned and looked out the narrow window with its picture-postcard view of the Mall, which ran from the Capitol straight as a plumb line to the Washington Monument. He spent hours in that room listening to his favorite music, reading classified documents, thumbing his way through mind-numbing staff reports from the Committee on Appropriations. He really did not enjoy serving on Appropriations. But that's where the power was in politics. That's where all the interest groups in the country ended their pilgrimage, at the money tree. And he was one of the few who decided which would receive, which be denied its fruit. So he stayed.

Besides, he thought, there was nothing on the Appropriations Committee quite as paralyzing as universal electromagnetic sensors. The very words were paralyzing! But then, he thought, sobered, so were the weapons that Russia and America were racing so desperately to develop.

He turned to the transcript of a recent briefing session by a Department of Defense physicist. ". . . We are working on an application of a principle that could achieve efficiency one hundred to a thousand times greater than the most powerful weapons in our inventory. Coupled with advances in microelectronics, we would have the potential . . ." The five short buzzes signaled seven and a half minutes to get to the floor.

Chandler placed the documents in his wall safe, spun the dial, and left the office, locking the door behind him. Two minutes later, he was on the Senate floor. He spotted Charles Walcott. "What's this vote, Charlie?"

"A motion to table Jack Sprague's amendment to the foreign aid bill."

"What's the amendment do?"

"He wants to terminate economic assistance to any country that fails to support our efforts to limit the transfer of technology to the Soviet Union."

"What do you think, Charlie? Sounds a little too inflexible."

"It is, but I think Jack's entitled to an up or down vote on his amendment."

Tom grinned. To Jack Sprague, every issue was clear-cut. There were no gray areas to cast shadows on his judgment, no nagging doubts to haunt him.

Walcott motioned for Tom to sit next to him at his desk in the last row of the Senate Chamber. "The Director asked me to stop by his office this morning," Walcott said softly, almost conspiratorially.

"What did our favorite spy want?" Chandler asked.

Walcott smiled but was immediately serious. "He didn't want anything—except to know what you're up to. Apparently someone told him you were looking into some of the Agency's past activities. All the way back to the early sixties." He waited to hear some expression of denial from Chandler. None came. "You know how the Director feels about the Agency."

"I know," Chandler said.

The Clerk of the Senate continued to call out the names of the senators alphabetically. "Mistah Anderson . . . Mistah Bender . . ."

"Trevor worries about morale out there."

"Oh, shit, Charlie. That's the oldest ruse in the book. Whenever they want to get back to their black-bag jobs or get Congress off their backs, they leak some sob story to a wet-eyed journalist—

who's probably on their payroll—about morale going all to hell! I put one lousy shovel into the dirt and they're calling the Chairman—"

"Look, I'm not—"

"I know. I'm sorry," Chandler said. "You know I don't want to do anything that's going to reflect discredit on you for recommending me to be in charge of this thing. But, Charlie, I can't get a grip on the investigation without doing some thorough backgrounding. Organized crime is mainlining drugs into every crossroads in Florida. The state's got a ten-billion-dollar habit."

"What does that have to do with the Agency?"

"I don't know. Maybe nothing. But there are a lot of ex-CIA operatives from the sixties down there—a lot of Cubans—helping to run those drugs."

"So?"

"And we know that Frank Terpil and Ed Wilson were organizing terrorist activities for the Libyans, and they're both ex-CIA."

Walcott frowned. "I don't see the connection."

"I don't either. Not yet. But if I'm going to conduct an investigation, I've got to know all of the players. I can't rule out any possibility, however wild it might seem."

"Why are you digging up the Kennedy assassination?"

Chandler looked directly at Walcott. His jaw muscles tightened. "Fabricante was murdered in Miami a month ago. He was involved somehow in the Senate's investigation into Kennedy's death. I just wanted to find out what the connection was." Walcott seemed satisfied. "There are a thousand pieces to this puzzle that I'm trying to lay out on the table, Charlie. If I'm going to be questioned every time I move one of the pieces around, then you'd better get somebody else."

"Now, hold on, Tom. I'm not—" Walcott was cut off by the calling out of Chandler's name.

Chandler decided to give one to Sprague. He boomed out "No," loud enough to ensure that his gift would not go unappreciated.

"I've got a lot of faith in you, Tom," Walcott continued. "You know that. I'm part of this investigation, too, and I don't want to get blindsided."

"You know I won't embarrass you." Chandler rose to his feet. "I've got to get back to the office, Charlie. Tell the Director that the Agency has nothing to fear"—he paused for effect—"for now."

He was angry. How had Trevor heard about his interest in the Kennedy assassination? Could someone on the staff be passing things on? He reviewed the names of the people who knew about that angle: Kevin O'Brien, Maude Duberstein, Elaine Dunham. He brushed the suspicion aside. Maybe a waiter in Miami had eavesdropped on their conversation, but they had been careful when anyone was within earshot. What about the man he had talked to— listened to, really—at the pool, then at the pavilion? Maybe he was one of Trevor's people. . . ?

He settled on no one suspect. But what bothered him more was what had prompted Trevor to call Walcott. Why was Trevor so concerned about something so relatively incidental?

As soon as Chandler entered his outer office he saw Ned Dempsey lying in wait for him right at the receptionist's desk. There was no way to slip past him.

"We've got to talk, Tom," Dempsey said, placing himself directly in his path.

"In half an hour, Ned. Give me a chance to—"

"We've got to talk *now*, Tom. Dave Krasner has done a number on you." He held a newspaper clipping in one hand, a file folder in the other.

"Okay, okay." Chandler admitted defeat. Dempsey stepped aside, then followed on Chandler's heels to the inner office, pausing long enough to say, "No calls until I come out, Margie."

Ned started before Chandler had even sat down at his desk. "I don't understand this son of a bitch, Tom. We keep feeding him leads for his column and he bites our arm off just below the elbow."

"There's not much we can do about it, Ned, except to tell Bob Tilley to feed any tips to one of his competitors. Maybe if his editor wonders why he keeps getting scooped, he'll be a little more grateful. What's he saying?"

"Oh, some idiot has written a letter to every paper in Connecticut saying you ducked the vote to deregulate natural gas. You had to give a speech in Phoenix that day, remember? We were under the impression that the leadership would protect you till Monday. Well, they didn't. Rice was managing the bill and he insisted that it be voted on. The leadership couldn't prevent it. Anyway, this kook has flatly stated that you ducked the vote because the Political Action Committee at Pacific and Western Gas contributed to your last campaign. This was supposed to be a payoff. Krasner has run the letter as his lead."

"Payoff?" Chandler was incredulous. "As I recall, they contributed all of a thousand dollars."

"That's right. And Krasner knows it. He also carefully fails to mention the fact that you were endorsed and supported by the Committee for an Effective Congress. *And* every consumer group in the country. You raised well over fifty thousand dollars through them. So if you were really in the business of selling your vote, you'd hardly have sold it to the gas producers. But the bastard isn't concerned with the truth. He only wants a juicy headline. And you know how many people read beyond the first paragraph—not to mention the first page—of any story."

Chandler sighed. "Well, there's not much we can do about it except ignore it. It'll pass. There'll be something else in tomorrow's paper. In the meantime, let's go on the offensive." He thought a moment. "Let's get out a release challenging the Secretary of the Navy's decision to transfer nuclear-submarine construction from Groton to Newport News. Call it crass politics—another example of the Administration aiding the flow of defense contracts from the North to the Sunbelt. Tell Bob to lead with, quote, 'I promise to lead the fight to restore the contracts to Connecticut, or cut the defense budget by the millions they're going to waste by the transfer.'"

"Okay. I'll get right on it."

"Anything else, Ned?"

"Plenty. A list a mile long. But it boils down to 'Remember the folks back home.' I'd like to set some things up for you."

"Can we talk about that later? I've got some task force work that won't wait."

"Sure. First things first," Dempsey muttered. As he walked to the door, Chandler was already on the phone.

"Margie," he was saying, "get Kevin over from the Intelligence Committee. I want a briefing on the car-bomb explosions outside Penn Station last night. And . . ."

Dempsey closed the door and smiled at Margie. He hated always being the bearer of bad news. But that's what he was paid for, and he knew he had Chandler's complete confidence. Still, he was beginning to worry about Chandler's political base back in Connecticut. People were starting to grumble that he was neglecting them while pursuing higher ambitions. If he was in contention for the presidential—or vice-presidential—nomination, that would bring credit to the state of Connecticut. They wanted him to have a higher national profile—but not at the expense of reducing his commitments at home. It had been tough enough to keep Chandler on a regular speaking schedule in Connecticut before the task force was created. Now it was almost impossible.

Ned hoped that Chandler would be able to complete the investigation quickly, and preferably in a blaze of good publicity. But he had a feeling it was somehow going to bring more pain than glory.

20

Wednesday, April 22 –Thursday, April 23

The explosion ripped the head of Seyni Ahmounche from his shoulders, and sent it caroming to the other side of West 75th Street. By the time the New York Police Department rescue unit arrived, Ahmounche's BMW 733i was engulfed in a fireball. Hours later, an arson specialist determined that there had been two people in the car. It would be twenty-four hours before Ahmounche and his passenger, a fashion model named Jessica Landis, were publicly identified. Because Ahmounche was black and Jessica Landis was white, city investigators put the murders down to racial hatred.

Colonel Cyril Metrinko knew better, and so did E. W. Trevor.

Ahmounche was an aide to the Nigerian Ambassador to the United Nations, a man whose policies tilted too much toward the West to suit some of his Third World colleagues. But the Ambassador's policies had nothing to do with the murder. Ahmounche was one of Trevor's best agents, recruited years ago out of Harvard Business School. He had been in deep cover, his identity known only to Trevor and a handful of Trevor's associates on the basis of need-to-know, highest-code-word clearance.

Somehow, Metrinko knew too. He had instructed the assassination unit to eliminate Ahmounche as violently as possible. They had followed orders with four sticks of dynamite.

Crestwood Lane is located in a heavy slash of woods between Chain Bridge and route 123 in McLean, Virginia. The trees there are so thick that direct sunlight is rarely able to penetrate in any season but winter. The residents who live on the lane like it that way. E. W. Trevor and his wife, a semi-invalid, liked the shadows and seclusion most of all.

Today, the Director was angry. But through years of disciplined effort he had learned to conceal his emotions, to arrange his face in an expression opposite to what he felt. The emotional discipline had produced a permanent kind of false placidity. On the surface, he remained as impassive as lake water untouched by the wind.

The call had come in from the night operations officer shortly after 2:00 A.M. Trevor had managed to sleep for another four hours. Now he was awake and thinking clearly, trying to see the pattern, trying to plan the response. He opened the front door of his large dark-brick home to gather in the newspapers. The air was thick with the smell of pine trees.

He laid the newspapers on the kitchen table, poured a glass of orange juice, filled the automatic coffee maker, and sat down to read. He scanned the lead stories on the front page. The killing of Ahmounche had happened too late for the *Post* to have anything on it. But Trevor was not looking for that story. He did not need newspaper accounts about acts of terror. Anyway, he doubted that any newspaper or television news show would be able to discern a pattern. First there was the station chief in Lagos, under diplomatic cover as cultural attaché. Shot in the head as he sat in the back seat of his car, stopped at a traffic light. Then there was the agent in Bangkok. Found face down in a pool of blood in the Temple of the Sleeping Buddha, his throat slashed. Two weeks later, an agent attached to the U.S. Embassy in Manila was found in one of those garish Philippine taxis, an icepick in the back of his neck. A man missing in Berlin. Now Ahmounche.

There could no longer be any doubt that someone had declared a secret war against the United States.

Trevor turned to *The New York Times*. He was looking for news of the war on another front: the leaking of secrets.

Late yesterday afternoon, Trevor had received a cable from the station chief in London. The London *Times* was going to run a story on the breakthrough the United States had just achieved in developing an electromagnetic sensor. *The Times* concluded that this development would give the United States a significant lead over the Soviet Union.

The story, as it happened, was not true. The breakthrough described was premature by several years. Besides, there were other projects of far more importance to the United States—and that was what was gnawing at Trevor. It occurred to him that the Soviet Union might be telling the United States that the Soviets knew what we were developing, that whatever we had would be appropriated by the Soviets because they had access to our secrets.

Trevor knew—*no, sensed*, he told himself. *Knowledge comes from specifics.* He sensed that the killing of his agents and the leaking of secrets were connected and that the threads led back to the Soviet Union. But there was no pattern, no *reasonable* pattern. On the Soviet policy plane, nothing was happening that matched this secret war. The Soviets were certainly as intransigent and their speeches as anti-American as ever. But the Agency analysts were reporting no changes in their estimates of Soviet intentions. Nothing was going on publicly. But *something* was going on, something without signals, without reasonable pattern.

Outside, a gray mist was just starting to lift. The sky overhead was turning from a deep purple into gradations of pink. Trevor was late for his row on the Potomac. His preoccupation had slowed his normally quick and precise movements. He forgot to push the toast down. The coffee measurements were not quite right. Too much water.

Trevor turned his mind to a situation closer to his own interests. Two days ago, he had met with President Christiansen in the Oval Office. Things had not gone well. Trevor had tried to get the President to authorize executive action against Juan Canstanda, the powerful young leader of the guerrillas in Venezuela.

"Mr. President," he had said in his most persuasive tone, "we could have had Khomeini eliminated for a few hundred dollars when he was in Paris. The Israelis offered to take out Qaddafi for us, and we turned them down. The world would have been a lot safer for everyone without those madmen. Now Canstanda is threatening to blow up the oil fields—"

131

The President had cut him off. "What happens when Canstanda sends his team of assassins for me? Maybe he already did for Mrs. Harrold and . . . Christ, haven't you learned anything from the past?"

Trevor was still smoldering. The President did not understand. He was just like all the moralists up on Capitol Hill or at the *Post* and *Times*. Why couldn't they see the equation in its complete perspective? The death of one man could save hundreds, maybe hundreds of thousands of lives. But no, they stuck their noses in the air, placed a hand on the Bible, and said it was unconscionable. *Unconscionable! What a load of sanctimonious bullshit.*

Was it any more unconscionable to spend thirty or forty billion dollars on a Rapid Deployment Force to ship soldiers off to the deserts of Saudi Arabia or the jungles of Central America or God-knows-where-next? And if Canstanda overthrows the Venezuelan government and shuts off the flow of oil to the West . . . are we prepared to go to war to protect American interests?

Trevor knew the answers. *Stalin was right*, he cynically told himself. The death of one person in a traffic accident is a national tragedy, the liquidation of half a million people a statistic. While these poor miserable moralists were standing on principle, the United States was being drawn into the bloody whirlpool of a major war.

Even more infuriating was the President's reference to the lessons of the past. He was quite specific, asking whether *he*, Trevor, had learned anything. Exactly what did he mean by that? The ambiguity troubled Trevor, particularly if it was deliberate. Was the President taunting him for a past mistake? No, he couldn't possibly know. No one knew.

But why the preoccupation with the past? What about the future? *We're faced with enemies who change the past if they don't like it—revise Stalin or Khrushchev right out of the picture. They're everywhere and they operate without restraint. We have to be twice as good just to stay even.* And now Chandler was digging up old mistakes—just when the American people finally seemed ready to give the Agency the opportunity to do its job. To protect them. How long was Kennedy going to haunt him?

Trevor walked to the hall closet and grabbed a light windbreaker. The day promised to be warm, but there was no guarantee in April. He would work up a sweat and then a breeze could come up and give him a chill. No sense taking chances.

And he wasn't going to take any chances with Chandler either. Men and women in the Agency put their lives on the line every minute of every day. Trevor was not going to let Chandler climb over their bodies on his way to the presidency. He could deal with Canstanda later; right now, he was more concerned with Chandler.

It was time to contact Elaine. He cursed to himself. Maybe he had made a mistake in putting her on the Intelligence Committee in the first place. She was supposed to be looking for leaks coming from the Committee and to be keeping an eye on Chandler. But his suspicion was growing that she was holding something back. *Elaine will have to be watched more closely*, he thought. She was starting to feel guilty about her job. And guilt was unacceptable in anyone engaged in the business of keeping secrets. It was a poisonous seed that one day could blossom into betrayal.

Outside a black Ford LTD waited, with two men and a driver inside. They would take Trevor down to the boat house just below Chain Bridge and watch while he slipped his single-seat scull into the brown water of the Potomac. One man's eyes would never leave Trevor. The others would constantly scan the river banks. And their hands would never be far from their not-quite-concealed weapons.

21

Friday April 24

The day promised to be unseasonably hot, the sudden chill of the previous night already gone. Even at 7:00 A.M. the stillness on the Potomac, unbroken by any breeze, bred a sense of indolence. Humid vapors suffused the spring air. Overhead, on the Whitehurst Freeway, early commuters from Bethesda and Cabin John were beating the heat. As Elaine parked and locked her car on Water Street, under the Freeway, perspiration made her crisp beige cotton dress cling to her shoulder blades. Was it the heat? she wondered. *Or am I afraid?*

Her previous meetings with the Director of Central Intelligence had been in fairly ordinary places, but this time her instructions really made her feel like a spy. As directed, she walked almost two blocks north on Water Street, under the traffic rumbling overhead.

At the end of the street she saw the black Ford, unobtrusive except for the thin antenna on its trunk. An unremarkable man dressed in a dark suit, white shirt, and striped tie stood silently near the driver's door. She remembered having seen him outside the inn in Pennsylvania the night she met Trevor. The man bowed his head slightly by way of greeting, then gestured toward the river. He said nothing. Elaine carefully negotiated the few narrow, broken steps down to the water's edge, grateful for her low-heeled shoes. She had also worn a broad-brimmed straw hat, partly as protection against the morning sun and partly for concealment.

At the bottom of the steps a light, freshly painted canoe rode high in the water. In the stern sat E. W. Trevor.

A second anonymous man silently took her elbow and guided her into the forward seat facing Trevor. He pushed the canoe away from the small run-down dock.

"Good morning, Miss Dunham," Trevor said. "It's good of you to be up so early to join me for my morning row. How nice you look! I'll do my best not to get your lovely dress wet." His compliments seemed forced to Elaine. "Actually, as you can see, this isn't so much a row as it is a paddle. Normally I would be out here in my scull, but two of us might have been something of a squeeze."

Trevor expertly guided the canoe out onto the river, effortlessly shifting the paddle from side to side. He was wearing lightweight warm-up trousers, a matching T-shirt, and expensive Docksider shoes. Elaine noticed how fit he looked for a man in his fifties. His full head of carefully trimmed hair, even though it was beginning to gray, made him look a decade younger. He had obviously taken care of himself over the years. *I wonder if Tom rows*, she thought, and hastily checked herself.

"Well, Miss Dunham, how is it going?" Trevor sounded almost lighthearted. Clearly, propelling a small boat through the water was a liberating experience for him. "Your efforts to find connecting links in all this terrorism—have they been any more successful than ours?"

What does he know about the letter? She had asked herself that question again and again in the forty-eight hours since she had found the letter. *"My life was—is—in danger. They might have killed you too."* She had told no one about it, certainly not Tom when they had met for lunch yesterday; and not even her half-sister or half-brother. She had started to call them, but she was afraid to talk. Trevor was perfectly capable of having bugged her phone. Now she was face to face with Trevor, trying to think of something to say. The canoe bucked slightly in a mid-river eddy, and she covered her genuine nervousness with a feigned look of panic.

"Mr. Trevor, if you tip this canoe over," she said, "you'll never find out what I know."

"You can trust me, Miss Dunham, I assure you." The echo burned in her mind: *"Trevor is not to be trusted. . . ."* "This is one place where I know what I'm doing." Trevor shipped the paddle, relaxed, and waited.

The canoe drifted pleasantly down the river. Passing motorists on Rock Creek Parkway, beside the overhanging Kennedy Center, might have remarked a resemblance to a painting by Monet or Seurat. But the canoe's occupants were too far away from either bank to be recognized.

Elaine mentally reviewed her options. *"I repeat. Do not trust him."* She would stick by her earlier decision not to tell Trevor of Chandler's midnight meeting in Miami. She suspected—mostly from what he *didn't* say—that Tom had established some means of continuing contact with the man. But she had to tell Trevor something. She took a deep breath.

"First of all," she began, "Senator Chandler seems to have developed an important source of his own. I'm not quite sure how it happened, and I don't know who it is. But whoever it is, they're certainly pointing Chandler in some interesting directions."

The canoe was drifting toward the shore. Trevor dipped the paddle effortlessly a few times and sent the canoe out toward the main channel. "What sort of 'interesting directions'?" he asked casually, shipping the paddle.

"Well, I mentioned the last time we talked that Chandler came back from Miami determined to look into Sam Fabricante's connection with the Agency and the Castro assassination plots—"

"Wouldn't it be easier simply to ask the Agency whether we maintained a relationship with Fabricante?" Trevor interrupted. He sounded genuinely irritated. "Why not simply ask us, instead of snooping around behind our backs?" He began to paddle the canoe vigorously, three strokes on one side, then three on the other. "Who does Chandler think he is anyway?" Trevor sounded like a querulous child.

Elaine realized there was real ire behind his calculated effect.

"Senator Chandler simply doesn't trust the Agency, Mr. Trevor. And he thinks that you see your responsibility as protecting the Agency rather than telling the truth—at least where Congress is concerned."

Trevor didn't like the trend of the conversation. Elaine Dunham was beginning to talk to him as an equal. It would take an effort to keep her in the role of agent. "Regardless of Senator Chandler's opinion of me, what about this source of his? It might be more than interesting to know why someone is trying to direct congressional attention to some fairly obscure twenty-year-old events. And, I might add, what kind of person would be interested in doing so? Do you have any idea what's behind all this, Miss Dunham?"

Trevor smoothly reversed the canoe's course, bending to the paddle, pulling right and left, right and left, against the diverse current. The hour was nearing eight, and the sun was dancing off the water. Elaine found her hat brim insufficient and reached into her bag for a pair of oversized sunglasses. The slight breeze stirred up by the movement of the canoe felt welcome on her hot cheeks.

"Senator Chandler is holding that information very closely," she said. "In fact, he's never told me that there *is* a source. Mostly, what I've told you is my own conjecture."

"Miss Dunham, I'm afraid I'm beginning to find this whole matter very tedious." Now Trevor was clearly playing angry. "Either there is a source or there isn't. Either you know something about it or you don't." Trevor pulled hard on the paddle, speaking in short, hard bursts with each stroke. "Candor, Miss Dunham, candor. Who is this source? And what is he telling Chandler? That is information I must have." Perspiration ran down Trevor's face and soaked his shirt. The canoe fairly skimmed across the water.

Elaine was disarmed by Trevor's vehemence. She felt vaguely like an errant daughter in the presence of a stern, demanding father. "I'll do my best, Mr. Trevor. But, frankly, if he's getting information outside normal channels, he's going to have to trust me a lot more than he does now before he tells me about it."

"I simply *have* to know whether someone is sending Chandler in search of buried matters," Trevor said. "And if so, *who* is doing it, and *why*. I have an ominous feeling that someone may be trying to settle old scores with the Agency. We have no need of that right now."

The canoe was nearing the disreputable little dock from which it had departed. The traffic had intensified on the Freeway over-head. And Trevor had gotten his workout and was winded. He spoke slowly, between breaths.

"It would be extremely unwise for Senator Chandler to believe he can make a national political reputation out of such a witch hunt. Frank Church tried it several years ago, and unfortunately, one or two of my predecessors cooperated. But it caught up with him—and them. They're all gone now, Miss Dunham, gone."

Despite the heat, Elaine shivered.

Trevor docked the canoe and stepped up onto the jetty. He dried his hand on his warm-up trousers, extended it to her, and lifted her almost bodily from the boat. "Of course, I don't intend to suggest how you undertake this particular task. But somehow"—he carefully underscored the word—"you must find out what links Senator Chandler believes exist between your current investiga-tion—particularly the Fabricante murder—and the Castro busi-ness. And it would be very helpful to know who is encouraging him to move in this particular direction. Perhaps if you were to develop a more . . . *personal* relationship?"

Elaine felt a sense of violation. She knew what he had in mind, but he was not honest enough to say it.

They made their way up the broken steps and stood not far from the Director's car. The chauffeur and his companion waited out of earshot, their backs discreetly turned. Workers were begin-ning to arrive at the warehouses and construction projects along this seedy section of K Street, and Trevor seemed anxious to be gone. "Do you fully understand the importance I attach to this?"

"I understand, Mr. Trevor, and I'll do my best. But *you* must understand that it won't be easy. Senator Chandler is becoming increasingly edgy. He seems preoccupied, and certainly not in the mood to develop a more personal relationship with me—or anyone else, as far as I can tell."

Trevor's smile was knowing. "I thought yesterday's lunch was a step in the right direction."

Elaine sucked in her breath.

The smile broadened. He leaned close to her ear. "I like your perfume, Elaine. Flora Danica, I believe?"

Elaine was furious. *You bastard,* she thought. *You might have a great nose for perfume, but not that great. You did wiretap my room in Miami. Do you know I didn't tell you everything about that night? About the man by the pool?*

"It's my wife's favorite. Very light and subtle." Trevor looked directly at Elaine now. "You obviously are a woman of good . . . judgment."

He bowed slightly, then turned to the man waiting beside the car. "Take the canoe back to the boat house, Bill." He got into the front seat of the Ford, beside the driver, and the car pulled away.

Elaine started up the dusty brick street, her mind crowded with a storm of conflicting emotions. *I am not going to prostitute myself—not for Trevor and not for his version of my patriotic duty.* But she knew that her attraction to Tom Chandler was steadily growing. *If anything happens between us now, Trevor's spoiled it. Made it cheap. Made it a lie.*

Three steelworkers turned and whistled, surprised by such an elegant woman in that unlikely neighborhood. Elaine hurried to her car.

The letter. "Help me clear my name," he said. But how? Chandler? Everything kept coming back to Senator Thomas Chandler. Trevor. Her father. Did every honest emotion have to be complicated by the needs of other people? Was there no future for just plain Tom and Elaine?

Damn Trevor. He had so subtly suggested that she use sex to get what Trevor wanted. And now *she* wanted something: help for her father.

22 *Thursday, April 30*

Gordon Nicholson always tried to be the first to arrive at his office on the second floor of the Russell Senate Office Building. If he was at his desk at seven-fifteen, he generally had a full hour before his staff began to file in through the mahogany door. That gave him time enough to sort the morning mail, scrutinizing the return addresses and satisfying himself that all the important letters would receive his personal attention. Only routine work was delegated to his staff.

His secretary, a stout woman who dressed invariably in black or dark blue—her only effort at slimming—kept a daily log of every incoming phone call. Nicholson returned each call as promptly as possible. Usually he waited until after four o'clock to answer the unimportant ones, thus making the most efficient use of his time. He made it a point always to be the last to leave the office at night.

Unlike Chandler, who was uninterested in the administrative operations of his office, Nicholson was obsessed by them. It was *his* office. He refused to hire an administrative assistant, an arrangement that did not make for fraternal happiness. Staff morale was low and there was a large turnover of personnel. Nicholson preferred things that way. While few staffers were able to build a solid foundation of expertise before they departed, they were also unable to build a base of opposition within the ranks. All the staffers knew they were dispensable. Thus everyone had a strong incentive to stay out of office politics.

Nicholson's dislike of Tom Chandler was growing. He believed that Chandler didn't deserve even to be on the task force, let alone be its chairman. Chandler was a self-anointed gadfly and, as far as Nicholson was concerned, a troublemaker on the Intelligence Committee. He was glory-bound, running for the presidency—probably on a platform of "cooperation" with the Soviet Union.

Nicholson sat behind his large mahogany desk and brooded. Then he skimmed the *Journal* and the *Post*, circling in red the news items he wanted photocopied.

Today was Thursday, the one day Nicholson skipped an early-morning workout at the Squash Club on D Street, not far from his office. Nicholson refused to go to the Senate gym, which he regarded as a place for old walruses to have their flabby flesh kneaded while they dozed off into glassy-eyed half-sleep. He preferred to pound a hard black ball against a wall as if he were trying to put a hole in it. Other players might angle the ball deftly, low and into a corner, so it would glance off, catching their opponents flatfooted. But not Nicholson. Power was important to him, not form or subtlety.

Senate staffers on the Intelligence Committee had a nickname for every senator, the more derisive the better. Jim Perkins was Cotton Mather; Charles Walcott, The Oil Rigger. Tom Chandler was Yankee Doodle. And Nicholson was The Bull. He always came directly at you, always on the attack. The staff might occasionally be amused by Nicholson's rough, manhandling technique in questioning witnesses, but no one ever laughed at him. He looked like a man who could hurt you.

Nicholson checked his watch: nearly eight. He was due to preside at a prayer breakfast meeting. He knew Clinton Atwood arrived early at his office. He dialed the number. After two rings Atwood answered, sounding annoyed that anyone would call while he was working on his column.

"Yes?" he said, his voice sharp with irritation.

"Hello, Clinton? Gordon Nicholson calling. Sorry to disturb you this early. That matter we talked about at lunch last week?"

"Yes," Atwood said, not so stiffly now.

"Well, I checked it out with my sources. Chandler has definitely decided to go back into the business of the 'Family Jewels'— and, I'm told, all the way to Dallas."

Atwood did not respond. Nicholson thought he heard the sound of a pencil snap over the telephone.

"Just thought you should know what he's up to. I'll keep you posted if I hear anything more."

"Er, thank you, Gordon. That's very helpful of you. Yes. Keep me posted."

Nicholson hung up, a tiny smile distorting his lips. Atwood was one journalist who was not going to give Chandler a free ride.

Nicholson was off to bestow a spiritual message on his colleagues. It occurred to him that he might call it "God and Man in the Senate." Bill Buckley would love it.

Tom Chandler had been angry ever since the FBI agent left his office. That was at eleven, and now it was late afternoon. He knew he'd be likely to find Charles Walcott at the Senate gym after four o'clock, and phoned him to make sure.

He decided to walk over. Some exercise and fresh air might help to cool his anger, to give him some perspective. Besides, he'd been complaining lately about his hermetically sealed existence, from underground garage to office to Senate subway to Capitol and back again, some days setting foot outdoors only between the front seat of his car and the front door of his house.

But this air could scarcely be called fresh. The sky had turned the color of a faded bruise, a strange yellow gray, and the air was heavy with humidity. Washington spring was once again masquerading as summer.

Chandler turned right on Constitution Avenue and walked past the Dirksen Senate Office Building. Traffic had already started to swell, and the Metro buses let out a hiss of brakes as they stopped to pick up passengers. Another right turn at the corner of Constitution and First Street, and Chandler entered the Russell Building. The police officer on duty tipped his hat. "Afternoon, Senator." Chandler wasn't carrying a briefcase, but if he had been, he wouldn't have had to open it. Senators were not suspected of smuggling dynamite into, or classified documents out of, the office buildings.

Chandler nodded and headed down the dark, high-ceilinged corridor. When he opened the unlabeled mahogany-stained door of what he called the "library," a bell was tripped, alerting the employees inside that a senator was coming. No sounds from within had penetrated into the corridor, yet the minute Chandler opened the door, he could hear activity: Someone was practicing his kick in one of the pools. On the portable radio that belonged to the Swedish chief masseur, a violin concerto—*the Mendelssohn?* Chandler asked himself—accompanied the rhythmic slapping of a vigorous massage. The familiar distinctive smell assailed Chandler's nostrils: the odor of staleness, combined with chlorine from the swimming pools, filled the air in an almost perceptible haze.

"Afternoon, Senator." Willie greeted Chandler enthusiastically. Willie was getting old now, but his wiry black body was as slim as ever, though streaks of gray marked his lacquered-back hair. His tinted black-rimmed glasses were the color and thickness of Coke bottles. "Whatcha gonna do today, Senator? Work out?"

"Not today, Willie. Think I'll just grab a steam." Chandler walked past a small warm-water pool. Senator Everett Feldaver was making a scissors motion with his thick arms and wasted legs.

"Hey, Ev, how's the water?"

"Not bad, Tom. Helps ease the aches a little."

"We miss you on the task force, Ev. It's good to see you back in action."

"Not quite in action yet, Tom, but the hip's improving. Give me another two weeks and I'll race you a lap in the big pool."

Stanley Jacobs from Nebraska was in that pool now, doing his daily fifty laps. Jacobs was seventy years old but could have passed for fifty-five. He had come to the Senate almost forty years ago, but still approached each day with undiminished enthusiasm. Chandler waved to him and walked on, to one of the small cubicles where privacy was not quite guaranteed by a French-style swinging door.

Chandler's first impression of the Senate gym, years ago—perhaps because of the marble walls—had been that it was elegant. By his third visit, he had realized that it was simply old. It couldn't compare with the private health clubs proliferating in and around Washington. But it offered something no other club in the city could offer: total isolation from beseeching citizens. It was the one place where he did not have to explain or justify his votes. No one could reach him there unless he wanted to be reached. It was better even than his hideaway office. No staff was allowed. All calls were screened. Every need was attended to. "Water? Aspirin? Razor? Anything I can get you, Senator?"

Chandler sat on a cot and stripped off his clothes. He usually spent twenty minutes lifting weights to keep in trim, but today he had to talk to Charlie Walcott. He grabbed a towel from the rack, wrapped it around his waist, and walked with an athlete's stride to the sauna room.

There, three old stuffed chairs that looked as if they might have been purchased at a rummage sale were draped with white sheets, which supposedly protected them from legislative sweat. A telephone sat on a small table between two chairs, and newspapers and magazines lay like dying leaves on a canvas-covered ottoman the color of dead grass. *Truly elegant*, thought Chandler, not for the first time.

Partially hidden by the *Washington Post* he was reading, Charles Walcott was enthroned on the middle chair. "Have a seat, Tom," he said without looking up from his paper. "You said it was urgent."

"It is, Charlie," Chandler said, pushing aside some magazines to perch on the edge of the ottoman. "I don't know what in hell is going on, and I need your advice." Walcott peered at him over the top of his paper.

"I got a call today from an FBI agent," Chandler continued. "She said she needed to talk to me but not over the phone. I asked her what about. She said it involved counterespionage."

Walcott showed no visible sign of surprise. He was perspiring heavily now, and his chest was turning pink in scattered patches.

"I don't need to tell you I was curious," Chandler said. "So I asked her to come to my office, and she did. She told me the FBI was aware that I had been in contact with someone attached to the Soviet Embassy and wanted to know if I'd be willing to discuss 'the substance of my conversations.' Damn it, Charlie, I was pissed. I said that the FBI was either tapping *my* phone or the Embassy's, and she just looked at me and smiled."

"Tom," Walcott said, "I've told you on a number of occasions that there is nothing you say on the phone that goes . . . unnoticed."

"I know, and I've never said anything on the phone that would put me in a compromising position. But damn it, I have a right to return phone calls, don't I? Without the FBI jumping out of the woodwork at me? The fact is I never talked to anyone at the Embassy. I just left a message that I'd returned the original call. I thought it might have something to do with the task-force investigation. I'll take information from *any* source."

"You should know, Tom," Walcott said, lowering his voice as if he assumed that his words might be recorded even in the sauna, "that someone who has access to Intelligence Committee information passed some on to a KGB agent. It was a summary of the briefing we got on that new neuron weapon the Air Force is developing."

Chandler felt his neck muscles tighten. "Christ! Am I the suspect? All I did was return a phone call. I didn't even get past the switchboard. Am I supposed to conclude that I should have no contact whatsoever with anyone at the Soviet Embassy?"

"No. All I'm saying is you should be aware of what's been going on, and you should be careful."

"Charlie," Chandler said, letting his exasperation roll out like the sweat from his pores. "We're in a position to blow each other to Mars and back and what you're saying is that a U.S. senator can't even talk to a Russian on the phone. Jesus, do we have to become like them? Tap every conversation, take loyalty oaths, inform on our friends and family—?"

"Come off it, Tom. Spare me the sanctimony. We're locked in a struggle with a nation that recognizes no God but the sword. They have vowed to destroy us. The Soviet Union doesn't recognize your right of free speech. It doesn't tolerate dissent—"

"Well, we can hardly wrap ourselves in a cloak of innocence. We've done some pretty foul things too."

"True. But we're not shipping intellectual dissenters off to the Gulag. And we're not training and supporting terrorists around the world who bomb and burn and torture and kill anyone in their line of fire—including the Pope. You're the one who's so concerned about terrorists, remember?"

"Charlie, I understand all that. All I'm asking is, do we have to adopt their tactics? Do we have to submit to lie detector tests? Do we have to have our phones tapped, undergo surveillance checks, live under the constant watch of the FBI or the CIA, all in order to preserve our freedom? If we have to use their methods, what are we preserving? Christ, if *we're* not safe from the FBI, who is?"

Walcott sighed. "Do you think that it's all right for the Soviets to know what you're doing and saying, but not our own law enforcement agencies?"

"Of course not. I'm saying we ought to put a stop to the Soviets' bugging our conversations. But we shouldn't tolerate the FBI or the CIA doing it either."

"Tom, you're being naïve. Free societies are always at a disadvantage when it comes to protecting their secrets. You have access to the most highly classified information in existence—"

Chandler interrupted. "Damn right I do. And what have I said or done that would call my loyalty into question?"

"Nothing that I'm aware of. But the FBI doesn't know that. They're not in a position to trust anyone. Not me. Not you. There's a leak somewhere in the Committee. It might be a staff member—"

"Yes, or it could be someone in the CIA."

"Or," Walcott said, not hiding his displeasure at being interrupted again, "it might be someone in the Senate." He paused for emphasis. "There is a dead drop at the base of Key Bridge, almost directly across from Charlie Byrd's jazz spot in Georgetown. Last month someone connected with our Committee—or *on* the Committee—deposited a summary of the briefing on the neuron weapon in that dead drop. Our men intercepted it. Afterward, they kept the spot under constant surveillance. An attaché from the Soviet Embassy was observed there. He was *photographed*, Tom, searching for the missing envelope."

Chandler hesitated to ask the next question. He felt as if he were opening a door into a darkened room and someone was hiding behind the door. Finally: "What's the attaché's name?" he asked.

"Boris Luganov."

"Christ!" Chandler blurted.

"What's the matter?" Walcott asked.

"That's the guy who called my office."

"Tom. The FBI hasn't been tapping your phone, if it'll make you feel any better. The Soviets have a great big electronic vacuum cleaner that sucks telephone transmissions up and puts them through a computer. Their intelligence units sift through the conversations, looking for whatever nuggets they can find."

"So, the Soviet Union listens to us and then we get the same information by listening to them. No wonder old J. Edgar stayed in power so long. He probably had a file on everyone."

"Yup. there wasn't anyone—including Jack Kennedy—who dared suggest to Hoover that he ought to step down."

Sweat was pouring down Chandler's body. He suddenly felt exhausted and depressed. He pulled himself up from the ottoman. "Charlie, I know it all looks suspicious. But I'm not leaking information to the Soviet Union. You've got to believe that. I've got a feeling somebody somewhere is out to get me. But I don't know who and I don't know why." He shrugged and grinned wryly. "Classic paranoia, case number two million and twelve."

Chandler opened the glass door, and the cool air rushed in, clouding the glass with moisture. He turned back to Walcott. "Thanks for the ear, Charlie. And for the advice."

23

Thursday, April 30

Chandler's anger had abated very little by the time he got back to his office shortly after five. He had not told Walcott the full story. He had omitted the part about two members of the FBI's counterespionage unit coming to his office a second time, just after lunch, with some crazy story that the Soviet attaché was bandying his name around town as a good friend. Chandler was sure that the Bureau had fabricated the story, but he couldn't understand why. Maybe Boris Luganov was a double agent. Maybe the Bureau was trying to compromise Chandler, and through him the task force. He was sure there had been a tape recorder in the gray Samsonite briefcase one of the agents had carried into his office. It might be a new kind of ABSCAM operation, he thought, to set him up as a traitor. On the other hand, the Soviets were hardly likely to be happy about his investigation either. Chandler felt as if he were walking through a maze of mirrors. He saw a thousand images and he couldn't distinguish reality from reflection. He felt panic creep up his throat. He swallowed hard, then clenched his jaw in a way that would have told anyone who knew him that he had reached a decision. He pressed the intercom button on his phone.

"Margie, get me Mr. Boris Luganov at the Soviet Embassy."

"Sure thing, Senator," Margie said cheerfully. Within seconds, she buzzed Chandler back. "Mr. Luganov is on the line," she said.

Chandler was surprised at the speed with which the call had gone through. A welcome mat had evidently been put out at the Soviet Embassy. *Why?* He was as wary as a fugitive on the run.

"Mr. Luganov, this is Tom Chandler."

"Hello, Senator Chandler. I'm delighted you were able to return my call. I know what a busy man you are." Chandler could detect only a trace of an accent. Luganov's English was flawless. "I was wondering if it would be possible for us to have lunch one day soon. There are some important matters facing our countries, and I know that you are a man who is highly regarded in foreign policy. . . ."

Chandler smiled. *The Soviets are so damned obvious*, he thought. *About as subtle as a hammerlock.*

"Thanks for your confidence, Mr. Luganov," he said aloud. "But I think your time might be better spent with the chairman of the Foreign Relations Committee. He would be in a better position to discuss those issues with you." Chandler intended his failure flatly to decline as encouragement to Luganov to pursue the invitation. The cue did not pass unrecognized.

"Yes, Senator, I know that Senator Zolnick would be an important person to speak with, and I hope to do so one day soon. But there are some issues that I know you feel quite strongly about. I remember the conversation we had in Georgetown some time ago."

Chandler remembered the occasion too, an extraordinarily innocent one. But mindful of listening ears on both sides of the ideological fence, he couldn't let such a reference to the past go by. Any ambiguity might be interpreted as incriminating if it was not explained.

"You mean the night the Congress destroyed your tennis team and you had to buy us dinner?" Chandler's laugh sounded unforced. "I guess we showed that the United States still retains a measure of superiority in certain things." As the star of the tournament, Chandler had been awarded a red T-shirt with the Cyrillic letters for U.S.S.R. printed on it.

"Yes, Senator," Luganov said, picking up the challenge. "Perhaps if we could exchange tennis balls for missiles, and choose athletics to settle our differences, the world would be a better place. Certainly a much safer one." Luganov did not wait for Chandler to reply. "But of course, that is just one of the issues I would like to discuss. Could we get together for lunch, say at Lion d'Or? It's not too far from here and the food, I'm told, is excellent."

"Lunch, yes," Chandler said, "but why not make it up here on the Hill? We've been doing a lot of voting lately, and frankly, I'd find it more convenient." Then he added deliberately, "Besides, it's my turn to treat. As I recall, when we last met—was it five years ago?—we made a little wager on the Soviet grain harvest. Seems you've been having a succession of bad winters." Chandler was determined to leave no doubt in any listener's mind about the straightforward nature of his limited past dealings with Luganov. "I'll check with my secretary on my schedule for next week and have her call you to confirm the date."

"Wonderful, Senator. I look forward to seeing you again."

Chandler hung up. Hastily sifting through the conversation, he concluded that there had been nothing sinister in anything Luganov had said—certainly no remark that might later prove embarrassing. Just the same, he pulled out a yellow pad, jotted down the date and time, and then recounted the conversation almost verbatim. He added a rationalization for his interest in talking to a man he now knew was a Soviet spy. Walcott was right: naïveté was no excuse for allowing himself to fall under suspicion. "I wish to talk to Luganov, he wrote, "to see if I can detect any Soviet reaction to leads we are pursuing about Soviet terrorist connections."

That ought to satisfy the FBI, he thought. He then buzzed Margie and asked her to open a new file, marked CONFIDENTIAL.

As Chandler pressed the intercom off, he wondered what flurry of activity had been set in motion down at that slightly scruffy-looking building on 16th Street. No doubt Luganov was making notes too. A file was being opened, a record compiled that later would be expanded. And at the J. Edgar Hoover Building, what agent was rushing to Judge Schumacher with a spool of tape this very moment?

Which mirror was he looking at? What were they after? Who was *they*?

24 To Craig Delvin, chief of staff of the Intelligence Committee, the man seated diagonally across from him looked like just another of the many smart young business executives and lobbyists who lunch with senators they are seeking to influence. The man wore a well-tailored dark-blue gabardine suit, and he was patiently reading *The Washington Post*. But Delvin knew this was no lobbyist sitting on the brown leather couch in the reception area of the Senate Dining Room. Delvin knew he was Boris Luganov, a Soviet diplomat and probably something more.

Delvin had seen Luganov, but had not met him, a couple of weeks before at the British Embassy, where a talented group of diplomats who called themselves the Embassy Players had put on a rousing Victorian music hall show. Delvin had wangled hard-to-get tickets from an intelligence officer assigned to the British Embassy. The officer had pointed out Luganov and whispered, "KGB chap, I hear." Now, seeing Luganov in the United States Senate, Delvin remembered the whispered remark and wondered what the man was doing here.

When Chandler arrived, late and on the run, he caught sight of Delvin and glanced quickly away. *Just my damn luck*, Chandler thought. It was not unusual for senators to meet with foreign diplomats in the Senate Dining Room. It was rare, however, for a senator, particularly one who sat on the Intelligence Committee, to be seen talking with a Soviet representative, especially when tensions were high. Senators were not in the business of conducting diplomacy with the Soviets, and certainly not with one identified by the FBI as a KGB agent.

Sensing a snub that he could nevertheless understand— Chandler's dislike of Delvin was cordially reciprocated—Delvin retreated, but not out of earshot.

"Hello, Boris," Chandler said. "Sorry to keep you waiting. I got tied up at the last minute with some constituents."

Luganov stubbed out his cigarette in the ashtray on the coffee table, where, Chandler noticed, three more distinctive Russian cigarette butts already reposed. Luganov smiled. "No problem. I arrived just minutes ago myself."

He saw Chandler's eyes go to the telltale evidence in the ashtray, and only winked. He was a good student of the art of the innocent lie.

A hostess showed Senator Chandler and his guest to their table.

"We'll need a minute to look over the menu," Chandler told the waiter, "but I'll have some coffee now. Mr. Luganov, how about you?"

Luganov asked to see the wine list, and was informed that wine was not served in the Senate Dining Room.

"In that case, I'll have coffee too." Luganov said amiably.

Chandler knew he was taking a chance by meeting with Luganov, but he had weighed the advantages and disadvantages. He might be able to get some feel for his prime thesis—that the impetus for international terrorism was coming from the Soviet Union. And, since he now knew that Luganov was a KGB agent, he could count on his questions about terrorism quickly getting back to Moscow. There might be a reaction that would give Chandler the lead he required.

This dangerous game had its other side. The lunch would give the FBI—and, inevitably, Trevor—another incident for their file on Senator Thomas Chandler. He had to take that risk.

But what better place for running that risk than here, he thought, as he looked around the Senate Dining Room. He had chosen as public a place as possible, to avoid any semblance of furtiveness. Visibility was his shield. Then too, the noise level reduced the likelihood of their being overheard.

"I'm glad to see you again," Luganov began genially. "Incidentally, Senator, you look in splended shape. You are still playing tennis?"

"As much as I can," Chandler said. "But things have been a little hectic."

"Of course. But you must take time for leisure too. All business can be depressing."

The waiter brought their coffee and went away with their food order. "You're right," Chandler said, "but I'm sure you didn't ask me to lunch just to talk about the therapeutic value of athletics. What's on your mind?"

"I'm going back to the Soviet Union next month," Luganov said.

"Oh?"

"So I thought it might be important for us to talk." Luganov lit another cigarette. "I'm concerned about what's happening between our two countries. I fear we are on the edge of catastrophe. You're a thoughtful man, Senator, and I consider myself quite reasonable too. Unless people like you and me start communicating, start to reverse our countries' policies, we are in danger of destroying humanity."

"Policies like Afghanistan and Poland?"

"I'm not interested in being baited, Senator," Luganov said evenly. There was no defensiveness in his voice. "We signed a SALT treaty, you may recall, and you, the Senate, were the ones who refused to ratify it. I could mention the neutron bomb, cruise missiles, China, Chile, El Salvador, South Africa . . ." Luganov took a long drag on his cigarette. ". . . But that would serve no purpose today. If we keep hurling old charges at each other, rather than agreeing that we must agree to live with each other, we are going to incinerate this planet."

Chandler reserved his assent. He had come to regard Soviet declarations of concern for human life with skepticism. Yet he was struck by the difference between Luganov's manner today and what he remembered of their first encounter five years earlier.

Then, Luganov had reacted angrily when Chandler goaded him about Helsinki and human rights. Chandler remembered his saying, "This is not your concern. It's a matter of our internal affairs. . . . The Backfire bomber is not the same as the B-1. It is not helpful to talk about state lies while your CIA is trying to execute foreign leaders. . . ." He had been hostile, combative, surly.

Today, he seemed cool, yet affable. But Chandler was only partly persuaded. "Isn't your concern a bit coincidental with our decision to rebuild our military capability?"

Luganov looked at him directly. His eyes were suddenly as hard and cold as ice. "And do you think we are remaining idle or are preparing to disarm?" It was not a question. "You built MIRVs. We built them. You developed neutron weapons. We increased our SS-20's. You have the shuttle. We have a space station. You want lasers. We prefer particle beams. How much more do we need?"

Chandler's response was deferred by the appearance of their lunch. In the quiet bustle that ensued as the waiter set down Chandler's chef's salad and his guest's cold salmon, his mind grappled with the issues Luganov had raised. The superpowers relentlessly, mindlessly, kept preparing for war while all over the world, the people of every nation continued to pray for peace. They wanted their children to live, to reproduce and prosper. But too often those children lived only as names engraved on the marble walls of memorials to yet another war.

And next time, the war would be different. The equivalent of fourteen billion tons of TNT was locked in the forty thousand warheads that stood poised on both sides, waiting for one last orgy of destruction. Hurricane winds of fire would sweep across continents. The seas would be clouded with a different kind of fog.

And all the while, both sides spoke of the option of thermonuclear war as if it were a mere game of chess. Who would move first?

"We don't need *any* more," Chandler said at last. "But I don't think there will be a change in policy here unless there is first some sign from your government—a sign that you are truly interested in peace."

"Such as?"

"Such as completely pulling out of Afghanistan. Or getting the Cubans out of Africa. Or better yet . . ." Chandler decided the time had come to probe for a reaction. "Better yet, stop supporting global terrorism—and trafficking in drugs."

Luganov's face remained impassive. "We do not support terrorism, Senator. We support wars of liberation. The fact that the oppressed people of the world must resort to terrorism to overthrow their enemies is not of our making. Do you support dictatorships, or do dictators merely ask for American support? I might just as well ask the United States to show some sign of good faith. Senator, if people like you cannot see the benefit of at least opening up new talks, serious talks about ways in which we can step back from the brink—cautiously, without sacrificing national pride—then nuclear holocaust is inevitable." Luganov shook his head.

Chandler tried another tack: "And the other issue? Drugs may be less violent than terrorism, but they take a lot of lives. What *about* drug smuggling?"

Luganov emitted a short bark of a laugh. "The international drug traffic, my dear Senator, is a very capitalist enterprise. And drug addiction is a very American problem. Our Soviet youth have no need of such false stimulants."

Chandler saw three possible reasons for Luganov's response: Chandler's suspicion of Soviet involvement in the drug trade were unfounded; or Luganov was ignorant of that particular activity; or he was a very good actor indeed. In any case, it was evident that any hoped-for reaction, any evidence that he was on the right track, would come, if it came at all, only after his questions were relayed to Moscow.

The waiter came to remove their empty plates and offered more coffee. Chandler figured he'd probed as far as he could today and shifted the conversation to neutral social ground. "What's happened to Georgi Tupolev?" he asked.

This time, when he least expected it, he got a reaction. Luganov looked as if he'd been slapped in the face. After a moment he said, "He . . . retired from the service."

"So I'd heard on the diplomatic grapevine. But where is he? What's he doing now?"

Luganov looked uncomfortable. "Unfortunately, he died several weeks ago. It is a great loss."

Chandler was surprised. He had met Tupolev for the first time about a year ago, at a dinner party given by the Swedish Ambassador. It was hard to believe that this chubby Russian with the large potato nose, this jolly man who reminded him of everyone's favorite uncle, was what he was rumored to be: the KGB station chief in Washington. Tupolev had made an unusual request that night, asking if Chandler could arrange for a record company to send his grandchildren some rock music records while they were visiting in Poland. Chandler had complied with the request; maybe American music could breach international walls more effectively than missiles.

"That's strange," Chandler said now. "I saw him about two months ago. He seemed in excellent health."

"It was an aneurysm, I'm told. It's a terrible thing, isn't it, Senator? The mere popping of an artery can take it all away."

Luganov was visibly impatient now to get away. "Let me return to a most important point, Senator, before I have to leave. I do not believe in supporting terrorism. There is nothing that can justify the wholesale murder of innocent people. It breeds only a bloodthirst for revenge and more terror. But we cannot always choose our friends—any more than you can choose your dictators. Both of us, our countries, have to find a way to stop the flow of weapons into the hands of nations that can drag us into war. Are we agreed?"

Chandler said nothing. He continued to search Luganov's eyes for indications of sincerity or deception.

Luganov decided he had made his point. "I hope to return to Washington one day," he said. "In the meantime, I hope I can tell my people that there are still some American leaders who are sincere in their desire to avoid a confrontation."

He started to rise, then abruptly sat down again. "I almost forgot. Here, this is for you." Luganov handed Chandler a small white envelope.

Luganov smiled at Chandler's questioning look. "It is a gift from Ambassador Brodovsky. As you know, he is an admirer of yours. The Bolshoi Ballet is playing at the Kennedy Center. The Ambassador thought you might like to see Saturday night's performance."

Chandler was taken by surprise. He didn't want to accept the tickets, but he didn't want to offend Ambassador Brodovsky either.

At the large table in the middle of the dining room the Senate photographer was organizing a group shot of some Hawaiian visitors. "Smile," he coaxed. *Click.* "There, that's great. Senator, move in just a little closer to the young lady in the striped dress. There. That's it. Got it." *Click.* "One more." *Click. Click.*

Chandler took the proffered envelope and put it in an inside pocket. He would give the tickets to Margie and her husband. He signed the guest check and walked out with Luganov.

At a table near the door Craig Delvin was having lunch with Gordon Nicholson. So that was who Delvin had been waiting for. Chandler would have liked to ignore them, but it was too late; eye contact had been made. The three men exchanged insincerely cordial greetings, and then Chandler moved to re-join Luganov, who had drifted quietly on and was waiting outside the door. He had deliberately avoided putting Chandler into a position where he would be forced to introduce him to these men, and to the other senators now coming into the dining room.

Luganov and Chandler made their way through the crowded

reception room, down the corridor, and out through the revolving door. Luganov hailed a passing cab. He turned to Chandler and extended his right hand. "Thank you for the lunch, Senator. I enjoyed it and hope that when I return to Washington you will permit me to repay your hospitality."

Chandler hesitated for a fraction of a second, then shook the outstretched hand. As Luganov drove off in the cab, Chandler stood in thought, hardly noticing the scores of tourists milling about in front of the Capitol, carrying souvenirs, snapping pictures of the dome.

Chandler was puzzled. He knew what he himself had hoped to accomplish with the meeting, but it was Luganov who had sought *him* out. *Why?* The conversation had been, for the most part, pleasant enough but unremarkable. Luganov appeared to be sincere, but to what end? The only new information he had imparted was that Georgi Tupolev was dead. And probably not from natural causes, if the unguarded expression on Luganov's face meant anything. But why should Chandler be concerned about the death of a high-ranking KGB agent? Tupolev meant little to him personally and nothing at all—as far as he knew—to his investigation.

At one point, Chandler had been tempted to mention the subject of neuron weapons, just to let Luganov know that Chandler was aware someone on Capitol Hill was feeding him information. But that would only alert Luganov to the fact that he was constantly followed by the FBI.

The thought sent Chandler down a new track. Luganov had undoubtedly been followed to the Hill, probably into the dining room. *The ballet tickets!* Someone had probably seen Luganov hand Chandler the anonymous white envelope. Chandler cursed himself for a fool—why hadn't he taken the tickets out of the envelope, made it obvious to any anonymous watcher that this was a totally innocent transaction? Had Nicholson and Delvin seen? God knew they were no fans of Thomas Chandler. And Nicholson, at least, was awfully cozy with E. W. Trevor.

A burden of quiet despair began to settle around Chandler's shoulders. *Am I being set up by the Soviets? Or by my own country?*

Chandler stood there, knowing he had just made a terrible mistake.

25

Chandler still had a long road ahead as he drove over the soaring Chesapeake Bay Bridge onto the Eastern Shore of Maryland. Checking his rearview mirror for the twentieth time since leaving Washington, he noted the sun over his shoulder. There would be an hour or two of daylight left to drive by, but it would be dark by the time he reached his destination. And that was as it should be.

At the end of the long drive and longer night that lay ahead, he might find some . . . what? revelation? He could hope. In the week since his meeting with Luganov, Chandler had begun to sense that his investigation had reached a turning point. Tonight was important, he thought, because he was becoming his own chief investigator, finally moving out from behind his desk. He grinned in recognition of a certain boyish enthusiasm. There was an element of risk involved in what he was doing, and that excited him.

Since the Harrold family tragedy and the formation of the task force, his mind had been numbed by mountains of files. With the exception of the Miami trip, Chandler's time for the last seven weeks had been spent in a continuous cycle of meetings with the task force staff and reviewing documents. The shelf behind his desk was piled with unclassified files and committee reports: documents on terrorism, on drugs, on the Warren Commission and the Church Committee investigations, on the activities of the CIA and the FBI during the fifties and sixties, on the KGB. On and on.

It had become his habit to spend the hours of four to six every afternoon in the sealed-off and closely guarded offices of the Senate Intelligence Committee. There, with either Kevin's or Elaine's assistance, he had plowed through page after page of classified information on the activities of various terrorist organizations and individuals, on psychological profiles of their leaders, speculation about intricate connections among the various groups and one or more foreign governments, the flow of arms and money, hiding

places, false identities and passports, routes of escape, potential targets for destruction or assassination, American sympathizers and
financiers. There were reports from American intelligence sources
and agencies, European police forces and security networks, and
Interpol. Some of them were consistent but most were contradictory.

Interspersed with the endless hours of reading, cross-checking,
backtracking, and reviewing were periodic meetings with the staff,
both his own and Co-Chairman Walcott's. Sometimes they reported new findings about real or possible connections among the
terrorists, but often their information merely confirmed impressions Chandler had acquired from his own research.

Chandler had come to understand, and strongly sympathize
with, real detective work—the tedious, undramatic, unromantic
piecing-together of a mosaic. Maybe panning for gold was a better
image, he thought as he drove north through the Maryland countryside. Bushels and bushels of gravel, rock, and sediment passing
across a little metal pan, until a tiny valuable grain glistens from the
bottom. The golden grain has to come from somewhere. You work
your way upstream, finding one or two other little flakes as you go,
knowing somewhere up in the hills is a vein where the truth lies
hidden.

Thirty miles down U.S. 50, Chandler turned left onto state
highway 404. Now he had a further drive of sixty miles, well over
an hour on the two-lane highway to the coast of Delaware. He
sifted the flakes of gold in his mind.

The Harrold family had been killed by a team probably composed of six men. They were almost certainly all foreigners who
had entered the country for the sole purpose of assassinating the
Secretary of State. All but one of the men had escaped the country
before exit points could be secured. Only the Palestinian Ahmad
Rashish had died.

Bits of evidence, isolated but beginning to connect, indicated
that the Harrold assassinations were related to a pattern of terrorist
acts carried out by an international network of organizations, pre-
viously autonomous and nationalistic, but recently brought together in some loose confederation by an unknown catalyst.

Chandler's task force had painstakingly pieced together data
from more than a dozen sources showing that this terrorism was
being financed by a new drug supply and distribution network.

There was ample evidence to suggest that Sam Fabricante, the old Mafia don, had been killed because he had found out about this market and, for some reason, had objected to it.

But then the gold specks ran out. The mountains of research yielded no new clues.

Except for the man from Miami. Except for Memory.

Chandler crossed the Delaware state line. The half-set sun in his rearview mirror blazed with a final burst of fire, igniting the low western sky. Chandler, now going well over the speed limit, pushed eastward in the gathering gloom.

Who was the man from Miami?

Even though he had met with Memory twice, Chandler still would have been unable to identify the man if he saw him in full light. Both meetings had taken place in very dark surroundings, obviously by design. Chandler guessed, mostly from the man's lightly accented voice, that he was of middle age and had probably come from a Spanish-speaking country. Given his apparent knowledge both of Miami and of intelligence activities in the early sixties, the man was likely to be a Cuban.

Chandler slowed the car as he entered the Delaware town of Georgetown, and picked up speed again on route 18, heading toward the town of Lewes, fourteen miles away on the coast.

The man had evidently been well enough placed in the Cuban exile community to know a great deal about plans for invasion and plots to overthrow Castro. That meant he would have had some knowledge of the Mafia connections. And he obviously had learned, then or since, about the CIA's executive-action capability. On the other hand, Chandler thought, the Church Committee reports contained a lot of information about all that. The man could be peddling used goods.

What about motive? There were clearly some facts or theories—well hidden—that Memory wanted brought out. He apparently saw the investigation as a way to do that. He had the connections needed to find out about Chandler's unpublicized trip to Miami, even to knowing where the investigators were staying. But wait. They had gone to Miami in response to an anonymous phone call to Woodrow Harrold, a call from a man who spoke with a Hispanic accent. Could it have been Memory who sent them there in the first place?

Chandler wondered if he would ever find out who the man was, why he was doing this, who he was afraid of—most of all, what he wanted Chandler to know. Chandler brooded as he followed the signs through the town of Lewes out toward Cape Henlopen State Park. It was almost totally dark when he came to a high gate and a tollbooth. As he paid the fare, the tollbooth clock read 8:56. Joining a double line of thirty or forty cars driving onto the Lewes–Cape May ferry, Chandler entered the final leg of his trip to a rendezvous on the far southern tip of New Jersey.

The spring evening was pleasant, but Chandler shivered. As the broad-beamed white ferry pushed out of its slip to begin the seventy-minute trip across Delaware Bay, Chandler suddenly realized he hadn't eaten since noon, when he'd shared a pastrami on rye with Elaine in the Intelligence Committee staff room. It looked like sandwiches again. He made his way to the enclosed upper deck, bought a stale, plastic-wrapped ham and cheese sandwich, two cartons of milk, and a chocolate bar, and took them out on the open forward deck. In his jeans, light windbreaker, and Irish tweed hat, he hoped he looked like an ordinary tourist.

During the meeting at the pavilion, now nearly a month past, Chandler had satisfied himself that Memory had invaluable information to share. Memory had confirmed, in his strange, Socratic way, that the terrorist acts were somehow related, that they were connected to the upsurge in drug traffic, that Fabricante had been killed because he knew too much, and finally and perhaps most importantly, that ZRRIFLE, the CIA assassination capability, was an important piece in the puzzle.

Since then, Chandler had been asking questions:

What had Fabricante found out about the new drug market and who had had him killed? The Miami police department and the FBI were still on that case, and neither had come up with much.

How had the terrorist Ahmad Rashish gotten into the country and how had he died? The Immigration and Naturalization Service confirmed that Rashish had been traveling under a skillfully forged passport that could have been produced by any of three or four expert sources. He had died by hanging, and the so-called lawyer who had visited him had almost assuredly arranged the death to look like a suicide.

What was ZRRIFLE and who was involved with it? Here, Chandler and his staff had scoured the Church Committee's classified and unclassified reports and files on assassination assets in the late fifties and early sixties. The principal unanswered questions centered on an agent code-named QJWIN. Chandler had personally interviewed five retired CIA officials and officers cognizant of ZRRIFLE and QJWIN. He had found out little more than what was in the reports of the mid-seventies' Senate investigation.

Finally, Memory's tantalizing "snake in the tower." Chandler had presented the phrase to Maude and Clarissa, the researchers, without attribution. It had proved agonizingly resistant to explication. Three tries at the Library of Congress had turned up nothing. The intelligence community computers also had drawn a blank. Then one evening, when he and Elaine were taking an unrelated-reading-and-ice-cream break from their labors, she had suddenly let out a gasp. "Listen to this!" she cried, holding up a slim volume of poetry she had purchased at a Capitol Hill bookstore that day. "It's Auden. A poem called *The Double Man:*

> "Why did the watchdog never bark?
> Why did the footsteps leave no mark?
> Where were the servants at that hour?
> *How did a snake get in the tower?*"

Her voice had stressed the last line, and she looked up at Chandler with shining eyes.

But when they sobered up from their initial excitement, they found themselves as much in the dark as ever. Even if Chandler could figure out what the "tower" was, he would still have to find and identify the snake.

At that point, he had summoned Memory. Following again the instructions he had received in Miami, Chandler had placed a brief notice in the Personals column of *The Washington Post* on the following day.

You can close your eyes to reality
But not to memories

Stanislaus Lec

Four days later Chandler had received, in the post office box he had taken in the name of Stanislaus Lec, a message typed on a plain card in an envelope without return address:

I can be found at the convent of St.
Mary-by-the-Sea, Cape May Point, New
Jersey, next Wednesday, 13 May, at 11 p.m.

The ferry drifted smoothly into its bumpered dock, and Chandler's borrowed Mustang followed the line of cars down the ramp. Fifteen minutes later he was in the center of Cape May. Following his map, he took a right fork in the road and drove until he spotted the lights of a drive-in ice-cream stand on the edge of town. The clock behind the soda fountain said 10:25. He ordered a chocolate milkshake and confirmed with the teenaged clerk that he was headed in the right direction.

Four miles down the dark, sand-shouldered road his headlights picked out, barely visible on the left, a small gateway marked CAPE MAY POINT. As he turned in he saw, looming a quarter of a mile farther on, the tall Cape May lighthouse, its beacon circling overhead every ten seconds. He drove toward the beach. Only a few old-fashioned street lamps resisted the night. By their light he could make out several dozen beach houses, most of them deserted this early in the season.

Little more than a block from the lighthouse, Chandler parked his car in front of a vacant lot, congratulating himself again on having borrowed Kevin O'Brien's old blue Mustang with its unremarkable District of Columbia plates. He got out, locked the door, and started walking toward the ocean.

Soon he found himself at the end of the deserted street. On his left stood the imposing lighthouse, surrounded by a high electric fence. Directly ahead lay a fifty-yard strip of rolling sandy beach. On his right was a dark-roofed, white, U-shaped building, its closed side facing the ocean. In the courtyard stood a tall crucifix, and on the nearer wing, barely visible in the light from a distant streetlamp, was a small wooden sign: SAINT MARY-BY-THE-SEA NO TRESPASSING.

Chandler looked around and saw no one. He checked his watch: 10:55. He started around the building. The night was pitch-black. He wished for a flashlight, then realized he couldn't have used it if he had one. He was around the front of the building, his shoes half buried in sand, when his eyes, adjusting to the moonless night, made out a wooden porch.

He listened a moment and, hearing nothing, leaped up onto the porch as quietly as he could. Though the air was cool, he could feel the perspiration under his arms and between his shoulder blades. He took three steps forward, the boards creaking under his feet. In the darkness he could just make out the convent's double screened front door. He pulled the knob, and the outer door opened with a squeak. Breathless, he pushed on the inner door, and slowly it opened.

"Are you there?" he whispered.

There was no answer.

He tiptoed into the total blackness. There was a slight rustle—a rat?—then silence. "I'm not coming any farther unless I know you're here," he whispered. Nothing. Suddenly panic was rising in his throat. He turned toward the door.

A light touch brushed his shoulder. "Chandler." It was Memory.

"Please come in quickly and close the door."

Chandler exhaled with a rush. He eased the door shut behind him. He could see nothing.

"We have some time, but not a lot," Memory said. "The watchman comes at midnight. We must be gone by then."

The man seemed to be speaking in poetry. Chandler felt giddy.

"How goes the eternal quest for truth?"

"I want to find QJWIN," Chandler said.

"You certainly do," Memory agreed.

Chandler's sense of unreality vanished on the instant. "Goddammit!" he snapped. "I didn't come here to be mocked by you. I need some answers and I need them fast."

The man sighed audibly. "Senator Chandler," he said, both pleading and exasperated, "why can't you be more patient? Secrets buried more than twenty years do not reveal themselves overnight. They must be found. They must be summoned."

"Is QJWIN still alive?" Chandler shot back, his voice low and tight.

"Yes," said Memory.

"I want to see him," Chandler demanded.

There was a silence. "When you are ready."

"I'm ready *now*," Chandler said. He wanted to grab Memory and shake him, hit him.

Outside, there was a slight scratching on the porch. The two men stood motionless. Chandler felt his nerves twanging.

Then a prowling cat gave out an angry yowl and sprinted off down the boardwalk.

As if there had been no interruption, Memory spoke from the dark. "It would do you little good now. It will be more helpful later."

"Later? How much later?"

"Later, when you can ask him the right questions. Like me, he will tell you very little. But he will help you with the questions. He will point you toward the information you must have." Chandler felt, more than saw, that Memory moved quietly across the floor. Then he caught a fleeting glimpse of a profile against a window dimly visible in a reflected fitful glow from the lighthouse. The man returned.

"How much does he know?" Chandler asked.

"He knows everything, I believe."

"About the past? About ZRRIFLE? About executive action?"

"Yes, about the past. He *was* ZRRIFLE—at least its principal asset. If there was a connection between executive action and Kennedy, he undoubtedly knows it," said Memory.

"What do you mean, 'If there was a connection'?"

"That is between you and QJWIN, Senator. I want to have nothing to do with that."

Chandler realized the man was getting nervous. "Does he know about the 'snake in the tower'?" he asked.

"I believe so," said Memory. "But if he does, he will not tell you directly what or who it is. You must know enough—about the terrorism and the drugs—so that when you meet him you'll understand what he's talking about."

"What is the 'tower'?" Chandler realized his voice had taken on a pleading note. He didn't care. "I have to have some clue."

Memory was silent again. Then he said, "It is a place, Senator Chandler."

"Who lives there?"

"Your adversary."

"My adversary? How do I find him?"

"Ask the right questions."

"The right questions about what?"

"The drugs."

"The drugs?" Chandler echoed. "What do you mean? Like: Where do they come from? Who's selling them? Who's buy-

ing them? Where are they going? Who profits? Whither the proceeds?"

"Those are all excellent questions," said Memory.

"When I get answers to them, will I be ready to talk to QJ-
WIN?"

"I believe so."

"When I get the answers, will you help me get in touch with
him?"

"I will do my best."

"How shall I contact you?" Chandler asked.

The man was quiet again. Then, "Get down!" A powerful hand
grabbed Chandler's shoulder and pushed him to the floor.

An automobile spotlight swept through the building from the
back to the front. Chandler watched the dust motes rise in its moving beam. They heard the motor of a car as it slowly drove on.

There was a grunt as Memory got up.

"Contact me as you have before," he said. "But it is getting very
dangerous for me. That is why I had you come all the way here. I
can talk to you only once or twice more." The man hesitated, then
appeared to relent. "It was stupid of you to have met with
Luganov."

Chandler was thunderstruck. "Jesus! How on earth did you
know?"

"Others know, so I know. You were very stupid indeed. It
could undermine everything you've been doing. Stay away from
the Soviets."

"Nothing much was said," Chandler assured him. "I hoped I
might get some reaction—something that would tie into the—"

Memory interrupted. "We must get away from here, quickly.
The watchman will be coming. And the police may start wondering about your car."

Chandler felt Memory's hand on his shoulder, a touch of
farewell or even camaraderie. "One more thing, Senator Chandler,"
he said. "You have a person on your staff. A Miss Dunham." He
paused, and the hand tightened its grip. "Be aware that she is seeking another kind of truth."

"What the hell does that mean?" Chandler asked. But the hand
had left his shoulder, and the wooden door was opening very
slowly, very carefully. Chandler could make out Memory's stocky
figure in profile.

"Wait until I'm gone," Memory said. "Then go back to your car and return as you came."

Chandler called softly after him: "What do I do when I find the snake?"

But Memory was gone, into the darkness, once again.

Thursday, May 14

26 Chandler came in late the next morning. He had spent the remainder of the night at a Howard Johnson's somewhere in New Jersey, and arrived at the office looking unaccustomedly gray and disheveled.

Ned Dempsey shook his head. "Man, you've either been cracking the books or a bottle. You look like hell."

"Thanks, Ned. Just what I needed." Chandler was clearly in no mood to play.

"I assume you've seen the *Post*?"

Chandler motioned Dempsey into his office and closed the door. He picked up the paper that lay on his desk, folded open to the op-ed page. His gaze locked onto Clinton Atwood's column, captioned in boldface TILTING AT WINDMILLS.

> Senator Thomas Chandler is a capable politician who is letting his ambition run away with his judgment. In fact, insiders say he is using his investigation into terrorist activities as a ploy to undermine the CIA's morale, which is already at a historically low level. . . .

"That son of a bitch," Chandler swore.

"Atwood?"

"No, Gordon Nicholson." Chandler knew that Nicholson had planted the story. In the past couple of weeks, Atwood had written two columns praising Nicholson, a sure sign that the columnist was getting something in return. There was nothing Chandler could do about Nicholson, but he knew he had to counter the attack. "Ned, I can't let this story stand."

"You're right about that," Dempsey agreed. "Atwood doesn't have much credibility in this town, but he's syndicated in more than a hundred papers, including three in Connecticut. We'll get a lot of mail on this one."

Chandler knew that if he did nothing, other reporters would pick up the blood scent. It took only one hound to start the whole pack baying in print. They would shake the story by the throat until it was dead—or *he* was. He had to act quickly.

"Ned, you know Rick Roberts. Get him for lunch or a drink and feed him some background on the task force. Try to see if we can get a break in the *Times*."

"Fine. But what am I supposed to say? I don't know what the hell is going on."

"It's no secret, Ned, that I'm trying to unravel a knot. To make my report thorough, to give it substance and credibility, I've got to ask questions. I've got to find out how the Puerto Rican FALN or the Cuban groups are structured and financed. How they can function almost with impunity. Whether their activities are monitored or tolerated by our law-enforcement and intelligence agencies. What the connection is between the mob and the heroin and cocaine traffic that's inundating this country. Whether the Soviets have a fat hand in—not only in terrorism but in the drug traffic itself."

"Fine. Let's say I can get all that across. But he's bound to ask why you're screwing around with the Kennedy assassination."

"You can just tell him that I'm updating the Church report of 1975. The report raised a lot of questions about CIA activities with reference to Kennedy. Those questions were never answered and probably never can be. But I had to start somewhere and that seemed to be as good a place as any. That's the line to take: It's simply a starting point." Chandler could feel his frustration with the press rushing to the surface. "Get Bob Tilley on it too. Same story. What I need is time to do the job without being eaten alive by the jackals at the FBI and the Agency. *And* the press corps."

Dempsey seemed satisfied. He had no reason to doubt Chandler's wish to do a competent job. "Okay. I'll pass that along. But in the meantime, you can do me a couple of favors."

"Sure," Chandler agreed—too quickly, he would later complain.

"Get back to Connecticut and take care of business there. Remind the people who elected you that you're working for them."

"And the other favor?" Chandler asked coldly.

"Try to appear to be a little more of a team player down here instead of running a one-man show."

After twelve years of give-and-take, Chandler knew that Ned was almost always right. He looked away from Dempsey's steady gaze.

"If you really want to get ahead in this place . . ."

"Yeah. I know. Join the club," Chandler said.

"Not a bad idea. But at a minimum, you ought to put more effort into the party's activities. Show that you care about your colleagues a little more than you do."

"Christ!" Chandler exploded. "What do you want me to do? Bend over and start licking their boots?" He was hurt and angry now. "The next thing you'll say is that I have to join Gordon Nicholson in the Senate prayer group."

"A little religion never hurts."

"Come on, Ned. You've known me long enough to know I'm no hypocrite."

"What makes *them* hypocrites?"

"All that plain food and fellowship and searching of souls. Then they go to the Intelligence Committee and approve covert wars. Damn it, I don't want any part of it."

"That's unfair, Tom, and you know it. There are decent people in that group—Mark Hillhouse for one, Alan Leighton for another. You're talking about Nicholson. Why do you let him get to you and prevent you from having—"

"A meaningful relationship with others?"

"A *working* relationship with others."

"Okay, Ned. Let's drop it." Chandler had had enough. He turned away and looked out the window into an overcast sky. The building across the street looked like a faded daguerreotype.

"Senator, it's your career. I'm only suggesting that sometimes it's easier to walk through open doors than it is to break them down."

"Maybe I can walk around them."

"You can't walk around doors to the National Convention." Dempsey pulled himself up out of the deep leather couch. "Incidentally, you've been invited to speak to a labor rally in Groton a week from Monday. They need an answer today. What should I tell them?"

"I want to think about it for a while."

"Okay." Dempsey sighed as he headed for the door. Ordinarily he would have urged Chandler to accept the invitation. But this was one of those days when he was as tired of giving advice as his boss was of hearing it.

Outside Chandler's office, Dempsey caught Margie's inquisitive eye, wordlessly asking him, *What kind of mood is he in today?* Dempsey's expression said, *Don't ask.* He lit another cigarette and walked over to Margie's desk. "Got any coffee left?"

"Sure, Ned. That bad, huh?"

"No. He's not that bad. I had to say something he didn't want to hear. It'll pass."

Moments later, Chandler slipped out of the side door of his office and fled to the Intelligence Committee's staff room. Here were the documents, most of them secret, that he believed could help him find his way through the dark maze of terrorism.

He stopped by most mornings to review the National Intelligence Daily, the NID, which contained a daily analysis of developments in trouble spots around the world. The NID was a composite analysis of every intelligence agency's information. The rules were strict in the room. He could make written notes, for instance, but he never did. Anyone seen making notes was bound to be a target of suspicion when information leaked to the newspapers. He knew he was being watched, especially by Craig Delvin.

"Good morning, Senator." Delvin had come in without Chandler's noticing him. "Do you want the NID?" Chandler nodded. Delvin left and quickly returned with a folder marked TOP SECRET.

Delvin, of course, would never dare reproach any senator, even if he broke a rule. Although Delvin did not understand Walcott's affectionate regard for Chandler, he knew enough not to challenge it. Delvin's personal opinions found expression in the columns of Clinton Atwood, to whom he fed morsels of damaging information and unflattering gossip.

Chandler flipped open the NID. On the third page he read, *London: Car-bomb. Two Members of Parliament killed. Carlton Hinssley (Labour). Geoffrey Herd (SDP). Libyan assets in UK suspected.*

Chandler felt his skin grow cold. Geoffrey Herd had been one of the brightest young leaders in British politics. He had been among the founders of the new Social Democratic Party and preached a brand of economic moderation and social liberalism not far from Chandler's own philosophy. The two of them had progressed from mutual respect to genuine friendship through several conferences they had attended at the Ditchley Foundation in Oxfordshire, and when Chandler had last visited London, in late February, Geoffrey had taken him out to dinner. They had closed London's most fashionable private dinner club at three in the morning.

And now Geoffrey was dead. Was this an early warning, perhaps aimed directly at him? Chandler wondered. Was the snake in the tower saying: Members of Parliament today, senators tomorrow?

Sunday, May 17

27 The Intelligence Committee was presumed to have unlimited access to a glamorous world of mystery and intrigue. In actuality, Committee members were admitted only to the periphery of that world. Testimony about CIA activities came to the Committee sanitized, wrapped in vague generalities. Witnesses usually managed to defer answers to specific questions: "We'll have to furnish that later, for the record, Senator." They knew, of course, that time was the enemy of investigation. Weeks would pass before the answers would be supplied, and then they would be ambiguously worded, not quite responsive. Members of the Intelligence Committee knew only as much as the Agency chose to disclose.

But for Senator Thomas Chandler, things were different now. He felt almost nostalgic for the days of his innocence. With the formation of the task force, Chandler had descended into a world of shadows and mirrors, where all the inhabitants wore masks—and some wore two. It was a world without order or sequence. Every mirror became a door leading to another room of mirrors, another room of doors. There was no sun here, no fixed horizon to help a wayfarer achieve a sense of direction. In this world of reflection, paranoia became as rational as logic. Friends were enemies; enemies, friends. The truth consisted of a mosaic of lies. There were no facts, only fleeting theories and surmises that were countered by equally valid assumptions and speculations. It was a world of silence and terror. Its commerce was carried on in code. And at its center pulsed the heartbeat of death and violence.

Was it simply paranoia that made Chandler so suspicious of the phone call that had brought him here this evening? Danielle had called on Friday and said she had to see him. It was only the second time he'd heard from her since the divorce was final. They had agreed to meet on neutral ground, and he had chosen public neutral ground: the Four Seasons restaurant. He could stop in New York on his way down from a weekend of fence-mending with his constituents in Connecticut.

He didn't know why he should suspect that Danielle's call had something to do with the investigation, but he did. Everything seemed to be connected with the investigation, he thought as he sat at the bar waiting for Danielle, wondering what she was going to say.

He had arrived about twenty minutes early for their seven-thirty engagement and ordered a J&B on the rocks. As he waited he watched, in the mirrors behind the bar, the mating rituals of the young executives and professional people who gathered there. His eyes momentarily met the reflected glance of a lovely brunette in a tailored suit, and he felt a sudden surge of desire for Elaine.

What was she doing tonight? he wondered. What did she do on all the other nights? And with whom? Anytime he'd asked her out to dinner or for an evening, she had put him off. Beyond their work, their only times together had been a few chaste lunches. Sometimes she seemed to relax with him; twice, alone together in the office, they had seemed on the breathless verge of a kiss. But always she had drawn back, set him at a distance with a little laugh or an impersonal return to business. There must be someone she cared for, some romantic or sexual entanglement to which she remained true.

What was it Memory had said to him in parting the other night? *"Be aware that she is seeking another kind of truth."* How did Memory know what Elaine was seeking, when Tom, who saw her almost every day, had not been able to get the smallest hint of what went on behind those cool green eyes? Was Memory the man she cared for? A wave of jealousy swept him, surprising him by its strength. He seemed to be getting in deeper than he'd thought, than he'd wanted to.

"Hello, Tom." Danielle's well-remembered voice startled him back to the present.

"Hello, Danielle." Chandler hoped he sounded friendly. "Let's sit at a table over there. You're far too elegantly dressed to perch on a barstool." He downed the last of his scotch and escorted Danielle to a nearby table. "A drink before dinner?"

They gave their drink orders to a passing waiter, and a slightly uncomfortable silence fell. At last Danielle spoke. "Tom," she said, reaching into her purse for a cigarette, "you look marvelous. More distinguished than ever."

"You look good yourself," he said. He was lying. Danielle was still attractive, but the lines at the corners of her eyes and mouth were deep now. Her voice had a throaty quality, a certain huskiness that Chandler associated with her heavy drinking. Her hair, as bright and brittle as Christmas tinsel, was pulled too tightly back from her face. And no amount of expensive oils and packs could put back what alcohol and tobacco had taken from her skin. Her face shone without softness.

Looking at her now, Chandler suddenly felt sad. From the beginning they'd had little in common but their age. Danielle had been rich and beautiful, spoiled and ambitious. Tom had come from a lower-middle-class family and had gone to Yale on a scholarship. He had been ambitious, too, but in a different way. He had wanted position, but not for the sake of entertaining rich kids who played at being rich adults.

Tom's father had perceived this. Jack Chandler had never approved of the marriage, perhaps because he saw it as a rejection of the values he himself held dear. He had gone to the wedding, but had taken no joy in it. Jack Chandler had advised his son not to lean on Danielle's wealth and thereby face a lifetime of doubt about his own ability. Though Tom respected his father, he had dismissed the warning, arguing that he could make it on his own— and still get a little help from his father-in-law.

Not long after the wedding he realized that perhaps Jack Chandler had been right. Tom was a good lawyer, but he was not fully accepted by his colleagues. His fellow attorneys seemed to be saying that success is easy if you know you can't fail.

Danielle's father, Raymond Fouchette, owned a shipping company in New Orleans. As a wedding present, he provided the capital and arranged the financing Tom needed to start an electronics firm in downtown Stamford. Fouchette had been frank about it: He said he wanted to make sure that his daughter was not dependent on the income from Tom's small law practice. The wedding present not only launched what became a prosperous business but also gave Tom Chandler the financial security he needed to enter politics. He began by winning appointment as a prosecuting attorney. His success in that office put him on a path that led to the governor's mansion and then to the Senate.

Danielle had viewed Tom's entrance into politics as a social climb rather than a commitment to public service. She cared little for any of the issues that moved him. Without children, their life together consisted largely of a series of trips to warm beaches.

Chandler had held on as long as he could. He had a deep-seated fear of failure, and given his family background, to be part of a failed marriage was something to avoid at almost any cost. But in the end not even political expediency could save the marriage. It had lasted for twenty-one years, though for the final few in name only. Love, if it had ever existed, had been replaced by indifference and increasingly empty displays of affection for the sake of appearances. In the end, all that remained for Chandler was an emptiness and silent resignation.

They parted finally, not with fury, but not without bitterness. Negotiations for the divorce began. What had been emotional soon became merely financial. Danielle's lawyer, another gift from Fouchette, arranged a complex settlement that enabled Tom to buy her share of the Washington house and retain some stock in the electronics company.

Then, suddenly, it was all over. He was alone in the house in Spring Valley and Danielle was back with her family in New Orleans. In the past three years, he had thought about her more than he had when they'd been married. Loneliness had done that, he knew now, looking across the table at Danielle.

"Cheers!" he said, raising his glass.

"Cheers." Chandler noticed a slight tremor in her hands.

"Tell me, what have you been up to?" Chandler sounded as if he'd just run into an old college friend.

"Not much, really."

"Sorry to hear that."

"I don't have to ask what you've been doing. I read about you a lot. You must have a new press secretary. He's good."

"Bob Tilley had better not hear that," Chandler said, laughing. "He says he's underpaid."

Diagonally across from them sat a well-dressed couple in their thirties. The man's dark hair was combed neatly back, his mustache carefully trimmed. The blond woman with him was smartly dressed and athletic-looking. Their manner and clothes identified them as people of means. For several minutes now, Chandler had been aware that the man was trying to catch his eye. Like most politicians, he had developed finely tuned antennae and had learned when to acknowledge or ignore such signals.

Finally the man pushed his chair away from his table, murmured something to the woman, and approached Tom and Danielle. He apologized for interrupting, introduced himself as a "fellow Nutmeg Stater." Congratulating Chandler on his work in the Senate, he touched him lightly on the shoulder and expressed the hope that Chandler would one day run for President.

The man returned to his table, and a minute later, as Tom and Danielle were being escorted to the main dining room, Tom noticed that the couple had left.

Seated at a table next to the central pool, Danielle seemed to expand and soften in the deferential attention granted to Senator Chandler.

"You handled that man very well, Tom," she said. "You're more patient with gushy constituents than you used to be."

Chandler flashed a half-smile but said nothing. A vague, indefinable feeling, almost a premonition, had entered his mind: Something about the man from Connecticut was not quite right, or was *too* right. . . .

"That did sound patronizing, didn't it?" Danielle apologized. "Tom," she said, becoming serious, "tell me what your committee is doing."

"Why do you ask?" Chandler's voice was edgy with suspicion.

"Just curious."

"Come on. You were never interested in my work when we were married. What's on your mind?"

His abruptness brought a flush to her cheeks. "All right. I have something to tell you. But I *did* have good reason for being curious about what you're doing. Do you have someone working for you named O'Brien?"

"Yes, he's a member of my task force staff. Why?"

"He's been poking around in New Orleans, asking a lot of questions about drugs and connections between organized crime and the anti-Castro groups down there."

"So?"

"So, there are some people in the city who don't like it."

"For example."

Danielle started to answer, but her voice faltered and stopped. Then, recovering, she leaned forward and said softly, "My father."

Chandler looked at her intently.

"He asked me to arrange a meeting with you. He says he wants to buy back the stock you still own in the DataLink Company."

"That stock isn't worth a hell of a lot."

"He thinks it is. He says he's prepared to offer you two million dollars."

"Two million!" Chandler gasped. "For the few shares the settlement left me with? They're not worth a fraction of that!"

"They are—to him."

"Now *I'm* curious. What if I decide to turn down your father's very generous offer?"

Danielle began tentatively. "This isn't easy for me, Tom." She was silent for a time, staring down at the table. Finally she looked up. "I don't know anything about my father's affairs. I really don't. But I do know my father. I know when he means business, and he means business now. He said he had some information that could damage your career, and if he has to, he's prepared to see that the story gets out."

Before the divorce, Chandler's relationship with Danielle's father had been cordial, if not close. Raymond Fouchette was a man whose sole talent was the making of money. While he didn't exactly flaunt his wealth, he certainly made no effort to hide it. He entertained lavishly at his homes in New Orleans and Palm Springs.

"What story?"

"I don't know."

"Come on." Chandler was angry now. His voice rose above those at the other tables. People turned to look.

Danielle, on the verge of tears and as mortified by their stares as she had earlier been gratified by them, lowered her voice almost to a whisper. "No, Tom. Really. He didn't say . . . but you know him. You know what he's like."

Indeed Chandler did. He knew that Fouchette was a tough son of a bitch who was capable of holding a grudge. And he held one against Tom Chandler for divorcing his daughter. But what could he possibly know that could hurt Chandler's career? There was nothing, absolutely nothing.

"So now your father is offering to bribe a United States senator. And he's making his daughter—my former wife—an accessory to the felony. Of course, he knows that if I report the bribe, he can claim he simply wanted to buy back full ownership of the company and was prepared to pay a high price. An accusation of bribery on my part might look like a personal vendetta against an ex-father-in-law." Chandler's gray eyes were cold and unflinching. "Well, what happens when I reject the bribe?"

"He said when you understood what was involved, you wouldn't refuse."

Chandler took his napkin from his lap and dropped it on the table. He pushed back his chair and stood up. "Danielle, I just did."

Chandler strode over to the maître d' and handed him money to cover the bill. Without a look back at Danielle, he left the restaurant and hailed a cab. He could still get to La Guardia and catch the last shuttle back to Washington.

28

Monday, May 18

The next morning Chandler called Kevin O'Brien into his office and asked for a briefing on the New Orleans trip. In twenty minutes, O'Brien gave him a quick rundown on what he had learned about drug operations there. They had turned out to be even more extensive than Chandler had imagined.

"Did you ever come across the name Raymond Fouchette?"

O'Brien looked surprised. "Sure." He paused. "Why?"

"Maybe you know why."

"I think this is called sparring, Senator. I thought we didn't bother with that. Fouchette was your father-in-law. I know that. But I didn't find out about him because of that."

"My name was mentioned down there, wasn't it? 'Linked with Fouchette's name,' as the newspapers would put it."

"I'm not sure what you're talking about, Senator. Yes, your name was mentioned. The cops naturally know that Fouchette was your father-in-law. And naturally they were a bit curious about why one of your guys was down there asking questions that got around to the subject of Fouchette. I was going to mention all this, by the way, in context."

"What kind of context?" Chandler asked irritably.

"I am trying to give you a sensible briefing," O'Brien said, speaking more slowly, his own manner of showing irritability. "I was going to put Fouchette in the context of the Agency. That's the context, not you. May I go on?"

Chandler nodded.

"Some of the locals I talked to—the good locals—say they've been trying to nail Fouchette for some time. He's tied in tight with the syndicate down there. There have been several investigations into his shipping company. Anybody with a lot of ships, or even a few boats, gets a good going over regularly by the federal drug guys and by the locals who are trying to stop drugs from coming into the country.

"But with Fouchette, nothing happens. They think they have something on him, but nothing holds up for a grand jury. Witnesses have a way of forgetting or disappearing."

"You mentioned the Agency," Chandler said. "You think he's being protected?"

"It figures. I talked to the FBI Special Agent in Charge of the New Orleans office. He says he has no doubt that Fouchette is being protected by the Agency. Here's a guy who may have been running people for the CIA in the sixties—when the Agency definitely was tied to the mob. Now maybe he's being patriotic again, running people into Nicaragua for them. And so he gets protection for his business, whatever that might be.

"Now the context," O'Brien continued. "With the Agency playing footsie with Fouchette, with you looking into the Agency's past deeds, and with the Agency knowing that he was your father-in-law—yes, in that context I'd say this is a bad mix. Fouchette can probably handle the locals, but he knows damn well that a Senate investigation is beyond his control. Unless he can figure a way to stop it."

Chandler wondered if O'Brien had heard about Fouchette's offer to buy him out. He almost told him about it right then, but decided to wait, at least until he heard Fouchette's response to his refusal.

"Thanks for the briefing, Kevin. Let me know if you hear anything more from New Orleans."

"You'll be the first to know, Senator." O'Brien turned and walked out of the office.

Chandler didn't have to wait long to discover that Raymond Fouchette didn't like taking no for an answer. Three days later, a letter arrived, addressed to Chandler and marked PERSONAL AND CONFIDENTIAL. It was postmarked Dallas, Texas. Margie left the letter lying on Chandler's desk unopened.

During a break in a committee hearing, Chandler returned to his office for coffee and to review his calls. He opened the letter. At first he thought it was a joke.

> Dear Senator Chandler,
>   Bacteria can be used to build microchips. Coca leaves and poppy seeds can work with computers. The formula makes some rich and leaves others poor.

The letter was dated but not signed.

Chandler read the letter again, slowly. *Bacteria . . . microchips . . . coca leaves . . .* Fouchette was saying in his quaint little code that unless Chandler kept his investigation out of New Orleans, Fouchette would see to it that the press learned the true source of the money that had launched Chandler's electronics firm. Now Chandler knew the basis of Fouchette's wealth. The money Fouchette had advanced him had come from coca leaves and poppy seeds. The mob's drug money.

Chandler felt a tightness spread across his chest, a prickling at the back of his neck. A net had just been dropped over his entire future and was being cinched tight. A scandal like that would provoke banner headlines: SENATOR'S WEALTH BUILT ON CRIME. DRUG PROFITS LEAD TO SENATE SEAT. No protestations of innocence could undo the damage of the initial stories. His pursuit of drug smugglers would strike the public as the height of hypocrisy. If he sold the stock, he would corrupt his office. If he failed to sell it, he would be charged with corruption. Either way, he was clearly the loser.

And Fouchette was relying on his Agency connections to keep him clean, whatever mud he threw at Chandler.

He buzzed Margie on the intercom and asked her to get Danielle on the phone. Seconds later, he heard Danielle's voice, cold and angry.

"Danielle, I'm sorry I walked out on you in New York."

"Really?"

"Yes. It's just that I'm not in the habit of receiving such . . . how shall I say it? . . . such generous offers from people."

"Oh? You sound as if you've—"

"I've had a chance to give it the consideration it deserves."

"And?"

"I want you to deliver a message to your father for me."

"Wonderful, Tom." Danielle sounded genuinely relieved.

"Yes. Tell your father . . . tell him I'm going to bust his balls."

PART THREE

The situation of our time
Surrounds us like a baffling crime.
There lies the body half-undressed.
We all had reason to detest . . .

29

Friday, May 22

IRRITABLE. IMPATIENT. ABSENT-MINDED. He knew the signs. How often Danielle had complained of them. When he was immersed in a subject, she said, he lived as if he were in a cave, and all he wanted for company in that cave was whatever project or mission obsessed him at the moment. Chandler had been in the cave for seven solid weeks now, ever since Miami.

He had rarely ventured out, though he would have done so happily if Elaine had consented to join him. But she'd never agreed to anything more than lunch, as if daylight constituted some sort of shield against desire.

Once she had suggested they lunch at the café in the National Gallery of Art. Then she had taken him to a room full of abstract metal sculptures by David Smith. Walking back to the office, she had told him David Smith's credo, which Chandler thought might be her own—"Each stroke more free because confidence is built by effort." And he had told her about living in a cave.

Now, on this early Friday morning, Chandler was sitting at his desk, trying to concentrate on his schedule for the holiday weekend. From the time his plane landed at Bradley Field near Hartford—less than four hours from now—till late Monday afternoon, every hour was filled. "Damn it," he said to his empty office, "the second weekend in a row. It's a campaign schedule, and I'm not even running until next year."

Friday's schedule was "tightly packed," as his state staff members liked to say. *Tightly packed, hell.* They treated him like some kind of mechanical man: Feed in computer program 32, out pops the appropriate speech, smile, handshake, joke, sympathetic response. The faster he ran, the more events they crammed into the program. And when he complained, they protested that he was spending too much time in Washington. One and often two weekends each month he would race through Connecticut from Friday till Monday morning. Next year it would be three, possibly four, weekends. Then he would return to Washington exhausted, but would be expected to shine brilliantly for the next four and a half days. His Washington staff, although sympathetic to the needs of the Connecticut team, wanted their boss to "measure up."

Chandler regretted giving in to Ned Dempsey's insistence that he take time away from the investigation. But he was resigned. It was a price every elected politician had to pay. Besides, it was too late to cancel anything now. His only consolation—and it was an important one—was that the weekend would wind up with his first evening date with Elaine.

When Elaine had told Chandler she was planning to spend the Memorial Day weekend in New York, she had half hoped, half feared that he would ask her to meet him for dinner on Monday. She had put him off so many times, afraid of compromising her own real and growing desire for him with the conflicting desire of Trevor for information. And if she gave in to the urgings of her own body, her own heart, how could she know for certain that she wasn't answering her father's cry for help? Why did something that ought to be so clean, so simple—the coming together of a man and a woman in mutual attraction and need—have to be complicated, sullied, by the demands of others?

Chandler *had* asked her to have dinner with him, and this time she had said yes. She wasn't sure why. Perhaps it was because they would be away from Washington, from the sense that everyone was watching them—Trevor's ubiquitous handymen, the rest of the task force staff, the Washington gossipmongers. Perhaps it was just that she could no longer deny that she was falling in love with Senator Thomas Chandler.

Now, on the Metroliner bound for New York, Greyfur restless in his carrying case at her feet, she was on her way to visit her half-sister, Betty. Betty's father was Jim, big laughing Jim Dunham. Elaine had always called Jim *Dad*, but one night, when she was about eleven, her mother had sat down on the edge of her bed and talked to her about the days before they had come to live in Massachusetts. "Your dad, Jim," she told Elaine, "well, he's not your real dad. Your real dad—well, I guess he's dead, honey."

Not dead. Yet not alive, not for Elaine. He was only words in a letter: *"I have lost myself as well as you. . . . Help me clear my name . . . perhaps come back to life again."* He had said he would contact her again. Soon, the letter said. But there were no more letters. No phone calls. Nothing. How could she help him if he continued to remain lost to her?

Elaine longed to tell someone about her father, to share the burden of her secret. Could she tell Betty? No. This would have to be just an ordinary visit: big sister to little sister, and the two of them out to the nursing home in Long Island to visit their mother. And she would stare at them without seeing them, and shake her head, and clutch at silence. But she would smile when they took turns brushing her long hair, which once had been so shining black.

Elaine shook herself out of reverie. Monday evening she would see Tom, and she had to think clearly about what she was doing, where she was going, not just bumble into bed, and into love. Trevor would be glad if she went to bed with Tom Chandler. That was reason enough not to. She did not like Trevor. To be more accurate, she didn't like herself or what she had become.

She felt unclean, like a voyeur standing in the darkness watching someone undress in a lighted window. She had to record all the naked details, the scars and imperfections, and then turn her mental notes over to Trevor. For the sake of her country, he had told her. But she was no longer sure about Trevor's motives.

Chandler had given no indication that he was out to jeopardize the Agency's operations. He was trying to do a job, an important one. He had some wild notions about the Kennedy assassination, but nothing she had observed would justify Trevor's fears. Nothing.

Elaine wished she could withdraw from her assignment, but she didn't know how, not without jeopardizing her career—and, perhaps, jeopardizing her father. If she quit the Intelligence Committee, she could never go back to the Agency. And if she quit her unwelcome task for the Agency and stayed on with the Committee, it would take just one phone call from Trevor to the chairman and she would be unemployed—and probably unemployable in Washington. It would mean returning to the investment world, almost certainly in some other city. Even then, Trevor's reach was long. And how could she help her father, once she was away from this shadow world she hated more every day?

30

When Elaine arrived at the Park Lane Hotel overlooking Central Park, Chandler was standing near the entrance to the dining room, waiting—nervously, it seemed—for her. He reached out awkwardly as if to shake her hand, then bent to kiss her lightly on the cheek. "Elaine. Glad you could make it," he said, trying to sound as if they were simply old acquaintances getting together.

The maître d' escorted them through the spacious dining room to a table with a view of the park and the couples, young and old, passing in horse-drawn carriages below. A cocktail pianist in the corner opposite was trying his hand at a Beethoven sonata.

"Oh Lord," Chandler said, putting his hands over his ears. "All we need is a little light background music. He's definitely not ready to audition for the Philharmonic."

Elaine sensed he'd had a bad day and tried to lighten his mood. "Reminds me of the passenger on the *Titanic* who said, 'I know I rang for ice, but this is ridiculous.'" She smiled.

An answering smile forced its way onto his lips. "I'm sorry," he apologized. "It's been a long day."

The waiter brought their drinks—a double scotch on the rocks for Tom, a Dubonnet over ice for Elaine. Chandler drank deeply; he didn't speak.

Elaine searched his face. "Tom, what's wrong?"

"The Pentagon," he said flatly.

"What?"

"The Pentagon destroyed its files on the Kennedy assassination. The Army intelligence file is simply gone. And we don't know why."

"Army? I thought Oswald was in the Marines."

"He was," Chandler said, "but it seems that on the day Kennedy was killed there were Army intelligence agents in Dallas, as part of the security setup. When a colonel in Army intelligence

184

heard about the assassination—he was near the Mexican border, by the way. Anyway, he found out that the name of the man being held as the assassin was already in military intelligence files under two names: Lee Harvey Oswald and A. J. Hidell. The colonel called the FBI in Dallas.

"All of this—the colonel's information, the phone call, the file on Oswald/Hidell—all of this is gone. Which means there are no incriminating pieces of paper to show that Oswald was mentioned in American intelligence files *before* the assassination.

"The files are just gone," he said. "It makes no sense. Washington is a city that sits on a mountain of paper. Files are kept forever—there's one on every dam and snail darter in America. And yet someone decided the records on Kennedy's assassination were dispensable—forever."

Chandler was clearly angry. "Frankly, I wonder. I wouldn't be surprised if some people at the Agency were deeply involved in the whole thing."

Elaine touched his hand soothingly. "Tom, the Warren Commission report said there was no evidence of any undercover operation, or any relationship between the U.S. government and Oswald at any time."

"Yes. And the former Director of the CIA—who, coincidentally, was a member of the Warren Commission—said that any CIA official would perjure himself under oath before he'd tell the truth to the Commission."

"What's the point, Tom? What difference does it make?"

"It makes a difference because some people in the Agency continued the ZRRIFLE operation after it was ordered terminated."

"ZRRIFLE?"

"Our officially approved assassination policy, the one set up to take out Castro."

"I still don't understand what the connection is now, today. I mean, what's the relevance?"

"Because President Kennedy, as a part of settling the Cuban missile crisis, made a pledge to disband the ZRRIFLE operation against Castro. Only somebody, or several somebodies, in the Agency refused to go along with that pledge. They maintained their own private executive-action capability without Kennedy's knowledge."

"I still don't understand . . ."

"Castro warned Kennedy that unless the plots against him stopped, he would retaliate in kind. Don't you see? If Kennedy didn't know about the renegade group within the Agency, then he was unaware that he was being set up—in essence—by his own people."

Elaine released Tom's hand, and there was a note of irritation in her voice. "Isn't it possible you're pushing the conspiracy theory too far? I mean, Kennedy was killed more than twenty years ago. We've practically destroyed our intelligence community, investigating it to death. Professional morale is abominable. Good people have quit. Congress has practically put the Agency in irons. Do you think it's responsible for a member of a Senate committee to raise this issue all over again?"

This was a side of Elaine that Chandler had never seen before, and it bothered him. He resented her tone of rebuke and her one-dimensional view of the CIA. And her references to the "intelligence community" and "professional morale" sounded for all the world like E. W. Trevor. *Good God!* Was she one of them, one of the mirror people? He shook the thought from his mind, but when he spoke his voice was angry: "A conspiracy doesn't cease to be one just because it hasn't been proved."

Elaine's calm, direct gaze said more clearly than words: "Don't lecture me like a child."

"I'm sorry," he said. "I don't mean to preach. It's just that there are too many unanswered questions, too many shadows, too many unconnected lines."

Elaine continued to study his face. "The whole thing sounds kind of bizarre to me, Tom. So many cranks have come up with crazy conspiracy theories about the assassination—I'm afraid that if you start talking like this in public, people are going to say you're just the latest in a long line of crackpots."

"Elaine. I haven't said a word yet to anyone but you. I don't know if I ever will. I know I can trust you." Chandler was surprised to hear himself say it, but he knew as he did that it was true. However reserved she might be, whatever the answer to Memory's enigmatic reference to her, and even though she had seemed to be parroting Trevor's line, Tom's instinct whispered *Trust*.

Elaine blushed to the roots of her hair. She was living a lie, but more than anything in the world she wanted to be worthy of his trust. She fought to control her tumultuous thoughts, to return to safely professional conversational ground.

At last she said, "Tom, the press is going to say you're either sensation-seeking or you're sick. Either way, you lose. You've got a real chance to be President of this country someday. Why throw it away on a dead . . . a dead issue?"

Chandler knew she was right, but he couldn't help himself. Like countless Americans, he had replayed the Zapruder film again and again in his mind. He didn't know how many gunmen there were, or where the second shot came from. But he was convinced that Oswald had not planned the assassination alone. There were too many coincidences, too many convenient lapses in intelligence and security. And there were too many groups who wanted Kennedy dead: the Mafia, the anti-Castro Cubans, Castro. And, just maybe, some people in the Agency itself.

"Elaine, there's a secret sitting in the middle of that maze out there, and I've got to find the answer to it. Because I believe there is *some* connection between those events and what is going on today. Nothing else matters to me right now. . . . Well, that's not quite true," he said, and he smiled deep into Elaine's eyes. For the first time he noticed the triangular fleck of red-brown in her right eye, an imperfection that enhanced her beauty.

He reached across the table and took her hand. "Elaine, *you* matter to me. You do. And . . . I need you."

When he touched her, it was as if a current of heat passed through her fingers and met an answering impulse deep within her. She felt her face go warm again. Guilt surged in her mind. But despite her every caution, she knew she was in love with Tom Chandler.

"You know I want you," he said.

She laced her fingers in his and, for a moment, gave herself up completely to joy.

But then it was just as she had feared it would be. The thought of Trevor's insinuating smile was in her mind, blotting out the light in Tom's eyes. She felt a rush of shame. That Trevor should have succeeded in recruiting her was at the moment more than she could bear.

"You mustn't want me," she blurted. "I . . . I'm . . ." Tears choked her voice, and before he could stop her she was gone.

31

Inching his way along in the stop-start weekend traffic, Chandler found himself whistling the overture to *The Marriage of Figaro*. He grinned as a red Corvair cut in front of him. *Nothing spoils my mood tonight.*

He had been bitterly confused by Elaine's abrupt departure on Monday evening, and had immediately retreated to his cave, taking refuge in the predictable solidity of government documents. On Tuesday he had passed Elaine in the hall. Their eyes met briefly and she looked for a moment as if she might speak, but then she lowered her glance and hurried on with a murmured "Excuse me." Wednesday's staff meeting had marked a return to reserved professionalism. She spoke to him without apparent embarrassment, but Chandler noticed ruefully that she addressed him only as "Senator."

On Thursday afternoon he had entered the Intelligence Committee staff room in search of the day's NID. Elaine looked up from her note-taking. "Hello," Chandler said tentatively. "Miss Dunham?"

"Hello." She cleared her throat. "Tom?"

His heart started to pound.

"Tom, can we try again? Dinner, I mean?"

"Damn," he said.

Immediately she withdrew. "I beg your pardon, Senator. I shouldn't have—"

He interrupted her with a laugh. "No, no. *Damn*, just meaning I can't make it tonight. I have to be on a panel at Georgetown University, and there's no way I can get out of it. Would tomorrow be okay with you?"

"It would," she said.

Which was why he found himself at seven o'clock on Friday evening, freshly showered and shaved, following Elaine's neatly

drawn map through the winding roads of Reston, Virginia, to a
row of town houses nestled in a cluster of pines.

Elaine opened the door in answer to his ring and led him into
her small living room. She poured him a scotch on the rocks, introduced him to her cat, and, promising to be back in ten minutes,
went into her bedroom to change.

Chandler engaged Greyfur in one-sided conversation for a few
minutes and then decided to explore. He inventoried the contents
of the living room, hoping to find clues to Elaine's elusive personality. On the walls, three large black-and-white prints with a quality of shadows on rough whitewash. A low glass coffee table with a
brass frame. Pale-green couch. Two overstuffed chairs slipcovered
in a floral print on midnight-blue. Fireplace, with a brass coal scut-
tle on the hearth. Bookshelf with turntable, tuner, no tape deck;
records mostly classical, some soft rock; books included a complete
set of Jane Austen bound in leather, three biographies (Queen Victoria, Richard Wagner, Theodore Roosevelt), a few references, the
one-volume *Oxford American History,* Schlesinger's book on Kennedy. Chandler picked it up and saw it was a Library of Congress
volume checked out to the Committee. In a Lucite box-frame, a
snapshot of a man with a little girl in a yellow sunsuit. Unmistakably Elaine. An open door into an adjoining room gave him a
glimpse of an elaborate home-computer setup. He went back to the
couch and was sitting, scratching Greyfur's blissful stomach, when
Elaine returned, radiant in a gauzy dress that matched her eyes.

He had asked her to choose a restaurant, and she had named a
favorite of his: La Niçoise, where Jean Pierre, the maître d', made
it a custom to kiss each woman who entered the door and where the
waiters all whipped around wildly on roller skates.

Chandler had not felt so relaxed in months. He and Elaine
joined in the laughter as Jean Pierre and the waiters performed outrageous skits on the small stage. Chandler even laughed when he
was splashed with the wine that Jean Pierre poured all over the
stage during the final skit.

After dinner, they went dancing at Charlie's Jazz. Elaine felt
detached from herself, floating in Tom's arms. *The hell with Trevor,*
she thought. And when Tom pulled her close to him, she knew
that for tonight at least, it would be just plain Tom and Elaine.

Later, back at her house, they made love. It was fierce, two rivers of energy rushing together, gloriously, powerfully. No words were needed.

Afterward they lay together in bed, listening to the sudden rain tapping against the window, and touching as if they were trying to memorize each other's bodies in the dark.

Just before dawn they made love again. Then Tom eased himself out of bed and, as quietly as he could, began searching likely places in the kitchen for coffee. Elaine found him ransacking a cabinet and laughed. She handed him bread, pointed out the toaster, and opened the refrigerator. "I keep the coffee in here. It stays fresher," she said. "Give it a few minutes before you start the toast." She filled the coffeepot and plugged it in.

"You're very efficient so early in the morning. And very beautiful," he said.

"I'll get the *Post*," she said.

Tom heard an exclamation from the direction of the front door. "What was that?" he called.

Elaine came back into the kitchen carrying the Saturday edition of *The Washington Post*. "Miserable cat!" she said. "He's off and running again. Won't be back for days."

They sat in companionable silence over their breakfast, trading off sections of the newspaper. Chandler looked up from an article about home computers. "You're a computer buff, I noticed." He gestured toward the other room.

"Yes," she said. "Once you get the hang of them, it's hard to go back to plain typewriters—not to mention balancing your checkbook. That one doesn't actually belong to me, though. It's hooked up to the Intelligence Committee's system, so I can work on a report here at home and feed it directly to the office."

He grinned at her. "A woman of unsuspected talents," he said.

A pang of guilt stabbed at her, and she hid her flushed face behind the pages of the business section.

Getting up to refill his coffee mug, Tom stooped and kissed her ear. "This doesn't have to end, you know."

Elaine looked up, startled. "What do you mean?" A sense of betrayal gnawed away in her mind: *Trevor will be happy about last night. And maybe my father will too.*

Chandler seemed surprised by her reaction. "I mean that just one phone call can move us to the wilderness for the rest of the

190

weekend. If my colleagues haven't gotten in ahead of us." He explained that the National Park Service operated a place called Camp Hoover, which was unofficially reserved for members of Congress and high federal officials. "It's in Shenandoah National Park. About a hundred and twenty miles from here on the Skyline Drive."

Elaine was delighted. In the late-spring countryside, perhaps she could forget for a time her duplicitous existence. While Tom called the Park Service duty officer for the home number of the Chief of Congressional Liaison, who assured him that the President's Cabin was available, she quickly showered and dressed in jeans and her favorite red-and-white checked shirt. Packing an overnight bag, she smiled to herself as she included a lace-trimmed white nightgown.

"I've been there a couple of times," Chandler said as they sped west on highway 66. "President Hoover bought the land and the Marines built the cabin and a dirt road as a training exercise. Hoover gave it to the nation when he left office, thinking that future Presidents would use it. But FDR discovered what became Camp David, so Camp Hoover became a place for humbler representatives of the people."

"Including *future* Presidents?"

Tom smiled. "We'll have to see about that," he said. "There's a lot of work to be done in the present. I'll wonder about the future after the task force job is done."

They drove a few more miles in silence. Chandler explored the radio dial for music, found only rock and country, and turned off the radio.

"Did you ever come up here with . . . with your wife?"

"Not very likely," Chandler said, a bitter memory of Danielle flaring in his mind. "My wife preferred bright lights and warm beaches." He turned to look at Elaine and smiled. "My previous companions up here have been United States senators looking for a couple of days of privacy, poker, and no shaving."

About thirty miles down the Skyline Drive, the long, high road that traverses Shenandoah National Park, Chandler pulled into the Timber Hollow Overlook and they got out to stretch their legs. Elaine pointed to white and pink blossoms peeking out of the wooded slopes before them. A breeze from the valley stirred her long, dark hair, and her beauty brought a catch to Tom's throat.

A few miles down the drive they stopped again while Chandler picked up a set of keys from a ranger in the Big Meadows Visitor Center. Past a locked gate, they drove for six miles up a dirt road closed in on both sides by dense forest, mostly evergreen with some stands of birch. Less than fifty yards ahead of them, a foolhardy deer dashed across the road. Elaine gasped, then laughed with delight.

The President's Cabin, a big log house, sat at the end of a long mountain meadow. Chandler parked the car around to the side so that their view from the huge front porch would be unobstructed. From the back seat of the car he took a bag full of groceries raided from Elaine's kitchen. He cast her a sheepish glance as he opened the trunk and lifted out a canvas weekend bag. "Always like to be prepared for any eventuality," he said, and she laughed at his discomfited look.

Unlocking the front door, they came into an L-shaped room: a living area with a large flagstone fireplace to the left, a smaller dining area with another fireplace straight ahead. Past the dining area, Elaine explored the kitchen. "A dishwasher!" she exclaimed. "An electric coffee percolator!" And Chandler, exploring elsewhere, exclaimed, "A double bed! Clean sheets!"

They made coffee and tunafish sandwiches—"on toast," Chandler insisted—and took them out onto the porch. From wicker chairs they looked out to the mountains.

"Shall we make this a working lunch?" Elaine asked.

"How can you be so businesslike?" Chandler said. At her mock reproving look, he made his face solemn. "Okay. I'll find the official government-issue ballpoint pens and legal pads. I'm sure they're here somewhere."

"I have some material on drugs," Elaine said. She fished a brown envelope from her oversize handbag.

"I suppose you were thinking about this a few hours ago, too," Chandler said, laughing. "I'm not flattered."

"All play and no work makes a dull playmate," Elaine said briskly, but her eyes were warm with memories. "To business."

She ticked off the latest information about the drug trade. "The best figure we can come up with is one hundred billion dollars. Heroin and cocaine are closing fast on marijuana in the middle-class market. Key spots: Colombia—which has a sort of *laissez-faire* attitude—and Cuba, which is actively helping drug runners. Cuba is using the money to help buy weapons for the guerrillas in Central America." She turned to Chandler. "You can say all this in the report. But you have to be careful you don't lose the focus on terrorism."

"I understand that, Elaine. I'm sure we'll get the connection, and we'll be able to spell it out."

"I hope so, Tom. But so far it isn't there."

"Well, so far we have Cuba, and that *is* a connection."

"Nothing new about Cuba," Elaine said. "It's always been a thorn in this country's side."

"Maybe not always," Chandler said, "but certainly for about as long as you've been on earth."

"Why do you say that?"

"Guessing your age, I suppose. I don't know much about you."

"I don't know much about myself."

"Mystery woman. Is that it?"

Elaine avoided his questioning eyes. "Tell me about Cuba, about the Bay of Pigs," she said quickly.

"Why do you ask?" *What other truth are you seeking, my beautiful Elaine?*

"Well, in Miami you said that everything goes back to Kennedy—that certainly seems to be one of your themes. But if your theory is right, then isn't the Bay of Pigs part of it, too? If the Bay of Pigs had succeeded, there would have been no 'executive action.' No Castro. No Kennedy assassination."

"That's about right," Chandler said. "But it didn't work out that way."

"What happened? What made the Bay of Pigs fail?"

Well, if Elaine wanted a history lesson, he'd give her one: "Someone leaked the invasion plans to a reporter. But the major newspapers ignored the story. Even *The New York Times*. The *Times* finally ran a watered-down story about ten days before the invasion. No reference was made to the timing of the invasion or the CIA's involvement. Can you imagine that happening today? But then someone, maybe the same person, got word to Castro. He was ready. And Kennedy backed down when the bombers were ready to fly. He called off air cover. A bunch of people got butchered. Those who survived spent some time in Fidel's hotels. They probably wished they'd never made it ashore."

Was my father one of them? Or was he the one who got word to Cas-

tro? How can I clear his name when I'm working in the dark this way?

Chandler was looking at her curiously. Elaine realized she'd been silent a long time. "Let's see what we have on the attack on the Vice-President's plane," she said hastily, "You'll need that in the report, I assume. . . ."

For more than an hour they talked about developing and classifying the information in such a way that it could be incorporated into the first draft of the task force report. Chandler was concerned with getting the job done as soon as possible. So was Elaine, but for different reasons.

In the middle of a review of known terrorist organizations, Chandler suddenly broke off, threw the papers down on the rustic log table, and said, "Let's get out of the cave and take a look around."

While he changed into jeans and the high-topped shoes he called his boondocks boots, Elaine organized their working papers and took them inside. Locking the front door behind them, Tom took Elaine's hand, and they set off down a trail that plunged into a dark patch of mountain laurel, still touched here and there with pink bloom. Elaine had found a wildflower book in the cabin and she announced her discoveries: "Large-flowered trillium . . . redbud . . . moss phlox . . . and, look, over there, joe-pye weed." They saw two deer, and, alongside a stream, Chandler insisted he had found a bear track. The trail led to another meadow, where Elaine picked a bouquet of buttercups.

They returned more slowly than they had started out, wanting to hold on to the magic of this day. They made love in the double bed, and Tom wondered aloud if the Hoovers had ever done the same. With a lot of laughter they contrived a spaghetti dinner, complete with red wine, and Girl Scout cookies for dessert. Elaine said Girl Scout cookies grew on the trees of Reston.

Chandler built a fire in the living room fireplace, less to ward off the evening chill than to heighten a romantic mood. They sat on the hearth rug and drank the last of the wine. Tom put his arm around Elaine's shoulders and watched the flitting shadows that danced on her dreaming face. Finally he asked, "Why did you leave me in New York?"

"I didn't know if you'd love me in the morning," Elaine said, with a flippant suggestion of a smile. When Tom failed to respond, she said, "Truth?" He nodded.

"I didn't want to lose you. And I didn't want to hurt you. I know the investigation is important to you. To me, too. I was afraid that there might be a lot of leering gossip—you know: 'Senator sleeping around with his staff. What kind of investigation is this committee up to?' I didn't want anything—even us—to jeopardize what you're doing. Or what you might become."

Elaine told herself she was speaking the truth. Everything she said was true. Except that Trevor would have liked what she said, and that made it less than the truth. She would have to find a way to get out of Trevor's reach. She would have to find a way to help her father. But Tom couldn't know these things. Not now. Not yet.

"Tom. There's more." She felt his shoulder stiffen. "I'm going to need your help on something very important to me. Later. After the task force is finished. Will you help me then?"

"Of course, Elaine," he said. He tightened his arm around her. "Whatever you want."

"Thank you." She touched his cheek and smiled. "Can I ask you something else? There's something that's been bothering me. It's about the investigation." She paused and took a deep breath. "You've been holding out some information."

Chandler drew back sharply. "What do you mean?"

"Someone's giving you information and you're not sharing it— or him—with the rest of us."

Chandler didn't answer. It was confession enough.

"I saw you with him in Miami. Down by the pool. And I suspect you've seen him since then." It was more question than statement.

"I can't tell you who he is, Elaine. I don't even *know* who he is. I've never seen his face, and I don't know his name. In my head, I call him Memory."

"Do you trust him?"

"I don't know. He keeps dropping little bread crumbs along a path, leading me on."

"Could it be a trap?"

"Sure. It could be. But my gut tells me it isn't."

"Why won't he say who he is?"

"Because he knows he'd be a dead man. I'd have to list him as a source, probably have to get a sworn affidavit, maybe call him as a witness before the Committee. And he'd probably be found floating in the Potomac, in a barrel like our friend Fabricante."

"Don't you think that's a bit paranoid?"

"Paranoids have real enemies, too, you know." Chandler smiled. "I'm sure Memory knows as well as I do that it isn't healthy to talk to people investigating assassinations. I've gone over all the old witness lists. A lot of scheduled witnesses never got a chance to testify. There were at least four alleged suicides. A hunting accident. And at least ten other people disappeared or were killed, most of them Mafia types and many of them just before they were going to be called to talk to the investigators. One of them got a bullet in the back of the head and then six more in a circle around his mouth. As long as I don't know who Memory is, he's safe. Or as safe as he's ever going to be."

"So he is in hiding?"

Chandler smiled. "That's putting it about as mildly as it can be put."

Elaine's eyes filled with tears. Tom pulled her close to him and gently kissed each eyelid. "Don't cry, my tender heart, don't cry," he murmured. "For someone you don't even know." He tasted the salt tears running down her cheeks. He touched her face and his hands were slow and gentle. She gave a little sob, and her lips parted as they sought his.

Two people became one silhouette against the firelight. At that moment, if the flames had leaped out to consume them, they might not have noticed. Or cared.

32

Monday, June 1

Kevin O'Brien thought that the location of his apartment was just right. He could walk to the office in eight minutes, if his pace was brisk. It usually was. A not inconsiderable advantage of being within walking distance was that he could keep his battered Mustang in the office garage, thereby avoiding the expense of garaging his car privately—at what he deemed exorbitant rates.

The neighborhood was reasonably safe. That was important to him. He often carried classified documents home at night so that he could keep Chandler constantly updated.

O'Brien's two-room second-floor apartment on D Street Southeast was just on the edge of the enclave of white-owned town houses that surrounded Capitol Hill. He was a block away from a neighborhood bar on Pennsylvania Avenue where he would occasionally go for a beer. He could get a hamburger there, better and cheaper than he could make for himself in his kitchenette. And the building was quiet. There were only two apartments, and the middle-aged secretary who lived on the ground floor had never been known to have a guest.

On this early Monday morning, O'Brien filled a saucepan with cold tap water and turned on the stove. He disliked instant coffee, but he needed only a cup or two to hold him until he got to the office. And it was easier and less wasteful than brewing a fresh pot.

He looked across the room at the stack of newspapers he had allowed to accumulate during the week. There were coffee-cup rings and cigarette ashes on the low wooden coffee table in front of the used sofa he had purchased at one of the Hecht Company's annual warehouse sales. He sighed. He never seemed able to keep abreast of the mess. On the other side of the couch was a bookcase filled with fictional accounts of the Vietnam War. He liked to compare his own bitter memories with the imaginings of novelists. He had no pets, or even plants. He seemed to have no need for companionship.

Reflexively, O'Brien snapped on the television set. It was 7:00 A.M. and the symphonic prelude to the CBS morning news was just concluding. "Good morning, ladies and gentlemen," came the genial voice of the commentator. "Today, we are going to talk about a report that has just been obtained which indicates that the United States is contemplating construction of one of the most exotic weapon systems ever conceived. It is called a neuron exchanger, and it would allow the United States to alter the brain patterns of its enemies so as to make them totally benign and nonthreatening. According to today's *New York Times*, the Pentagon has been working on this weapon for over fifteen years and recently achieved a remarkable breakthrough."

O'Brien felt as if he had been hit in the face with a dash of ice water. He swallowed his coffee in one gulp and raced down the stairs to the front door. In the holder just under his mailbox was a tightly rolled copy of *The New York Times*. He took the stairs back up two at a time, reading as he ran. There it was—a front-page story on the latest weapon system that the United States was counting on to gain the edge in warfare against the Soviet Union. How the hell did the *Times* get the story? Only a few senators and congressmen had been briefed about it, including the members of the Intelligence Committee. "Shit," he muttered and slammed the paper down. Now he would have a problem on how to cope with responding to the report. Denial would only whet the press's appetite. There would be follow-up stories, with references to key documents. Any denials would be held up as official lies.

But what really troubled O'Brien was a gnawing suspicion that someone might be trying to discredit the Intelligence Committee. That meant his boss would be tarred with the same sticky brush. His forehead wrinkled in concentration as he went on reading.

The timing didn't seem coincidental. The CIA had given the Committee members the classified report on electromagnetic sensors and transmitters—the one Trevor had raised hell about after it appeared in *The Times* of London. Less than six weeks had passed since the Committee had received a briefing on the developments in the neuron exchange program. Where were the leaks coming from? The Agency or the Hill?

O'Brien didn't have the answers. But he decided it was important for him to find out.

What had been a plan of action had become an obsession by the time O'Brien reached the office. He had to be sure that no one on the Committee staff was feeding top-secret information to the *Times*. If the Agency or the White House started questioning the security of information going to the Hill, they would devise even cleverer ways to divert and reduce the flow. Already there were grumblings that Congress could not be trusted with national secrets, that the intelligence committees of the House and Senate were anachronisms left over from Watergate. Responsibility for protecting the national security interests of the American people was the President's—not that of a bunch of vote-seeking headline-hunters moved by the narrow interests of their states. Let Congress appropriate the dollars and execute effective scrutiny, let the people pay their taxes, and let the intelligence experts do their job. No, O'Brien did not like the trend of things.

The Agency had some valid complaints. Too many people on

the Hill had access to sensitive information. The Agency had to report to the House Armed Services Committee and even the Energy Committee. Too many staffers were too eager to ingratiate themselves with reporters in order to get their bosses more favorable attention. And some staffers even opposed the premise of a strong intelligence agency.

O'Brien wanted to see the United States regain a reputation for reliability with governments throughout the world. Intelligence had to be strengthened, morale restored. But he was satisfied that intelligence also had to be restrained. Without congressional oversight, intelligence could become a dark, closed, violent circle, where arrogance would inevitably lead to abuse.

The Soviets did not have to account to the Russian people. There were no restraints on the KGB in Russia. *And,* he thought, *there are damn few restraints on the KGB in America. The bastards are everywhere. They practically run the United Nations!* Anyone attached to the Soviet Embassy in any capital was presumptively KGB.

Christ, he muttered to himself. A couple of years ago Vladimir Krasov, a Soviet naval attaché, walked right into the General Accounting Office and requested reports by their numbers. And some of them weren't even printed yet! Krasov even requested a classified report on the electronic jamming system of the EF-111A fighter-bomber. Someone was feeding him numbers even before the U.S. government had them. Someone on the inside. And that was not just leaking stories to the *Times.* That was helping a spy. That was treason.

There was a growing consensus in Washington that the KGB had managed to penetrate the Agency itself. James Angleton, the former head of Counterintelligence, had believed it—and possibly lost his job trying to prove it. O'Brien didn't know what to believe. Angleton was right on some things. He had always maintained that Soviet defectors to the United States were frauds. He said that "Fedora" and "Top Hat" were not double agents. *He was right on that, too. We got taken, suckered.* Maybe he was right about there being a mole near the top of the Agency.

O'Brien knew that if the Soviets could penetrate the Agency, then penetrating the Hill would be a piece of cake.

The FBI made extensive background checks on people seeking staff positions on committees that received intelligence information. But there were no initial or annual "flutters"—no lie detector tests to determine the integrity and trustworthiness of the applicants. And once they got their jobs, they were home free. There were no effective internal procedures for protecting the flow of information from the Hill. Briefcases were checked on entering and leaving, but only for weapons, not documents. Not national secrets.

O'Brien had no real basis for suspicion of anyone on the Committee. But he sensed the presence of someone or something alien. There were nights when he had been on watch in Vietnam and it had been so dark and so quiet that the silence had begun to ring in his ears like a siren. But he had known there were people out there, moving without a sound, dressed in black like part of the night. He had always followed his instincts in Nam. Something in his mind would say *Now*, and he would fire, and the silence would be shattered by the screams of men who had come to kill him.

The same voice that had said *Now* was telling him that here, in this office, there was someone moving like a cloud across a moonless night. He picked up an alphabetical list of all the staff members from the full committee, together with their home addresses and phones. He scanned the names: All but three had worked for the Intelligence Committee since its inception. The three newer members he had recruited from the Defense Department himself. He was satisfied they were loyal. What about the senior staff members, the ones who came in on the ground floor?

Jeff McCoy? No. McCoy had been shot down on a bombing mission over Hanoi in 1966 and spent six and a half years as a prisoner of war. He had been beaten and tortured but he had never agreed to be part of North Vietnam's propaganda campaign. If the Viet Cong couldn't break McCoy, neither could the Soviets.

Sam Kaplan? Unlikely. He was a true professional, hired by Charles Walcott personally. He loved Israel as much as America, and the Soviet Union was the implacable enemy of Israel. He would never release information to the Russians. No, not Kaplan . . .

This was not going to be easy, O'Brien told himself. He couldn't just reach into a drawer and get personnel folders and results of security checks on these people. Walcott and Delvin sat on those records, and O'Brien had no plausible—or even implausible—reason to ask for them. Besides, the security checks themselves were highly classified. He was on his own.

But he continued going through each of the staffers in the same way, satisfying himself as to their background and loyalty. There was only one person on the list who troubled him.

He didn't know why, but there was something about Elaine Dunham that just didn't ring true. Maybe it was her extraordinary beauty. A woman that striking should have been married or living with someone, or at least have a lot of male friends. But she was strictly career.

Maybe that was it. She was too professional. She came to work, did her job, and went home, instead of hanging around the office or going out for drinks after work. At times she seemed incredibly innocent, at others worldly and aloof. But she was always cool.

Her work was outstanding—thorough, logical, penetrating, well organized. It was just .   . just that O'Brien didn't know anything about her. He decided to find out who Elaine Dunham was.

33 *Tuesday, June 2*

As dusk deepened into night, clouds gathered like a flock of giant crows across the sky. Colonel Cyril Metrinko looked up at the most famous cathedral in all of Moscow. The domes of St. Basil's were even more dramatic and beautiful at night, when the powerful lights trained on them made them seem to glow from within.

"Brilliant stroke, was it not?" Metrinko said to Captain Dmitri Natashin.

"Truly brilliant, Colonel. Especially at night."

"I speak, Captain, of the concept of Ivan—the blinding of the architects Barma and Postnik afterwards, so they could never again create anything so beautiful."

"Ivan the Terrible," Natashin said. "So terrible."

"The word is *grozny*, Captain. Ivan the *mighty*, Ivan the *awesome*."

"Whatever, Colonel. It was a cruel act. Pitiless."

"Glorious, Dmitri."

"It is only a legend. Not fact."

"Russia is a land of legends," Metrinko said. He laughed harshly.

They had decided to meet in public, in the very shadow of the Kremlin walls, because this was a safe place for two men in uniform carrying bulky briefcases. They had arrived separately, Natashin from inside the Kremlin, Metrinko from Dzerzhinsky Square, to mingle with all the other uniformed men making their way through the twilight at the end of another working day.

Metrinko was quite sure that no one would ever dare follow him, but he had taken certain precautions nevertheless. He had ducked into the huge Child's World department store, plunged into the crush of shoppers, and bought a bear puppet for his nephew. Then he left the store by a different exit and joined the stream of Muscovites walking down the broad stairway to the subterranean network of pedestrian tunnels. The stream branched at the Metro. Metrinko went with that stream, then suddenly veered away and joined the stream surging up the stairway that led to a broad street at the edge of Red Square.

Captain Dmitri Natashin had less of a journey to the rendezvous and more reason to believe he might be followed. Kremlin officers always believe they are being followed. He left his office and walked to the assigned doorway next to the Kremlin gate, where the big black cars sped in and out on presumably urgent missions of state. The enlisted man at the door cursorily checked the briefcase. Natashin told himself again that if he were followed it would not look suspicious for him to stop and talk to Metrinko, whom he knew as part of his official duties.

Now, as they strolled near St. Basil's, Natashin felt relieved. Here at Red Square, in this mass of people from every republic and from most of the nations of the world, the security people were paying little attention to men in uniform. As the bells in the tower above them tolled the hour, the civilians massed before Lenin's Tomb to watch the stiff-legged choreography of the changing of the guard. And the security men watched the audience.

As the bells tolled, Metrinko and Natashin wandered to the edge of the crowd. "My admiration of Ivan the Mighty disturbs you, Dmitri?"

"No, Colonel. It is merely that I cannot share your admiration. There is one legend about him that I remember from my childhood. Ivan saw an omen in the sky, a fiery comet that looked like a burning cross suspended over Moscow. He said it was a death sign. Now, was there really a comet at that time?"

"Does it matter?" Metrinko said. "He lives on. The witches of Lapland were wrong. He lives."

"Colonel, I will grant you that Ivan was brilliant. But he was a tormented man. I read of him once that it was as if 'a terrible storm came from afar and broke the repose of his good heart, so that he became a rebel in his own land.'"

"Yes, Dmitri. He was a rebel. Tragic perhaps. But surely heroic forever in the eyes of all Russians." *As perhaps one day, one day soon*, he thought, *I will become heroic in the eyes of all Russians, when my Eagle plucks out the eyes of America.*

Natashin waited patiently for Metrinko to tell him the reason he had requested this meeting. Metrinko had calculated the risk of meeting Natashin, even here, where it was seemingly safe. Natashin was mentally rehearsing what he might tell a security officer if he were questioned, when Metrinko grabbed his arm. "What is the Politburo reaction to the information they are getting?"

"You are a candidate for new honors, Colonel. They talk of you and your source as the finest—"

"Never mind the flattery, Dmitri. Is it *useful*, being put to *use*?"

"Yes. There is talk of great potential use."

"Good. Then they perceive the value. And they would perceive the loss if they were to be told that Eagle may not be able to supply more information?"

"They would be gravely concerned, Colonel."

"Good. Then they may have to support an activity."

Natashin involuntarily looked around. *Activity* was Metrinko's word for a terrorist operation. The Politburo had no direct knowledge of these operations. He wondered why an "activity" was going to become something the Politburo would have to "support."

"Support, Colonel? They are not officially aware of your activities."

"It may be necessary, Dmitri, for me to go before them, for I am thinking of an unusually sensitive activity. It is going to be necessary, Dmitri, to strike very, very hard at one of Washington's own activities."

"I assume you fear a Central Intelligence Agency operation against your source?"

"No, Dmitri. Not the Central Intelligence Agency. Some politicians, Dmitri—or one politician, in the United States Senate."

34 Chandler had long ago grown weary of Washington parties. After a few spins around the social circuit, the guests and cuisine became tediously familiar. And ever since he had taken over the task force, he had declined all dinner party invitations. But tonight was different. The party was at the home of Secretary of State Woodrow Harrold, who was emerging from the shadows of grief. He had resumed the helm at the Department of State, and was trying some personal diplomacy by hosting a birthday party for the Soviet Ambassador, Andrei Brodovsky.

Tensions between the United States and the Soviet Union were running fever-high. Relations were nearly as bad as they had been after the Korean airliner was shot down. Western Europeans appeared to be on the verge of accepting more new American-made and American-controlled nuclear missiles. Brodovsky just might take this opportunity to signal Soviet readiness to consider some accommodation with the West. The publisher of *Time* magazine would be in attendance, and Brodovsky never missed a chance to try to influence the opinion makers in America. Nor did rising national politicians like Thomas Chandler.

As Chandler entered the high-ceilinged hall of Harrold's home his eyes were immediately drawn, as they always were, to the walls. Matisse, Gauguin, Renoir. On the staircase wall was a Picasso, and in a niche a small Rodin bronze.

Chandler accepted a glass of white wine from the tray of a floating waiter hired for the evening, and soon found himself talking to a rather arch woman in her sixties with bleached-blond hair that framed her face like spaniel ears. She made polite talk about how important it was for politicians' families to live in Washington rather than back in their home states. But the seeming innocence of her observation slipped quickly into gossip.

Kathy Bender's red head appeared out of the crowd. She took Chandler's arm, skillfully detached him from his partner, and steered him into a relatively quiet corner of the dining room. "Where have you been?" she asked. "We've missed you—Doug and I."

In answer, Chandler kissed her cheek. "I miss you too. But—"

"I know. You're busy with your terrorists. But you've got to have *some* relaxation. Now it just happens that an old college friend is in town for a few weeks. How about dropping over this weekend for dinner?"

"Matchmaking again, Kathy? Remember the last blind date you arranged for me?"

She giggled. "That *was* a disaster, wasn't it? But this one's different, Tom. She may not be gorgeous, but she's fun and really quite attractive . . . in her own way . . ." Her voice trailed off.

"Forget it, dear. I may never need the services of a matchmaker again."

Kathy looked up at him sharply. "Tom! There's someone? Oh, I'm so glad! Who?"

"I can't tell you that yet. Especially not here, with all these ears around. I shouldn't even have told you she exists, but I know you won't tell anyone—except Doug, of course. But one of these days, when various problems have been settled, I'll bring her over. I think you'll like her." He sounded suddenly shy.

Kathy put her arms around him and hugged him tight. Over her head he caught the eye of the spaniel-eared blonde. "Kathy, I suspect that you and I are about to become the newest item in the gossip mill."

"Frankly, my dear," she said in a vague stab at a Clark Gable impersonation, "I don't give a damn." She winked at him. "But I'll throw up a smokescreen." She surveyed the chattering crowd. Her eyes came to rest on a broad-shouldered man who managed to suggest, even in evening clothes, that he had just finished felling a tree. "A likely candidate. Come see us soon, Tom. And bring what's-her-name. I can't wait to meet her."

She vanished in the throng.

Ambassador Brodovsky, wineglass in hand, was standing with Woodrow Harrold in the ornately carved archway that led to the living room. Brodovsky had replaced the dean of Washington diplomats, Anatoly Dobrynin, eleven months ago, when Dobrynin had been abruptly recalled to Moscow. For some reason, never disclosed to a dismayed diplomatic corps, Dobrynin had fallen into disfavor with a powerful figure in the Soviet hierarchy.

Brodovsky, like Dobrynin, was a large man, but more square-shouldered and noticeably slimmer in the waist. Whereas Dobrynin's oval face sagged into pudginess, Brodovsky's jawline was strong and well-defined. But Brodovsky was a carbon copy of his predecessor in the qualities that mattered. Intelligent, skillful, and suave, he possessed a broad smile that seemed always present and genuine.

He was laughing when Chandler caught sight of him. In public he was always seen laughing. His eyes narrowed into slits and his mouth turned up in a jack-o'-lantern smile. How could anyone so jocular represent a country that was anything less than well-meaning? But Chandler always saw the cruelty in Brodovsky's smile. He was a crafty diplomat well versed in the Washington power game.

The Soviet Union was at present threatening to shut down air-travel rights into West Berlin and was mobilizing thousands of East German and Warsaw Pact troops on the Central Front. This show of force was intended to discourage the West Europeans from deploying on European soil more of the new long-range missiles, which could strike the Soviet Motherland. Growing unrest in East Germany had inspired more trouble. The Soviets had accused the United States of malicious propaganda designed to undermine the internal stability of the U.S.S.R. and her allies. It was a dangerous time. Millions of people worried that the two superpowers were heading toward nuclear confrontation.

But Brodovsky gave the impression that peace and harmony were just around the corner, next to the nearest buffet table. Brodovsky said something to Harrold and laughed uproariously. Harrold also laughed, but weakly, Chandler thought. The grief was still there, would always be there. But to Brodovsky—and, granted, to most Americans too—the blowing up of Harrold's family was an event of the past, a regrettable incident in a world full of such tragedies. With a sense of disgust, Chandler made his way to one of the bars and requested a scotch.

At that moment there was a hush and then a stirring. All the guests turned toward the door. Two large men in evening clothes appeared in the entrance hall and scanned the crowd. The men were unmistakably Secret Service agents, first-stringers from the White House detail. A moment later two more appeared, and directly behind them came Arthur Christiansen, the President of the United States. Even the most sophisticated group in Washington stands in awe when the President enters a room. *The hush is as good as "Hail to the Chief,"* Chandler thought.

The agents wordlessly made a path for Christiansen, who walked directly to Harrold and Brodovsky and shook each man's hand. A television camera crew popped out of the library, which had been designated an impromptu press and security room, and shot a few seconds of pool film for distribution to the networks. Then two still photographers recorded the meeting for newspaper and wire-service coverage. Harrold and Brodovsky had not been standing at that spot by accident, Chandler realized. Christiansen was endorsing Harrold's gesture of friendship toward Brodovsky and, indirectly, toward Brodovsky's country. And the gesture was being signalized by presidentially controlled publicity.

Chandler watched with admiration as the President worked the room, shaking every proffered hand, conferring a few words on anyone he chose so to honor, lingering where lingering would do him the most good, telling a quick joke to a columnist, saying something special to the Chairman of the Joint Chiefs of Staff (thereby balancing the détente moment with Brodovsky), assuring a congressman from Pennsylvania that he had received his letter and the Secretary of the Interior would be calling the congressman tomorrow, sticking his head into the library to call a hello to the newspeople and the security staff. Finally he reached Chandler and clasped his hand firmly. "Tom, I hear you're doing a fine job on the task force. I know it's in good hands."

"Just as our country is, Mr. President," Chandler said.

Christiansen smiled, moved on, and five minutes later was gone as quickly as he had come.

There were too many guests to permit a formal dinner, so they all lined up to fill their gold-rimmed plates at buffet tables. Chandler saw Richard Dalton, the *Time* publisher, take a seat near the Steinway grand, on which he set his glass while he coped with the plate on his lap. Chandler was about to drop out of the buffet line, on the premise that dinner was worth forgoing for a chance to chat privately with a major influence on public opinion, when the Soviet Ambassador settled himself in a chair next to Dalton's. By the time Chandler had filled his plate, Brodovsky had moved on to sit with his host. But before Chandler could reach Dalton, a television newscaster had occupied the vacant chair and was paying elaborate compliments to Mrs. Dalton.

Frustrated, Chandler sat down next to a rosewood end table that once, he remembered, had held framed photographs of Harrold's family. He looked around, hoping to spot one or both of the Benders. An Undersecretary for Economic Development in the State Department approached him. "Mind if I join you?"

Of course Chandler minded. The last thing he wanted was to be distracted with esoteric discussions of American economic policy in the Caribbean Basin, but it would have been rude to decline. He forced a smile and said, without enthusiasm, "Pull up a chair."

For the next twenty minutes he listened to a recital, couched in near-perfect Oxonian tonal conceits, of the initiatives the Christiansen Administration had taken to relieve poverty in Honduras, Guatemala, and Costa Rica. "This has been no easy task, particularly in view of the pressure being received from congressmen who are unwilling to open up U.S. markets to low-priced Latin products that are in direct competition with their constituents. . . ."

Chandler ate and nodded automatically, his mind occupied with thoughts of Elaine. He wished she were with him.

After dessert, the glasses of the guests were filled with champagne. Woodrow Harrold picked up a fork and lightly tapped his glass, calling for silence. "Though I could toast tonight the hope that the Soviet Union and the United States will soon have a new dialogue, tonight is a night of personal friendship. Therefore I raise my glass to a friend of mine, a friend of my country. Happy birthday, Andrei."

Brodovsky broke into his patented grin and thanked his host for his generous reception. He praised Harrold's art collection, particularly a piece of eighteenth-century Russian sculpture, and then singled out Senator Thomas Chandler for his statesmanship and his efforts to promote peace between the Soviet Union and the United States.

Chandler was visibly embarrassed by Brodovsky's effusions. Even the guests who hopped from one social event to another in Washington seemed impressed. But if anyone expected to hear any special foreign-policy message, they were disappointed. Brodovsky told several well-rehearsed jokes, light and nonpolitical. He was predictably self-effacing with respect to his accomplishments and equally predictable in his praise of the United States as a world power. He never indulged in chauvinistic chest-beating. He was so cultivated, so charming, so unthreatening. So un-Russian.

After Brodovsky had concluded with a toast to world peace and prosperity, coffee was served in demitasse cups along with a choice of brandy or a liqueur. Cigars were offered, a tacit signal to the guests that soon the party would be officially at an end. Ordinarily, Chandler would have been among the first to leave. But he managed to maneuver Ambassador Brodovsky to a corner of the oak-paneled study.

Before he could explain to Brodovsky what he wanted to talk about, the Soviet Ambassador said, charmingly and without hint of criticism, "Senator Chandler, I'm sorry you were unable to attend the Bolshoi."

Taken by surprise, Chandler flushed. Of course Brodovsky would know he had not attended the ballet. Officials from the Soviet Embassy would have taken note of the occupants of seats reserved for the Ambassador's special guests.

"Ah, yes," Chandler said, recovering quickly, "I'm sorry, too. I was looking forward to the performance, but I was called out of town at the last moment." It was not a lie, even though he'd had no intention of attending the performance. He *had* been called out of town—to meet Memory at Cape May.

He had planned to give the tickets to Margie, but later had decided against it: If Ambassador Brodovsky's gift was sincere, he might have been insulted to see that Tom had passed the tickets on to his secretary. And if he'd had an ulterior motive, for any of Tom's staff to have used the tickets might have proved embarrassing at a later time.

"Mr. Ambassador," Chandler said, "I was hoping you would speak tonight to the issue of our deteriorating relations, that you might offer some hope for working our way out of the corner we both seem to be in."

Brodovsky looked at him querulously. "Well, my good Senator, you might have avoided the problem by not threatening the Soviet Union with more missiles in Europe. There is still time for you to correct the mistake."

"That is, of course, for Secretary Harrold to discuss, but speaking only for myself, I am afraid that what you propose will not be possible unless you agree not to target Europe." Keeping his eyes fixed on Brodovsky, Chandler paused to sip his brandy. "I believe there are other things going on that are just as dangerous to whatever remains of our relationship."

"And they are?"

"The question of terrorism, and what I believe to be the related issue of narcotics coming into this country—"

Brodovsky, his mood shifting mercurially, cut Chandler off in mid-sentence. "Now do not blame us for that! Senator, please. You disappoint me."

Chandler was unprepared for the vehemence of Brodovsky's response. He decided to try the subject that had served him unexpectedly well with Luganov. "Mr. Ambassador," he lied, "Georgi Tupolev sent me a letter shortly before he returned to Moscow."

Brodovsky stiffened. "What did the letter say, Senator?" The tone of the question was slightly menacing.

"I am not at liberty to disclose that, but he knew something was wrong in your country." Chandler went for broke: "He suspected that there was a snake in the tower. Your tower, Mr. Ambassador." A thin blue vein was beating in Brodovsky's temple.

In a sudden burst of chatter, Woodrow Harrold and several of the guests came into the study. Brodovsky abruptly began to laugh. He slapped Chandler on the back. His laugh became a wide grin and his eyes narrowed into horizontal slits that served to reassure the others that he and Senator Chandler were merely sharing a good joke.

Then, his lips barely moving, Brodovsky said in a bone-chilling whisper, "Senator, I think you should be more prudent with your investigation. *Much* more prudent."

He laughed once more for all to hear. Then he thanked the Secretary of State for his gracious hospitality and took his departure.

Outside, his chauffeured limousine was waiting. An aide opened the rear door for the Ambassador and then got quickly into the front seat. With a smooth and powerful roar, the black limousine pulled away from the curb and sped off into the night.

Monday, June 8

35 Over the weekend and all day Monday, Chandler worked in his office, reviewing the information that O'Brien had been collecting. His desk was cluttered with articles on narcotics statistics, sea and air routes into the United States, and projections for poppy crop yields in Iran, Afghanistan, Pakistan, and Thailand. A stack of clippings on the most recent bombings and assassinations, filed by location and date in legal-size red folders, rested on the shelf behind his desk. Smoke from the cigars he had puffed blurred the air. The radio on his bookcase played softly in the background.

He looked up at the clock and cursed. He had forgotten to call Elaine, to tell her he would drop off a rough draft of the interim terrorism report at her home in Reston. They had worked until midnight the previous evening putting some preliminary information into her computer, which was connected, through a secure phone line, to the Intelligence Committee data bank. The report itself was to be put into the computer this week.

He had called too late. She said she was sorry; she had a commitment for dinner and couldn't break it. But she would be home by ten. Looking over the stacks of papers on his desk, Chandler said it would probably be eleven before he reached Reston.

"See you then," she said. "I'll have plenty of coffee." Coffee was one of their private jokes. He was drinking so much coffee that she worried about it and urged him at least to switch to tea. He enjoyed the feeling of having someone worry over him. It had been a long time.

He hung up, wondering jealously whom she was meeting for dinner. But he'd promised not to intrude upon her life beyond her invitation—not until the task force job was finished. He went into the utility room and poured himself another cup of coffee. By now it tasted rancid, and he softened it with cream and a half teaspoon of sugar.

Back at his desk, he reviewed the emerging pattern in the evidence he and the staff had accumulated during the last two and a half months. He traced all the apparent targets among the assassination victims—their nationalities, political parties and philosophies, their last living statements. Each targeted victim had urged moderation in the West's conduct toward the Soviet Union and each had called for resumption of the spirit of détente. Each victim had also been rising in political popularity.

The pattern was clear. But what was its purpose? To eliminate every voice of reason? Were there people who actually wanted to see a confrontation between the United States and the Soviet Union? Did they plan to take two of every living thing into their underground arks? Did they really believe there would be survivors, or that what would be left would be worth surviving for?

Everyone fit into the pattern except Fabricante. Fabricante must have found out something about the drug market. New sources or, more likely, new dealers, new competition . . . And Georgi Tupolev. Perhaps he *had* discovered something that bothered him. Had it bothered someone else too? Kevin O'Brien had learned that Tupolev had not been scheduled to return to Moscow before June. And his death may or may not have been caused by an aneurysm.

Then there was Brodovsky. Chandler had lied when he told the Ambassador that he had received a letter from Tupolev. He had hoped for a reaction, but he had not expected a veiled threat. Tupolev *must* have known something. Something that cost him his life. . . .

For three more hours, Chandler kept reviewing the reports, recalling every conversation he had had with Memory. Damn, but he was frustrated with that man. Ask questions, he said. Which questions? Of whom? When could he see QJWIN? Memory had said at Cape May that they could meet only once or twice more. And only when Chandler was ready. But there was insufficient time left to keep stumbling around in the dark, literally and figuratively. There were barely sixty days before the final draft of the report would have to reach the Government Printing Office.

Chandler continued to read, index, cross-reference, reorganize his notes—all with the intensity of a prosecutor preparing a murder case for trial. He kept returning to the Kennedy assassination, to the leads that were never pursued by the CIA and FBI.

On December 1, 1963, the CIA received information that a November 22 Cuban Airlines flight from Mexico City to Cuba was delayed some five hours, from 6:00 P.M. to 11:00 P.M. E.S.T., awaiting an unidentified passenger. This un-identified passenger arrived at the airport in a twin-engine aircraft at 10:30 P.M. and boarded the Cubana Airlines plane without passing through customs, where he would have needed to identify himself by displaying a passport. The individual traveled to Cuba in the cockpit of the Cubana Airlines plane, thus avoiding identification by the pas-sengers. . . .

Why had the CIA ignored this information? Why hadn't they ever told the Warren Commission about it? Or about the Cuban-American who had passed from Tampa through Texas into Mexico on November 23, 1963, before he flew to Havana using a "courtesy visa" and an expired U.S. passport? What was the CIA hiding?

Chandler kept sifting through the pages, marking dates, draw-ing lines, trying to force his mind to make logical connections. But nothing seemed to add up.

When the dull ache that dwelt just behind his forehead stabbed deep into his brain, he stubbed out his cigar, shrugged into his suit coat, and tightened his tie. He filled his briefcase with the pages assembled for the interim report, closed up the office—as usual of late, he was the last one out—and took the elevator down to the garage. Maybe the drive to Elaine's would clear his head.

Forty minutes later, Chandler reached the familiar row of Res-ton town houses and parked near one end. The moon and stars had disappeared behind a sheet of clouds. The night air felt cool against his face. It was a beautiful early-June evening, the air filled with the fragrance of the pines he walked past and, from somewhere, the scent of roses.

The distant roar of a westbound jet disturbed the silence. The only other sound was a faint whine of traffic on the Dulles access road. No dogs barked on Quail Hollow Run. It was as peaceful as a cemetery.

Chandler had passed between the last trees and was on the darkened path to the house when suddenly he felt a terrible pain on the left side of his chest, over his heart. It felt as if a blade had slammed through his rib cage. A cry was trapped, frozen, in his throat and he sank to his knees, gasping for breath.

Then a sharp pain bit into his neck, just under his right ear. He groaned, fighting off the darkness inside his head. The next blow was not quite on target, and Chandler struggled to his feet.

Fear and anger surged through his veins. He was being attacked. Was there just one? Two? he swing his fists wildly, trying desperately to connect. "You bastards," he swore, "you—"

A foot caught him deep in the stomach. Air exploded from his lungs. He didn't even feel the second kick, which came a split-second later and landed with speed and precision, heel first on his jaw.

Elaine, startled by the shouting, flicked on the front door light. She paused for a moment, then ran to the still body on the path. There was no one else in evidence, no sound to break the silence. As she knelt, cradling his head, Chandler began to moan, then stir.

"Lie still," she commanded, but Chandler struggled stubbornly to his feet. He grabbed at her shoulder for support, and she managed to get him through the front door. She guided him into her bedroom, pulled back the covers, and lowered him gently to the pillows.

"The briefcase," Chandler groaned. "I had a briefcase."

Elaine returned from the kitchen with a handful of ice cubes wrapped in a dish towel. She held the towel to the livid bruise on his jaw, wincing in empathy as she touched it. Again Chandler said, "The briefcase . . ."

She nodded, and when she went to look for the briefcase, she carried a butcher knife in her right hand.

Who did this thing? Not ordinary muggers. At the cabin he had told her about Danielle's message, about Fouchette. *His men? Their kind of work.* She found the briefcase a few feet from where Chandler had been struck down. She ran back into the house. As she locked the door, another, more terrifying thought came into her mind: *Trevor.*

Chandler forbade her to call the police, a doctor, anyone. Then he lost consciousness, but his regular breathing seemed to indicate sleep rather than coma. She would keep watch.

An hour later, satisfied that he was deeply asleep, she went to the kitchen. Wisps of hair had fallen across her forehead, and her eyes were deeply shadowed. She had the look of a nurse who had been on duty too long.

The briefcase lay on the kitchen table. *I suppose I should open it. Get the key out of his pocket and open it. And call Trevor. Tell him all about the treasure inside. Finish up the night of lies.*

She had had no dinner date. Her engagement had been with Trevor at the Georgetown home she now knew so well. *Not much to report.* But he had probed. "Enjoy your weekend?" And she had finally told him about going to the cabin, though she knew it must be no news to him, as she knew he was aware of every step she took. "Fine, Elaine, fine. And don't worry. It will soon be over, this little masquerade." *He called him Memory. He doesn't know his name.* Trevor had shown no reaction. She accepted further instructions: "I'd like a digest of what will be in that interim report." And then, soothingly: "Don't worry. This happens. An agent gets close to an asset and they think they have fallen in love." *So fatherly.*

Janus. Trevor meant it as an insult. Two faces. One to look forward, the other backward. To the Romans, Janus was a god of foresight and hindsight. But I have no power to see into the future.

She sighed. *And into the past?*

All she had was her own memory. The man in the photograph—*Memory?*—was a man she did not remember. Her mother had told her a little about him. They had lived in Florida, the three of them, until the early sixties, when her father disappeared. They moved back to Gloucester, Massachusetts, her mother's hometown. Her mother got a job as a waitress and, after Elaine's father was declared legally dead, married Jim Dunham, who worked on the wharves.

Betty came along, then Paul. The drunk driver who smashed into Jim's car had killed him, and effectively put an end to her mother's life as well. She suffered a severe stroke that left her partially paralyzed and unable to communicate. There was no insurance. When she was finally placed in a nursing home, the children were distributed around foster homes.

A year later, Elaine turned sixteen and went out on her own. The authorities said she could take one sibling into her two-room apartment near the high school. Paul seemed to be doing okay where he was, but Betty needed her.

The kettle's insistent whistle interrupted Elaine's thoughts. She poured the boiling water into her teacup and gazed blindly at the rising steam.

*   *   *

215

She had done well in high school. She was such a responsible girl, they all said, and aptitude tests showed she was gifted in languages. That was Middlebury's specialty, and when she got a scholarship to Middlebury, she took Betty along. The seven-year-old became a kind of mascot for the Spanish dorm, until she was old enough to win a scholarship of her own, to boarding school.

The CIA recruited strenuously among the seniors at Middlebury, which had federal contracts to teach languages in which the government was interested. Elaine had studied Russian and German as well as Spanish. An Agency recruiter had requested Middlebury's recommendations, and Elaine had said, *Why not? Sounds exciting. Probably lots of travel. Intrigue. I'll stand for freedom, justice, and the American Way.*

Now she wanted to quit, and she would have if she had not received the letter from her father. Why was he hiding from her now? Why the silence? Only the photograph gave her any hope.

Elaine took a sip of her cooling tea, then pushed herself away from the table. She went to the window and looked out. She could see only her ghostly image staring back at her.

She had thought she could live with her deception. Trevor kept assuring her that it was an act of patriotism. But she didn't feel like a patriot. She had never wanted to hurt anyone, most of all not Tom. She didn't want to love him either, but she did. Against every instinct in her soul, she did.

Yet she still couldn't tell him the truth, not about anything. Two nights ago, she'd had a creepy feeling that someone was watching her, watching the house from outside. If she had told Tom, he might have asked the Senate Sergeant at Arms to provide protection . . . and maybe he wouldn't have been hurt.

She was too confused to think about what she should have done. Self-pity started to well up within her, and hot tears spilled down her cheeks.

Startled by the sound of a car engine idling outside, she ran into the dark hall, went to the window, and parted the curtains.

Not more than forty feet away was a car she did not recognize. She thought she could see the silhouettes of two men inside.

Elaine stood in the darkness, weeping with self-pity and anger. And with fear.

*   *   *

It was nearly eight when Chandler awoke, stiff and sore but somewhat refreshed by his long sleep. He called his office to say he wouldn't be in, but insisted that Elaine go to work; he didn't want anyone drawing conclusions from their mutual absence. Reluctantly, she went. He ached all over. In the bathroom mirror he inspected a large, horseshoe-shaped bruise on the left side of his chest and another on his abdomen. His neck was so stiff he could barely turn his head. And his jaw: Although the discoloration was limited in size, he could open his mouth scarcely wide enough to admit a toothbrush.

In the afternoon, when Chandler felt able to talk, he called Ned Dempsey and surprised him by saying he had decided to go to Connecticut next weekend after all. He told Dempsey he would spend the next few days holed up at home working on the interim report and then, on Friday, would head north. He asked to be switched over to Margie, and told her to book him on a Friday morning flight for New Haven.

Then he wrote a note to Elaine, telling her where he'd be: A weekend in Connecticut would help him recuperate better than one in Washington. And it would be safer for Elaine to stay away from him if someone was out to get him. He left the note on her bed, pasted a Band-Aid over the bruise on his chin—he could call it a shaving accident if anyone saw him—and went out to his car. He eased himself into the seat and drove home, where he put himself to bed, painfully propped up, with the contents of the briefcase scattered around him. If he still walked a little stiffly by Friday, he thought, he could blame it on tennis, an alibi that would never hold up in Washington, where his staff had seen him putting in fourteen-hour days for the past two months.

Chandler felt as if he had been hit by a moving van. Yet there were few obvious signs of the beating, no cuts or bruises around his eyes or lips. He knew he had been beaten by professionals. Someone wanted to send him a message without telling the world about it.

Tuesday, June 9

36

Kevin O'Brien began his investigation of Elaine Dunham by calling a bank. In his view, everything could be explained by sex, money, or religion, and money was the only one of the three he could easily explore. He could see no likelihood that religion played a part in any of this, except perhaps a kind of love-of-nation religion. As for sex, he had been wondering if sex was involved ever since the trip to Miami. But he wasn't yet ready to raise that delicate matter with Chandler.

So money would be his starting point. He remembered having seen one of Elaine's checks on her desk. The name of the bank, Federal Sun Trust, had stayed with him because John Hagget, a friend who had served with him in Vietnam, was now one of its senior vice-presidents.

O'Brien phoned and said he needed to talk about a confidential matter involving national security. Hagget told him to come over, and within fifteen minutes, O'Brien presented himself at the bank.

"Kevin," Hagget said as O'Brien came into his office, "it's good to see you." The men shook hands. They had kept in touch since the war, and before O'Brien's divorce the Federal Sun Trust had held the mortgage on his house in Alexandria.

O'Brien told Hagget what he wanted.

"It's against our policy, Kevin. I'm sorry. We're a fiduciary when it comes to handling our depositors' accounts."

"John, I don't want her money, damn it. I just need to see how she's been spending it over the past few years." Hagget shrugged in a gesture of helplessness.

O'Brien persisted. "Look, you talk about being a fiduciary. What in hell do you think I'm supposed to be as far as the country's national security is concerned? I didn't fight in that friggin' war just to turn around and give it all away to the Soviets." O'Brien allowed his anger to rise visibly to the surface. It was an old technique. An angry appeal to honor.

"But, Kevin," Hagget said, somewhat less righteously now, "no one is entitled to see a person's bank statement without permission."

"The IRS is," O'Brien snapped.

"You're not the IRS," Hagget shot back.

O'Brien knew he had overstepped the bounds. He decided to shift tactics. Softening his tone to avoid the implication of threat, he said, "No, John, but I can get the IRS to do it. I do have some friends there." He was careful not to imply that he didn't have one here. "But that would involve more people. That's why I came to you first. The more people who know why I'm looking into bank records, the more likely she is to be embarrassed by word getting out. It also could ruin her career."

"Aren't you endangering that career yourself?"

"John," O'Brien said, pleadingly now, "look. I may be way off-base on this. She may be totally aboveboard. I don't know. But someone has been leaking top-secret information and it may be coming out of our staff. I'm going to be checking out a number of people. She just happens to be the first. I've got to do it in a way that minimizes the risk of anyone's finding out—for her sake as well as my own."

"No matter how you cut it, Kevin, it's still an invasion of privacy." Hagget was starting to dig in his heels again.

"If we don't stop the leaks, there isn't going to be any privacy left to protect for the American people." O'Brien decided to make one final appeal to Hagget. "John, I've never asked you for anything before. I never expected to ask you for anything. But you trusted me once a long time ago. I have the same feeling in my bones that I did that night."

The allusion was unmistakable, and both men knew it.

"Okay." Hagget sighed. He wished he could have been angry with O'Brien for reminding him of a debt owed, but he couldn't. Anyone else would have come to a banker and asked for money on favorable terms. But not O'Brien. That was not the kind of security that motivated him. In the war, it had been physical survival; now it was the nation's. He had to admire O'Brien.

"But you'll have to give me a couple of days to go through the microfilm records and make copies."

"That's fine, John. Listen, I really appreciate this. I know how strongly you feel about your customers'—"

"It's okay, Kevin," Hagget said softly.

"No one will ever know. I guarantee you."

But Hagget would always know—that he had compromised an absolute principle. On the other hand, he knew that O'Brien would never be back seeking another favor. As O'Brien used to say, "A card laid is a card played."

Friday, June 12

37

Except for one particularly firm handshake and a couple of ribald responses to his tennis alibi, Chandler managed to get through his annual lunch-and-questions appearance at the New Haven Chamber of Commerce with a smile. He then prevailed through a series of meetings with special-interest groups in his New Haven office.

With no commitments until that night's City Labor Council dinner, he decided to walk back to his hotel and relax. He spotted a vaguely familiar figure coming toward him. The next moment he shouted, "Richard, you bristle-faced old son of a bitch!" and threw his arms around the bearded, balding figure six inches shorter than he.

"Tom, how are you? It's been fifteen years at least."

Chandler was flipping through the Rolodex of his mind, searching for a last name. He settled on *S* and then thought *Sanders, born Santorelli.* "What are you doing here in New Haven, Dick? The last alumni newsletter had you practicing down in Florida someplace, as I recall. Haven't you been living down there since graduation?"

"I just moved back to New Haven to set up my own practice. I don't expect you'd remember, Tom—particularly since you've gone big time, you big horse's ass—but I grew up here. The Miami firm belonged to a couple of uncles of mine. I did all the damage down there I could and then moved out. Came back home."

"It's great to see you after all this time, Dick. I'd sure like to catch up on what you've been doing."

Richard Sanders had been Chandler's law school classmate and a good friend. Born and raised in an old Connecticut Italian family, Sanders had made reasonable grades but had majored in billiards, good Burgundy, and beautiful women. Chandler had stayed close enough to reap the benefits. Together with three or four other kindred souls, they had represented the driving social force of an otherwise colorless law school class. They had last seen each other at the only class reunion Chandler had ever attended.

The two men stood on the sidewalk in front of the Courthouse on the New Haven Green, and Chandler knew if he stayed there much longer a small crowd would gather—including, inevitably, some constituents with problems. "Let's go down to Sherman's and I'll let you buy me a drink, Richard." Chandler had a brief vision, like an oasis in an endless desert, of an hour or two without thought of terrorists, mayhem, or drugs.

"My God, Chandler, are you serious?" Sanders said. "United States senators drink? I'm appalled! No wonder the republic is collapsing. Drink and party—that's all you politicians ever do. Shame on you. Let's go!"

They started down Elm Street. Occasional passersby recognized Senator Chandler. One or two honked in passing cars. Chandler purposely kept the pace fast to discourage greetings and conversation, and Sanders double-timed to keep up.

Chandler was genuinely delighted to see his old friend. Memories flooded into his mind, of law school escapades, and the two men traded stories, each one more exaggerated, laughing all the way to Sherman's. They arrived just ahead of the after-work crowd, and the proprietor gave them Chandler's customary darkest table in the back corner. Chandler felt comfortable in the place. It was small and relatively quiet, even during the cocktail hour, and the proprietor protected Chandler's privacy when he dropped in with friends after a hard day of campaigning.

"What a surprise, Tom," Sanders said for the third time, after their beers had arrived. "Actually, I've been hoping to bump into you since I moved up here. I didn't know whether to call your office—I didn't know if you'd dare to be seen with disreputable people like me anymore."

His tone was half-mocking, but contained an element of seriousness that Chandler was accustomed to, from old friends who wanted to be reassured.

"Oh, come on, Richard. Don't give me that 'disreputable character' horseshit! I read the alumni magazine. I know you're making three times the money I am, your house is twice the size, and your kids go to the most expensive private schools in New England. Disreputable, indeed. Since your old friend Nixon, we politicians are the disreputable ones. Be serious for a minute. What brought you back to New Haven?"

"Well, it's strange, Tom. I was in Miami when you started this investigation that's taking you to stardom. . . ." Chandler winced. "And I thought about getting in touch when you first came down to Miami. But I knew you'd be busy, so I didn't call."

A small cloud of uneasiness took shape in the back of Chandler's mind. *How did he know I was in Miami? It didn't come out in the papers until later.*

"And of course I've been dying to talk to you—just like a couple of million other people. Tell me what you're up to and where this thing is going. But I guess you can't. I'm sure it's all hush-hush, and you're not about to tell some untrustworthy type like me any of those highly classified secrets."

"Sanders, if you don't come off that 'untrustworthy' crap, I'm going to pour that beer down your throat and follow it with the bottle." Chandler made a mock lunge at the smaller man.

"Actually, Tom, I am interested. Shit, I'm intrigued—just like everybody else. All this terrorism and cloak-and-dagger stuff you're doing. But, I'll tell you, when the newspapers started reporting that maybe some drugs were hooked up in all of this, I thought maybe you'd be giving this old Italian a call." He leaned toward Chandler and stage-whispered menacingly: "You know we *all* belong to one of the 'families,' don't you?"

Sanders laughed, rather too loudly. Behind the beard and still-broad grin, Chandler thought he detected a glint of implication—almost a signal. The cloud in his mind grew slightly larger.

"Come on, Richard, I'm not even permitted to joke about stuff like that—particularly representing this state. You guys can joke among yourselves, but not us WASPs." He took a long drink of his beer. Without intending to, he found himself reflecting out loud about the investigation. "Actually, I didn't anticipate the drug thing. We started with the Harrold assassinations. Then all of a sudden there was poor old Fabricante floating around Biscayne Bay all chopped up in that barrel—horrible sight. . . ."

He paused, remembering those haunting pictures.

"Then the recollection that Fabricante was tied in with all that CIA-Cuban-Mafia—excuse me—anti-Castro business back in the sixties. Then a big surge in the drugs and the terrorism. One damn thing leads to another."

Sanders moved to the edge of his chair, intense, waiting. Chandler recognized that Sanders was exhibiting more than casual interest, and the growing cloud in his mind became an overwhelming suspicion. This was another setup, another low blow, another warning or threat. *My God, they're everywhere.*

"Richard, old friend." Chandler's voice was low and even, totally lacking the camaraderie of minutes before. "Were you waiting for me? Do you have a message for me?"

Sanders's grin vanished. He tried to recapture the lighthearted tone: "Now, Tom, what makes you think that?" It didn't work.

"How long did it take you to arrange that 'accidental' reunion out there on the Green, Richard? You had to plan this for some time. Had to have my travel schedule, my appointments, my habits." Suddenly Chandler flared, sick of being stalked, boxed in, set up, manipulated—apparently by the whole goddam world. There was no escape. He wasn't paranoid. Everyone *was* after him! Reflexively, he began to rub the bruise on his chest.

"Goddam it, Richard, you planned this. You arranged this meeting, you son of a bitch. What's going on? Can't *anybody* deal with me straight anymore?" Chandler rose half out of his chair and was stopped from leaving only by Sanders's strong clamp on his arm.

"Tom, ease up." Sanders's voice was low but insistent.

Chandler subsided into his chair. "You've got thirty seconds, Richard, to clear this up. Am I right or wrong? And you'd better be honest."

"You're right—as usual, Tom. I did arrange this meeting, and it took some doing. When you find out why, I think you'll appreciate the effort."

Relaxing a degree, Chandler said, "All right, you have thirty more seconds to tell me why."

"It's simple," Sanders said quietly, leaning forward. "I know something about the drugs."

Chandler sat back in his chair, stunned.

"I have connections in Miami."

"What connections?" he asked.

"The firm of Santorelli and Santorelli, Miami, Florida. My uncles. We represented a variety of people in the Miami area on civil and criminal matters—people who were often alleged by both the press and the police to have ties to organized crime." Sanders was all business now, the carefree law school classmate gone. "All in all, we made a great deal of money at it. And in the process I picked up a great deal of information."

Outrage gave way entirely to curiosity. Chandler the investigator surfaced. "What kind of information?"

"Information about narcotics—among other things. Where they're coming from, where they're going, who's buying, who's selling, and who's making the money."

Chandler loosened his tie and signaled for another round of beers. "Now you're talking, Richard. I apologize for blowing up, but for reasons I can't begin to explain now, this investigation has my back to the wall. I shouldn't have taken it out on you, but—"

Sanders raised a hand. "Not a word, Tom. I'm sorry I had to approach you the way I did. But what I have to tell you is such that I couldn't—I didn't dare leave messages around. I don't trust your staff. I don't trust anyone. You have to protect me. If it gets out that I've talked to you about this, it'll go *very* rough on me and my family. Besides, I was afraid you'd think I was just another long-lost classmate trying to cash in on your fame if I tried to set up an appointment in the normal way. This way, if anyone did see us, it was just an accidental meeting that led to a friendly drink for old times' sake."

"That's good enough for me, Dick. I think you exercised good judgment. Let's get down to business. What do you have?"

"What I have doesn't look good for you, Tom. You've walked right into the middle of a minefield. Whether you know it or not, you're up to your ass in a world of trouble. If you care to preserve any options on a long life—as a friend, I'd suggest you back out as carefully and as quickly as possible."

"Come on, Dick. It doesn't work that way. I just don't run. Besides, I'm in too deep to get out now. Spit it out."

After-work professionals were starting to drift into the bar. The noise level rose slightly and the two men put their heads close together.

"Lots of new drugs, Tom. You know that. Started about six months ago. Almost all of it is coming through South Florida and the Miami area. The market is Europe, almost entirely Amsterdam. That's not new. But what *is* new is that there is just one source, one seller. For the volume of stuff, that's unique. It is all high-quality

Golden Triangle stuff. What's also unique is that the seller controls the supply from the beginning."

Chandler was nodding and making notes on the back of an envelope.

"Tom, you remember anti-trust law and corporate structures? This outfit is *vertically integrated.* The people I talk to in Miami say it's the damnedest thing in the history of the drug trade. These guys, whoever they are, own the whole thing from beginning to end, top to bottom, from the goddam poppy field to the goddam blood vessel. They're dealing here in this country with a younger generation in the business. They've gone off the reservation and set up shop on their own, outside the families. It's a handful of kids who are making a fast buck—an awful lot of fast bucks. But the oldtimers are mad as a nest of hornets. Big trouble inside, all hell to pay. The capos have got war councils set up all over the place. They're sending lynching parties out and they're demanding scalps."

"What happened to Fabricante?" Chandler asked.

"That's the thing. No one knows. Two possible motives: The youngsters may have done it because the old man was ready to blow the whistle on their neat little operation—maybe because he was sick and wanted to clean his slate before he kicked off. Or some say the old chieftains may have done it to shut him up."

"Shut him up about what, Richard?"

"Tom, please, don't push on that one."

"I'm pushing, Richard."

"Oh, God. You've *got* to protect me on this, Tom. The word is—and it's *very* hush-hush—that old Sam was ready to spill something about some of the boys turning on Kennedy after he called off the Castro operation. The families were super-upset. No Havana, no casinos. No casinos, much fewer dollars. Simple financial problem, but one of great proportion."

"Which do you believe, Richard?"

"I am not here as a believer, just a humble reporter. And if *any* of this gets back, this humble reporter's ass is grass. I mean grass!"

"Who owns the vertically integrated drug operation, Richard?"

"How do I say this—particularly so I don't sound like a lunatic?"

Chandler sighed. "Given all I've heard and seen in the past few months, nothing you could say would surprise me."

"Well, I know this sounds nutty, Tom, but this is exactly why I came to you." Sanders checked the room nervously. "The word among my clients is this: It's the goddam Russians."

"The Russians?" Chandler's excitement mounted. "Are you sure? The Russians?"

"I'm not sure about anything—except that I'm doing a very stupid thing talking to you. But, damn it, Tom, I've got teenage kids. And life is tough enough without a bunch of goddam Russians trying to fill our kids' veins with junk."

"Is there any way you can help me prove this?"

Sanders shook his head violently. "Not if I want to stay alive. The capos are going to deal with it themselves, one way or the other. They're not about to stand for the young guys' going it alone. So if they can't scare them into shutting down, *they* will shut them down, with serious loss of life all around.

"Furthermore, they're absolutely bullshit about the idea of dealing with Russian communists. It's driving the oldtimers absolutely crazy. So one way or the other, it will be stopped. In the meantime, an enormous amount of money has changed hands and is still changing hands. The young guys have exported tens of millions of good Yankee dollars to whoever is the mastermind of this unit. Whoever he is, he's an absolute goddam genius."

"Any idea who that genius is, Richard—assuming it isn't Drachinsky himself?"

"You know, that's the funny part, Tom. A couple of my uncles' friends got hold of one of the younger guys involved in this operation and dealt with him very severely—bent him into some odd shapes to find that out. The kid didn't know for sure, but from his contacts in Amsterdam, when he was conducting negotiations for the drug deals, he came to believe it was not an official operation. The kid heard some rumors—which he was finally willing to divulge with some sophisticated persuasion—that the head man was some crazy colonel operating on his own."

Chandler started to ask another question and Sanders stopped him.

"That's all, Tom. I swear to God, that's all I know. What I've told you here is enough to put my ass in a permanent sling. It's the principal reason I had to get my family out of Miami. I knew too much. And now I've talked too much. But you've got to do something—somebody's got to do something! We can't go on like this: Everybody on his own, cowboy groups springing up all over the place. There's no order, no structure anymore. Nobody plays by the rules. It's every man for himself, and the world's gone crazy."

Chandler said, "Richard, this information is absolutely invaluable. Unfortunately, it fits into the pattern—which makes me believe it's probably true. You've been a great help. I don't know how to thank you."

"You can thank me two ways, Tom," Sanders said, rising to his feet.

"How's that, Richard?"

"You can pay for the beers . . . and you can forget this conversation ever happened." Sanders waved over his shoulder as he went out the door.

When Chandler got back to his hotel, he found a message to call Senator Walcott at a number in Tulsa. Chandler placed the call the minute he reached his room.

"Tom. Thanks for calling. I wanted to tell you that I'm scheduling a meeting of the Committee for Monday morning at ten."

"That's pretty sudden, Charlie. Why such short notice?" Chandler asked. There was something in Walcott's voice that put Tom on his guard.

"I'll have to tell you that rather quickly. I'm about to leave for the airport," Walcott said. "I think it's time that you—we— brought the Committee up to date on the investigation. I've been getting some complaints from the members. They say they've been kept in the dark."

"You mean Gordon Nicholson wants a report," Chandler said angrily.

"Tom, he and the others are entitled to know where we are on this thing. Sorry I can't talk more about it right now. I've got to run."

Hanging up the phone, Chandler thought, *Craig Delvin has been working hard.* And Walcott's voice. Chandler didn't like the chill in Walcott's voice.

38 Shortly after ten o'clock on Monday morning, Chandler settled himself behind the witness table, Kevin O'Brien at his side, and arranged his notes. He felt a brief tug of sympathy for all the witnesses who had appeared before the Committee, particularly those he had subjected to a grilling. It was very different on this side of the table. He was grateful for the waves of support he could feel emanating from Elaine, who was both figuratively and literally behind him.

"Now, Senator Chandler, before you proceed, I would like to say a few words," Walcott intoned. "I should like to advise the members that while I serve as co-chairman of the task force, time constraints have forced me to delegate most of the basic investigative work to Senator Chandler. And for that reason, what Senator Chandler has to say today is based on his own work." Walcott turned to Chandler. "Senator, this Committee eagerly awaits what you have to say. We are well aware of the enormous investment of your own time and considerable talent in this effort. And you have our heartfelt appreciation for undertaking this difficult, even thankless, task on behalf of all of us."

You don't know the half of it, Charlie, Chandler thought. *And after you hear what I have to say, you're probably going to wish this investigation had never begun.*

Walcott asked if any other member wanted to make an opening statement. Only one hand went up: that of the junior senator from California.

"Mr. Chairman," Gordon Nicholson said, an unaccustomed warmth pervading his voice, "as one initially opposed to this investigation, one of three dissenting votes, I feel obliged to add a word of appreciation and to extend a word almost of apology to our colleague from Connecticut."

Chandler noted the subtle emphasis on *almost.*

"Senator Chandler— No. We are among friends. *Tom* Chandler

has done an absolutely extraordinary job at keeping this highly sensitive, this explosive inquiry under wraps. Some of us might have been tempted to make a little political capital out of such a sensational subject, get a little free publicity. But, Tom, if I may say so, you've been just terrific. And as an early doubter—you know we haven't always seen eye to eye—my hat is off to you."

Nicholson's unexpected and uncharacteristic tribute raised eyebrows around the table and, predictably, set off a round of similar remarks from other members. Chandler wondered what was up Nicholson's sleeve. He girded himself for trouble.

Finally Chairman Walcott nodded to Chandler to begin his presentation.

"Mr. Chairman and colleagues," Chandler began. "I have heard such warm remarks from senators only on the occasion of one of our colleagues' retirement. I hope, after you hear this report, that is not what you'll have in mind for me." There was laughter around the table. "Since our time is brief and—as you know—my style is direct, I will dispense with the preliminaries."

Chandler cleared his throat and turned to his notes. "Let me first summarize our findings to date, and then attempt to answer any questions you may have. The wave of terrorism—particularly political assassinations—that triggered this inquiry continues. Yesterday, for example, the Libyan Ambassador to West Germany was shot to death while driving to work, probably by the Mossad in retaliation for the recently discovered documentation of Qaddafi's support for the PLO hijacking and execution of the Israeli trade mission to Greece. The question all along has been, is there any connection, any pattern, to all these seemingly random events? And if so, who or what is behind them? I believe that in most, but not all, of the incidents of high-level political terrorism there is a common thread."

Two or three of the older committee members were already looking drowsy. But most of the others, particularly Nicholson, moved forward in their chairs.

"I believe that many of the operations carried out by most of the national terrorist gangs have a common source of financing. That source seems to be a major new supply of narcotics that started to move into the international marketplace approximately six months ago. Our investigation into the drug market led us to the Mafia in this country and to international markets in Europe particularly.

To be more specific, the major arena for sales seems to be Amsterdam, and the major purchasers seem to be a younger generation of
American mob figures. Thus, the distribution throughout this
country seems to run through Mafia channels, but involves some
new faces. Some of these people the FBI and DEA don't even have
files on yet. No known criminal records."

Chandler observed that Gordon Nicholson was rapidly making
notes. "Mr. Chairman, I wonder if the Chair might remind me
what the ground rules are regarding keeping this report classified,"
Chandler asked.

"Certainly, Senator Chandler. I would remind all of our colleagues that this matter is highly classified, that any outside discussion of any matter we are considering here today will be looked
upon with severe disapproval by the Chair, the Committee, and the
Senate. And furthermore, background discussions with reporters—
or whatever you call this leaking—will simply not be condoned.
Now, members can of course keep whatever records they wish. But
for the sake of the Committee's integrity, and your own protection,
I would urge you to have the staff place any notes you may take in
the Committee's classified safe. And, of course, the reporter will
have a complete transcript of these proceedings. Proceed, Tom."

One for me, Chandler thought as he saw Nicholson resume his
normal stony stare.

"As to the more important question—who is marketing the
drugs?—the trail gets very confused." Chandler had already decided not to share with the committee the information passed on by
Richard Sanders. Too soon, too dangerous. He needed more proof,
and the whole thing could be blown away by an early leak—one he
was sure Nicholson would love to make. For now, Chandler would
show he was closely pursuing the matter without disclosing his theory. "We are checking all the angles, and with the help of international police and narcotics agencies, we may be able to turn
something up in the next few weeks."

"Mr. Chairman." It was Nicholson. "Of course I don't want to
interrupt Senator Chandler's presentation, but a number of questions have already arisen. I wonder whether this might be a good
point at which to simply open up the subject to discussion."

Chandler could tell that his old adversary, for all his elaborate
politeness, was itching to get at him. "It's entirely up to you,
Tom," the Chairman said.

"As the members wish, Mr. Chairman," Chandler said. "I know many have followed and supported this investigation, particularly Senator Nicholson, and have questions to ask. So why don't we just go to those immediately?"

The Chairman, observing seniority, called on Senator Arch Waldorf.

"Now, Senator, exactly what is it you think this project of yours is all about?" Waldorf asked. "I mean, is it some wild-goose chase that could embarrass this Committee? I guess what I'm saying is: Do you really think this whole thing is worthwhile? Is it worth all the money we're spending on it? By the way, how much have you spent so far and how much more is it going to cost? You know what I mean. Is it something we ought to be doing?"

Old Arch really had a knack for getting to the point, Chandler mused. "Senator, you've asked a number of very important questions. First of all, we have spent just under"—here he consulted his notes and got a whispered confirmation from Kevin O'Brien— "three hundred and twenty thousand dollars. That primarily includes a pro-rata share of staff salaries, travel, and reproduction of documents. My best estimate is that we will require another one to one hundred and fifty thousand to complete our work, including the cost of printing and reproducing our report.

"Yes, I believe this effort is necessary and vital. Given this Committee's conclusion that a very possible link exists between international terrorism and intelligence activities, and our conclusion that we were peculiarly the committee of jurisdiction in this matter, I believe we had no choice but to look into this issue. As you'll recall, the Committee voted overwhelmingly to undertake the investigation." After all these years, Chandler was still amazed at the time taken up in the Senate restating the obvious.

The Chairman intervened. "If that's all, Senator Waldorf, I'll recognize Senator Lewis."

"Senator Lewis has no questions."

"Senator Mrozek?"

"Senator Chandler, where are the drugs coming from that are being sold to finance terrorist activities?" Ray Mrozek had voted with the majority and was in no way hostile now.

"Geographically," Chandler replied, "they seem to come from the general areas that have traditionally been the sources for hard drugs: the so-called Golden Triangle region in Southeast Asia—

including Laos, Cambodia, and Thailand—and from certain parts of Turkey. What is peculiar, according to international drug enforcement experts, is the opening up of new growing and processing facilities in these areas. That is to say, the new large supplies apparently are the result of totally new operations begun within the last year in those regions."

"Who started these operations?" Mrozek asked.

"We don't know," Chandler said, not entirely truthfully, "but we're trying to find out." He couldn't afford to tip his hand yet regarding the information he had on the Soviets. If anything were to get out before the circumstances were entirely clear, it could be used by members of the Committee or the press to justify God-knows-what international escapade. He had to buy time and hope his colleagues would understand later.

The Chair recognized Senator Balcomb.

"Tom, you surely must have your own theory. I think that's all that any of us really want. Can't you simply give us an educated guess?" Balcomb leaned forward.

"Alan, I truly wish I could. I'm not trying to be coy with you. I'm just not prepared to come down on any one villain or set of villains here. We're looking at every possible angle. Criminal syndicates, international crime groups, neo-fascist organizations—"

"If the Senator would yield, Mr. Chairman; if the Senator would kindly yield for just one moment . . ." Nicholson's hand was waving frantically.

The Chairman addressed Balcomb: "Does the Senator yield?"

"Certainly, Mr. Chairman," Balcomb testily agreed. "I yield to the always-eager Senator from California. I can't stand the sight of apoplexy."

"I thank the Senator from Delaware for yielding," Nicholson said, ignoring the affront. "Mr. Chairman, it's difficult to know where to begin. There are so many unanswered questions here. In fact, Tom's progress report is remarkable in that it raises more questions than it answers. My intervention at this point is occasioned by the listing of all the possible sources of new supplies of drugs—and, therefore, assassinations—without even a mention, not even a notion, of the possibility of communist—that is to say *Soviet*—involvement. How can that be, I ask the Senator from Connecticut? How can it be that the most likely culprit is always the one least noticed? That's how we've gotten into this terrible mess, by constantly glossing over, for some presumed crumb of détente, the arch-villains, the perpetrators of the most heinous crimes . . ." Nicholson was reaching full flight.

Chandler broke in. "Based on experience, I knew that sooner or later the Senator would have to come up for air, so I will seize that opportunity to respond. May I remind my colleagues that my earlier listing of possible suspects was interrupted. Therefore, I guess the Senator from California will never know whether, voluntarily, I would have listed his principal evildoers. Nevertheless, now I will do so. We are indeed looking into the possible involvement of the Soviets, *very* thoroughly. I am well aware of previous theories, with some documentation, that the Soviets have sponsored most, if not all, terrorism for some years. There still seem to be differences of opinion among qualified experts on this, however. In any case, there is no occasion to believe that whatever involvement the Soviets have had in terrorism has abated over the years. The key question is whether they are involved in this recent dramatic upsurge in really vicious and seemingly random assassinations."

Nicholson attempted to regain the initiative. "What bothers me about this report by our distinguished colleague," he said, now addressing the whole Committee, "is the predominance of words like *seems* and *believe*. We either know who's behind all this or we don't. I, for one, am not willing to spend a half-million dollars of the taxpayers' hard-earned money on guesswork and speculation. With all due respect to our colleague, this Committee shouldn't pussyfoot around a tough issue like this. Why not tell it like it is and say what we all know to be the case: The Russians are engaged in political murders as they have been since the Bolsheviks came to power. Why does my friend from Connecticut find it so difficult to state the bald truth?"

Chandler paused for effect. "Because, as the Senator knows, some of us don't find the truth invariably bald, as he does. More often than not it has a little hair on it—a tuft here, a fringe there. Those fringes and tufts cause the trouble. Senator, if you want to march out of here and state *your* conclusion that the Soviets are behind the recent acts of terrorism, be my guest. But be prepared to support those charges with your own set of facts. Because nothing I've said here today leads to that conclusion—yet."

Nicholson was furious. "I'm not sure my able colleague quite understands what's going on here. The burden of proof is not on those who wish to indict the Soviets. They stand indicted in the court of world opinion by their own bloody history of murder and subversion. Let's put the blame for these current acts where it truly belongs—at the doorstep of the Kremlin. Then they can figure out their own defense. Why should the United States Senate be in the business of protecting murderers? We ought to use this investigation to point the finger of blame at those criminals."

Chandler responded with some heat: "Mr. Chairman, it was my understanding that this Committee was convened to receive an update on my investigation and to discover the truth, not to receive lectures on Soviet perfidy. If some members want to turn this project into a propagandistic kangaroo court, as I've already indicated, that is their prerogative. But count me out. I have better uses for my time than to be lectured by the Senator from California, or to have the result of the task force's—if I may say so—incredible effort perverted for the purpose of a private political vendetta."

"Mr. Chairman, a point of personal privilege." Nicholson's tone was softer, almost pleading. "Our able colleague from Connecticut has worked so hard, has put so much of himself into this investigation, that he senses at every turn opposition from those who may not be prepared to accept every qualification, every neat turn of phrase, that he uses perhaps to protect himself from any charge of lack of objectivity."

A tiny sound of indignation escaped Elaine.

Nicholson went on: "We all must accept and appreciate the enormous strain this effort has placed on Senator Chandler. Unquestionably, he is doing his best, as he has defined it."

Chandler didn't like the trend the debate was taking. Nicholson clearly was maneuvering to establish a case that Chandler was pulling his punches on International Communism, and further, perhaps, that the investigation itself had mentally unbalanced him.

"Mr. Chairman." Nicholson almost whispered. "Given the very personal nature of this discussion, it might be well if we cleared the committee room of all but members—in the interest of a free and candid discussion."

"All right," Walcott said. "I think I agree with that suggestion. So if there is no objection from you, Tom, or from anyone else? We'll ask our able staff to excuse itself—of course with our continued thanks and appreciation." Walcott nodded an apology, embarrassed that even a shirt-tail of dirty senatorial linen had been exposed.

When the room had been cleared of all but the eleven attending Committee members—Elaine flashing Chandler a surreptitious thumbs-up signal as she left—Nicholson again sought recognition. It was granted.

"All right, let's not beat around the bush," he began. "Tom, I think you've gone about as far as you can go with this thing. I don't like to say it, but I do call your objectivity into question. For whatever reason, I don't believe you are prepared to call a spade a spade. I think even if you had cold, hard facts in hand that the Russians were dead guilty, you would be inclined to qualify them. What I don't know is why—"

"Now, just a minute, Nicholson." Chandler started out of his seat. "I've listened to your horseshit long enough. I'm not going to sit here calmly and have you or anyone else call my sanity or my patriotism into question. You're way out of line and every man in this room knows it."

The Chairman started banging his gavel to restore order, but Chandler stormed on. "You either get off my case, or we'll find some other way to settle this."

"There will be order in this room," Walcott boomed. "I'll call the Sergeant-at-Arms if I have to. You both behave as gentlemen and senators, or I'll have you off this Committee—and I can do it!"

But Chandler wasn't through. "Nicholson, for whatever reason, you've been out to undermine this investigation from the start. If you want members of this Committee to ask questions, they can begin right there. What's your agenda, Nicholson? What's your angle?"

Nicholson smiled benignly, almost angelically. "Angle? Agenda? Only the truth, Tom. Which is something you seem to be afraid of. You are not fooling anyone by shifting the questions to me. This is still your investigation. It's not getting anyplace. Is it a failure? Or are you hiding something? Which is it?"

Nicholson turned to Walcott. "I propose, Mr. Chairman, that the Committee order this investigation terminated here and now, and that Senator Chandler be discharged of any and all authority and responsibility in this matter forthwith. I offer this proposal in the nature of a resolution for the Committee's immediate consideration."

So that's it, Chandler thought. *The son of a bitch has been headed for this showdown all along. He's softened me up and now he's moving in for the kill.*

Having no counteroffer to make, Chandler said merely, "I don't care to debate this matter. I put the question of my integrity and professionalism squarely to my colleagues on this Committee. Be warned of one thing, however: If you choose to terminate this investigation now, you will be accused of sixteen different kinds of cover-up. Put it to a vote, Mr. Chairman. The question is clear."

"Just a minute, Mr. Chairman." It was Alan Balcomb again. "I strongly supported the resolution authorizing this investigation. I genuinely believe Tom's done a good job, under very difficult and trying circumstances. And I would say to my colleague from California that I think he is way off-base. But we cannot permit the Committee to fragment on this question. I sense and fear a close vote on Senator Nicholson's proposal. So, by way of compromise, I will offer my own resolution and an amendment to the pending proposal. That is, that we authorize the investigation to continue, but that a final report must be delivered in no more than thirty days."

Chandler rose in protest. There was no way he could finish his work and file a report in a month. It was almost worse than being stopped now.

The Chairman, sensing a way out of a very sticky situation, gaveled him down. "I think the Senator from Delaware has come forward with a very constructive idea. I don't think we need to call the roll on this. Let's have a voice vote. All those in favor say 'aye'; all those opposed 'nay.' The ayes clearly have it."

Nicholson and three others had shouted 'nay.'

"That's it, then," Walcott said with relief. "Tom, I think that you—we—can conclude this report within thirty days. We'll have the full Committee staff to help us wrap it up. If there are no other comments, the Committee will stand in adjournment."

As the members collected their papers and made for the door behind the witness table, Chandler started for Nicholson. Alan Balcomb headed him off. "Tom, don't let that bastard get your dander up. You're bigger than that. I'm sorry I had to put up that proposal, but, frankly, I was afraid Nicholson had a chance to carry his own. It was the only thing I could think of to stop him."

Chandler was partly appeased. "That's all right, Alan. You did the right thing. Maybe the best thing would have been to end this project right now. I'm not sure I can finish up in a month anyway. And given the way things are going on this Committee, I'm not sure I can *ever* prepare a report a majority can sign off on."

He sighed. "Fixing the blame for assassinations—Nicholson wants to turn it into an ideological taffy pull. He's never going to be satisfied until the whole thing points to Moscow. I'll tell you this, though. If he doesn't stay out of my way, there'll be blood on the floor. He's obviously trying to provoke me, and at this point, he's succeeding."

Chandler was the last to leave the room. Something in him wondered when and how he would see the inside of it again.

39

Tuesday, June 16

"Mr. Director, as you know, I've tried to stay out of your hair while carrying out my work on terrorism." Chandler adopted a smoothly neutral tone for his opening gambit with E. W. Trevor. "When we had to make an exception, the Agency was most cooperative with my staff, particularly Miss Dunham, and I want you to know how appreciative I am."

"Not at all, Senator." The Director's flat glasses gleamed back at him. "I told you we would cooperate, and I meant it. What brings you here today? You were uncommonly mysterious when you called."

"I apologize for that, but it's something perhaps only you can help with. That's why I wanted to see you personally. It has to do with Executive Action."

When the Intelligence Committee hearing had ended yesterday morning, Chandler had known that, despite Walcott's formal offer of help, he was really on his own. He rejected the proffered assistance of both O'Brien and Elaine, who wanted to help plan a counterattack. But Chandler felt the investigation had come down to a duel between him and Nicholson. Perhaps his best ploy would be to start with the man he thought of as Nicholson's puppet-master, E. W. Trevor.

He had called Trevor and, in a surprisingly cordial exchange, made an appointment for the next morning.

Chandler spent most of the night reviewing once again the accumulated data that directly involved the Agency. That part of his investigation went back to 1975, when the Senate Select Committee on Intelligence had discovered that some elements of the U.S. government had been in the assassination business. From approximately the late 1950s to the mid-1960s, plots had been conceived and, in a few cases, operations undertaken to assassinate as many as five foreign leaders. The plots and operations surfaced in CIA internal investigations undertaken in 1967, later incorporated into a review of questionable CIA activities compiled in 1973 and called, appropriately enough, the Family Jewels.

Fumbling its way through the rank jungle of espionage, the Select Committee addressed to the CIA what Chandler thought of as the most naïve question he had ever heard: "Is there anything we ought to know about?" It struck Chandler as the equivalent of a parent's telling an errant child: "I want to know all the bad things you've done this week."

To its credit—and to the dismay of many denizens of its netherworld—the CIA leadership had chosen candor. There had been plots to "eliminate," "take care of," and mostly "get rid of" Patrice Lumumba, the Marxist firebrand of the Congo; Rafael Trujillo, President of the Dominican Republic; Ngo Dinh Diem, President of South Vietnam; Chilean General Rene Schneider; and, with almost demented persistence, the thorn in Uncle Sam's Latin American side, Cuba's Fidel Castro.

As in most human undertakings involving highly imaginative people, zeal had outrun judgment. License had led to excess. Given the American penchant for organization, in early 1961 the people tasked with hatching and nurturing those plots had formed a tightly compartmented, closely held operation directly overseen by the CIA Deputy Directorate for Plans. It was called "Executive Action," after its counterpart in the KGB's Department V.

With two exceptions, the handful of men involved in Executive Action did not seek resources beyond their own ranks—which perhaps explained, Chandler thought, why no foreign leader ever perished as a result of their efforts. One exception was the Deputy Director's involvement with three key Mafia chieftains in the most sustained of the assassination efforts, the eight plots to kill Castro.

Chandler had spent almost a month's time early in his own investigation personally reviewing all the records of the Select Committee for 1975 and 1976. He read the entire five-volume report thoroughly, examined the accompanying volumes of official documents, then, hour after hour, painstakingly scoured the files of the Committee. He particularly focused on the assassination plots, the CIA-Mafia-Cuban-exile efforts to overthrow Castro, and the separate study linking all of this to the assassination of John F. Kennedy.

In the course of this research, Chandler discovered the other exception to the use of outside resources in Executive Action. "QJ-WIN" was the CIA code name given to the free-lance espionage agent who, according to Committee files, had been placed under contract by the CIA sometime in 1960. The few records containing any reference to QJWIN were still, some twenty-odd years later, marked TOP SECRET, CODE-WORD CLEARANCE, or EYES ONLY.

In Cape May, Memory had agreed to help Chandler contact QJWIN—when he was ready. Now the need was urgent.

"Senator," Trevor said now, "excuse me. But as I told the Intelligence Committee during my confirmation hearings, Executive Action and all its ramifications happened during my salad days. The closest I got was during my involvement in JMWAVE—the headquarters for the operations against Cuba—and my work as a middle-level officer with the Cuban exiles in the plans to overthrow Castro. I've testified under oath that I was not aware of any plot to assassinate Castro during that period."

"I'm aware of that, Mr. Trevor," Chandler said. "But my interest is somewhat more specific. I want access to all the information you have on QJWIN—and I may want your help in finding him."

Trevor's placid features showed nothing beyond a faint look of puzzlement around the eyes. "I'm sorry," he said. "QJWIN didn't register with me at first. Of course, he's the fellow the Church Committee claimed was under contract in connection with Executive Action."

With grudging respect Chandler noted that Trevor had protected both himself and the Agency, neither admitting that he recalled QJWIN nor admitting that QJWIN had ever in fact worked for the CIA.

"Of course, I'll be glad to help on both requests. I doubt we have very much around here in our records, but you're welcome to what we have. We're not particularly proud of that operation or our association with that fellow, but it's ancient history." Trevor paused to buzz his secretary, Mrs. Brinkley. "Would you see if Harry is in, and if so, let me speak to him." Then, returning to Chandler, he said, "I'll just order up the file while you're here, if you have the time. Save you the trip."

The buzzer on his desk sounded. "Hello, Harry? Could you have someone bring around anything we have on a contract agent from the 1960 to '63 period, code name QJWIN? That's right. The very same." Chandler fancied he heard swearing on the other end. "Have the file sent around quick as you can. I have Senator Chandler here, who would like to have a look. Thanks.

"Now, Senator," Trevor continued, "the second part of your request will be more difficult. To the best of my knowledge, we never used QJWIN for *anything* after the mid-sixties. Certainly after our preoccupation in Southeast Asia, the mess about Watergate, and the congressional investigations, we would never have had an occasion to call on this individual's talents. If he was the world-class assassin that legend claims, he has been deep underground with a lot of identity changes over the past twenty years. But we can certainly do our best.

"I feel somewhat constrained to ask, however, why you want to find him. You can't possibly believe he is somehow involved in recent assassinations, can you? If you do, we should certainly know about it. Also, you would do all of us here a great favor, and contribute to rebuilding Agency morale, if you wouldn't dredge up all that muck from the past—at least in public. I ask you that as a friend and public servant."

Trevor seemed genuinely sincere, but Chandler had anticipated the request and framed his response: "Our evidence so far shows a remarkable pattern of . . . I guess I should say 'professionalism' in the high-level assassinations over the past few months. Although different groups with different political motives seem to be involved, their methods of operation and planning are remarkably similar. I'm chasing a theory that there are not that many professional assassins in the world, and that this QJWIN character might know something about them, or at the very least, about their training methods. It's just a hunch I have, but I'd like to pursue it."

Chandler knew it sounded pretty lame. But he was not about to tell Trevor that he also wanted to talk to QJWIN about the Executive Action assassination operations code-named ZRRIFLE, and about E. W. Trevor.

Mrs. Brinkley was at Chandler's elbow before he was even aware she was in the room. "Senator." She acknowledged his presence unsmilingly. Chandler was shown to a private room and given the file. When the door had closed behind Mrs. Brinkley, he read carefully but hurriedly, as if afraid this valuable information might be too quickly taken away.

The file contained fifteen pages, mostly single-spaced, typewritten interoffice memos. There was surprisingly little on QJWIN the man. In 1960 he was thirty-nine years old. In the early 1940s he had been a member of several underground resistance organizations in occupied France. He spoke half a dozen languages fluently and had obtained and kept current at least that many passports, none bearing his real name. It was believed that his parents were White Russian nobility who had settled in Belgium. That would account for his anti-communism, but not necessarily for his early anti-fascist actions, Chandler thought. He had emerged from World War II a legend throughout Europe.

After the war, unable to settle down, the young man was soon under contract for special projects with a variety of intelligence services. He immediately established and consistently maintained a reputation for never doubling or tripling his clients. He would never work against or betray a service that was paying him. In that, as well as in the degree of his professionalism, he was unique. In the chaos of postwar Europe, he became the Continent's premier assassin.

He had performed a variety of services for the OSS and the CIA over the years. When ZRRIFLE—the code name for proposed Executive Action associations—was being planned in late 1960, the Agency turned to this extraordinary figure, and gave him the new code name QJWIN.

QJWIN's first job, the report continued, was to carry out the assassination of Patrice Lumumba. A CIA assassination attempt on Lumumba's life in September 1960 had been botched, both because the Agency was new at the game and because Lumumba was under the protection of the United Nations. But Lumumba's Congolese enemies captured him in January 1961, and killed him. The CIA took no credit, but since QJWIN worked on his own, he may or may not have planned the operation.

During the spring of 1961, three pistols and three rifles made their way through CIA channels to dissidents in the Dominican Republic who admitted their purpose was to kill President Rafael Trujillo. Once again the CIA washed its hands of the operation, but with the silent QJWIN in the background, the dissidents ambushed and killed Trujillo on May 30, 1961.

The most elaborate schemes began in the summer of 1960—the plots to kill Fidel Castro. Here QJWIN's involvement was greatest, and curiously, here the already vague records became almost meaningless. Chandler knew he would have to find this man, if he was still alive, in order to find the truth.

Chandler closed the file, returned it to Trevor's office with thanks, and with a warm good-bye to Mrs. Brinkley, left the building under Trevor's personal escort.

Thursday, June 18

40

With a low, grating squeak the iron gate swung slowly inward. Chandler was startled out of reverie. He heard a soft oath. A familiar, slightly baggy silhouette materialized inside the shadows of the crypt, and Memory eased the gate more quietly back to its closed position. He locked it.

"Senator," said the vaguely Latin voice as Memory seated himself on the slate bench near Chandler. "I fear for my own sake we are becoming too friendly. But you have not abused my offer, so I believed I owed you at least this one more meeting. I fear it may be our last."

"How much time do we have?"

"Very little. About like the last time."

"I need your help."

"You certainly do, Senator."

Chandler controlled his irritation and mentally congratulated himself on increased maturity.

"I did what you told me to do during our last meeting at Cape May," Chandler said. "I followed the drugs. And I've got pretty good evidence connecting the drugs with terrorism. Some network—it's more than one person—brings the drugs out of Southeast Asia. They've set up an independent market in Amsterdam, selling primarily to younger elements in the American Mafia. Proceeds from the sales are being used to finance a number of terrorist groups—with special targets here in the United States and with the special purpose of destabilizing Soviet-American relations."

Memory tapped him warningly on the shoulder. A moment later, Chandler could hear the night watchman whistling his way down the sidewalk on the northwest Capitol grounds.

They waited until the guard was well beyond the pavilion. Then Memory said simply, "Yes."

"I'm ready to talk to QJWIN. I've done what you told me. I *have* to talk to him." Chandler's whisper was a plea.

"Yes," Memory repeated. "Yes, I believe now you are ready. What will you ask him?"

"Two things," Chandler said quickly. "First, how do the events and the people I'm looking into today relate to what took place more than twenty years ago? Clearly, a lot of people today are afraid of something from the early sixties.

"And second, who is the snake in the tower?"

Memory was silent. Then he said, "I would be very surprised if QJWIN answers your second question."

"Does he know the answer?" Chandler pressed.

"*Verdad,*" Memory said softly, almost to himself.

"Does he have a reason to tell me?"

"If he likes you. If he believes you are honest."

"Do you believe I am honest?"

Memory was silent again. Then: "Yes, Senator, or I would not be here. I believe you are honest, but naïve. Perhaps they are the same. I don't know any more. But you are soon to become less naïve. The trick is to become no less honest in the process. Very few are able."

"What about the first question—about the past?"

Memory said, "He has information for you. If he likes you and trusts you, he will tell you." After a moment's pause he went on: "QJWIN is like me. He may not give you the kind of answers, the kind of facts you Yankees seem to need. But he will lead you to even more important information. What you call motives, *why* people did what they did and are doing what they are doing."

The Capitol Hill chimes signaled eleven-thirty. Chandler knew his time with Memory was almost over.

"Your search for truth, Senator, is directed too much to facts.

Facts are important, yes. But sometimes they obscure the truth. Facts are less important than the reasons for them. *Why* people do what they do. You have now learned most of the facts. But you cannot determine what they mean. I told you when we first met that I could help you ask the right questions. You had to find those facts yourself, so that you would know what to make of them. Now you have the facts, but they—"

Memory stopped suddenly. In the intensity of their discussion, the guard had arrived almost on top of them unnoticed. They held their breath as the guard's footsteps approached. He shook the gate roughly, tested the lock. Chandler considered the option of identifying himself and taking his chances with the Capitol police, but Memory's hand covered his mouth before he could speak. They heard a succession of small clicks and a muttered oath as the guard evidently discovered that his flashlight batteries were dead. Finally he walked on. But chances were good he would be back soon, with a flashlight and, probably, reinforcements.

Memory whispered quickly. "You will meet QJWIN. You will receive your instructions soon. Your two questions are the correct ones. But remember: You are near the end of 'what.' Now you must ask 'why.' The answers lie in what the mystery writers call motivation. Motivation." His relish of the word suggested he had just discovered it after long search.

Memory stood up, and Chandler with him. They moved quickly to the gate. Memory produced a small wire and popped the lock.

In the urgency of escape, Chandler suddenly experienced a wave of desperation at losing this link to the past.

"One more question," he whispered. "Not about the investigation." Memory did not respond. Chandler grabbed his arm. "Elaine. You said I should be careful of Elaine. Why?"

"Not careful, Senator. *Aware.* Aware that she is seeking another kind of truth."

"And she will do her seeking after the investigation is over?"

"I cannot answer that, Senator."

Memory pulled him forward through the gate, closed it, and reattached the lock. In the increased light from the Capitol grounds, Chandler caught a quick glimpse of Memory's face before he turned his head away from Chandler's gaze. There was a fleeting, disturbing sense of familiarity about it.

"Where does all this end?" Chandler asked.

"It ends in no good—as it began, Senator."

The two men walked quickly away from each other. Neither looked back.

Thirty seconds later four Capitol policemen converged on the pavilion. They found it dark and empty.

PART FOUR

And all are suspects and involved
Until the mystery is solved
And under lock and key the cause
That makes a nonsense of our laws.

41

Friday–Monday, June 19–22

A CLOCK HAD BEGUN TO TICK persistently in Tom Chandler's mental cave. When he met Memory in the pavilion, Chandler had only twenty-seven days left to complete the investigation and file his report. Realistically, that meant about two and a half weeks of investigation. He suffered an agony of irritated suspense until he found the instructions from Memory in the Stanislaus Lec post office box on Saturday. The next day he was checking into the luxurious Amstel Hotel in Amsterdam and waiting again, this time for instructions from QJWIN. Twenty-four days left.

Although Chandler had briefly stopped over in Amsterdam three years earlier, with a congressional delegation returning from the Soviet Union, he had forgotten the civilized beauty of the city. From his fourth-floor corner suite in the south end of the hotel, he looked out across the Amstel—the great canal, the principal water artery of the city. The hotel stood between two land passages across the canal, the Sarphatistraat Bridge and the Torontobrug. Across the Amstel were rows of narrow, four-story town houses with gleaming white doors and window frames. One block beyond was the giant NederlandBank, and across the Sarphatistraat, the Frederiksplein Park. Wherever there was not water, it seemed, there were trees. Chandler believed he had never seen so many lovely trees in a city. For a moment loneliness overcame him. He ached for Elaine.

The awaited instructions were brought to him by the porter when he got up on Monday morning. Nobody knew who had delivered the anonymous envelope in the early hours. Chandler tore open the envelope and withdrew a three-by-five-inch file card. On it were typed his instructions, and at the bottom the letters "Q.J.W."

Shortly after three that afternoon, Chandler left the hotel, carrying a small shopping bag, and caught the bright-yellow tram traveling along the Sarphatistraat. Five minutes later he alighted. With a sense of unreality, but in accordance with his instructions, he performed a complicated series of maneuvers, changing forms of transportation, entering buildings by one entrance and exiting by another, all intended to shake off possible pursuers. In the men's room of the railway station he removed his tie, changed his navy-blue blazer for a lightweight tan sweater, donned a pair of sunglasses and a tweed cap, and dumped the shopping bag in a trash receptacle.

At exactly 4:55 P.M., when the guards signaled the closing hour at the Rijksmuseum, a tallish man with a slight scholarly stoop took one last look at Rembrandt's colossal "Night Watch," then moved with the crowd to the main entrance. Precisely at five, Chandler made his way outside as the doors were closed.

Careful to maintain the stoop that helped to disguise his height, Chandler walked two long blocks down the main thoroughfare of the Stadhouderskade, back across the Singelgracht, then through the park at the foot of the bridge. There he found a passenger dock for canal tour boats. A boat was just loading, and Chandler was the first passenger aboard.

He walked to the stern of the boat and took a seat in the last row. About a dozen other people, all tourists from the look of them, boarded before the boat got under way. Chandler had now completed his instructions and was feeling both nervous and slightly silly. For all he knew, he was the victim of an elaborate hoax. The whole exercise would mean nothing unless QJWIN— who might even be a figment of the CIA's imagination—was indeed master of a nexus of intrigue that had lasted for more than twenty years.

The tour boat moved grandly up the Singelgracht canal, past the Rijksmuseum, and on toward the Leidseplein.

"Murder." The voice came from the far end of the back row of seats. Until he spoke, Chandler had not noticed the rather nondescript man, who might have been a country parson on a holiday. "Murder," he sighed again and sadly shook his head. The man gazed out of the glass-covered boat at a small group of unkempt youths gathered at the edge of the canal, under the bridge connecting the American Hotel with the Leidseplein. They were exchanging money and small white packets. "These kids get away with murder," the man muttered.

Chandler tried unsuccessfully to place the man's accent and, with more assurance, to judge his age—perhaps early to mid-sixties. He turned a grave face toward Chandler. "This beautiful city, petrified by drugs." The man wore a brown tweed suit and a narrow-brimmed hat of a darker tweed. "Something surely must be done," he said. His eyes looked so forlorn that Chandler feared he might cry.

The man slid closer, with a murmured "If you don't mind." Chandler nodded indulgently, but felt rather as he did when buttonholed by a constituent. *In for it.*

"This city is known around the world for three things: diamonds, sex, and drugs. Now me, I am not from this city, so perhaps it is not my place to say. Diamonds are for commerce, like banking. And sex—sex is all right too. But drugs will lead to all sorts of crime . . . and other bad things. Amsterdam is businesslike. It is clean and friendly, rather livelier than the States. But drugs . . ." He lowered his voice. "Incidentally, Fabricante sent the message."

Chandler turned sharply in his seat. The man looked absently out the window as the boat passed under the Marinstraat bridge. Chandler, appalled at his own stupidity, stared at the country parson benignly nodding next to him. Rather breathlessly he said, "You're the man I've been looking for. You're the man I came to see."

"Indeed, I am afraid I am." The voice hardened. "I have followed at some distance your . . . odyssey. But I am not sure what I can do for you."

Above their conversation, the descant of the tour guide's monologue assured their privacy.

Chandler took a moment to recover his wits. Then he said, "I simply want to ask you some questions about the past, and the present—the past having to do with some of your activities, and the present having to do with some of mine." Chandler hoped he sounded both senatorial and ingratiating.

"Sir," the older man said, "I have nothing to say to you about the past. That has always been my policy. It is the key to survival in my field. Though the events of twenty years ago may interest *you*, I will not discuss them. Perhaps I will leave a memoir for posterity, after what I hope will be my natural death."

The boat was traversing a tiny passage barely wide enough for its beam. QJWIN rose from his seat, moved forward, and said something to the pilot at the wheel. As Chandler followed, the boat approached a landing on the far side of the broader canal it had just entered. The man quickly debarked, favoring a stiff left leg. Unsure of what to expect, Chandler followed again. The man glanced back at him, then led the way into a short, broad street, the Spuistraat, and crossed it to enter the secluded courtyard of a thirteenth-century convent. He took a seat on a stone bench and motioned for Chandler to join him.

"I've been told about your background," Chandler said, "and your reluctance to discuss it."

"Not reluctance, sir," QJWIN broke in. "Refusal. Few people in the world have my 'background,' as you say, and no one who has had that background has survived for long. The others talked too much."

"All right," Chandler sighed. "I'll state my problem and leave it to you to decide how you can help, if you can. I started out investigating terrorism. I kept finding links between now and the early sixties. In 1961, after the Bay of Pigs, the CIA created a unit called ZRRIFLE. By contract, you became part of that unit for almost three years. During that period, more than half a dozen attempts were made on Fidel Castro's life. On the very day that the CIA passed equipment for one of the attempts to a prospective assassin whose code name was AMLASH—on that same day, John Kennedy was killed.

"Now, none of the records I've seen indicate that you were involved in any of those attempts against Castro. But I must find out if any of the assets—the people—involved in ZRRIFLE might have known of a counterplot against Kennedy, and if so, were any of those same assets involved—Cubans or Mafia or whatever? And what is the connection between them and what's happening now?"

"Sir," QJWIN said, "I played no part at all in that sloppy endeavor to eliminate Castro. If I had, that gentleman would surely not be strutting around today. Nonetheless, I was called upon occasionally to advise on this and that, and sometimes to help your Agency uncover 'assets,' as you call them." QJWIN paused to reflect. "You may wonder, given my reputation, why I agreed to see you at all."

"Indeed," Chandler said.

"One simple reason. What I said on that boat, I meant. I have felt total affection for only one human being in my life. She was a beautiful young girl. I was not married to her mother, but I *was* her father. She lived here in Amsterdam. I visited her often, as her 'uncle.' I wished to marry her mother and adopt our daughter, to make her truly my own. But if others had known of her importance to me, there was always the chance she might have been harmed."

QJWIN's eyes were haunted. "One day some people who had a grudge against me got hold of her and forced her into addiction. She was barely fourteen. Now, many years later, she is in a sanitarium. She has been cured many times. . . ."

Here QJWIN stood up, took a step or two, then turned and sat down again on the bench. "The doctors say she was so young and the doses they gave her were so large that she may never get well." The hard blue eyes glistened. "I have done many bad things in my life. But there are worse things than assassination. That is a form of war. What is worse is to turn an innocent child into a vegetable."

QJWIN stood again and began to pace slowly across the courtyard. Chandler followed a step behind.

"I meant what I said on the boat," QJWIN repeated. "Drugs are murder. And I have a score to settle. So, the reason I talk to you, an American politician, is because I have heard you are following the drugs. And"—he turned to look Chandler squarely in the face—"I know something about that."

"There's a large, new supply of drugs flowing through this city," Chandler said. "That's established fact. The international narcotics agencies also know generally what countries they're coming from, and where they're going. They've traced many sales to the United States, particularly to Mafia sources in the South."

"Ah," said QJWIN, "I told you I had nothing to do with the Castro plots, and that is the reason why. Those Mafia men the CIA was conniving with were already drug merchants then, corrupting many young girls like mine. I would have none of it. Those jackals!" he spat.

Chandler pressed on. "To stop all this corruption of young people, to put an end to it—or at least this new part of it—I have to find the link between the drugs coming into Amsterdam and the drugs going out: who pays for them and who sells them and where the money is going."

"You know where the money is going, sir," QJWIN said slyly. "You have made the connection between drugs and assassinations. That is why you looked for me. I am no expert on drugs. You did not even know of my interest in such things until just now. You looked for me because I am an expert, shall we say, in the craft of assassination."

By now the two men had emerged from the quiet courtyard, and were walking slowly along the broad Voorburgwal toward the Royal Palace. As they strolled, QJWIN talked: "You suspect the Russians. Yet you can't quite believe they are systematic terrorists, or perhaps that they would take the risks involved. It is almost amusing to watch you Americans, and the Russians also, dance around each other. You are both naïve, sentimental people. You both have generosity and big hearts. But you are afraid to trust each other. Yet neither of you has learned to use force like the Germans, or to hate like the Italians, or to have contempt like the French.

"Your lack of sophistication leaves you in a quandary. You can't separate the good from the bad. You must learn to think like us Europeans. We know that good and evil can mix, in nations even more than in people.

"You are right: It makes no sense for the KGB to involve itself in these assassinations. Yet there are some KGB fingerprints there. How can this be explained?"

Chandler took the question as rhetorical and was silent.

QJWIN continued: "For your answer, you have only to look at your own country. Twenty years ago you were supreme in the world. Nuclear weapons. Ordinary weapons. Wealth, influence, power. Yet some things were happening which you couldn't control. Nationalism. The decay of colonialism. The rise of the Third World. None of your weapons could stop that tide. With money and guns you could slow it for a while. But sooner or later the waves of nationalism washed away your favorite dictators. In desperation you thought, 'Maybe we can simply kill the revolutionaries.' So you turned to the people who were experts in this field. You hired the Mafia—never mind what kind of people they were or what else they were doing. And you hired me."

They walked on in silence for a while.

"Sometimes we professionals perform." QJWIN turned his chilly smile in Chandler's direction. "And sometimes we do not. In the case of our efforts for your CIA some years ago, I am afraid we did not perform very well. Some of your prospective victims may have perished as a result of our efforts, or they may have perished at the hands of their more natural enemies. Other attempts failed. And the rest—well, the efforts were so comical the victims must even today be doubled up with laughter. Those Mafia men in particular were dunces.

"But what is important here, you see, is that a *capability* was created. Men are not like machines. They cannot be simply shut off. That is especially true if they have some personal interest, some passion about what they are doing. Me? I was safe. I had no passion. But some did, and it becomes very dangerous for those who pay them and point them in a direction, and then try to shut them off. They cannot *be* shut off. Even worse, they come to hate anyone who tries. That person becomes their enemy. My friend, men of passion, of fanaticism, are the most dangerous kind."

"Mr.—" Chandler stopped. "I don't know what to call you."

"By any name you wish, sir," QJWIN said. "That is one advantage of my profession. I can be anyone I choose."

"Well, Mr. Win, then," Chandler said. "Let's stick to the names we have. Is that what happened in 1963? Did the CIA create an assassination capability that turned its guns on Kennedy?"

By now the two men had reached the seventeenth-century Royal Palace. QJWIN led the way to a low stone wall in a corner near the dam behind the Palace. "You already know," he said, "that the code name for the capability was ZRRIFLE. It was composed of only about half a dozen senior Agency men. They, in turn, hired me and I recruited one or two other people on special assignments—running equipment into a country past customs and so forth. In the case of Castro, however, there were these Mafia dunces and a few Cubans, like AMLASH. I couldn't believe the CIA was so stupid as to hire well-known gangsters." QJWIN shook his head. "But they did it.

"The gangsters cooperated with the CIA not because they were loyal Americans but because, with Castro out of the way, they had a chance to reenter Cuba and reopen their casinos. I am told by those who know that the Mafia casinos in Havana, with their prostitution and everything else that goes with it, were the largest source of revenue for the Mafia in the entire Western Hemisphere. No small change. Castro's coming to power cost them maybe one hundred million dollars a year. That was in the days when a hundred million was a lot of money." A thin smile came and went across QJWIN's face.

"The Mafia had financial reasons for wanting Castro dead. The exiled Cubans had their own reasons for wanting Castro dead. And certain right-wing millionaires in the United States had ideological reasons for wanting Castro dead. All those interests were content so long as efforts were under way to ensure Castro's death. But when President Kennedy changed that policy after the missile crisis, then all those interests were very unhappy with him. He became an obstacle to their plans."

"That's a popular theory," Chandler broke in, "and one I've heard before. What I want to know is, do you have any proof of it? *Were* the plots against Castro turned around on Jack Kennedy?"

The enigmatic smile played across QJWIN's face again. "I have no proof. I was not directly involved, as I told you. I am speaking only of motive . . . and motive is the most important thing to know about any human act. But even though I was not involved in the Castro plots, I do know this: Sam Fabricante was one of three key Mafia men hired by the CIA. More than twenty years later, Sam Fabricante is killed—an old retired man. He was killed when he threatened to get in touch with your federal authorities. Should this not tell us something?"

QJWIN's manner was increasingly uneasy. "I have only one more thing to say to you on this matter. Whether your records show it or not, I continued to be carried on the ZRRIFLE account until the fall of 1963. So did Sam Fabricante. That is the year President Kennedy began closing down operations to overthrow Castro. Word had gone out over the network that the policy had changed. No more missiles, no more assassination attempts. That was the deal Kennedy had struck with Khrushchev."

A nondescript man had settled himself against the low stone wall some thirty yards distant. QJWIN began to walk slowly but deliberately away from the Palace. His voice was almost a whisper. "Few people then, and fewer alive today, knew that the ZRRIFLE capability was kept alive well after Kennedy ordered it shut down. One of those people has now become *very* important in your Agency. And that is all I will say."

"Could that person be the one Memory called 'the snake in the tower'?"

"Memory?"

"Oh. That's a sort of code name I've given to the man who sent me to you. I don't know his real name. But he told me to look for 'the snake in the tower.' Is it the person at the Agency? Or is it someone—maybe someplace—else?"

"I have told you that I have said all I will say."

Chandler's mind was racing. He felt his elusive companion about to slip irretrievably through his fingers. "A few minutes ago, you said the reason you were willing to talk was your hatred of drugs. How does any of this fit with what I am investigating?"

The two men, heads close together, had reached a grove of poplars near the Victoria Hotel. QJWIN was openly wary now With his back to a tree, he maintained a constant watch over Chandler's broad shoulder.

"If you can help to stop this new flow of drugs, it will not restore my daughter. But I will have some measure of revenge. So I talk. I tell you about capabilities that get out of hand, become uncontrollable. I talk about passionate men who let nothing get in the way of achieving their goal. I talk about how blindly the Americans and the Russians misunderstand each other. And you ask me about a connection between then and now." He paused, and Chandler held his breath.

"The connection is this: When the United States was at the height of its power, it created a means to kill foreign leaders who could not be controlled. For all its power, it saw no other way. It was desperate. The world wouldn't behave the American way. But that capability is the worst one for any nation to possess. It is sinister. It cannot be controlled.

"But the effort Kennedy had begun, to achieve some kind of accommodation with the Russians, continued also after his death. Now the Russians have their rigid ideologues, too. And they have their ability to liquidate those who won't do what *they* want.

"So you might wish to ask yourself, is there a Russian ZRRI-FLE now? Could *it* possibly have gotten out of control? Is there perhaps a snake in the Kremlin tower?"

Chandler strained to hear QJWIN's whisper. "I spoke to you about motive. What is the result of all this? Your country and the Russians are in a new Cold War. You must ask yourself, who wants this to happen? Who has an interest in creating tension, in destroying good relations?"

QJWIN took Chandler's arm and guided him across the busy Damrak to the landing stage of the Plas canal boats. A boat was just beginning to load. QJWIN bought a ticket and took Chandler aside for a last word.

"You will not see me again. I go now to see my daughter. Then I will return to my underground existence . . . which promises to become very precarious when information gets out that I have talked to you. And it will.

"There are two other men who have also stumbled onto the things I have told you. One is the head KGB man in Rome. His name is Alexei Kucharov. The other is your own CIA man, Alfred Rizzuli, in that same city. They do not know what they are onto, but soon they will."

QJWIN's strange smile returned. "Finally, my young, ambitious, eager friend, take care of yourself. You seem too sincere to live in the world you are in. You may not be able to live with the truth you find. And if you are not careful, you will not live to find the truth at all. *Au revoir.*"

Before Chandler could recover his balance, he had been thrust into the canal boat and QJWIN was gone.

Monday, June 22

42 Alfred Rizzuli, chief of the CIA's Rome station, rarely left the city. His was a big station, and he had plenty of trained professionals to cover problems wherever they might arise in his Italian jurisdiction. Twenty-six years in the Agency, a good record, and his Italian heritage and language competency had won him the Rome station as a preretirement benefit. Normally he left his desk only to attend the obligatory social functions expected of a senior embassy official in the "political" branch.

It had been at such a function, six weeks after the Harrold family assassinations, that he had learned from his British counterpart that the KGB contingent at the Russian Embassy in Rome had suffered a major shakeup. Reportedly, the number one had fallen out with the number two and sent him home. Blood had been spilled as a result. It was the kind of story that reverberated throughout the intelligence population in any major city of the world. Now, Rizzuli wondered if it had had anything to do with the Chandler theory about the Soviet Union and narcotics.

Rizzuli had developed an intense interest in the Chandler investigation, attending closely to the Agency's ever-growing cable traffic on Chandler's activities. The Agency had recently confirmed that Chandler was working on a general theory about drugs and the Russians, a theory that Rizzuli found of particular interest. During his three tours of duty in Italy, Rizzuli had developed good personal sources within the Sicilian underworld, and they not only confirmed a major spurt in drug traffic from new suppliers, but also, curiously, suggested some Russian involvement.

High-ranking Agency officials had scoffed at Rizzuli's reports in 1981 that the attempted assassination of the Pope might have been a plot masterminded by the Bulgarian secret police, possibly with the knowledge of the KGB. But Rizzuli had closely followed the long, painstaking Italian investigation that proved he had been right all along. And now he wondered again. There might be a rogue element in the KGB capable of dangerous and demented acts.

On this June Monday, Rizzuli was about to do some sleuthing on his own. He had carefully put out word among the loyal elements of his Sicilian network that he needed to know about any possible Soviet connection. Within a few weeks, his squeezing had produced some juice. He discovered that there apparently was indeed a high-level Russian drug connection, linked somehow to systematic terrorism. No one knew whether or not it was officially sanctioned by the Kremlin. Rizzuli sometimes played a deep and private game, keeping information to himself until he felt the time had come to share it. Now, believing he had reached his limit in Italy on this strange affair, he was ready to pass his personal file on to Washington. But more juice—one last drop—came.

Alexei Kucharov, his KGB counterpart in Rome, reportedly was somehow involved. Not exactly involved, said Rizzuli's Sicilian sources, but searching—trying, by himself, to put odd pieces together.

Kucharov was the only Russian, particularly the only KGB operative, Rizzuli had ever liked. They were the same age, with similar career paths, and over the years their postings had several times coincided. They had a genuine respect for each other, though usually at arm's length. What appealed to Rizzuli most was Kucharov's sense of humor. Rare enough in the business, it was unheard of among Soviet operatives. But Kucharov—pure Slav, almost Scandinavian—had somehow become Westernized enough in his traveled career to appreciate the absurdity of his line of work. He was also shrewd enough to know that his openness and wit were an effective front that facilitated important contacts.

Rizzuli had pressed his underworld sources further, and one day got the word that Kucharov was preparing to make a personal contact in Venice—without the knowledge of his KGB colleagues and political superiors—with an informant who had an urgent need to share what he knew about drugs, the Soviet Union, and terrorism. No Russian station chief in a major capital worked agents or informants personally, particularly halfway across the country. In that fact lay the significance of Kucharov's reported trip.

To verify his Sicilian sources, Rizzuli had asked Italian intelligence to check on any travel Kucharov might be planning. Sure enough, on Friday, Kucharov had left the Russian Embassy on foot at midday. After some standard evasive maneuvers, he ended up at a busy downtown Alitalia ticket office. The tail followed him back to the Embassy, then returned to the ticket office. Kucharov had paid in cash for a round-trip ticket to Venice for Monday, June 22, traveling under the name Dottore Domanda.

And so Rizzuli was doing something he had rarely done in his own career. He was breaking the rules. He checked himself out of his office, giving a vague excuse to his secretary about spending the day shopping with his wife. He told his wife, on the other hand, that he would be out of the office in meetings with the Ambassador all day. He then visited a different Alitalia office, booked an earlier flight to Venice than Kucharov's, and a later return. He paid in cash, giving his name as Dottore Risposta.

The Sicilian had given him the key: Kucharov was meeting his informant in the armory of the Doge's Palace on the Piazza San Marco at two o'clock.

Rizzuli settled himself in the far northeast corner of the Doge's Palace inner courtyard. He leaned against one of the massive support columns, half-sitting on its square foundation block. He could see everyone entering the courtyard, but in the pillar's shadow he himself was next to invisible.

From his position under the archway at the base of the Giants' Staircase, Rizzuli commanded a view of the flamboyant fifteenth-century Porta Della Carta, named for the scribes and copyists who had worked near the gothic gateway centuries before. The only other street entrance to the palace—the Porta del Frumento, or "Wheat Gate"—was closed. Thus all tourists, including Kucharov, would have to pass before Rizzuli's view.

Rizzuli loved Venice more than any other city. The ancient buildings, the remarkable canals, the extraordinary pastel aura that blanketed the city at sunset, the dwindling number of pure Venetians, the women with their Veronese oval faces, all enchanted him. Rizzuli often thought he might retire to Venice.

Nothing represented Venice more forcefully to him than its world-famous centerpiece—the Piazza San Marco and its San Marco Basilica and golden Doge's Palace. For fully a thousand years, this sublime structure had been the public and private residence of the Doge, his government, the courts of justice, and prisoners of state. For a moment, contemplating the intrigues of ancient Venetian politics seemed more real to him than deciphering the intrigues of the Soviets.

After landing at the Marco Polo Airport in mid-morning, Rizzuli had confirmed the 1:00 P.M. ETA of Kucharov's flight. He had timed the motorboat passage from the airport to the quay of the Piazzetta. He had scouted the palace to verify the timing and pattern of the tours, and had memorized convenient hiding places and shortcuts he might need to track Kucharov and his contact. Having reacquainted himself with the palace floor plan, he still had an hour before the scheduled meeting time of two o'clock and had treated himself to a capuccino at an outdoor table in the Piazza.

Now he waited. And as the hour approached, his stomach tensed and his nerves tightened. He was reminded of a long-ago time when he had met his first agent in a little park in Rome during his first tour of duty. He had forgotten how much fun it was.

Finally he thought he spotted Kucharov's distinctive bald head in a noisy group of German tourists. Reflexively, Rizzuli slipped around the pillar until he was totally in its shadow. The group filed past the ticket counter and turnstile, then headed into the sunlight across the courtyard—directly for Rizzuli.

He had anticipated this and had positioned himself accordingly. He needed to establish positive, close-up confirmation of Kucharov's identity, so he would not trail the wrong man at a distance.

The tour group, with Kucharov almost hidden in its midst, filed through the portico under the clock in the northwest corner of the courtyard, then through the Foscari Arch and up the Giants' Staircase to the Loggia. As the group emerged from the Arch and approached the foot of the Staircase, its attention was directed to the left, to the tiny Senator's Courtyard and the little Church of San Nicolo. From his shadowy hiding place twenty paces away, Rizzuli saw Kucharov's profile and knew he had his man.

Rizzuli waited until the tour guide moved past the statues of Mars and Neptune that guarded the top of the staircase, then followed the group up the steps and down the eastern Loggia to the Golden Staircase. The tour then proceeded to the Gallery and next to the Doge's Apartment.

Rizzuli stayed one room behind, watching just enough to ensure that Kucharov did not bolt. Through the magnificent halls Rizzuli tailed his quarry, at one point hiding behind the doorway that led from the Erizzo Room to Priuzi Hall.

Evidently satisfied that he was not being observed, Kucharov casually wandered off from the tour group and made his way to the Golden Staircase, back down the Loggia to the Landing of the Censors' Staircase, and then up a separate stairway leading to the four halls that comprised the Doge's Armory.

Rizzuli followed, always waiting until Kucharov had turned a corner before pursuing. He knew the contact was waiting in the armory, and had no fear of losing his prey. Cautiously he peered around the corner of the Hall of Arms, where four excited schoolboys raced from halberd to battleax to spiked shield. Quickly he crossed the hall and scanned the Hall of Henry III. There, next to the niche containing the magnificent battle armor of the French king, he saw Kucharov engaged in the polite, age-old ritual of making contact.

Leaning casually against the doorway to the hall, his face buried in a guidebook, Rizzuli could catch only pieces of their conversation. They spoke in Italian. Was the armor authentic? Kucharov seemed to ask. The contact—an absolutely colorless man of indeterminate age—assured him that it was, pointing to the plaque above the niche. Kucharov seemed to raise another question, indicating the golden medallion on the breastplate. The contact nodded, stating in tones Rizzuli could clearly hear that it was the Order of the Holy Spirit.

These two crucial signals having been exchanged, Rizzuli noted the only distinguishing character of the contact's dress. He wore a 1940s-style fedora with its wide brim turned down on the left side, away from Rizzuli. Still earnestly studying the guidebook and the armor in the Hall of Arms, Rizzuli heard the contact ask Kucharov if he would care to visit the "Wells," the tiny cells on the ground floor of the palace, next to the Rio di Palazzo Canal.

Gambling correctly that Kucharov and his contact would approach the Wells by the Golden Staircase, Rizzuli made straight for the prison block, taking the back stairs that led directly from the Hall of the Three Chiefs of the Council of Ten. From his earlier survey, Rizzuli judged that Kucharov and his informant would have to pass by a small guardroom off the Wells and he secreted himself there just seconds before Kucharov and his companion went by.

As they passed, Rizzuli saw the contact close up. The left side of his face, partly covered by the hat's brim, was hideously scarred by fire or chemicals. No chance that Kucharov—or anyone else— could have mistaken his identity.

They paused near the doorway, and Rizzuli heard Scarface whisper instructions to Kucharov. "Signore, follow the corridor around the cell block counterclockwise until you come to the third cell on the other side. It will have the Roman numeral 'VI' above it, upside down, as all the cell numbers are. The door will seem to be shut. Push it hard but slowly. It will open. I will wait one minute, then join you."

Kucharov did as he was bidden. Some minutes later, after carefully checking adjoining hallways and watching the last of a tourist group depart down the exit corridor, Scarface followed.

Rizzuli waited for fifteen seconds, then followed Scarface. He crept down the dark corridor, cautiously turned the first corner of the block, came to the second corner ten steps later, and very carefully eased his way around it. Four steps brought him to Cell VI, which was totally dark, its vented door closed. He brought his ear as close as he dared to the narrow vent.

Scarface was speaking urgently, a tremor of fear in his voice: ". . . danger, signore, more danger than ever before in my dangerous life. They know I have tried to make contact with you, and are trying desperately this very moment to find me and kill me. My cousin has a fast boat at the Rialto Bridge to take me to the airport so I can get out of Italy. So I must hurry. For the money and passport you have given me, I will tell you what I know.

"You have serious troubles in the KGB. Don't ask me how I know. I know. My information tells me you suspect it, too, or you wouldn't be here. Some number of your people—I don't know how many—are running wild. They want to start World War III. They think your Russian bear has gone soft, that you fear the American cowboy. They mean to pick a fight and stiffen your spine. You've got big—"

Kucharov swore in Russian, cutting him off. "Cut the shit," he said in Italian. "You're giving me nothing. I come all this way and pay all this money and you give me shit!" Rizzuli heard soft foot-scuffling and a strangled protest from Scarface. "I want a name. I want the biggest name you've got. And I want it now!" Rizzuli knew the Russian could kill Scarface and lose not a moment's sleep.

"Metrinko. Colonel Cyril Metrinko," Scarface gasped.

"What about Metrinko?" Kucharov demanded.

"I am in drugs, signore. This terrible business caused me to be as disfigured as you see. Two weeks ago my partner goes to Amsterdam. We hear there is a new market opening up. Perfect drugs. Some Russians buying, even KGB. Maybe to peddle in the U.S.A. and cause more trouble to their enemies. My partner called to tell me he had made contact. Then he didn't come home as he said. I got worried and flew up there. I went to his hotel room. He was dead, signore. Very sharp knife in his back."

"I don't care about your partner. Where did you get the name Metrinko?" Kucharov sounded almost apoplectic.

"Quiet, signore. Remember they are looking for me right now. There are tricks in my business, just as in yours. My partner and I had an agreement. We would avenge each other if anything happened. That is why I contacted you. You are my revenge. Our secret was—*look under my tongue*. Signore, I opened my partner's mouth and pushed up his tongue. There was a scrap of paper torn from his passport with two words written before he died: *Metrinko* and *renegade*."

"Anything else?" Kucharov demanded.

"There was one more thing, signore—"

A split-second before the two men in the cell became aware of them, Rizzuli heard soft, rapidly approaching footsteps. They were clearly the steps of a searcher. Quick steps. Step and look. Stop and listen. More soft, quick steps, close by. Then silence.

Rizzuli quickly backed around the corner into a darkened niche—and bumped into the searcher. Both grunted with surprise, then fell together in a tangled heap. Rizzuli felt himself swept aside by a powerful arm. The butt of a pistol struck sparks on the stone just inches from his head.

Simultaneously the door to Cell VI sprang open with a wrenching screech and two sets of footsteps rang down the dark corridor and out onto the stairway leading up to the Hall of the Three Chiefs. Rizzuli's assailant bolted out of the niche and ran off in pursuit.

Rizzuli picked himself off the stone floor and headed as fast as he could for the only palace exit, the Porta Della Carta. As he raced from hall to hall, he could see the others, thirty or more paces ahead, apparently possessed of the same idea. Everywhere the palace was in chaos. Tour groups scattered from the runners. Tourists gaped and pointed at the two men in the lead, then at a third, then a fourth. Assuming that a priceless antiquity was being stolen, a guide shrieked for a palace guard.

Rizzuli raced down the Golden Staircase and scrambled out onto the Loggia—just in time to see Scarface, with Kucharov close on his heels, burst out of the courtyard, into the Piazzetta, and through the Porta Della Carta, knocking down an elderly couple. The unknown assailant was halfway down the Giants' Staircase, and as Rizzuli sprinted after him, he saw the man hurl himself full speed through the Foscari Arch and lunge down the Portico, scattering the people who had come to the aid of the elderly couple.

Rizzuli, beginning to puff now from unaccustomed exertion, pursued the stranger. In the daylight it was evident that the man was considerably younger, longer-legged, and more powerfully built than he. Blond hair. *Nordic*, Rizzuli thought. Leather jacket. *A merchant seaman, perhaps a Swede.*

Rizzuli's greatest worry was losing the others in the Piazza crowd. In a second or two, all the options ran through his trained mind. Scarface would not head for the quay; too little room to maneuver. A long line waited to get into the Basilica; too easy to get trapped in there. Only two other choices: the entrance to the Piazza at its far, western end, leading to commercial and residential areas of Venice. Or the other way, past the Basilica, out the northeast corner of the Piazza.

Scarface had said his cousin had a boat waiting at the Rialto

Bridge. As Rizzuli reached the edge of the Piazza, pushing past the corner cabaret tables and the crowds entering from the side streets, he knew his spy's instinct had not deserted him. Thirty yards ahead he saw the blond head and leather-jacketed shoulders of the pursuer pushing through the crowd.

Now the narrow streets proved almost impassable. Rizzuli was consoled by the knowledge that his strung-out quarry could move no faster than he, and the slower pace gave him a chance to catch his breath and marshal his thoughts. He made headway around the Chiesa Mercerie, sometimes losing, always regaining, sight of the blond man now shoving his way more violently through the crowd ahead.

Seeing an opening down a side street over the bridge beyond the church, Rizzuli took a gamble that the blond pursuer would not catch the other two before the Rialto. He took the shortcut, racing the block to the Salizzaoa S. Lio, and the block and a half from there to the bridge leading into the Campo S. Bartolomeo and the open-air bazaar next to the Rialto Bridge.

Fifty yards ahead, over the heads of scores of tourists, Rizzuli saw a scuffle overturn several market stalls. His shortcut had gained him nothing. Leather handbags flew, then scarves. Another stall collapsed. A woman screamed. Rizzuli pushed ahead. Fists flew and a man went down. The blond man broke away. As the Campo rose to the foot of the bridge, Rizzuli saw Scarface and Kucharov run from behind a vegetable stand and cross the street behind a row of jewelry shops.

The market area leading to the bridge was flanked by stalls on both sides. Kucharov and Scarface were ducking back and forth, feinting between stalls from street to portico. Suddenly, Scarface—the fedora still miraculously on his head—dashed from behind a shop and ran the last few yards to the top of the bridge. There were screams and cries of *"Polizìa! Polizìa!"* as the blond man, arms swinging wildly, a revolver in one hand, bludgeoned his way through the crowd, up the middle of the bridge.

Rizzuli raced after him, watchful for any sign that the gun might turn, lightning-quick, on him. As the gunman reached the bridge's peak he stopped, crouched, and leveled the gun at Scarface, who was now heading down the other side. Simultaneously, Kucharov sprang from an alley between two shops directly to the gunman's left. Without a second's hesitation, the gunman turned his weapon on Kucharov and fired a bullet through his forehead.

Rizzuli shouted, "No!" In all his years with the Agency, this was the first time he had seen a shot fired in anger. Kucharov, knocked backward by the bullet's impact, toppled over the crest of the rail and plunged into the Grand Canal twenty-five feet below. The killer bolted.

As Rizzuli rushed to the rail, his foot struck an object that clattered away. The killer had dropped his gun. Rizzuli picked it up. He looked down at the canal and saw nothing. He dashed to the other side and looked down again. A stunned gondolier appeared. In the stern of the gondola, face up, partly impaled on the ornate aft ornament, lay the body of Alexei Kucharov, a small dark hole in the middle of his forehead. His eyes were open in an expression of horrified surprise.

For a moment Rizzuli stood there, his own face mirroring the horror in the face below. In another moment he was surrounded by policemen, guns drawn. One barked a command, and Rizzuli dropped the gun he held. He had almost forgotten the gun.

Two policemen grabbed his shoulders and spread-eagled him against the railing. A police vaporetto roared up, and the two men who held him shoved him aboard. He realized that they thought he had shot Kucharov, but as the police launch sped away, he felt he would be able to explain what had happened. He was, he thought wryly, an innocent bystander.

The launch came to a stop near a small bridge. Rizzuli was yanked off as roughly as he had been shoved aboard, and hustled into the Carcere Venezia—the Venice jail.

As he went through the booking procedure, he said in Italian, on a rising note of exasperation: "I am not only an American citizen, I am a high official in the American Embassy in Rome. If you weren't such thick-headed bureaucrats, you'd pick up the telephone and find that out."

"Si, signore, you say you are Alfred Rizzuli and so say some documents in your wallet. But why then this airline ticket which you carry in the name of Dottore Risposta? What kind of name is that, 'Doctor Answer'? And if that is your name, what is the answer to possessing the gun that killed this strange foreign gentleman on the Rialto Bridge. A man carrying an airline ticket issued to Dottore Domanda. 'Doctor Question'? 'Doctor Answer'?"

"It's *not* my gun, I told you," Rizzuli shouted.

"We shall see, signore. We have much to sort out here. In the meantime, we have one of our better cells for you."

Two gorillalike policemen half-carried him out the door as he continued to yell: "Call the Ambassador, I said. Call the Am—" The iron door clanged shut.

"Goddam it! I want to call the American Ambassador!" Rizzuli paced his cell, sufficiently recovered from shock to be outraged. "I work for the United States Government. I didn't kill anyone. I demand to talk to the American Ambassador in Rome!"

About two hours after he was booked, Rizzuli looked up from his cot to see a visitor standing outside his cell door. Rizzuli did not recognize the man in the dark-gray suit, but he looked like a lawyer. And he was being treated like a lawyer. The man spoke a few sharp words in passable Italian and handed some American bills to the gorilla, who unlocked the cell door and disappeared.

As Rizzuli started to explain what had happened, the visitor took a pack of Marlboros from his pocket and offered it to Rizzuli.

"Thanks," Rizzuli said, accepting a cigarette. "You speak English, I assume?"

The man nodded and held out a Dunhill lighter.

Rizzuli bent forward to accept the light. As the lighter opened, he instantly knew it was not a lighter. He drew his head back—but too late. A jet of vapor shot straight into his nostrils and deep into his lungs. Rizzuli's eyes rolled back. As if in a dream, he heard the last words he would ever hear: "Metrinko says good night."

The visitor swiftly took off Rizzuli's belt and necktie and tied them together. He pulled the belt tight around Rizzuli's throat, dragged the body to the window, and tied the necktie securely to the bars. He went out, closing the cell door behind him. It was half an hour before the gorilla found Rizzuli's body and cut it down.

43

Someone had once asked Kevin O'Brien whether all Irishmen were born in South Boston and then formed a conspiracy to infiltrate every fire and police department in the country. O'Brien had resented the slur, even if it was meant as a joke. He was no fireman and he had never been to Boston. He had had no reason to go—until now.

The Delta flight from Washington took barely long enough for the flight attendants to serve breakfast. As soon as he arrived at Boston's Logan Airport, O'Brien rented a car. He had only a short drive to make—to Gloucester, where Elaine had graduated from high school. He had got that nugget of information by calling a friend at the Senate Placement Office, where job-seekers' applications are processed. He told the friend that an insistent constituent had inquired about how many Connecticut citizens were on the various staffs. The friend looked up Elaine's original application and reported that she was born in Miami, Florida, went to high school in Gloucester, and graduated with honors from Middlebury College. O'Brien then tracked down the high school's former guidance counselor and made a date to meet him at his home.

Displaying his Senate staff identification card to Fred Giles, a slight man with a disappearing hairline, O'Brien opened with a standard pitch: "We're doing a background check, Mr. Giles. Elaine is being considered for a high-level government position that will require her to be cleared for the highest classified information there is."

"Well, there's not much I can tell you about her that you don't already know," Giles said. "I remember her well. A brave little girl. Very brave. But, as I said, I'm sure you know the story."

"Yes, I do," O'Brien solemnly lied, "but I'd like to hear it from you." He lied again: "I know that you helped her a great deal."

Giles nodded, puffed at his pipe, and pushed the smoke through his nose. "Well, I had to make a big decision. I know I did right, but of course I couldn't know at the time. I mean, letting a little high school girl and her baby sister live in an apartment, arranging for that, telling the damn social worker to keep her nose out of it, and the principal—"

"Perhaps you could start at the beginning," O'Brien said.

Giles began with Jim Dunham's fatal automobile accident, went on to the placement of Mrs. Dunham in a nursing home, and the distribution of the three Dunham kids to foster homes.

When Giles had finished, O'Brien said, "I had only known the basic story, without these human details. Elaine is so modest, so unassuming." He took a breath and plunged: "You said that Mr. Jim Dunham was Elaine's stepfather. She . . . she always refers to him as 'father.' But her real father?"

"Thought you government fellows knew everything," Giles said, laughing and knocking out his pipe against a ceramic toadstool in the middle of a bright-orange ashtray. "He's dead. I remember we tried to find him, after the kids became wards of the state and all. We were looking for next of kin, and checked down in Miami."

"Where Elaine was born," O'Brien said, feeling he had to indicate *some* knowledge of her background.

"Right. Well, we checked and found that he had been declared legally dead. So he was dead. A Cuban. I guess you know that," Giles said, a bit suspiciously.

O'Brien nodded. He had attributed her dark beauty to a strain of what his father had called "black Irish." He took another plunge: "Because he was declared legally dead and because Mr. Dunham was her legal father, well, the truth of the matter, Mr. Giles, is that the government *doesn't* know everything. Elaine doesn't know his name, and—well, there it sits, a blank on the security-check form. Would there be any record at the school?"

"No need to go there," Giles said. "It's here," and he tapped the side of his head with the stem of his pipe. "I used to teach World Lit. Literature, that is. Never came across the name outside of literature. You know, the name of Don Quixote's squire, Sanchez. Her father's name was Immanuel Sanchez. Now I don't know why I remember the 'Immanuel.' But the Sanchez—that was right out of *Don Quixote*."

Sancho, O'Brien wanted to blurt. *Sancho Panza, you idiot!* But he said, "Thank you very much, Mr. Giles. You've helped us very much. You have a remarkable memory."

O'Brien tried to remain calm as he swung his car out of Giles's driveway and headed back toward Logan Airport. But his heart was pounding with excitement.

It all began to make sense. Her flawless Spanish. Someone in Miami said she spoke it like a native. *She isn't who she said she was.* But who was she? She had a double identity, probably a whole set of identification papers in her father's name. Somehow, the Cubans and the Soviets must have gotten to her, God knows when. Maybe at Middlebury. O'Brien had heard about the Agency's recruiting there. Maybe the KGB did too. Maybe they kept her on ice for years. The monthly payments—more than her salary—didn't start appearing in her bank account until a little while ago. All deposits with no matching withdrawals. *Pretty clever. She looks like she's living on her salary. But she has enough stashed away to make a getaway anytime she wants.*

O'Brien remembered reading something a KGB defector had once said: Unmarried female secretaries in their thirties or forties were the easiest targets for recruitment as agents. How about a professional staffer on the Senate Intelligence Committee? How about an unmarried female in her late twenties who was cozy with the boss? Who spoke Spanish flawlessly—and, he remembered her once saying, "a little Russian"?

He had to warn Chandler. But not just yet. There was one more thing he needed to know: Who was Immanuel Sanchez?

Tuesday, June 23

44

The insistent ringing of the telephone caused Chandler to hesitate at the door of his Amsterdam hotel suite. A taxi was waiting at the entrance to rush him to Schiphol Airport; otherwise he would miss the morning flight to Washington. So few people knew he was in Amsterdam that it must be important. He couldn't risk not answering.

"Senator Chandler." The voice unmistakably combined the several European accents that produced the unique sound of QJWIN. Chandler's adrenaline started to pump.

"As many as a dozen or more intensely interested parties are now listening to this conversation. Therefore I shall merely report to you briefly and sadly that our Roman friend, about whom I spoke to you last night, Mr. Senator, was, exactly at the time we were meeting, relieved of his command—with extreme prejudice."

Chandler made the mental connection between "our Roman friend" and the name of Alfred Rizzuli. "How could that have happened?" he said. "Did anyone else know that he was working on"— Chandler groped for a circumlocution and only later realized how revealingly personal it had been—"on my problem?"

The voice continued, unmoved: "Several hours ago a captain of the Venice police signed an official paper certifying that this unfortunate gentleman took his own life by the act of hanging in the Carcere Venezia. Italian authorities had arrested him for murder yesterday in Venice.

"You might wish to ask yourself—if not the Italian authorities—how a man can hang himself whose heart has not been beating for several minutes.

"*Au revoir*, Mr. Senator. It will be useless for you to pursue this matter with me. I have come to place a certain belated value on my life as I've grown older, and what you have become involved in is much too incompatible with a decent respect for personal safety.

"Only one thing more, since by now many of our auditors are desperately tracing this phone from which I speak. Our friend, who has gone away in such an untimely manner and so unhappily for you, was taken into custody by the polizìa for the murder of the head of the KGB in Rome. Myself, I don't think our friend was that stupid."

The phone in Chandler's hand clicked and buzzed. QJWIN was gone into permanent retirement.

Chandler flew immediately to Italy. Talking to the Venice police got him nowhere. They insisted Alfred Rizzuli, head of the CIA/Rome, had stalked and killed his long-time rival Alexei Kucharov, head of the KGB/Rome, in some apparent blood feud. Apprehended for murder, caught in the act, weapon in hand, career and reputation ruined. Rizzuli naturally had taken the easy way out.

Yes, the gentleman had made a statement, but it was full of nonsense. A scar-faced man, a high-speed boat. Yes, the *Senatore* could have a copy of the worthless statement. And the report of the policeman who had arrested the man who said he was Doctor Answer. A strange man.

In Rome, one of Rizzuli's men translated the statement and the report for Chandler. He received little more aid from the American Embassy, which treated him as an embarrassing and perhaps dangerous nuisance.

Chandler could not believe that Rizzuli had killed Kucharov. Rizzuli had to be telling the truth in his statement: The man pursuing Scarface had killed Kucharov. Chandler assumed that Scarface was permanently in hiding, or dead, and that the real killer had made it across the border or to a friendly ship. And the visitor to the cell—a replay of the killing of Rashish in Miami.

QJWIN had been right. The one man in Europe, perhaps in the world, who could offer any support for Chandler's bizarre theory of drugs, Russians, Mafia, and terrorism was dead.

As Chandler waited at Fiumicino airport for his flight to London, the first leg of his hastily rearranged return to Washington, he began to realize more clearly than ever that he must uncover some concrete proof of his theory, or soon be crushed under the weight of Mafia blackmail, CIA retaliation, a crumbling political career, and—given poor Rizzuli's fate—a premature and unpleasant death.

He thought how increasingly detached and unemotional he had become. His Dante-like descent into hell had turned almost into an intellectual adventure, a passionless pursuit with an infernal life of its own.

He pondered the brilliant madness of the Soviet mastermind behind this. Chandler had come to believe that there was one man, one extraordinary man, somewhere high in the Soviet structure. He remembered the conversation with Richard Sanders in New Haven: a KGB colonel. With one stroke this madman had killed Scarface or sent him permanently underground, had eliminated what must have been a suspicious Kucharov, had framed a high-level CIA operative for Kucharov's murder, and then had eliminated him. He had also confounded Chandler and, most diabolically, caused worldwide chaos in the intelligence community.

Threats and counterthreats, Chandler knew, would be flying back and forth from Washington to Moscow along diplomatic and intelligence circuits. The Rizzuli-Kucharov affair would set back civilized behavior in the international intelligence community forty years—to the back-alley days of Marseilles after World War II. And in the chaos, this madman would thrive—starting fires here, spreading mayhem there. Always blaming the other side. Maybe the Russian who was running this had discovered the key to destabilization, the way to start World War III, Chandler thought. Spying was essential to predictability. Predictability was essential to stability. Stability was essential to survival. And intelligence was the glue holding it all together. Now some madman had apparently found the formula to dissolve it.

The Rome flight arrived in London at 7:30 P.M. Chandler had almost two hours before catching the Concorde to Washington-Dulles. He checked in at the ticket counter, and was directed to the Concorde Club's VIP lounge. The secretary there placed his call to Washington and soon had his office on the phone. It was not quite 3:00 P.M. at home.

"Oh, Senator, how are you? I'm so glad you called. We tried desperately to reach you in Rome before you left, but I'm afraid my Italian just wasn't good enough." Chandler was glad to hear Margie's voice, one of the few dependable points of reference in his decaying world. "Early this morning you got a call from London, having something to do with *your project*." Margie's efforts at euphemism always amused Chandler, as he was sure they did those listening on his line.

"Naturally I gave the call to Kevin. He says it was a man named—just a minute. Let me get the slip. Oh, yes, a man calling himself Arthur Simpson. He told Kevin he's a free-lance journalist and he needs to talk to you. Kevin quizzed him pretty carefully, and he's convinced you should see him. Simpson talked vaguely about 'interviewing' you, but Kevin says it sounds like he has more to say to you than you do to him."

"Margie, I'm exhausted. All I want to do is come home. I've been over here three days and three countries' worth now. I'm still strung out by jet lag and a lot of blind alleys. Did Kevin check this guy out?"

"He sure did. British Embassy, Library of Congress, *and* Agency. He's legitimate, but not exactly well known. No Pulitzer Prize, I'm afraid. Mid-fifties, bounced around a few papers and journals. He's published a few things recently on intelligence—

nothing profound. Popular stuff. But he has an interest. And his one area of specialization has always been Soviet politics.

"The Agency has no official record that Simpson ever worked for the Soviets—or any intelligence service. But they say 'watch out.' He's apparently developed some high-level sources on the other side, and he may be fishing."

"I'll give him a call," Chandler said resignedly. "Give me the number."

Margie relayed the number and, anticipating such circumstances in typical fashion, assured Chandler that if he had to stop over in London, Ned Dempsey said he would miss only a few inconsequential votes in the Senate.

"Thanks," Chandler said. "If I have to stay, I'll try to get into Brown's. If you need to reach me, you can start there. And let's leave our embassy here out of this."

From the VIP lounge, Chandler called the number Margie had given him. Simpson answered on the second ring, as if anticipating the call.

"Senator, how honored I am to hear from you. You are so kind to call back. You are here in London by the sound of your voice. What a coincidence."

Chandler was unconvinced. "It certainly is, isn't it? What can I do for you, Mr. Simpson?"

"As I explained to your assistant in Washington, Senator, I thought it might be mutually helpful for us to get together. You see, I'm keen to do a piece for British readers on your task force. You've stirred up a bit of interest over here with your snooping about—sorry. Investigation. And I'm not sure we've quite got it right what you're up to, you see. So if you had just a moment— lunch tomorrow perhaps?—I might just be able to put it down properly for all those who are so interested here."

"Mr. Simpson," Chandler sighed, "I'm afraid my office didn't quite explain things properly to you. My policy is no publicity until the ivestigation is completed. I appreciate your generosity and interest, but I've turned down all sorts of inquiries in the States and I'm afraid it would be unfair to talk to you now. Why don't we just take a rain check and perhaps talk on your next visit to the States, once our work on this subject is completed."

"But, Senator," Simpson broke in like a man playing an ace. "I've done a lot of work on this project already, you see, and I've interviewed many people who have a great interest in what you're doing. If you did nothing more than confirm or deny the information I have it would be an *enormous* help. Besides, Senator Chandler, who knows, perhaps some information I've gained might be of some help to you. Amsterdam. The Kennedy assassination. That sort of thing. One never knows, really, does one? I mean, a bit here and a bit there—"

Chandler cut him off: "Lunch tomorrow then. Why don't you meet me at Brown's at one, in the waiting room?"

Wearily, and with an increasing distrust of all the world around him, Chandler postponed his Concorde flight for twenty-four hours and made a reservation at Brown's.

Wednesday, June 24

45

Exhausted, Chandler slept until almost noon. Awakening in the strange hotel room, he was totally disoriented. Now, as on more than one occasion during a political campaign, he had to fumble on the bedside table for a telephone directory to find out where he was. He was startled when he saw LONDON on the cover. Then the events of the last few days came back to him. He cursed to himself for staying over to meet Simpson. Probably some crackpot who had made a lucky guess or two.

Rested, showered, and shaved, he felt considerably better as he descended in the lift promptly at one. He walked into the parlor off the hotel's lobby with some of his confidence restored.

A man rose to greet him. "Ah, Senator, there you are. Would have recognized you anywhere. But much younger than your pictures. You Americans do favor the wholesome look in your politicians."

Simpson wore a baggy tweed suit, blue shirt with curled-up white collar, and regimental tie knotted off-center. A lock of lank, dirty-blond hair fell over his left eyebrow. He bared yellowing, overlapped teeth and, as he approached with an "Arthur Simpson, pleased to meet you," exhaled the worst breath Chandler had ever encountered.

Chandler led him across Brown's small lobby into the dining

room, where the maître d' showed them to a remote table. Seating himself in the corner facing the room, as he habitually did, Chandler pondered whether to place Simpson across from him, with the risk of their being overheard, or next to him, with the halitosis. Unasked, Simpson opted for the latter position, and Chandler shifted to the far edge of his chair.

"Well, this is a great honor, I must say," Simpson said. "And I do so much appreciate the time you've taken to speak with me." They ordered lunch, Chandler politely following Simpson's suggestions. "Actually, as I said last night, there is great interest over here in you and your investigation. We are a spy-loving nation, after all—third man, fourth man, fifth man. It never stops. There is all manner of speculation as to what you are up to and whether you have discovered what's behind all the terrorism. For my money—"

Chandler interrupted him. "Mr. Simpson, I genuinely appreciate your interest. But as I told you last night, I'm not free to discuss any aspect of my activities in this area."

"Right, Senator, righto!" Simpson was unchastened. "But, on the other hand, I have pieced together a few things that are simply extraordinary. And these pieces must be of as much interest to you as they are to me. With your forbearance, Senator, I thought I might just sketch out for you, so to speak, my findings and, if I may, a few theories."

Chandler had been studying Simpson. He couldn't decide whether the journalist had more broken blood vessels in his eyes or on his nose. Yet for all his pathetic seediness, Simpson gave off a counterfeit air. Chandler, by now honing his character-judging skills almost daily, did not trust the man. There was a twisted quality in Simpson. The deeper Chandler took his search, the less things turned out to be what they seemed.

Simpson rattled on: "Now, if I understand correctly, you have traced certain connections among most of the acts of terrorism—random assassinations—over the past few months. Apparently you believe there is some association of these terrorist acts with a new supply of narcotics. My sources indicate you traced the distribution point of the narcotics to Amsterdam . . ."

Simpson trailed off as his luncheon arrived. Then, with the waiter's departure, he dug in voraciously while continuing his narrative. ". . . and from Amsterdam into the United States through established Mafia channels. Now here it seems to become complicated. My sources tell me the Mafia has become upset with your efforts to pin this new drug traffic on them, particularly as it does tend to associate them—although in an indirect way—with a number of political assassinations which they do not wish to be identified with."

Chandler's appetite was rapidly waning. This man—whoever he was—knew too much. But how? Chandler felt his neck muscles tensing, as if for a blow. He forced his expression to remain placid, even unconcerned.

"Now you see, Senator, this is a sticky thing. Most complicated, and most unpleasant, I am sure, for you. My sniffing 'round also tells me you are in hot water with your intelligence people, especially the high panjandrums at your CIA. Seems it's something to do with—dear me—that old chestnut, the Kennedy assassination. Apparently there's something to hide . . . shall we say 'cover up'? about the CIA spooks, the Cubans, and the Mafia. And lots of people have lots of reasons to let all that stay quiet. Senator Church's investigation in 1975 caused enough heart attacks for several generations, all right."

Given what Simpson had already said, Chandler began calculating the sources that might be available to Simpson and for whom the Englishman might be broker. Simpson increasingly seemed a shrewd and clever animal, a ferret.

"Now, Senator, you are such a gracious man, I wonder how to proceed . . . shall we say, diplomatically?" The noisome breath gusted at Chandler.

"Simply proceed, Mr. Simpson," Chandler said.

"Quite so." Simpson shifted in his chair. "Well, for all sorts of reasons there is mounting interest in the Soviet Union in your activities."

Chandler heard Margie's voice in his mind: *His one area of specialization has always been Soviet politics.*

"Accordingly, as you are an experienced man, you will not be surprised to learn that certain of your movements have been observed—"

"Monitored. Intercepted. Spied on, Mr. Simpson." Chandler's voice cut like a knife.

"As you wish, Senator. Among these movements was a meeting between you and your former wife at the . . ." Here Simpson furtively consulted a reporter's notebook fetched from his rumpled coat. ". . . Four Seasons in New York on—"

"May seventeenth at seven-thirty P.M." Chandler interrupted. He tried to call back the scene. *Who? Danielle? A waiter?* And then he remembered the friendly constituent who had come over to their table and patted him on the shoulder. A planted transmitter?

"Ahem, yes. Quite so," Simpson said, watching Chandler's tightening jaw. "Now, during this meeting, and according to my sources in a subsequent telephone conversation you had with your wife after she spoke to your ex-father-in-law—a Mr. Fouchette, I believe it is—it was made clear to you that your investigation— at least to the extent it touched on the Mafia, either its present drug distribution or previous involvement in Castro assassination plots—was to be abandoned. The reward for your cooperation was, shall we say, forbearance on the part of organized crime— gangsters."

Simpson, gaining confidence, was clearly enjoying his new-found power over his host. "Yes, gangsters, who would refrain from disclosing the fact that your own wealth, your early financial success, was based entirely on financing arranged through Mafia conduits, financing traceable to gambling, drugs, extortion, and prostitution. Now, disclosure of that information would clearly doom your political career, ruling out any thought you may have had about becoming President."

"What do you want, Mr. Simpson? Just what is it you want from me?" Chandler spoke with ominous softness.

"Ah, Senator, sir. I see you are in a mood to slay the messenger. A most unpleasant prospect for us both, especially after such a pleasant lunch." Simpson raised his hand as if in defense and spoke conspiratorially. "My sources—"

"Your *bosses*."

"My *sources* want you to know they are equally concerned with your investigation. They feel your mucking about in Soviet intelligence to be very harmful and disruptive. They wish you to know they feel *very* strongly about this. So strongly, in fact, that *they* are prepared to release the information they have, ah, acquired about your financial background and the Mafia connections, even if the Mafia should not. They want you to know they can do this very discreetly through normal American journalistic channels without a Soviet fingerprint anywhere. In a word, Senator, they want you to stop. Senator, you are a nice, sincere man. For your own sake, I beg of you—"

"Mr. Simpson, you've done your job. You've delivered your goddam blackmailer's message. I hope you were well paid.

"You are right. I am in a mood to slay the messenger. Therefore"—Chandler paused briefly—"I intend to close my eyes and pretend you don't exist while I count rapidly to ten." Chandler closed his eyes.

"One . . ." He heard the scrape of Simpson's chair.

"Two . . ." Hurrying footsteps died away.

Chandler opened his eyes to see Simpson's deplorable tweed back disappearing into the lobby.

Wednesday, June 24

46

Metrinko had chosen to hold the meeting at his dacha in Zhukovo, to emphasize to his deputies that they were working for him, not for the large, unwieldy apparatus at Dzerzhinsky Square or the glass box beyond Moscow. He sat behind the plain table in the room with the stark white walls. The other two men occupied straight-backed wooden chairs, like pupils before the master.

They had spent many days and nights standing over chairs like these, shouting at or cajoling people who sat as they did now, stiff, nervous, wishing for a cigarette or—so unlikely in this monk's dacha—a vodka.

The three men in the room were old friends. They had worked together all their adult lives in the KGB. The two men facing Colonel Metrinko shared his hard-line ideology. They had followed him up the intelligence ladder to the command of a special unit of Department V. Tightly compartmented, its existence known to only a handful of officials in the Kremlin, it was the operational unit responsible for dirty tricks.

Cyril Metrinko's reputation was known far beyond Department V, and his reputation was steadily, stealthily growing. Had he been a priest, he would have been the most devout in any order. He would have demanded the restoration of hairshirts and flagellation. He was brilliant, gifted, and totally committed. His dedication to the spread of Leninism was total, even feverish, and his hatred of capitalism and Western democracies was equally passionate.

The deputies had heard that the younger men in Department V called him The Monk Metrinko. The nickname had apparently not got back to Metrinko, or if it had, he had taken no action against these insubordinate cubs. Actually, a sycophant, feigning shock, had reported it to him. The sobriquet had amused Metrinko, but he did not see himself as a monk. He saw himself as a savior.

Ever since the first SALT pact, the opening of trade and exchange with the West, and the Vladivostok Accords, Metrinko had brooded. Something must be done to reverse this destructive course, this outrageous cooperation with the enemy. True communism had gone out of style. Now it was all refrigerators, television, motor cars. There were even reports of marijuana smoking among the young. The signs of decay were everywhere, and almost no one seemed to care. Near the top, there were only Metrinko and his disciples.

Those who shared his purity of faith, he knew, would organize themselves at the local level. Indeed, some had already done so. They were beginning to make their pressure felt within the Party, but in the meantime, Metrinko increasingly felt some cataclysmic event was needed to restore polarization between East and West. A Cold War of controlled terrorism would be a test for both systems, and Metrinko was determined that the United States would buckle and ultimately collapse.

He had said all this in his powerful voice and then, finally, he had come to the real purpose of the meeting. He told his deputies how he intended to remove "one more barrier to the restoration of Communism Militant: United States Senator Thomas Bowen Chandler."

Metrinko had followed Chandler's investigation from the beginning, and from the beginning he had treated it seriously. He had carefully studied the dossiers of every member of the Senate Intelligence Committee and he knew Chandler to be one of the brightest, hardest-working, and most ambitious. Equally, he knew Chandler had too much at stake not to treat the subject of terrorism seriously. With the authority to demand files and documents, to interview and if necessary subpoena witnesses, Chandler could look almost anywhere. And when one lifted the lid on a snakepit, one never knew what might crawl out.

Metrinko had carefully and methodically developed his contacts with terrorist organizations. Working through KGB channels, he had identified the most driven, the most radical, members of radical organizations and quietly established his own network of agents and informers. Once their trustworthiness had been unmistakably established, he and his small group of followers had planned and coordinated assassinations. But all these efforts, as well as his creation of a new drug market to finance the operation, involved the connivance of a growing body of untrustworthy people. He had been forced to conclude that enough tracks now existed for Chandler to stumble across at least one. One set of tracks would lead to another, and sooner or later the entire scheme could be traced back to Colonel Cyril Metrinko.

If that should happen, then the universal discredit brought down on his cause would weaken the case for militant communism and strengthen the hands of the détentists.

Chandler had become a problem. He had been sighted and then lost in Amsterdam. A wiretap had turned up a call from a disaffected, and therefore dangerous, international assassin. Very bad business. Chandler was getting much too close.

The deputies nodded in agreement.

The man was a menace and had to be dealt with. But simple assassination would make Chandler a martyr. It would be attributed to his investigation. That meant that others would pick up the effort where Chandler left off. Even more trouble would ensue. No, something infinitely more subtle was required.

The deputies agreed.

Metrinko had found a solution to the problem posed by Thomas Chandler, a solution that in one bold masterstroke would dispose of the senator and further the cause of conflict. He revealed it now to his deputies, who saw at once both the cunning and the feasibility of the plan.

Only one final step remained before the wheels were set in motion: Metrinko must go before President Drachinsky to sell his scheme to the Kremlin.

Wednesday, June 24

47 Glancing often in her rearview mirror, Elaine followed the circuitous route Trevor had dictated. Since her duties took her regularly from the Committee offices to the CIA anyway, she didn't understand why on this particular evening she had to worry about being followed. Mafia? KGB? FBI? CIA? She didn't know and she no longer cared. She could barely think beyond what she would be doing in the next few minutes. She was almost past fear now. To keep her sanity, to be any good to herself or to Tom or her father or to anyone else, she had to do it.

She pulled to a stop at the eastern guardhouse of the Central Intelligence Agency in Langley, Virginia, and handed her Senate credentials to the guard. He took them into the stone and glass guardhouse, checked a clipboard, examined her identification, turned to glance at her face, and then returned with a visitor's pass for her windshield. As he started to give directions to the main building, she sped off down the familiar road to the main office building. It was past seven and she was late.

Elaine pushed open a glass door to the office building where she had once worked with considerable patriotic and professional pride. Passing through clearance procedures with the guards at the lobby checkpoint, she felt distinctly unpatriotic and unprofessional. Back came her recurrent desire to bolt, to return as fast as she could to a simpler, cleaner world.

Elaine's access to certain CIA files on terrorism had been granted ostensibly in connection with the Chandler investigation, but primarily to give her entrée to Agency headquarters at odd hours. Now she had merely to call the Director's private number, tell his executive secretary his pictures were developed and would be delivered at a particular hour, and she was cleared through to his office with only Mrs. Brinkley the wiser.

This evening, as usual, Mrs. Brinkley occupied the Director's outer suite alone. She gestured Elaine into Trevor's office with a frown. Mrs. Brinkley disapproved of Elaine's age and beauty, but mostly of her immediate access to the Director on what clearly was one of the few high-level projects Mrs. Brinkley did not know about.

The door was closed and, Elaine was sure, the tape recorder activated. Trevor offered her a sherry, which she declined.

She began without ceremony: "Chandler's in trouble. The closer we get to the connection between narcotics trading and terrorism, and the linkage between the Mafia and the Soviet Union, the greater becomes his personal danger. I know the mob has tried either to bribe him or blackmail him through his former father-in-law.

"Now Chandler's on the trail of QJWIN. He thinks if he can locate QJWIN he can somehow persuade him to confess that whoever hired him to carry out the Agency's Executive Action plans more than twenty years ago was connected to the Kennedy assassination."

Elaine watched Trevor closely. Except for a remote flame in his deep-set eyes, and the slight exasperated shrug he gave every time this subject came up, she saw nothing. He waited patiently, his hands folded primly on his desk. Elaine suddenly realized how much the desk resembled an operating table.

"Anyway, on Sunday, Chandler suddenly took off for Amsterdam. He seemed to think he could locate QJWIN there—as if maybe he'd had a tip. I tried to find out what the rush was, or whom he'd talked to, or even whether I could go. But he said no. On some things"—Elaine looked down at her lap—"on some things he won't talk, even to me."

The calculator in Trevor's mind was clicking over furiously.

"He did call me early this morning to tell me what he'd learned," Elaine went on. "He'd just finished having lunch with some Englishman who said he was a journalist. He called himself Simpson. Chandler said he was a phony and that he sounded like a Soviet mouthpiece."

As usual, Trevor was ahead of her. *So the Russians are using him again. Curious. They dropped him for years. Must be hard-pressed.*

"Whether Chandler ever got together with QJWIN over there or not I can't say," Elaine continued.

Neither can I, for sure, Trevor thought wryly. *He got away from us in Amsterdam. But that last phone call sounded as though he did.*

"He won't talk," she said, fighting the betraying catch in her voice. "I think he feels he's in so deep he can't trust anyone, including me."

With the insight that had saved his life on several occasions early in his career and that he hoped would save his career as DCI, Trevor reached a conclusion. *It had to happen,* he thought. *Now she's in love, and he no longer trusts her, poor paranoid bastard.* Trevor knew that Elaine's utility to him was at an end.

"So here he is. Mafia on one side. Soviets on the other. Finally, Mr. Trevor, he now suspects you as well. He's asking me more and more about the Agency. He wants to know everything he can find out about you, and particularly your career in the late fifties and early sixties. I think he believes he's found a trail that may lead right to the Agency's doorstep. He's very close to piecing together a scenario in which Executive Action generally and AMLASH in particular led to the assassination of President Kennedy. I think he believes he's found the key."

Her voice rising, she added, "Is that why everyone in the world is trying to shut Tom Chandler up? Because he may uncover the big secret?"

The flame flickered again deep in Trevor's eyes. Elaine drew a short breath. She had never been so afraid in her life. She feared for herself, but mostly for Chandler. She thought, almost irrationally, that if she put all the cards on Trevor's desk—including some aces she wasn't even sure Chandler held—it might frighten Trevor off.

But Trevor was ahead of her, unsurprised and unafraid. He knew that everything hung on Chandler's credibility, and that was eroding fast. Nor, Trevor knew, could there be any conclusive evidence without actual testimony from QJWIN.

"I don't know whether you're trying to protect the Agency or yourself, Mr. Trevor. But I know that I'm through with the whole filthy business. I quit. You find out what Tom Chandler's up to on your own. Wiretap him. Bug him. Put someone else in his bed if you can." She was weeping with anger now. "I quit."

Trevor touched a button on his console and asked Mrs. Brinkley to get a glass of water and an aspirin for Elaine. Then, in a most uncharacteristic display of cold fury, he began to speak rapidly: "So you quit. The apple falls close to the tree. You're no better than your father."

Elaine gasped. "What do you know about my father?" She almost screamed the words.

"Oh, I know a great deal, Elaine. His name was Immanuel Sanchez and he betrayed his country. And I pray to God that he is dead. He deserved execution for his treason."

But the letter— The words started to form in Elaine's mind, but she bit them back. *Maybe Trevor really doesn't know about it.* She grabbed the edge of his desk, something solid to hold on to in a reeling world. Faintly she could hear Trevor's voice going on and on.

". . . the most despicable man I have ever had the misfortune to know. That was your father, Elaine. Like father, like daughter. You say you have quit? It's not that easy in this business. It wasn't for your father, and it won't be for you."

She looked up into those hard eyes and somehow took strength from them. When Mrs. Brinkley came in, Elaine waved aside the glass. She stood up and walked out of Trevor's office. She could hear him issuing instructions behind her, and in a moment a security man was at her elbow, walking her out of the building and to her car. As she turned out of the horseshoe drive, she saw him get into a compact black car. It stayed in her rearview mirror all the way to her house, then drove off.

She went to the kitchen and dialed a number written on the little blackboard next to the phone. It would be close, but she would be able to see Tom tonight before she escaped.

PART FIVE

So, hidden in his hocus-pocus,
There lies the gift of double focus,
That magic lamp which looks so dull
And utterly impractical.
Yet, if Aladdin use it right,
Can be a Sesame to light.

48

Wednesday, June 24

THE BIG, BIRD-NOSED PLANE taxied up to the Dulles terminal at 7:00 P.M. Chandler shook his head as he reset his watch to Washington time. It was hard to get used to landing somewhere several hours *earlier* than you had taken off. A scrawled message was handed to him by a gate attendant: *Please call Mr. O'Brien at his apt. Urgent.*

Urgent or not, he was so tired he decided to let it go until morning. But, passing a bank of telephones on his way to pick up his luggage, he changed his mind. It would take at least fifteen minutes for his bags to arrive and another ten to clear customs. He dialed O'Brien's number. No answer.

While he waited wearily at the baggage-claim area, Chandler heard his name being paged on the public address system. He picked up a courtesy phone. "Senator Chandler," a voice said, "we just received a call from a Miss Elaine Dunham. She asked that you meet her at the Eastern Airlines Terminal at National Airport as soon as possible. She's leaving for New York on the nine o'clock shuttle and says it is urgent she speak with you before she leaves."

Chandler hung up and cursed under his breath. Even more than he wanted to see Elaine, he wanted to go home and crawl into bed. But it must be really important for Elaine to have tracked him down here. *And why the hell is she going to New York on a Wednesday night? Has something happened to her mother, or Betty? Or is it the investigation?*

The bags were delayed in arriving at the claims area. Chandler shifted his weight onto his right leg, then onto his left. He kept glancing anxiously at his watch. Finally his luggage appeared on the snakelike conveyor belt. He pushed between a woman and her young daughter, apologizing as he grabbed his bags. He strode quickly toward one of the customs officials and handed him his diplomatic passport.

"How long were you in Europe?" the officer asked, pretending to take no special notice of Chandler's senatorial status.

"Four days."

"Anything to declare?"

Chandler shook his head, trying to look less impatient than he was. Since his election to the Senate, he'd never had his baggage inspected, and he didn't want to give this man an excuse to show how impartial he could be in carrying out his duties. "No. Nothing. Unfortunately, the trip was strictly business."

The official continued to flip through the passport noting the stamps of all the countries Chandler had visited in the last two years. Then, with an air of calculated indifference, he closed it, handed it back to Chandler, and motioned him through the gate.

Chandler looked up at the large digital clock over the exit. It was 7:52 P.M. *Damn*, he swore to himself, *it's going to be close.* He headed for the taxi stand at a run.

A battered blue Mustang came tearing up to the front of the taxi line. The driver jumped out and when he saw Chandler, a look of relief spread across his face. It was O'Brien. "Senator. Jesus, I'm glad I caught you. Listen," he said, picking up Chandler's bags and tossing them into the back seat of his car, "there's something I've got to discuss with you. It's about the Committee and it can't wait."

He opened the passenger door and motioned Chandler in, ran around to the driver's side, and sped away from the terminal before Chandler could muster a word. He was bone-tired, but he wanted to see Elaine.

"Kevin, I've got to get to National Airport. Elaine's leaving on the nine o'clock shuttle, and she needs to talk to me tonight."

The way Chandler sat forward in his seat told O'Brien to hurry. O'Brien didn't take his eyes off the road as he roared off the ramp and headed down the Dulles Airport access highway. An accident had closed route 66 southbound. It was thirteen miles to route 123 in McLean, Virginia, he figured, and from there, another seventeen miles to National Airport. O'Brien shot a glance at his rearview mirror. Traffic was light. There were no signs of police vehicles. "Okay," he said. "I'll get you there in time. But there's something I have to tell you . . . about Elaine."

O'Brien began slowly. He told Chandler what had prompted his investigation—the leak about the neuron exchanger—and then he told him what he had learned from the bank.

"I can't prove it. But she's on someone's payroll. Maybe the Soviets."

Chandler said nothing. He breathed deeply and stared at the windshield wipers as they clicked methodically against the glass, against his mind, rhythmically repeating *someone's payroll, someone's payroll.*

He wanted to scream at O'Brien. *Who in hell asked you to investigate members of the staff? You're supposed to be investigating terrorism and drug dealers. Now you suspect . . .* Chandler had to clench his teeth to keep his thoughts from jumping out.

He had a sudden and terrible conviction that O'Brien was right. *She is seeking another kind of truth.* Elaine had been in on the investigation from the very beginning. She knew so much. . . . Christ, he had even told her about the threat from Fouchette! Maybe she had passed that on to the KGB! Maybe it wasn't Fouchette's thugs who beat him that night. And Simpson. How else could Simpson have known about the blackmail threat?

"She's a plant, Tom," O'Brien said. He told of going to Gloucester, learning the name Immanuel Sanchez, and then, in desperation, asking Craig Delvin to check the name through the Intelligence Committee files.

"I wanted information fast, and I knew I could get it from him. I figured that Sanchez, given the time frame, was somehow involved in the Bay of Pigs, and that Delvin, being a right-wing nut who still fumes about the Bay of Pigs, would have something. He did."

Chandler stiffened in the passenger's seat. He felt as if a knife was being twisted in his gut. But whose hand was on the knife? *Not Elaine's. Not my lovely Elaine. . . .*

O'Brien went on, his voice hard. "Delvin said that Sanchez was a double agent, recruited by our side out of the Cuban DGI. He slipped out of Cuba just before the Bay of Pigs and was stationed in Florida. I assume that's where he met Elaine's mother, but I didn't mention anything about Elaine to Delvin. I just said that the name had cropped up. Anyway, Sanchez apparently got turned again by the Cubans and tipped off Castro to the invasion. Then he disappeared, and the assumption is that he's dead. Could have been killed by either side."

"Or he could be very much alive."

"Why do you say that? Why don't you sound surprised?" O'Brien asked.

"Shock comes easier to me these days than surprise, Kevin. Where does Elaine fit into the Sanchez story?"

"Blackmail after she got into the Agency? Soviet recruitment through Cuban connections? I don't know. But it's going to be easy to find the answers when someone stumbles on this the way I did."

"Trevor?"

"Sure. Maybe he even knows already. Or the FBI. Or both. This is very, very big trouble. She is getting paid for something— at best, for leaking to somebody. I say Soviet plant." O'Brien avoided the word *spy*.

O'Brien felt uncomfortable inside Chandler's silence. He reached over and snapped on the radio.

Chandler continued to worry at his pain. *Maybe she's not even American.* He had seen a file on a young woman from South Africa who had burned up the Washington society pages in the early seventies, dating diplomats and congressmen. *Turned out she was a spy for the Cubans. . . . God, think about what it would mean for Moscow to have a direct line into the Senate Intelligence Committee. How incredibly easy it would be to set up. How easy it would be to walk out of the Senate with our top secrets in her briefcase or in her beautiful head. . . .*

His mind kept looking for an escape from this inexorable logic, the terrible voice that said Elaine had betrayed him, the investigation, everything. "The security checks," he said. "It would have shown up. She never would have been cleared with her father—"

"Her father of record was Jim Dunham. He legally adopted her. Her birth certificate will say that. My sister adopted a kid, and she showed me the birth certificate. It has her name and my brother-in-law's name on it. The kid's original birth certificate is officially nonexistent. Adoptees' records are sealed, and in most states the original birth certificate can't be found. There would be no record of Sanchez being her father. And her mother can't talk."

"I know that, Kevin," Chandler said sharply. "She told me that. She got her mother out of a state-run home and put her in a private place on Long Island. Why would she tell me that if she was trying to hide something?"

"Those private places cost a lot of money, Senator."

How much did he really know about her, anyway? Chandler asked himself. The few times they had talked at all about her childhood and background, she had been vague. He had assumed she had a reason not to talk about her past. *She certainly did*, he thought.

"When we get to National," Chandler said, "I want you to stay in the car. I want to talk to her alone." He turned up the volume on the radio, slumped down in the seat, and closed his eyes. He didn't want to talk—or think—anymore.

A fine mist was swirling across the riverside runways when they reached the airport. The midsummer twilight was as dark as night in the low overcast.

As soon as Chandler walked into the enclosed, seldom-used observation roof of the main terminal building, Elaine rushed toward him. She was dressed in jeans and a raincoat. She looked like a Botticelli, he thought. She had never looked more beautiful—or more desperate.

"Thank God you were able to make it," she said, throwing her arms around him. The reverse-engine roar of the arriving jets almost drowned out her words.

Chandler stiffened slightly in her embrace and she drew back, searching his face.

"What's wrong?"

"Kevin tells me you've been keeping a secret."

"What do you mean?"

"You've been moonlighting."

"What?"

"For Christ's sake, Elaine, don't make this worse than it is. You've been spying on the Committee, spying on me. And getting a nice monthly salary for it."

"Oh, Tom." Elaine put her arms around him, but he pulled away. Tears welled in her eyes. "I've been eaten up by this. I wanted to tell you before, but I . . . I couldn't."

So it was true. He'd hoped against hope that she'd have some explanation, but . . .

"I've been spying for Trevor. I've been reporting on you and the investigation all along. I haven't told him everything, but I've told him a lot. Whatever I told him or didn't tell him, the point is I've deceived you. Tom, I'm so sorry. I'm so sorry. I can't tell you how sorry I am. . . ." The tears were streaming down her face now.

Chandler was stunned. The revelations were coming too thick and fast to absorb. "I don't get it," he said. "You've been spying for *Trevor*? What the hell are you talking about?"

The wind was gathering force now, pounding against the windows. It would be a rough flight to New York.

Elaine turned away, wiping her eyes. "At the beginning, I was convinced it was right. Trevor told me it was necessary, to protect the intelligence community. I got into it without really thinking it through—what I was really doing. Then when I began to realize what it was—spying, actual spying, on you, and the Committee, the Senate—I was in so deep. But I've gotten out. I've—"

"Elaine, shut up a minute. Do you mean that son of a bitch Trevor planted you on the Committee? That he penetrated our Committee and the investigation from the very beginning? I can't believe it! That sanctimonious, sleazy, buttoned-down shit. I'm going to nail his ass to the wall."

"Tom, the plane's leaving. I have to go. I quit tonight. I told Trevor. It was horrible. Horrible. I'm frightened. But I feel strong too. I'm going to New York and try to figure things out. My sister's graduating from school next weekend. We'll go somewhere together. I'll . . . if you want me to . . I'll call you." She began to cry again.

Chandler's emotions were warring within him. It was impossible to think, to talk. He had come to the airport believing that Elaine had sold information to the Soviets. Now she was saying that she had betrayed him to Trevor. He was furious with Trevor. And he felt bitter disappointment with Elaine, but at the same time, he wanted to comfort her, relieve her grief, her self-disgust. He remained silent.

Elaine buried her face in his shoulder. He held her tight. He could feel her body shake with sobs.

"Tom, I'm sorry. This whole business . . . I'm afraid of something for the first time in my life, and I don't know why. I quit, Tom." She gave a shaky little laugh. "I told Trevor to take his job and shove it. Please believe me, Tom."

He took her wet face in his hands and looked deep into her pleading eyes. He bent his head and kissed her long and tenderly.

"I love you, Tom."

He cradled her in his arms. "I need to sort this out, Elaine." He took her shoulders and held her at arm's distance. "Just tell me this," he said. "Why did Trevor do it? What is he trying to find out?"

"I don't know. Originally, everything. Then, I think, the Kennedy assassination. Something to do with that."

"And your father? Immanuel Sanchez? Did he want to know about him?"

"My God, Tom! Tonight. Only tonight. He told me my father was a traitor and hoped—prayed—that he had been executed. But I got a letter from my father. I don't understand. . . . I don't understand."

She pulled away and ran toward the stairs leading to the shuttle. A clock on the wall showed three minutes to nine. At the top of the stairs she turned, looked at Tom for a moment, and disappeared behind the stairwell barrier.

Chandler gazed through the dark window at the streaking lights of a plane coming in for a landing. The runway glistened. The mist had turned to rain.

Thursday, June 25

49 When the phone rang at 1:30 A.M., Chandler was only half asleep. He was expecting Elaine to call. Instead, he heard O'Brien's voice. Chandler listened, exhausted, his mind still in turmoil. Why the hell was O'Brien calling him at this hour? Then the voice began to penetrate.

He started to speak, but stopped as abruptly as if his tongue had been severed. He listened. O'Brien had been watching the late news. *Always watching the news or reading the news. Day and night and early . . . Chandler's numbed brain clutched at irrelevancies.*

His lips began to move, but no words came out. At last he found his voice. "You're sure? You checked? The shuttle? It was the shuttle?" A thin line of pain began behind his forehead. "No survivors? . . . Damn . . . Damn . . . No, no. I'm all right."

Slowly, methodically, O'Brien gave him the details. The plane first was reported missing. He saw that report in a bulletin on

Nightline. Then he started working the phone. The airline said the plane was unreported. He called the FAA emergency office. They told him the plane went down off Atlantic City. A fisherman had heard an explosion. He saw it hit—or saw the flash. When he got there, he turned his lights on a lot of debris. He radioed the Coast Guard. The duty officer told O'Brien there was no sign of survivors. "He said," O'Brien explained, "that there couldn't be anybody alive after a crash like that."

"Yes," Chandler said. "Yes. Thanks for calling, Kevin. . . . Yes. Good night."

Chandler lowered the receiver onto the cradle.

Dead. All dead. Oh, God, how could you let this happen? How? A sob began to grow in his chest. He fell back into his empty bed.

I never told her that I loved her.

Only parts of eighteen identifiable bodies were found. Investigators said the indications were that there had been an explosion in the air. Not enough wreckage to establish a definite cause. The investigation would go on, but . . . The disaster went into the task force's incident file as a probable act of terrorism, but only Tom Chandler and Kevin O'Brien knew why.

Selecting a place for a memorial service was a problem. Washington was not really Elaine's home, as it was not the home of so many who came—and went. But there was no other place. No one was left in Massachusetts. Paul had been adopted by a Gloucester family who had moved to Illinois. Betty was in New York—and, Chandler thought, she would be on her own as a teenager, only a little older than Elaine had been. From teenager to woman overnight. Chandler sent her some flowers, with a note offering help if she had need of it.

He made arrangements for the service to be held in the Washington Cathedral's Chapel of Saint Joseph, directly beneath the Crossing. In the back, huddled near one of the great pillars, were a few senators from the Intelligence Committee and some other staff people, mostly women. The priest was a woman, too. *Elaine would have liked that*, Chandler thought.

Betty was there with a tall, thin young man. She had told her mother of Elaine's death, but no understanding had lit the vacant eyes. Paul's parents had not permitted him to come. Kevin O'Brien, Maude Duberstein, Clarissa Logan, and Tom Chandler sat in the pew behind Betty and her boyfriend. Margie and her husband were with Ned Dempsey in the row behind the task force staff.

The priest stood before a painting of the Entombment of Christ. "Unto Almighty God we commend the soul of Elaine Dunham," she said. "And to her family we say . . ."

Chandler had been seated at the end of the pew. As he turned up the aisle to leave at the end of the service, he saw a man slip out of the last pew and walk rapidly out of the chapel. There was something familiar about the stocky, scurrying figure, but Chandler lacked the will to follow him.

He stood aside until all the others had gone. Then he walked out alone. Going down the Cathedral's broad steps, he wished the day had been gray. But the sun hung like a gold medallion against the deep blue of a June sky.

Chandler was tempted to call a press conference, to blame Trevor for the explosion and mass death. But he had no proof of anything. The press corps would probably think him mad. *And perhaps I am.* He thought of driving out to Langley, bursting in on Trevor and confronting him directly. He would beat the truth out of him if necessary. But that idea was as insane as the first. Assuming he could get by the guards at the gate and in the lobby, the security people would be on him before he got halfway past Mrs. Brinkley's desk.

Besides, the more he thought about it, it was just as plausible an explanation that the Soviets had planted the bomb. If they knew about his meeting with Danielle, they undoubtedly knew about his involvement with Elaine. Or, it might have been the Mafia, hoping to get at Chandler through someone he cared about. . . .

But why would *anyone* blow up a plane and kill eighty-two people if all they wanted was one? If they wanted to kill Elaine, why not put a bullet in the back of her head one night while she was going home? Maybe just to show how ruthless they are, how big the stakes are . . . Maybe, it was just an accident. Like Howard Hunt's wife. A coincidence . . .

50

For the next week, every time Chandler closed his eyes, the nightmare was there. In his mind he imagined he heard the explosion, the shriek of steel spinning through the night, spilling carnage into the sea. What was Elaine doing during those final seconds? Did she scream? Or pray? Did she hold the hand of the stranger next to her? Did she cry out for him. . . . ?

He tried sleeping pills, painkillers, whiskey. Nothing worked. He would lie there in the darkness and feel himself slipping back into the horror of his thoughts, like a drowning man going under. He would kick and struggle to pull his head above the water line, the terror line. He would open his eyes and try to orient himself in the dark room. Always, after a few minutes, he would slip back again.

Elaine's death was not the whole of his waking nightmare. For the first time in his life he had been thrust into recognition of his own weakness, his egotism and smug conceit. How could he have allowed his outrage at Elaine's betrayal prevent him from telling her that he forgave her, that he understood? Yes, that he loved her, and that was all that really mattered. He had always waited too long to say what he really felt, even to admit it to himself. It was a politician's affliction, he told himself, but in these tortured hours, it seemed a pitiful excuse.

A week after the memorial service, he came home from another day of trying to work in the emptiness of the holiday-weekend office and began what had become a ritual. He filled a glass with scotch and drank it in one long swallow. His throat felt as if it were on fire, an image that had been filling his mind. He poured another full glass, this time over ice cubes he took from a barren refrigerator. He sipped this drink, then set it on a table next to a chair in his den. He sat down and drank. He got up, repeated the procedure, and returned to the chair.

The silence in the house became a sound—a high-pitched ringing in his ears. He began to hear more and more sounds: the whir of the air conditioning, the ice cubes cracking in the glass, the brush of a pine branch against a window.

His thoughts fluttered like phantom bats, brushing his mind with their dark wings. He thought of death, and then could hardly think at all. He felt bloodless.

The photographs on the walls of the den were whirling. He sat up in the chair, shook his head, blinked his eyes. He reached for something far away, the television set, and with an effort turned it on. There was a blur of color, a murmur of sounds Chandler could not understand. He drifted.

From somewhere came a new sound. He thought he recognized it and waited for it to come again. Nothing. *What was it?* He struggled to his feet and walked unsteadily to the front door. *The chimes.* Someone had rung the front door's chimes. He had a visitor. He laughed and flung open the door.

No one was there.

Chandler fumbled for a switch. The lanterns on either side of the door bathed the porch in soft light. A van was just pulling away from the curb. Chandler could read FEDERAL EXPRESS emblazoned on its side.

On the stiff bristles of the doormat was a large white, orange, and blue Federal Express envelope. He picked it up and closed the door. He wondered vaguely why the delivery was made so late at night and why the driver hadn't waited for him to sign the delivery receipt.

But there was no delivery receipt. There was only a name neatly lettered in the corner of the envelope: STANISLAUS LEC, the name he used to contact Memory.

Chandler went into the kitchen, measured out enough coffee and water for eight cups, switched on the automatic coffee maker, and opened the envelope. He took out a thick file folder and opened it on the kitchen table. The first page of the file was a plain sheet of paper. Taped to it was a five-by-four-inch card that read: INFORMATION COMPLIMENTS OF TWO FRIENDS. BE AT THE CHURCH YOU CAN SEE FROM YOUR WINDOW. 9 O'CLOCK TOMORROW NIGHT.

Two friends. Memory and.   ? In Amsterdam, QJWIN had

spoken of a memoir "after what I hope will be my natural death."
Chandler wondered if QJWIN had died, and if his death had been
natural.

Chandler lifted the blank piece of paper, and out of the words
on the page below, one emerged: *Rizzuli.*

Tuesday, July 7

51

"Are you still alive?" The buoyant voice of Doug
Bender interrupted the drone of another senator making a speech on the Senate floor. Chandler, slumped in his chair,
had been thinking about the manuscript he had spent most of the
night reading. When he had finally gone to bed, he had slept immediately, without dreams of horror and shame, and he had awakened
feeling refreshed from only three hours of sleep.

Doug dropped into the chair beside him. "Where've you been
the last few weeks? We were about to call for a special election up
there in Connecticut to fill this seat. It's a damn good thing you
decided to show up again—if nothin' else, just so we could recollect
what you looked like."

Doug Bender was so popular in his home state of Alabama that
some said he could be elected to any office he wanted—for life.
Although he constantly complained that his moderate voting record
would lead to his recall and hanging, he had the ease of manner
shared by the politically secure.

"If you don't mind me sayin' so, you look lower than whale
shit. I've seen happier people than you at their own execution. Say,
did you hear about this fella that was so miserable he was gonna
jump off a bridge? He'd been fired from his job, his wife ran away
with the mailman, and he was heavy into Atari stock. So there he
was, ready to jump, when this car pulled up and a woman jumped
out and yelled, 'Wait, wait, don't jump, I can help you.' She was
the ugliest woman he'd ever seen, but he got down to see what she
had to say. Well, she says, 'I'm a witch and I can give you any
three wishes you want.' And he says, 'What's the catch?' And she
says 'You have to make love to me.'"

Characteristically, Doug began laughing at his own joke. This amused Chandler even more than Doug's stories. The funnier Doug found his jokes, the more Tom enjoyed them.

"So this guy says, *ha ha hahaha;* he says, 'Okay, I'll do it.' And she says, 'Tell me your three wishes.' He says, 'Bring my wife back from the mailman.' She says, 'Done.' And he says, 'Get my job back.' And she says, 'Done.' Then he says, 'I want a portfolio of sure-fire growth stock.' And she says, 'Done. Now get in my car and let's go to my place for the rest of the deal.' So the guy goes with her, and he is holding his nose because she is *really* ugly. *Ha ha ha.*

"So afterwards she drives him back to the bridge where she found him and he says, 'When do I start getting my wishes?' And she says, 'How old did you say you were?' And he says, 'How old? What's that got to do with anything? I'm thirty-five.' And she says, *aha aha;* she says, 'Thirty-five. That's pretty old to believe in witches.'"

Doug doubled over in his chair, his face contorted. If Chandler hadn't known him so well, he might have suspected a heart attack. Several visitors in the galleries pointed at his quaking figure and nudged their neighbors. Doug wheezed and spluttered, trying to smother his laughter. ". . . pretty old to believe in witches!"

His foolishness was ordinarily sufficient to bring responsive laughter from Chandler. But this time, Chandler only smiled fleetingly.

Aware that his strategy hadn't worked, Doug grew serious. "Now, Tom, what's up? There are still one or two of us around here—I couldn't honestly say more than that—who give a damn about what's going on with you. What can you tell me about this woolly investigation of yours?"

Around them droned the desultory debate over the foreign aid appropriations bill. Senator Warren Henson of Indiana was proposing, in his most earnest, houndlike way, an amendment prohibiting abortion in any nation receiving foreign assistance from the United States.

Chandler genuinely appreciated his colleague's concern, but he knew Doug well enough to realize a full disclosure would convince him his old friend had gone crazy.

"Doug, I really didn't intend to get so deep into this thing. I sure didn't intend to let it wreck my political career. When I first got the idea, in fact, I saw it as an opportunity. You know how restless I've been. The last thing any politician wants to do is get lost in the shuffle—except when a tough one comes, when almost all of us run for cover." Chandler stood up. "Let's get out of here." In the background, Warren Henson's voice waxed eloquent on the evils of abortion, sex, and liberalism.

The two men walked out the east door of the Senate chamber and down the long flight of steps. The guard held up traffic as they crossed the east parking area and started around the oval sidewalk surrounding the green behind the Senate building. This was Chandler's favorite place to clear his thoughts between votes or during a particularly slow debate.

"Tom, the problem is that too many people just think you've gone off the deep end on this thing. It's a mystery to them how anyone with your talent and range of interests could become so damn preoccupied with any single issue—even as glamorous and exciting a one as this."

Doug puffed on his ever-present Anthony & Cleopatra Grenadier as if trying to see how fast he could burn it down. "I've had people—people who are not your enemies—come up to me and say they think you've become some kind of fanatic. They're concerned. They don't know what's going on. Well, I tell 'em I don't know either, but I trust your judgment—that you're too smart to go off on some tangent. But let me tell you, my friend, this town will eat you alive if you keep on this way.

"Ordinarily, our system squeezes out zealots—and that's the way it should be. But right now too many people think this terrorism thing has made you kind of wacky. Now the only thing that's saved you so far is the fact that you've been quiet. If you start going on television or giving interviews, that'll be it. The boys in white coats will show up with one of those jackets with endless sleeves."

"Doug, I know you're right and I appreciate your advice," Chandler said. "But I can't quit now. I've gone too far—and frankly, just between us, I'm too close to something really big to back off. I know it's hard to understand, but this is the first thing in my life I've ever believed in besides myself and my own career.

"I know this will sound corny, and I wouldn't say it to anyone but you, but what I'm finding out is important to the country. I've run across some stuff that's downright scary, and it has to be brought out."

Doug stood still. "Obviously, I don't know what you're talking about specifically, Tom, and I'm not so sure I want to." He shrugged. "But if you're onto something that big, you better get some help, boy. I don't think you're crazy or I wouldn't be here talking to you. But if you're into some kind of briar patch, you'd better turn this whole thing over to the CIA or the FBI. You're no one-man army. You gotta look out for yourself."

"I wish I could, Doug. But it's not that simple." The two men resumed their stroll.

"Frankly, somebody at the top of the CIA is in this."

Doug looked startled.

"So I can't really trust anyone over there. And the FBI is so paranoid about the Russians they can't make any distinctions—particularly not the kind required by this investigation. This is not a crusade, Doug, and it's sure not turning into a career—even if I want it to, which I don't. I know my limits, believe me. And I'm very near them."

Chandler's voice grew hoarse, and he came to a halt on the sidewalk. "It's been particularly hard in the last few days because . . . Elaine Dunham was killed."

"That was a terrible thing," Doug said. "I thought you two maybe had something going . . ." He saw that Chandler's eyes were glistening with held-back tears. "Hey, man, what's going on?" He put his arm around Tom's shoulders. "You really did care about her, didn't you? Kathy told me you said something about . . . Hey, Tom, I'm sorry. I'm so very sorry. I didn't mean to stick my nose into something that wasn't my business."

Chandler regained control of himself and looked his friend straight in the eye. "You're going to think I'm crazy and maybe I am. But I think Elaine's death wasn't an accident. I think someone or some group took her out. I know she was directed to penetrate my investigation from the beginning by the Agency."

"Trevor?" Doug blurted. "Come on, Tom. That *is* paranoid. He's not that stupid."

"It isn't paranoid, Doug. Elaine told me about it before she died. And it isn't stupid of him if he has something terrible to hide. I believe he's scared enough, and has enough to be scared about, to have tried to penetrate a congressional investigation. The stakes in this business couldn't be higher. They seem to be even high enough to kill."

Doug put his arm around Tom's shoulders again and urged him into motion. "Tom," he said, as they walked, "I'd do anything I can to help you. I just don't know how. Except to tell you to give it up. Get out—now. Go back up to Connecticut. Build up that base again. You're still one of the great white hopes of this town."

Chandler looked up at a vertical string of lights in the right-hand window of the Senate building that indicated a roll-call vote was in progress. The two men headed for the chamber. "Doug, I hear you. And coming from you, believe me, it means a lot. But I told you this wasn't a crusade, and I meant it. Nothing would make me happier than to get out. But I can't, not until this investigation is over with. I just have to look into a few more things and talk to a couple more people, and then I'll issue a report. What the Senate, or the President, or the CIA, or the FBI chooses to do with it then is up to them.

"But I'll tell you this. It will be a *public* report, and a lot of people don't want that. A lot of people. What I know and what I believe are too important to collect dust in some classified committee file. And I'm at the point where leaking is too ridiculous and juvenile."

They had reached the top of the steps to the Senate, and their colleagues were beginning to pass them in the rush to vote. Chandler pulled Doug behind a marble pillar. He suddenly realized they stood only a few feet from where the 1983 bomb had gone off.

"I have only one favor to ask, Doug. Some pretty vicious things are going to be said about me in the next couple of weeks. My sanity, my integrity, and probably my loyalty are going to be questioned. It will get *very* rough. I don't expect you to stick up for me. But it will be very important to me to know that you and Kathy don't believe that stuff. All I ask is that *you* trust me. In the long run, it will all turn out right."

For the second time Doug saw moisture in his friend's eyes. "How old are you, Tom?" he asked quizzically, eyebrows raised.

"Forty-eight, Doug. You know that," Chandler said, surprised.

"That's pretty old to believe in witches," Doug whispered.

This time he was not laughing.

Tuesday, July 7

52 After the vote, Chandler returned to his office. Margie met him at the door to say the Director of the FBI wanted Chandler to call him as soon as possible. Chandler told her to put the call through and went into his own office, wondering why Schumacher wanted to speak to him.

The phone rang, and Margie told him the Director was on the line. Chandler was surprised that the who-waits-on-the-line game had gone his way. *Schumacher must need my vote for something,* he thought.

"Good afternoon, Judge," Chandler said. "Caught any fine Wisconsin trout lately?"

"I very much need to see you, Senator."

Edwin Schumacher was not known in Washington as a raconteur, but he had an affable manner. It was unusual for him not to chat at least for a moment before getting to business.

Chandler's guard went up. "What can I do for you?"

"I would like to talk to you, in your office, as soon as possible, Senator."

Senator was strange too. The last time Schumacher had spoken to Chandler, it had been *Tom.* The tapes are rolling, Chandler figured.

"Walk in when you get here, Judge. I'll clear the calendar for you."

"I'll be there in fifteen minutes."

Chandler called in Ned Dempsey, who had remarked earlier that morning that Chandler was acting like his old self again. Chandler hadn't told Dempsey about the envelope or its contents. But he knew that the arrival of the manuscript had transformed him. He could feel life surging back within him.

Ned's back to normal too, Chandler thought when Dempsey entered the room. He seemed cocky again, no longer compelled to defer to his boss's depression. Chandler told him about Schumacher's request for an immediate appointment and asked if Dempsey had any ideas about what might be behind it.

Dempsey drummed a pencil on the yellow pad in his lap. "This isn't one of his courtesy calls, that's for sure. It's not appropriations time and the visit wasn't set up by the FBI's congressional liaison guy. Something sensitive?"

"And personal." Chandler added.

Dempsey nodded slowly. His eyes on Chandler's face, he said, "You've been wandering around a bit lately. Anything happen to you that would prove to be embarrassing?"

"Like being caught in a bordello in Amsterdam?" Chandler laughed. "No, Ned. I'm afraid I've been terribly discreet lately."

"Then it's the task force. Have you got something on the FBI?"

"No. And it's not likely we will. In fact, the agents in Miami and New Orleans were very helpful."

"You got that FBI visitation over your contact with Luganov. Maybe Schumacher's coming over to apologize." Dempsey smiled at his joke.

With a questioning look, he held up his right hand and made circular motions with his index finger. Chandler shook his head. In Washington sign language, Dempsey had asked if Chandler wanted a tape recorder set up to record the meeting with Schumacher. He couldn't ask the question out loud. The FBI—or someone else— might at that very moment have been taping their own meeting.

Margie showed Schumacher into the office, and he took a seat on the couch opposite Chandler's desk. From his red leather chair on Schumacher's right, Chandler could look past him out the window to the stubby brownstone tower of the church where tonight he would be meeting Memory.

"I'll get right to the point, Senator. I want to know just what you're up to with this task force of yours." Schumacher lit his pipe.

"I think you know the purpose of the investigation, Judge. Terrorism. If you have something specific to ask about some part of the investigation, please do so."

"Now, now, Senator, let's not get huffy. Sometimes I think there are too many investigations going on in this town. We tend to bump into each other." He leaned forward. "For instance, an envelope was delivered to your home last night. I would—"

"Wait a goddam minute, Schumacher," Chandler said. "What

the hell are you doing? How many United States senators do you have under surveillance? And where's your fishing license?"

"*You* are not under surveillance, Senator. Nor are any of your colleagues."

"Well then, how in hell do you know what was delivered to my home last night?" It was more challenge than question. "Unless, of course, you've been watching me, or stalking me, or tapping me, or . . ." Chandler unconsciously rubbed his chest. He decided not to voice another accusation.

"We do watch people and places and we do have crisscrossing inquiries. For instance, we have been keeping a watch on certain items that enter the United States from certain places. Such as Amsterdam. Such as what was delivered to your home."

"So you think I'm a dope peddler? Who tipped you off? Trevor?"

"Director Trevor and I do not have a good working relationship, Senator. I do not believe you are trafficking in narcotics." Schumacher tapped his pipe against the ashtray and sighed. "And I am sure you do not know that you received a phony Federal Express delivery from a stolen Federal Express van. It was found on a Georgetown street this morning."

"That may be interesting to the FBI," Chandler said. "But what I'm interested in is why the FBI had the home of a United States senator under surveillance."

"We had reason to believe that someone on the Committee was leaking information to the Soviets."

"*Had* reason to believe?"

"No. As a matter of fact, still *have*."

"And you thought I was the source—the spy? Why? Because I got a stupid phone call from Boris Luganov? Someone I hadn't seen or talked to in more than five years?"

"No. Actually, we . . ." Schumacher looked away from Chandler and studied the Oriental carpet. "We prompted that call. We were trying to double Luganov. We thought he was ripe to come over to us. We were close. But he was pulled back to Moscow too soon. We may have a shot at him again if he ever gets reassigned here."

"Did you come as close as you came to turning Georgi Tupolev?" Chandler asked contemptuously.

"You don't stop hauling in the nets just because you lose a big one, Senator. Not in fishing and not in this business."

"So you thought you might bait me with your little would-be double agent. Isn't that called entrapment, Judge?"

Schumacher busied himself with his pipe.

Finally, Chandler said, "When I didn't swallow the bait, why did you continue to follow me?"

"Because the leaks kept up and we couldn't rule you out."

"And now?"

"You are no longer . . . We believe we have ruled you out, Senator."

"Thank you very much. Is there anything else?"

"Yes. There is. Something is up, Senator. Something terrible. We are about to become a country besieged. I need—the Bureau needs—all the help we can get. I can't wait until your report is made public if that report has information in it that I can use *now*."

"On what subject, Judge? I told you, I am working on terrorism. I am seeing certain general lines of connection. I can go over them with you if—"

"Drugs, Senator, drugs. We've had forty-four people die in the last three days. In San Francisco, Chicago, Houston . . ."

"Overdosed?"

"No. The drugs were contaminated. Someone mixed strychnine with heroin."

"What's the point? Why would they want to kill their market?"

"We don't know."

"But I don't understand what this has to do with me, Judge."

Schumacher leaned forward and jabbed his pipestem in Chandler's direction. "You said you're investigating terrorism. This may be another form of it. It could be systematic."

"Why systematic? It could just as easily be some nut—"

"We're assuming the worst. God knows what kind of a chain reaction this is going to set off if it is." Schumacher moved closer and grasped Chandler's arm. "All we have been able to find out is that the contaminated shipment originated in Amsterdam." His eyes bored into Chandler's.

"I know nothing, Judge. Nothing. What you're telling me is terrifying. But I've heard nothing on it."

There was no response. "You believe me, don't you?" Chandler asked, trying to keep from his voice the desperation he was feeling in his mind. *He doesn't believe me.*

"That envelope came from Amsterdam. I want to see the contents of that envelope, Senator."

"Not yet, Judge. As soon as I finish my report I'll be happy to turn over that envelope and everything in it. But not yet. I'm sorry."

Chandler stood up. Schumacher stayed where he was, knocking the ashes from his pipe.

"You're playing a dangerous game, Senator," he said at last. "A very dangerous game."

"It is no game, Judge."

"No, Senator. It is more like a war." Schumacher got up and moved to the door. He turned back. "A war," he repeated. "And until now I thought we were on the same side. Good-bye, Senator."

Tuesday, July 7

53 The glass and marble Hart Senate Office Building towers over its brownstone neighbor, Saint Joseph's Church. Chandler looked down at the church from a corner window of his office and wondered how Memory had known of this view. Chandler envisioned him passing the security guards one day, taking the elevator up to the third floor, noting the location of Chandler's suite of offices, and then figuring out what could be seen from the windows. The choice of the church intrigued Chandler— he had so few clues to Memory's identity or life. *Another Catholic rendezvous*, he thought, remembering the darkened convent. *Ex-Cuban, ex-Catholic, ex-what else?*

He had decided to be late. He'd picked up a beer and a take-out dinner from a Chinese restaurant and eaten at his desk in the deserted office. At 8:45 he went to the window and watched until the chimes of the Taft Carillon struck nine times. In those fifteen minutes, a woman in a yellow hat had entered the church; she came out shortly before nine. No one else had entered or left. Chandler gave up at five minutes past the hour. *As I am watching for Memory, he is somewhere watching for me. And I must be first.*

As he mounted the church's steps and went inside, he listened to the echo of his footsteps on the stone floor. He crossed the vestibule into the red-carpeted silence of the sanctuary, walked down the central aisle, and slipped into a pew on the left, about halfway down the nave.

He was alone in the church. On a tall, gleaming holder a votive candle burned, its flame barely visible in the soft light that flowed from recesses high in the ceiling. Chandler wondered if an evening service was scheduled. *If so,* he thought, smiling to himself, *Memory has slipped a bit. He must have expected a darkened church at this hour. I'll be able to see him this time.*

About two minutes after he had come in, Chandler heard the sound of a footstep on the stone of the vestibule. He turned. There were several loud clicks, and the lights went out. Chandler could see nothing but the tiny gleam of the single candle.

Though he was expecting it, a touch on his right shoulder startled him. "You were late, Senator." Memory's voice came from behind Chandler. "Please move into the pew a bit. I am kneeling, and I find it painful."

"How did you . . . ?"

"The lights? Reconnaissance, Senator. Reconnaissance. It keeps me alive, even in church." Memory sat down next to him.

"I had a visit from the FBI today."

"Yes. Schumacher. I know."

"And I suppose you know he tracked that envelope to my front door?"

"Special handling by Federal Express. I imagine the FBI is more curious about you than ever. But enough of appearances. We must speak of contents."

"I found the contents very enlightening, Memory."

"That is your name for me? Memory? Very poetic."

"I could call you by your real name, Immanuel Sanchez."

"Yes. You could do that. And you might be right, or you—"

"So you *were* Elaine's father. You were the secret you said she—"

"This is not on our agenda, Senator."

"I must know. If you are Sanchez—"

"I would be a traitor. And if I were Sanchez, Senator, I would be dead. As Trevor wanted Sanchez dead. He made Sanchez a prey to both sides. Because he knew the truth. But that is history. Ask questions of today. Quickly."

Chandler obeyed. "In the envelope. The report from Rizzuli. He was onto the truth? And Kucharov was too?"

"Yes. The truth that is at the heart of your search. And do you now believe your search is over?"

"No, Memory. Not quite. I need to know more about AMLASH."

"That was long ago."

"But it connects to today, Memory."

Chandler heard Memory sigh. He spoke now in a hoarse whisper, as if what he had to say were being forced from deep within him. "Trevor was involved in running AMLASH. He ignored Kennedy's orders to terminate the project. Then, when he received information that Castro had arranged to retaliate against the AMLASH plots, Trevor dismissed it as an empty threat."

"And so," Chandler said, not whispering, "Kennedy was killed. Who else knew that Trevor had received specific information about a retaliation plot?"

"Georgi Tupolev and QJWIN and . . . me."

"Did Oswald act on his own?"

"There were others."

"Who?"

"The names are not important—now."

Chandler sensed that Memory would talk no more about the past. "Yes," Chandler said. "What is important now is another name—the name of the snake in the tower. The name of the man at the heart of this."

"You already have a great deal of information, Senator. Certainly your institutions, with all their resources—they can get that name. Give them what you have and let them pursue it further . . . to the name."

"You mean give this to Trevor? Or Schumacher? Absolutely not." Chandler grabbed Memory's arm and felt the instantaneous spasm of tension. Memory was ready to spring away.

"Already great cost has been paid for you to get this much information, Senator. Rizzuli, Kucharov, your Elaine, eighty-one passengers . . ."

"And QJWIN? Is he still alive?"

"That, Senator, I cannot say."

"You mean, *will* not say."

"As you wish. A moment please." Memory removed his arm

from Chandler's grasp and seemed to take something out of his pocket. From the rustle of his movements, Chandler thought that Memory was writing something.

"For many reasons, Senator, this has been our most dangerous meeting. The circle is closing in on all of us. I must leave you—and all of this—for what I hope will be all time. You passed your last test, Senator, and asked your last good question: What is the name? You were right in wanting it, right in not having someone else do the work that you must do, at whatever cost. Your hand, please."

Chandler reached out his right hand and felt the touch of Memory's. Chandler assumed that this was a sort of ritual, a final handshake. But he felt something placed in his hand.

The sound of a step came from the vestibule. In that instant, the figure of Memory moved swiftly, as a shadow in shadows, across the pews and through a side door. The lights clicked on, two by two, and a wave of soft light swelled from the altar to the rear of the church.

Chandler turned to see a tall black priest bearing down on him. "What's going on here?" the priest asked angrily.

"I have no idea, Father. I am Senator Chandler. I . . . stopped in to . . . meditate. And the lights went out. I thought it was some kind of time-switch."

"Sorry, Senator. I didn't recognize you. It was some kind of vandal. Opened a locked switch box in the vestibule. At least, it's usually locked. I noticed the lights were out from the rectory around the corner. Thought I might find a mugging victim. These are terrible times we live in, Senator. Terrible times."

He genuflected, stood, and with a "Good night, Senator," returned to the vestibule.

Chandler waited until he heard the priest's steps on the stone and the opening and closing of the church door. Then he looked down at what he held in his hand.

It was a card—another one of Memory's file cards, Chandler thought at first. But it was smaller and printed in colors. On one side was a painting of Jesus, hand raised in blessing. On the back were lines of printing. It was a Mass card, evidently taken from a rack in the vestibule. On the top of the card was printed the church's name and address. Below that was NAME OF DECEASED:_____ and DATE OF DEATH:__/__/__.

Written in ink in the first blank was *Cyril Metrinko*. In the second blank was written *???*. Under that, at the bottom of the card, was written *Proverbs, 22:20-21. Adios.*

Chandler ran back to the Hart Building, startling the security guard. He went into his office, rummaged through the bookshelves till he located a Revised Standard Version of the Bible, and flipped through it to Proverbs 22. He ran his finger down the numbered verses until he came to 20:

In the past, haven't I been right? Then believe what I am telling you now and share it with others.

54

Metrinko's polished boots clicked through the long marbled corridor that led to President Drachinsky's office in the Kremlin. He walked rapidly past the glass-enclosed walnut cases containing gifts from visiting heads of state. There were jewel-handled swords from Arabian kings, ivory carvings and uncut diamonds from African satellite nations. Metrinko smiled contemptuously as he passed the American President Richard Nixon's pitiful commemoration of his policy of détente: a chessboard with facing rows of ornately sculpted pieces of jade. *Chess, indeed.*

When he entered the anteroom of Drachinsky's office, Metrinko adopted the manner of a condemned man determined to face execution unafraid. Metrinko was under no threat of death. But what he was about to ask of Drachinsky was so daring that only a man beyond fear could lay out the plan.

Within a matter of minutes, Metrinko was escorted into a large, high-ceilinged, modestly furnished office. Leonid Drachinsky rose slowly from his desk and took his place at an oval table in the center of the room, joining eight other stone-faced men sitting around it.

An elderly retainer came in and served tea to the men. Metrinko stared at their faces. Old men. All of them. Metrinko's eyes moved methodically around the table, recording every weakness, as if he were a jackal approaching a herd of prey, preparing his line of attack. Alexandrov was eighty-three, but still vigorous looking; his high cheekbones and tawny skin placed his birth in central Russia. Time had not been as kind to Serge Ivanovich; his bald pate was covered with dark freckles. Only the deep wrinkles in his gleaming scalp discouraged a comparison to a large gray goose egg. Kuzentiski's rheumy eyes and bulbous nóse, streaked with purple veins, testified to his heavy drinking. Metrinko knew them all, and he knew their sins.

Alcoholism; promiscuity; black marketeering . . . It was all locked away in the files he had kept on each of them over the years. Knowledge was power. He knew it and they knew it.

It was the sense of power he felt in his very veins that permitted him to speak to them, not as some fawning subordinate, but as an equal.

Drachinsky began. "You said, Colonel, that you have a bold plan. We are here to listen."

Metrinko could not tell them he was running unauthorized attacks upon Western political leaders. These old walruses were too cautious, too timid for that. He knew he could keep his secret by telling only a part of it. He listed, chronologically, the remarkable successes he had scored through Eagle, his source in Washington: the names of American double agents, "some of them right here in Moscow . . . the Pentagon's targeting strategies for the MX missile . . . blueprints of the Air Force's latest cruise missiles and anti-satellite weapons . . . the biotechnical breakthrough that altered neurons in brain cells . . .

"I tell of these achievements," Metrinko concluded, "not to remind you of past successes but to warn you of grave future losses. All that is to come is in jeopardy. My Eagle will be exposed unless we move and move quickly."

He told them of Chandler's investigation, providing elementary facts about the American system for most of them who had no working knowledge of it. He said that the investigation must be terminated and Chandler himself removed. And he told them how he proposed to remove him.

Yes, he had considered the risks. And of course the proposal was not unprecedented. He reminded his audience of the incident involving the chief of West Germany's intelligence agency.

"That was West Berlin, not Washington," Alexandrov scoffed.

Metrinko did not retreat. "Distance is only a matter of miles, Comrade, a matter of a few hours. Unless we move quickly, years of work will be destroyed, years of promise wiped out by one foolish senator. There is no other way. Not unless we are prepared to sacrifice our highest agent in the United States government. An agent who may one day go even higher." With the word *we*, Metrinko made the old men his partners in a scheme they had never heard of before this moment.

Drachinsky was the key. Metrinko could see distress and doubt in the President's narrowing eyes.

Metrinko paused and then dropped his voice. Speaking directly to Drachinsky, he said, "The United States is developing a space-based laser system that will enable them to destroy every one of our ICBMs within minutes after they are launched. Do you realize what it would mean to our security to have knowledge of that system?"

Metrinko paused again, for what seemed an agonizingly long time to the men around the table. He stared at each of them in turn. "Do you realize what it will mean if we *fail* to get that system?"

Drachinsky spoke in his reedy voice: "And how will you convince the American authorities that we are not responsible for the . . . the *termination* of Chandler's investigation?"

"The Americans are stupid. They love scandal. Remember the stupid scandal that got rid of President Nixon? Americans make an art of persuading themselves of the improbable. They will not blame us, because we will not seem improbable."

Drachinsky slowly shook his head. He was still skeptical. "What you propose is extremely dangerous."

"A failure to act is *more* dangerous," Metrinko said, iron in his voice now. He knew he would have to press harder or he would lose them. "Remember what happened to the Americans at the Bay of Pigs?"

"Yes," Drachinsky said, "I remember. It was the CIA's plan. It was *not* the American President who authorized the plan."

Unmoved, Metrinko continued to stare stolidly at the President. "Perhaps a better historical example is that of the Cuban missile deployment. Perhaps you also remember the humiliation when *we* hesitated in the face of threats. Then it was only our honor that we lost. Today we may well lose our Motherland. I remind you that we are contemplating an activity against only *one* American. Weigh him and whatever the consequences against our beloved *Motherland*." He invoked the last word as a sacrament.

Drachinsky's gaze finally broke. He glanced quickly around the table. The others were waiting for his leadership. Metrinko knew there was only one answer he could give. Turning to Metrinko, the President said, "Tell us, Colonel, how can you possibly carry out this bizarre plan without detection?"

Metrinko suppressed a smile. His pale-green eyes took the measure of the old men. He had done it. Then, lowering his voice almost to a whisper, he laid out the details of his plan. Their heads bent forward, drawn by his words into a circle of conspiracy.

Wednesday, July 8

55 When columnist Clinton Atwood entered his third-floor office on 16th Street, he left a tidy footprint on a large manila envelope that someone had slipped under his door. This was not an unusual kind of delivery. Atwood frequently received information in this way from "friends of the cause."

He picked up the envelope and brushed it off. There was no direct or return address, on front or back. He moved behind his desk to open the venetian blinds, and sat down in the high-backed leather chair he had ordered more than twenty years ago from an antique store in London. The chair dominated the small desk, whose top was finished in green leather and gold leaf. Only a yellow legal pad and a black phone marred its pristine surface: the tools of his trade. He got most of his information by phone. He wrote his column in longhand, enjoying the tactile sensation of ink flowing through the tip of the pen onto the paper.

The office was a luxury that Atwood did not need. He could have written his column at home, but he liked a change of location to get his creative venom flowing. Besides, the office was an important symbol to his colleagues—and his informants.

He broke the envelope's seal with an ornate gold letter opener given him by the Iranian Ambasssador in 1972. He slid the contents onto the desktop and frowned. The envelope contained a series of eight-by-twelve black-and-white glossy photographs. The first showed a group of smiling Hawaiians seated at a table in what Atwood saw was the Senate Dining Room. He recognized

Senator Danny Kanawa immediately. *It must be a joke*, he thought.

He turned to the second photograph. The Hawaiians seemed a bit fuzzy and out of focus. In the third one, he could see a stained-glass portrait of George Washington at the rear of the dining room. Two men were sitting at the table directly beneath it. Atwood reached for his reading glasses in his breast pocket. *Is that Senator Thomas Chandler?*

His pulse quickened. Yes, it was Chandler. His right hand was raised, as if to give something to or receive something from the other man.

In the last photograph, it became clear that an envelope was being passed from one man to the other. Atwood flipped back through the photographs in the exact sequence he had received them. The other man at the table was passing the envelope to Chandler. It was unmistakable.

Atwood's heart was pounding now. A torrent of questions flooded his mind. Why were these photographs delivered to him? When were they taken? Who was the man with Chandler? What was in the envelope?

Atwood picked up the phone and dialed.

Maybe some of his friends at the Agency could identify the other man in the photograph.

56

Thursday, July 9

"Is it true?" Dempsey asked in a plaintive, almost pitiful voice.

He slapped down *The Washington Post*. The lead story on page one was headlined SENATOR ALLEGED TO HAVE BUILT FORTUNE ON COCAINE.

"Is what true? That Raymond Fouchette is involved with distributing narcotics? Yes, that's true."

"Don't bullshit me, Tom," Dempsey shouted, his anger rising. "Is it true that Fouchette set you up in business?"

"Yes. But, Christ, that was twenty years ago."

"Why didn't you tell me?"

"Tell you what?" It was Chandler's turn to be angry now. "Tell you that my ex-father-in-law was . . . is . . . a crook? I just found that out myself." Chandler smacked his fist down hard on his desk.

He stood up quickly and turned toward the window, away from Dempsey. He saw the black priest standing with a knot of people on the steps of Saint Joseph's, waiting for a casket to be unloaded from a hearse. *Dead.* I'm dead. He wondered if Fouchette did it directly or if the man named Metrinko did it. *What does it matter?* He turned back to Dempsey.

Ned checked his indignation and lowered his voice. "How did you find out?" His tone was resigned.

"I met Danielle in New York in May. She said she had to talk to me. My instincts told me her call was more than social, but I was curious. She told me her father wanted me to call off my investigation into the drug operations in New Orleans."

Chandler looked out again at the funeral group. "He offered to buy out the stock I still own in DataLink for two million dollars. If I refused to sell and refused to call off the investigation, he would see to it that a story was planted that my money came—indirectly—from narcotics."

"Why don't you say that publicly?"

"Because Fouchette is a clever bastard," Chandler snapped. "He'll deny it and say I tried to shake him down for two million dollars in return for calling off my investigation. Then he'll insist the investigation go forward, saying he has nothing to hide. Either way, I lose on this one."

"Then why don't you deny the story, period?" Dempsey asked, not quite thinking his suggestion through.

Chandler rounded on him with an accusing look. "Because I'd be lying. That's how Nixon got into a jam, remember? He lied and then got caught in his own web."

"Maybe you're right, Tom. But there's one very big difference. You're not the President. And the public doesn't put senators or congressmen on much of a pedestal. . . ."

Chandler slumped into a chair, deciding against telling Ned that an agent for the Soviet Union had tried to blackmail him too. "I know. But I won't lie. And I can't say 'No comment.' Christ, that's like pleading the Fifth. I'll just have to take my chances with the press."

"Tom, I'd skip a conference on this one. Let's try to find a friendly ear and go with an exclusive." Ned was grasping at straws now. There *were* no friendly ears. There could be nothing exclusive about a scandal.

Chandler shot him a glance of incredulity, but softened it when he saw the sadness in Dempsey's face. "Little chance, Ned. Might be worth a try. We've got to stall them for a while. I've got only six days left to finish the report on the investigation. Then I can make a full statement."

"Okay, Tom. I'll have Bob Tilley put up a wall like the one in Berlin. But it won't hold for long." He took a deep breath. "I'm going to do something I've never done before."

Chandler looked at him hopefully.

"I'll set up a press conference for tomorrow morning—"

"There's no way I can be finished with the report by then."

"I know. I'll send Bob to read a statement instead, and then have him say that you'll make a full report next week."

It was risky. But the press would never come if they knew in advance they'd be hearing Chandler's press secretary read a canned statement. And if a conference was not set soon, they would be camped out at Chandler's office *and* home. It was a chance that Dempsey thought worth taking.

It was a disaster.

Right from the beginning, when Bob Tilley walked into the glare of the television lights, the people who showed up at the press conference knew something was phony.

Tilley was superb at preparing his boss for appearances before the press. He could tell Chandler what questions to anticipate, what follow-ups were likely, whom to avoid, what responses might catch a headline. But his skills were purely advisory. He was totally unprepared to survive the experience himself. It was as if a fight manager had been thrown into the ring against his boxer's opponent.

The members of the press were angry that a deception had been perpetrated upon them. As Tilley tried to read his statement, someone shouted, "Where's Chandler?"

Tilley looked up momentarily from the page in front of him, then lost his place. He stammered, "Senator Chandler needs just a few more days to complete his investigation and then will make a complete report. He believes the results of that report to be of vital importance to the country."

"More important than the truth?" another reporter shouted.

"The truth is what I just stated, Ben," Tilley said, offended. But he knew that under a searchlight, the truth almost always looks naked, and embarrassed to be so. "He has some devastating information about drugs, about organized crime, terrorism, about the Kennedy assassination—"

Someone in the back row laughed. "Oh, shit," another said.

The eye of the camera did not blink. The lights continued to blaze. Panic began to pop out in beads of sweat on Tilley's forehead. The accusations struck him like stones.

It was a disaster.

57

Friday, July 10

Something happens when the hot wind of scandal hits Capitol Hill. It doesn't matter if the scandal involves money, sex, bribery, or kickbacks; the same drumbeat of retribution sounds for the breach of trust.

Network camera crews arrive early in the morning, their vans weighted with heavy equipment. They set up their one-eyed weapons in the wide corridors, and the thick black electrical cables snake across the marble floors like boa constrictors waiting for new prey.

Electricity crackles in the air. The news correspondents try to out-hustle their competitors from rival networks. Outside the hearing rooms they collar emerging senators for comment. Senators who used to backslap and laugh with their beleaguered colleague now step around or over the body. They become more timid—and more pious. "Let's not prejudge the case." "I want to wait until all of the facts are in." "I need the benefit of the Committee's judgment on this." In the camera eye, no one dares to state flatly that he believes the allegations to be without foundation, lest he look to the watching nation like a co-conspirator.

Chandler had done his share of sidestepping in the past. Now there were no hedges to hide behind. In one day his confident stride and hard intelligent gaze were gone. He appeared somehow disconnected. He had forgotten to shave, and the shadow of his heavy beard added a hint of quiet desperation to his face. His eyes seemed more deeply recessed. And where his colleagues had once resented his habit of eating alone, on this day they welcomed it.

Reporters and TV crews had his office in the Hart Building surrounded. For as long as he could, he would work desperately to finish the report, secluded in his hideaway office. The name had never seemed so appropriate.

Margie put through to him just two phone calls. The first was from Doug Bender. "I see what you were talking about the other day, old friend," he said. "I won't keep you on the phone, but Kathy and I just want you to know that we *do* trust you. Whatever happens, we . . . we love you, ol' buddy."

Chandler's voice was thick with emotion. "Thanks, Doug. Same here." He tried to laugh. "Give a kiss from me to my favorite redhead."

The second call was from Danielle.

"Tom, Daddy didn't do this. You must believe me."

"Why *should* I believe you, Danielle? You told me he'd release that information to the press—now he's done it."

"Yes, but don't you see? Your career may be ruined, but this news doesn't exactly do wonders for his, either. When he saw the paper this morning he said, 'Oh, God! The feds will be all over me!' And he's been closeted with a whole army of lawyers ever since."

"He's managed to get around the feds so far. He'll do it again. You don't need to worry about *him*."

"But I want you to believe me that he didn't release this information to the papers."

"Okay, Danielle. I believe you." Chandler sighed heavily. "Someone else knew about this too. Mr. Arthur Simpson of London and Moscow seems to have been extraordinarily busy."

"Mr. who?"

"Never mind. Thanks for calling, Danielle." He was surprised to realize he meant that.

There was no call from Charlie Walcott. And Woodrow Harrold was in the Middle East on another round of shuttle diplomacy. Chandler hardly expected to hear from him.

From the White House there was only ominous silence.

* * *

The news about Tom Chandler's mob connection had shocked and angered Arthur Christiansen. The shock came from a feeling of personal betrayal. He had trusted Tom Chandler, had even expected that someday he might succeed him in the Oval Office. Going over his recollections of various meetings he'd had with Chandler, the President found it hard to believe what he had read in *The Washington Post*. The anger came from the infuriatingly frequent experience of reading about an event in a newspaper instead of knowing about it in advance.

As he had told Trevor an hour ago, the experience was becoming too common. Time and again in recent months he had seen some of his country's most precious secrets—details of new weapons systems, defense plans, intelligence findings—appearing in newspapers in the United States, England, and France. Worse still, he had been told too often by Trevor that the Soviets were making moves that strongly suggested knowledge of American secrets

He had railed at Trevor and at Schumacher. Security had been tightened at the Agency, the Bureau, the Defense Department, and the White House. Several dozen key people with knowledge of the leaked programs and plans had been summarily fired. Fingers were being pointed throughout the national security network. No one was above suspicion. The most devastating result of it all was that fewer and fewer people at the top were willing to trust anyone. It was far and away the most destructive problem the President had faced since his election.

Now this—Chandler tied to the mob; Chandler and the suspicion voiced by Schumacher that Chandler might be the leak, the mole that had penetrated every secret niche in the federal government, from the Pentagon to the Oval Office.

With these disturbing thoughts, the President sat down to write an entry in his private journal. He switched on the radio, but the strains of Albinoni's Adagio in G Minor were almost too poignant. He closed his eyes and tried to open his mind to the music.

The phone rang. "The Prime Minister, Mr. President."

He was immediately alert, thoughts of disaster beginning to form. There was only one Prime Minister who might call, and she never called merely to pass the time of day.

"Good day, Mr. President."

"Good day, Madame Prime Minister. Secure here."

"Yes. Secure here. Mr. President, I must apologize for the

abrupt nature of my call and for my failure to use normal channels of communication."

"You need never apologize to me for person-to-person communication. You are always welcome, Madame Prime Minister."

"Thank you. This call is of a rather extraordinary nature. When you understand the purpose, I believe you will agree that it was necessary to go outside channels. I am calling to request that you receive a very special messenger from me. He will have information that is to be given directly to you. I urge you to tell no one of this call or his visit. I realize this is an extraordinary request, but . . ."

"I trust you and I trust your good sense. No one will hear of the call. We will be able to receive your messenger without any of the leaks that have been plaguing us. You have my word on that."

"Thank you, Mr. President. The messenger will contact your personal secretary shortly. He will identify himself as Christopher Marlowe."

"I will receive him by any name, but this one is certainly memorable."

"And pertinent, Mr. President. Thank you and good-bye."

"I expect that I will be thanking *you*, Madame Prime Minister. Good-bye."

The President went to his private bookshelves, where he kept a small part of what was regarded as one of the nation's finest collections of books and manuscripts on espionage, from modern thrillers to his prize, the transcript of the trial of the only American caught as a saboteur in England during the Revolutionary War.

He picked up *A History of British Secret Service*, and turning to a section on Sir Francis Walsingham, a diplomat considered to be the father of British espionage, he read:

> In the sixteenth century the most celebrated writer to spy for Walsingham was Christopher Marlowe, a poet and dramatist. His actual role in espionage is still wrapped in mystery to some extent, but it was an important and patriotic, though somewhat cynical and Machiavellian enterprise.

On Saturday evening, the Christiansens were entertaining congressional leaders and their wives with a preview screening of a new movie in the East Wing theater, starting promptly at eight-thirty. A little after nine, the President's secretary responded to the blinking telephone light in the rear of the screening room, then quietly moved forward to the President's chair and whispered briefly in his ear. So unobtrusively did Christiansen slip out of the room that most of those watching the film didn't even realize he'd gone.

The man called Christopher Marlowe was about forty years old, Christiansen judged. He was good-looking—somewhat bushy brown hair, chiseled features, slight build—but not a man who would be remembered for any one feature. *Could be a ladies' man,* the President thought, taking the measure of what the Prime Minister had called England's best agent.

"Did you pick your name?" the President asked, showing the way into his private inner sanctum off the Oval Office.

"Yes, sir. Rather silly, I suppose. But one needs a light touch now and then." With the door firmly closed, he sat down opposite the President's writing desk and politely declined offers of refreshment. He went straight to the point:

"For a number of years we have had a very high-level source inside the permanent cadre of the Soviet Union's hierarchy. He is mine. I run him, and as I am sure you can imagine, we do not make contact idly or often.

"I have received from him, on a most urgent basis, extraordinary information. He said that there is a KGB plot in motion to kidnap a United States senator. The senator is Thomas Chandler."

"Good God! And your government vouches for this information?"

"Yes, sir—and if I might say so, *I* vouch for it. This information is so valid, and was passed at such hazard, that I am sure my source is at great risk and possibly of limited future usefulness."

"What else does he know about the kidnapping?"

"Little else, sir. Except that it is to take place very shortly. We received the news on Wednesday."

The President was tempted to remark on how slowly the news had come to him, but he said nothing. Three days was relatively swift for the passage of information between governments, after all.

"My source, sir, took an enormous risk in getting even this limited information to me. He indicated that the planning is extremely secret. He was able to learn about it only because there is some high-level disagreement in the KGB. One faction is against it, and some information got out because of the dissension. He said that the man planning the kidnapping is apparently invulnerable, but nevertheless a renegade."

"You can get no further information?"

"No, sir. I am afraid the cost of this information is so high that we can attempt no further contacts. By this moment, my source may be gone. He may even be dead."

"I can go directly to President Drachinsky on this one," the President said, his eyes turning toward the phone. "And I can get Secret Service protection for Senator Chandler immediately."

"With all due respect, sir," Marlowe said quickly, "that would surely destroy my source. As an added difficulty, it would do nothing to help uncover the Soviet agent in your own government."

"My government?"

"Yes, sir. Actually, we believe it is someone in the Senate."

"Not Chandler? I mean, it seems to me that 'kidnapping' him would be a way to extricate him."

"No, sir. Certainly not Chandler. Chandler is definitely one of us, sir. My source says that Chandler is being kidnapped to stop him from doing damage to the Soviets. The 'kidnapping' will be staged to look like flight and defection. I believe some groundwork has already been laid with a scandal in the press?"

Oh, my God, Christiansen thought. *So that's it.* He spoke: "Why not thwart the kidnapping?"

Even as Marlowe began—"The Prime Minister wishes me to suggest a plan"—the President was beginning to see an answer to his question.

58

Sunday, July 12

At 6:00 A.M., a rumpled and sleepless Tom Chandler pulled himself off the couch and snapped on the television set to catch the early news. A reporter stood in front of Chandler's home in the Spring Valley section of Washington, speaking into a hand-held microphone: "According to reliable sources, Senator Thomas Chandler of Connecticut is still heavily involved in drug-related activities with organized crime. Chandler reportedly is coming under pressure from the White House itself to

consider resigning so as to spare his political party further em-
bar—"

Chandler switched channels. Same story. He snapped off the
set. They were trying to get something on the air to justify their
having staked out his home last night.

After leaving the White House, where he had been called to an
urgent 10:00 P.M. meeting with the President, Chandler had driven
to Spring Valley around 1:00 A.M. About a hundred yards away
from the driveway to his house, he became aware of the floodlights
blazing on nearly a dozen people he knew had to be reporters and
television crews.

He had quickly spun his car around, sped back to Capitol Hill,
and parked in the underground garage of the Hart Building. From
his office he placed a call to Kevin O'Brien. Apologizing for the
late-night call, he asked O'Brien if he could borrow the Mustang
again, if it was in its customary slot in the Hart Building garage.
Assured that it was, he told O'Brien that he was going to Elaine's
house in Reston to finish the report for the Intelligence Committee,
and asked him not to reveal to anyone—other than the President
himself—where he would be for the next forty-eight hours. With
thanks, he hung up the phone.

Chandler had kept his key to Elaine's house. With luck, the
utilities would still be working. He figured he could type the report
on Elaine's computer with its link to the Senate Intelligence Committee's computer system, and transmit it directly to the data bank,
where O'Brien could retrieve it.

The switch in cars successfully deceived the young wire-service
reporter staked out at the entrance to the Hart Building. But
Chandler had made a serious mistake. Amid all the turbulence in
his mind following his meeting with President Christiansen, he had
forgotten about the vulnerability of phone calls to interception.
When Chandler turned down Constitution Avenue, the telephone-
tap duty officer at the Soviet Embassy alerted a car parked on a side
street near the Hart Building. It pulled into the sparse late-night
traffic behind O'Brien's car.

There was no need for the driver to follow so closely that
Chandler would become suspicious of the headlights in his rearview
mirror. The Embassy had told him where Senator Chandler was
going.

*　　*　　*

Now, at ten past six on a muggy Sunday morning, Chandler went into Elaine's kitchen to see if he could find anything to call breakfast. Taking the coffee from the refrigerator— *"It stays fresher"*—he experienced such a jolt of nostalgic despair that he buried his face in his arms at the kitchen table and gave himself up to racking sobs. Memories of Elaine were everywhere in this house, in everything he looked at, everything he touched. Here they'd had breakfast, there they'd made love, there she'd taught him how to use the computer, there she'd nursed his beaten body, there she'd introduced him to her cat. . . .

It was the memory of Greyfur that brought him back to the present. *What became of the cat?* Elaine would never have set off for New York without making some arrangement for Greyfur. Did she take him with her? Was he yet another victim of terrorism? Chandler found himself laughing, not far from the edge of hysteria. *So many people have died. And here I am, in the worst danger of my life— damn near of anyone's life—and I'm crying over a cat.*

He pulled himself to his feet and wiped his face on his shirt-sleeve. Resolutely he started the coffee maker and went into the bathroom to shower and shave.

Chandler spent the morning fueled by strong black coffee, surrounded by drifts of papers, organizing his notes and his thoughts on yellow pads. At noon, his stomach crying out for food, he located an unopened box of reasonably crisp crackers and a jar of peanut butter, and switched to tea fortified with bottled lemon juice and honey.

Then he turned on the computer and its disk drive. The screen lit up greenly, and the prompter appeared:

HELLO

Aπ

Following the instructions Elaine had given him, he lifted the secure phone off its cradle and placed it upon a . . . *what did she call it?—modem. That was it. Modem.* He dialed the data bank number and tapped out three lines of instructions on the computer. There was no acknowledgment from the data base; it was wired so that information could enter it but not leave it.

He put the system disk in one drive, a new blank disk in the other, went through another ritual that Elaine had patiently taught him, and began to type. He couldn't be sure it would reach only those for whom it was intended. But he could try.

This report is for Kevin O'Brien's eyes only.

Kevin, take this directly to President Christiansen. Do *not*, repeat *not*, share it with anyone but the President. Here goes.

He worked for six hours, pouring words into the computer, speaking the words as he wrote them, speaking in a whisper that after a while only he could hear because the words were only in his mind. After every few paragraphs, he punched a control key, *KS*—"kissing the memory storage," Elaine had said—and the words went deep enough into the machine to be preserved on the disk.

Four months ago I undertook an investigation into the causes of the current epidemic of terrorism and violence in this country and around the world. The roots of this malignancy turn out to be anything but routine and more profound than anything I might have originally comprehended. I believe I have discovered links among some of the most sinister agencies and elements in our civilization and between the violent events of today and certain shattering events in our recent past.

I now believe beyond doubt that Department V of the KGB (the division exclusively responsible for political assassinations and the highest security "black" operations) has spawned a renegade unit. This unit is operating without authorization, totally out of the control of the Kremlin or the political direction of the KGB.

Chandler detailed his discovery that the renegade unit was run by "a brilliant, probably mad, certainly dedicated career officer of the KGB known as Colonel Cyril Metrinko," and he reviewed the events that culminated in Rizzuli's death.

He continued:

Before my source confirmed my theory that such a "rogue elephant" KGB unit actually existed, I had been following the track of the tremendous increase in hard drugs in the United States . . . underground drug networks operated by well-known Mafia figures. My investigation leads me to conclude that the KGB group I have identified has acquired massive amounts of drugs—mostly heroin and cocaine—from new sources it has developed in the Middle East and Asia. Using various terrorist organizations as carriers and dealers, the KGB unit has established a central point of contact with some up-and-coming young American Mafia figures in Amsterdam . . .

Metrinko's secret KGB outfit benefits two ways: First, an already serious social problem in the United States—drugs—is exacerbated by these very large supplies coming into the country. Second, the enormous sums of money paid by the mob for the drugs are then used by Colonel Metrinko to finance terrorist training operations, political assassinations, and other terrorist activities.

Chandler told of Fabricante's murder. Drawing upon what he had learned from QJWIN, from Memory, and posthumously from Alfred Rizzuli, he wrote that the semi-retired Mafia chief had "smelled a rat" when a new wave of drugs hit the market.

Fabricante contacted an acquaintance in Havana. Fabricante and his contact had worked together on the plot (code-named AMLASH) to kill Castro for the CIA back in the early 1960s.

Fabricante had recruited his contact (call him Trackshoe) from the exiled Cuban community in Miami in 1961 for the AMLASH operation. In fact, Fabricante had saved Trackshoe's life. The exile Cubans thought Trackshoe was one of Castro's spies because he maintained a lot of contacts in Cuba after the revolution. They had Trackshoe on a hit list of their own and were ready to kill him when he sought Fabricante out to save his life. Fabricante, tasked by the CIA with recruiting a couple of inside men for the assassination attempts, was convinced that Trackshoe was perfect for the job and committed to the cause, and so signed him up for AMLASH. Trackshoe was sent to Cuba in 1962 as part of a five-man team trained to kill Castro.

In fact, Fabricante was wrong and the exiled Cubans were right. Trackshoe was Castro's man all along. His job was to penetrate the exiles in Miami, learn of their counterrevolutionary plans, and report back to Fidel Castro. And that's exactly what he did in December 1962. When Trackshoe's boat hit the northern beaches of Cuba, he headed straight for Havana. Using all his high-level code passwords, he was in Castro's office within a few hours. He outlined the AMLASH plot and fingered his four compatriots. They were rounded up that night at the rendezvous point, tortured until they confirmed Trackshoe's story, and summarily shot.

Trackshoe has been one of Castro's closest friends ever since. But he never forgot the favor Fabricante did in saving his life. So when Fabricante got suspicious of the drug source, he sent a message to Trackshoe, whom he had not seen or heard from in more than twenty years: "Help me find out where these drugs are coming from—particularly find out if there is a Russian connection. You owe me."

Within one week, at a prearranged meeting point, an intermediary delivered the answer: "Trackshoe says to tell you this—'your suspicions are correct. Some of our cousins are involved.'" Fabricante knew the "cousins" were the Russians.

Now, Mafiosi consider themselves both businessmen and patriots. To the degree that they have a political ideology, it is decidedly conservative, if not right-wing. Fabricante was going to demand the Amsterdam trade be cut off and the Russian connection severed. He had just left his house to attend a high-level meeting of the *capo regimes* when he disappeared. He ended up in a barrel in Biscayne Bay—mutilated and dismembered—a week before my investigation began.

Either the Metrinko outfit or the younger Mafia elements intercepted his inquiry to, and answer from, Trackshoe and had him brutally murdered. If it was the Russians, they did it to protect their operation and sources of funds. If it was the younger mob members, they wanted to protect their new, lucrative drug operation. The brutality of the murder sent a signal throughout the Mafia not to nose around the Amsterdam operation.

Chandler started suddenly and quickly typed *KS* again. Either the recollection of Fabricante's mutilated corpse or his own mounting paranoia convinced him he had heard a peculiar sound—a thin, long scratch on glass—from the kitchen. He investigated, found nothing, and persuaded himself it was only a low tree branch brushing the window. Outside, the wind was picking up.

Chandler returned to the computer and typed: "But my investigation of Fabricante's murder focused Mafia attention on me." He told of Raymond Fouchette's blackmail attempt.

Fouchette tried to blackmail me, then—I believe it was his work—had me beaten up. Even if I had gone after him, through the task force investigation, he felt he had immunity because of his work for the Agency in Nicaragua; part of the payoff for this work was a kind of license to deal in drugs. But apparently it was not Fouchette but Metrinko—who has at least one British journalist in his employ—who engineered the "leak" of my alleged "drug connection" with Fouchette. Metrinko knew of Fouchette's blackmail threat, apparently through an agent who bugged my conversation with my ex-wife, Fouchette's daughter, at a New York restaurant.

By planting the story about the "Chandler-Fouchette link," Metrinko effectively destroyed my career—and probably Fouchette's drug business into the bargain. This served Metrinko's purposes in two ways: He got rid of a competitor in the drug business, and he punished a man who, through the aid he was giving the CIA, was hurting Soviet interests in Central America.

Chandler hit *KS* again, stood up, walked to the window, and peered into the gathering twilight. He had come to the part of the report that dealt with Elaine. *Elaine*, he thought, *Elaine*. He stood there, looking out, for a few melancholy minutes, then went back to the computer keyboard.

He told of Trevor's recruiting of Elaine. "Disclosure of this penetration of a working component of the United States Congress," he wrote, "could lead to his dismissal in disgrace and the discrediting of the Agency for years to come." Chandler ended that paragraph with a question: "Why did Trevor take such a risk?"

"With the help of my sources, especially information from Rizzuli, a brave man who happened on a trail that led to his death, I found the answer."

Chandler traced Trevor's career from the ZRRIFLE operation, particularly AMLASH, to the Kennedy Administration's decision to cancel both AMLASH and the proposed invasion of Cuba, all the way to the Kennedy assassination. He continued:

I do not believe that Oswald acted totally on his own. There were many who had both the motive and opportunity to act in concert with Oswald—the Soviet Union, Castro, the Mafia, anti-Castro Cubans, and right-wing assets of ZR-RIFLE. But we will never know. The trail has gone cold. Evidence has been deliberately withheld and destroyed; witnesses have either died or been killed. The secret of Kennedy's death will lie like lost treasure on the bottom of the ocean.

But there is one secret that I did discover. Word that an attempt would be made to assassinate Kennedy was passed to Trevor by a Soviet agent, Georgi Tupelov, through a man named Immanuel Sanchez. Trevor either did not believe it or chose to disregard it. It might have been a mistake. It might have been murder. But that's a riddle to which only Trevor has the answer.

I learned that immediately after the assassination of President Kennedy, Trevor wanted to eliminate any evidence of the warning he had received. He passed word to the Cuban community in Miami that Sanchez was a Castro agent who had tipped Castro off about the Bay of Pigs operation. He knew they would seek blood revenge against Sanchez for all the lost lives and the lost opportunity to free Cuba. Then he passed word through his channels into Havana that Sanchez was a CIA double agent who was part of the ZRRIFLE operation. Castro put a price on his head.

Sanchez has been hiding for more than twenty years. He is, I believe, the same man who has been providing me with information linking the present reign of Soviet-sponsored terror with our own assassination operations of the past, the man I have referred to as Memory.

I also believe him to be the real father of Elaine Dunham—which is the only explanation I can offer for his decision to help me. Routine security checks did not reveal what even Elaine did not know: the identity of her father. But deeper security checks showed that she was Sanchez's daughter. Trevor, sensing a future use for this information covered up the security discoveries. He later decided he might be able to use her to kill two birds with one stone—to ferret out the Soviet mole and finally to find the keeper of his secret. No birds were killed. Only Elaine, in that mysterious airplane explosion.

Trevor penetrated my investigation because he needed to know where it was going. His uncanny instinct for survival was strong enough to justify the risk—so he took it. Terrorism led us to drugs. Drugs led to the mob. The mob led to the Cubans. And the Cubans led to Trevor.

Many people do not want this report published. But it must come out. Regardless of the consequences, it

Chandler heard the floor creak behind him. Instantly he typed *KS*. As the words on the screen disappeared, he felt a hand going around his throat and a needle going into his right arm. Someone was gagging him. He was having trouble breathing. He was falling asleep . . . asleep. . . .

59

Sunday, July 12

The long limousine with the diplomatic license plates glided down the Dulles Airport access road. The Soviet Ambassador to the United States sat in one corner of the back seat. In the other corner was one of Colonel Cyril Metrinko's trusted deputies. Between them, barely conscious, sat Senator Thomas Chandler.

When Chandler had gone to Elaine's house on Saturday night, Metrinko's men had had to make some hasty alterations in their elaborately detailed plan to kidnap him from his Spring Valley home. The Embassy, in extremely guarded language, had cabled Moscow for a delay, so that Chandler could later be "extracted" from his own house. But Metrinko was adamant: The extraction must be carried out on the scheduled date.

The original plan had called for them to get Chandler's luggage from his closet, pack some clothes, take his passport, and leave behind a receipt for an airlines ticket. The media stake-out at

Chandler's home had made surreptitious entry impossible. But a downtown travel agency still had a record that a one-way ticket, from Washington to London, London to Amsterdam, Amsterdam to Helsinki, had been issued to Thomas Chandler on Friday. It had been picked up by a commercial messenger who, according to his instructions, had paid cash.

So, although some risks were increased, there were compensations: No news people were anywhere near Elaine's house, and there would be only a short drive from Reston to Dulles Airport.

Metrinko's men had found no difficulty in breaking into the Reston house through the kitchen door, or in taking the deeply concentrating Chandler unawares. They had injected him with a powerful relaxant that would keep him relatively mobile but mentally anesthetized for at least four hours. Working quickly and professionally, the two men propped Chandler in a chair, knotted a necktie under his shirt collar, and eased him into his jacket.

By then, Chandler had regained consciousness, but he stared unseeingly into space. The men stood him up and, one under each arm, half walked, half dragged him through the house to the garage. They settled him in the front passenger seat of O'Brien's Mustang.

One of the men then checked the house. Their gloved hands had left no fingerprints, but he replaced the desk chair that had fallen over when Chandler was injected, and gathered up all the papers in sight, stuffing them into Chandler's briefcase. He worried about the computer, but its screen yielded no clue of what Chandler had been working on. With a shrug he turned it off and hung up the telephone handset on its cradle. He switched off all the lights and, with the briefcase under his arm, returned to the garage and crouched down in the back seat of O'Brien's car.

The other man, in the driver's seat, had been studying the automobile's mechanisms. O'Brien's old Mustang was not exactly like the Oldsmobile he had practiced on in the KGB garage in Moscow, but he thought he could handle it. He got out of the car and looked out the small garage window to ensure there was no movement in the street outside. After backing the car out, he closed the door behind them.

Chandler did not stir. As they drove through the dark streets, he sat straight up in his seat staring silently out through the windshield. Once the car had left Reston, the KGB man in the back got up off the floor, but the two Russians did not converse.

The driver constantly watched the rearview mirror, but traffic was light and there were no signs of police vehicles. He continued on route 7 for a few miles to the Dulles Access Road, then, slowing to let a few cars pass, pulled into a breakdown lane where Ambassador Brodovsky's limousine was waiting with its lights off. Quickly Chandler was transferred from the front seat of O'Brien's car to the back seat of the Ambassador's.

The two cars, O'Brien's in the lead, continued about a half-mile apart for the remaining eight miles to the airport. The Russian driving O'Brien's car parked it in the area reserved for members of Congress and the diplomatic corps. He put the time-stamped parking slip in his pocket and walked out to the main service roadway where the Ambassador's car was waiting. He got into the front seat next to the driver, and the limousine purred around a curve and down the last hundred yards to a gate in the high metal fence that the service road separated from the runways. Overhead a slight breeze curled the American flag illuminated on its tall flagpole by spotlights. On the runway near the far service area sat the equally illuminated Soviet Ilyushin airliner.

Two uniformed guards attended this seldom-used gate. One of them, a short young man with a clipboard, noticed the diplomatic license plates. "May I help you?" he asked politely.

The driver's thickly accented explanation was cut off by the Ambassador himself, who leaned forward, smiling, and said in his fluent English, "I am Andrei Brodovsky, the Soviet Ambassador to the United States. I have come to see off the three leaders of our trade delegation who are leaving for Moscow tonight. I believe you have received notice of our arrival from my Embassy?"

"Yes, sir," the young guard responded. He consulted his clipboard. "Besides yourself, Mr. Ambassador, and your driver, that would be Mr. Simionev, Mr. Gorshnikov, and Mr. Levontiev." The guard peered into the darkened limousine, uncertain of the limits of his authority or how he was expected to determine identities.

Brodovsky smoothly filled the vacuum: "Of course I vouch for the identity of these gentlemen, as is usually the custom in such cases. In addition, you may wish to examine their passports."

As the guard fumbled awkwardly with the documents, trying to match pictures with faces in the dark interior of the limousine, Brodovsky leaned across Chandler in animated Russian conversation with the KGB man on Chandler's other side. The guard handed the three passports back to the Ambassador. "Thank you very much, sir. You and your guests may proceed. Please tell the gentlemen from your government we hope they have enjoyed their visit to the United States and that they will come back soon." He saluted smartly.

The gate swung inward. The Ambassador translated the guard's farewell, and as the limousine moved out onto the lighted runway, its Soviet flags fluttering on the front fenders, the guard thought he heard laughter.

The long car pulled up directly at the foot of the steps leading to the main cabin of the giant airliner. Two husky attendants came down the steps and, carefully supporting the tallest of the three visitors, helped him up the steep ramp. One of the young guards watching from the gate said to the other, "Those Russkies. Never can hold their liquor. The vodka gets them every time."

They watched the Ambassador exchange a few brief words with the other two men before they went up the steps. Then, with a wave, the Ambassador got back into his limousine and drove toward the gate.

A little way up the service road, the Ambassador's car paused. The ramp and service vehicles pulled away from the Soviet airliner. Its doors closed, and the airliner lumbered out to the long east-west runway and stopped there. For a few brief seconds, the Ambassador held his breath. At first gradually, then with increasing speed and noise, the plane roared down the runway and lifted into the night.

The Ambassador sighed.

Thomas Chandler was on his way to Moscow.

60

Tuesday, July 14

On the highly polished oak surface of the President's desk lay a copy of *The Washington Post*, its front page dominated by one of the biggest and blackest headlines in its publishing history: SENATOR DEFECTS TO THE SOVIET UNION. Two subheads proclaimed: MISSING CHANDLER SURFACES AT MOSCOW PRESS CONFERENCE and FBI SUSPECTED SENATOR AS LEAK SOURCE. Photographs accompanied the stories. The first was of Chandler and Boris Luganov in the Senate Dining Room. The other showed Chandler shaking hands with the President of the United States; President Christiansen had signed the photograph: "With best wishes for your future success."

The President did not touch the paper, as if to do so would burn his hand. He leaned forward and skimmed a secondary story that was headlined KGB'S STUNNING TRIUMPH: AN AMERICAN MOLE.

> For years the Soviets have tried to penetrate America's intelligence operations at the highest levels, as they have successfully done in England, Germany, France, and, some speculate, Canada. To date they have achieved some success in recruiting spies in our armed services and high-technology firms that provide sophisticated satellite and defense equipment to the Pentagon. . . . Only one known attempt has been made to infiltrate our political system. In 1962 the Soviet Union tried to encourage a young law school graduate to run for the New York State Assembly. . . . But the attempt to corrupt our political system has never been so bold or potentially disastrous for the free world.

Christiansen then read the story on the FBI. He smiled at one paragraph:

> After obtaining a search warrant to Chandler's Spring Valley home, the FBI recovered further evidence that may confirm his private sympathies. Among the items recovered was a letter from former Soviet KGB station chief Georgi Tupolev, thanking Chandler for his courtesies; a tennis shirt with CCCP (Cyrillic for USSR) stamped on it in red block letters; a Minox B camera, which is a common tool of the trade for spies; a black fur hat made in the Soviet Union, and several volumes written by the poet Pablo Neruda, a notorious communist sympathizer.

But no report, the President thought, frowning. *They didn't find the report. It must have gone with him.*

President Arthur Christiansen was a man of unbounded optimism. It proceeded not from a simplistic view of the world, but as a reflection of his belief that adversity was only a challenge waiting to be overcome. The doubts that sometimes plagued him he swatted away like moths. He was too American ever to approach the Platonic model of philosopher. He was a man who thought about things with the common sense, wisdom, and shrewdness that the American social mill was especially capable of grinding out in times of stress.

What a wonderful country this is, he thought now, on this awful day. *But what a terrible price some of us have to pay for loving her.*

Tuesday, July 14

61

The news of Chandler's defection disrupted few lives. In Washington's many residential districts, the reaction was the same as in any other American neighborhood: disbelief, shock, anger. But ordinary lives went on as they always had.

In the Washington area of Mount Pleasant some people, the government people, talked excitedly, looking forward to office coffee-break and lunchtime gossip sessions about the new big Washington scandal. Mount Pleasant, once seedy, was showing signs of gentrification, as the realtors called it. Professionals were buying the run-down two-story brick row houses at bargain prices, transforming them inside and out. New cars appeared at the curbs. Kids sped by on ten-speeds, and their parents jogged. Many black residents disliked the change in their old neighborhood, but most of them accepted it as progress. They would live through the coming of the black and white Yuppies, just as they had lived through the coming of the Hispanics.

For one of the many Spanish-speaking people who lived in Mount Pleasant, however, any change meant danger, a threat to his anonymity and thus to his life.

He lived alone in a basement apartment, and, as his neighbors said, he kept to himself. They said hello to him in one language or another, they waved and nodded, but they knew nothing about his life or his past. That was the way of Mount Pleasant: You kept your nose out of other people's business. Now the old ways were changing, and for months he had been wondering where he would live next. But today he had more than another disappearing act on his mind.

The digital clock on the top of the television set registered 9:22 A.M., but the apartment was dim behind drawn blinds. Immanuel Sanchez—a name that did not appear on his mailbox downstairs—preferred the darkness.

He had phoned his office to say he was sick, and as he made the call he had thought of suicide. Now, staring into the bathroom mirror, he thought it was senseless to go on living, to go on running.

The running had started when President Kennedy was killed. The instant he heard, he knew he had to run. Something had gone wrong. He had warned the CIA that Kennedy was going to be hit—and somehow it still had happened. Just as the Bay of Pigs still had happened.

He had run everywhere. New York. Chicago. Los Angeles. Finally he had made it to Europe and found a man who understood what it meant to be hunted and who knew how to stay alive. QJ-WIN had told Sanchez he needed a permanent change of identity. At first, Sanchez had resisted. He was proud of his aquiline nose and strong jaw. "Proud enough of your face to die for it?" QJWIN had asked.

QJWIN had arranged for everything. Sanchez traveled to Munich and submitted himself to a plastic surgeon who was, as QJWIN promised, a master of his craft. After the bruises and swelling were gone, Sanchez had not recognized himself. Even now, staring into the mirror, he could not remember the face he had lost.

A loud pounding on his door brought him instantly to the present. He whirled away from the mirror, ran into the bedroom, and took from under his pillow a .38-caliber revolver. He was not an assassin, like QJWIN, but he knew how to kill.

Beads of perspiration formed along his receding hairline. The pounding on the door continued. He slipped off the safety and raised the .38 until it nearly touched his right ear. For a moment he wondered whether this was the way to do it: now, before the capture, the questioning, the inevitable death at their hands.

A voice with a Caribbean lilt spoke through the door: "Hey, mon! You deaf? The Mon is comin' to tow away your car. You better move it. The Mon's on the street."

He sounded young, lyrical. Maybe Jamaican. Sanchez waited, not even breathing. He didn't own a car. *Trevor has found me. Or Metrinko.*

How many times did he have to die, at every sound—the popping of a balloon, the hissing of a bus's brakes, a knock upon his door?

He waited, a minute that seemed like an hour. Finally, the voice died away, taunting, "Okay, mon. They take your car."

Sanchez did not risk a peek through the blinds.

He cursed himself again and again. Why was he still afraid? What was there left for him to lose but his own worthless life? He had lost everything that mattered, beginning with his wife.

When he had returned from Europe with his new face, he had begun the search for her and for his little Elena. He had found his wife, but the woman he knew as Maria Sanchez had somehow become the woman named Mary Dunham, who could only stare vacantly at a blank wall. She did not recognize him.

He hadn't tried to see Elaine then. There might be danger for her. But he had watched her from a distance. He had once spent a weekend at her college town in Vermont, had even spoken to her in Spanish when she waited on his table in the Middlebury Inn. Her Spanish had been faultless, and he had felt a fatherly pride.

His fears for Elaine were confirmed when she was recruited into the CIA. He had known this was no coincidence. The rigorous security check would have told the Agency who she really was. He concluded that Trevor was using her to bait a trap for the father she didn't know she had. He wanted to warn her, but he couldn't take the chance, and he didn't ask himself if his caution was for his sake or for hers. He decided to move to Washington, wait in the shadows, and watch. Occasionally he would sharpen his old skills by following her, riding the same subway, eating in the same restaurant, visible but invisible.

QJWIN had once told him the secret of the art of hiding: "You must stay in plain sight, that you will not be seen." So Sanchez had boldly tested the credentials QJWIN had forged: He applied for a job at the Pentagon and was hired to translate training manuals into Spanish. He had recently been promoted and was supervising the publication of manuals for the use of American personnel in Central America. He had also tapped into a network of Cuban anti-Castro groups headquartered in Washington.

When he learned, through a newspaper story, that Elaine was on Chandler's task force staff, he gave Trevor credit for another move of his unwitting pawn. But what could he do? Tell Chairman Walcott that the Agency had planted a mole inside his Senate Committee? Walcott had to be aware, involved, Sanchez concluded. And even if he were not, he would surely have dismissed Sanchez as a crank. (QUESTION: *How do you know she's a mole?* ANSWER: *She's my daughter, but she doesn't know it.*)

There had to be another way, and he found it. It would be his last chance to clear his name and to expose Trevor. But, like his other warnings in that deadly past, this one had again led to tragedy: his sweet Elena killed in an accident that he knew in his soul was no accident, and now . . . Again, he held a secret shared by few others. Sanchez knew of Colonel Cyril Metrinko, and he knew that Thomas Chandler was no traitor. Metrinko had stolen him.

And as before, there was no one to tell. He felt himself succumbing to despair, like a drowning man slipping under a silent wave.

The gun was heavy in his hand.

62

Tuesday, July 14

President Arthur Christiansen's eyes were still on the big black headlines of the front page of *The Washington Post*, but he was no longer seeing them. He was remembering Saturday night, and his meeting with Tom Chandler after Marlowe had gone.

Their talk had lasted for more than two hours. Because of the likelihood that Chandler was under Soviet surveillance, the President had decided on an official explanation for the late-night meeting: His press secretary would announce that Chandler had been summoned to the White House and closely questioned by the President about his mob associations.

Chandler had outlined the most important elements of his findings about the link between drugs and terrorism and told the President about Trevor's placement of Elaine Dunham on the task force staff. He agreed that he would finish up his report at home on Sunday and deliver it to the President, for use as he saw fit. Assuming, that was, that the Soviets didn't have other plans for Chandler's weekend. Contemplating the disaster area that had until so recently been a life full of promise, Chandler was still understandably leery of going along with the kidnap plan.

"The risks are enormous," the President said. "It's a long shot at best. But it may be the only way we can find out who their mole is. We've *got* to do that, Tom, before he gives away the keys to the goddam space shuttle."

"I can see the sense of your plan, Mr. President. But I keep going back to the idea of the kidnapping itself. Why would they kidnap me? The KGB could just take me out and make it look like a suicide. They've had a little experience with that."

"Right now you're a prime candidate for suicide *or* defection," the President said. "Look at yourself as a defector: You've had access to our top secrets; your career is shot; scandal is hanging over your head. Whoever is planning this operation has probably figured that you will be a perfect stand-in for the *real* mole. By making you look like a defector, he's given golden protection to his source. Why should we look for anyone else when you're such a perfect scapegoat?

"Let's say they murdered you and made it look like a suicide. If the leaks were to start up again, some of us might come to the conclusion that you *were* murdered and we might start looking for a motive. But with you as a defector, if the leaks continue we'll still blame *you*. We'll assume that the leaks were already in your pipeline, so to speak." Christiansen smiled at his pun, but the frown hadn't left Chandler's face.

"A defection gives them a major international coup while they still protect their source. It's quite brilliant."

"But what do *we* gain by my so-called defection?" Chandler asked.

The President spoke slowly and deliberately. "I'm afraid that if we try to stop them, they'll have a backup plan to kill you." He let that sink in. Then he said urgently, "There's a good chance that whoever is planning this operation has to keep you alive long enough to give the defection credibility. And there's an outside chance he may go for the ultimate score and try to turn you. My guess is he'll try to convince you that you can't go home again anyway, and that life in the Kremlin can be pretty good for people who cooperate.

"It will take some acting on your part—anger, depression, ultimately resignation, perhaps even a modicum of enthusiasm for the job. It will take weeks, maybe even a couple of months. But every good politician has a little bit of actor in him, doesn't he, Tom?"

Chandler nodded but he didn't smile.

As the reality overwhelmed him, he fell silent. He asked to write a note. Christiansen handed him a piece of White House stationery and an envelope.

"Something for your collection," Chandler said with a bitter smile. "The last words of America's highest-ranking double agent." He said that if a time came when the President could speak of this—a time, as they were both aware, unlikely to come at all unless Chandler was dead—he would like the note made public.

The President was happy to accede to the request.

Later, in his personal diary, not only for the future but also to have an immediate record, Arthur Christiansen recounted the call from the Prime Minister, the visit with Marlowe, and finally the plotting with Tom Chandler:

> We decided to "mark the money." Key people in the Administration and the Congress—particularly the Intelligence Committee—will be given new, but false, information on weapons or satellite systems. Only specific information will be given to specific people. Then, when and if the information shows up in Moscow, Chandler will probably be asked to authenticate it. If Chandler can let me know which piece of false information has reached Moscow, the mole's "fingerprints" should give him away.
>
> We also worked out a system for us to communicate. Obviously we can't bring anyone else into this scheme because we don't know whom we can trust. Certainly not Trevor or the CIA and certainly not the Intelligence Committee, since one of them might be the mole. So I told Chandler that the British agent, a Russian working in the Kremlin, would establish contact with him. Once Chandler is asked to confirm the existence of the new satellite or weapons system—and please God he will be—he need pass only one word, the name of the system, to the agent. That name will be relayed to George Hanrahan, our Ambassador in Moscow. George was my roommate at Princeton and my most trusted friend in the world. George won't know what's going on, but he'll follow his instructions to communicate the message to me directly, bypassing all other channels.

The President tossed the *Post* aside. The paper slid to the floor. He picked it up and placed it carefully on a stack of other papers, all with black headlines about Chandler's defection.

The phone console on his desk buzzed. "Yes?" he said to his secretary.

"Director Trevor is on his way up from the gate, Mr. President," she said.

"Send him in as soon as he arrives, Phyllis."

"Yes, sir. And, Mr. President?" She cut in before he could hang up. "There have been several calls from a Mr. Kevin O'Brien of the Senate Intelligence Committee staff. I wouldn't bother you with it, but he called yesterday and again three times this morning. He won't tell me what it's about—says he can't. He just said he had something for you he was sure you'd want. He said to tell you: 'I didn't trust Elaine Dunham, and I don't want to make the same mistake twice.'"

"I see. Thanks, Phyllis. Tell him to come over at noon."

"Will do. And here's Mr. Trevor now."

Trevor, carrying a slim black briefcase, took a seat in front of the elaborately carved oak desk. The sun gleamed on his eyeglasses, so that his eyes seemed strangely blank. For nearly a minute, the President looked at him in silence. Then he said, "Can you give me more than I just read in the *Post*?"

"There is a report here from our Moscow station chief about the Kremlin press conference, Mr. President. Chandler appeared drugged," Trevor said. "And with it is my preliminary damage assessment." He reached into the briefcase and handed two folders to the President.

Christiansen looked at him coldly. "I want an assessment that goes back at least a couple of years, to when that man in California gave up the plans for defending the Minuteman missiles," he said. "And I want a report that will give me all the answers I'll need for my press conference today."

"Yes, sir."

"At the very minimum, I want to be able to say that the leaks will stop. Can I say that?"

"I believe so, Mr. President. You may also say, sir, that both the Agency and the Bureau have had suspicions about Chandler for some time."

"Oh. I can say that, can I?"

"Yes, sir."

"And what else can I say, Mr. Director? How badly did we get hurt? How much secret material did Chandler have?"

"We do not believe that it was a matter of technical material, Mr. President. The loss is in how the defection will be perceived.

We believe that eventually you will have to address the question of Chandler's knowledge. I would recommend that a presidential commission be established to assess recent intelligence losses and—"

"And pin them all on Chandler?"

"You should be able, Mr. President, to assure the public that—"

"That our prime intelligence agency is so good that it is caught unaware when one of our high-level leaders—a potential President—steals secrets and defects?"

"I admit, Mr. President, that there is substantial embarrassment . . ."

"*Embarrassment?* That's your word for this catastrophe?" He let Trevor stew in presidential wrath while Christiansen swiftly went through his options. He certainly didn't want Trevor to know that Chandler had written a report—which was still missing, unless this O'Brien fellow knew something about it. Nor did he want Trevor to know that Chandler was the President's own double agent. He had to get rid of Trevor, to keep him from damaging the Chandler mole operation—inadvertently or deliberately.

"At this point, Mr. Director, there is only one thing that I know I can say at my press conference."

"What is that, sir?"

"That you are fired, Mr. Trevor. Yours is the first head to roll. Sit down with McLaughlin and help him piece together my opening statement for the press conference. Then start cleaning your desk."

Perhaps the blade had fallen too swiftly for Trevor to react, to protest. He showed absolutely no chagrin or resentment.

"Mr. President, I still believe you can turn this thing around, to your advantage," he said. "You can stress that Senator Chandler had *limited* access to secret information. The danger would have been if he had gone undetected, picking us apart bone by bone like a barracuda. The ultimate tragedy has been avoided—Chandler might have become President. Imagine, our Commander in Chief—the man with total control of our security—a Soviet spy!"

"So, I should tell the press and the American people that we've snatched victory from the jaws of defeat?" Christiansen's voice was savage.

"Not exactly, Mr. President," Trevor said with undiminished assurance. He was playing the role of the consummate good soldier now. Rigidly upright in his chair, he seemed prepared to

346

swallow cyanide if the President so commanded him. In the very hour of his humiliation, he wore his honor like a badge. "But I believe you can claim credit for flushing out a traitor . . . and saving the country from an unparalleled tragedy. It will be a political embarrassment to our system temporarily, but not a major injury to our national security. I believe it is possible to turn the joker into an ace, sir."

Christiansen had to suppress a laugh at the irony of it all. Politically embarrassing indeed! *Flushing out a traitor is precisely what we haven't done! At least not so far* . . . He wanted to tell Trevor what an ass he was, and yet . . .

And yet he knew that he would have to do exactly what Trevor was suggesting. To calm the fears of the American people. Downplay the impact upon our national secrets. Give them hope for the future. After all, that's what had characterized his administration: the persistent sense of optimism.

The President got up from his desk and went to the windows on the south side of the Oval Office. He dismissed Trevor without a further glance, and stood gazing out the green-tinted, bulletproof windows. He could hear a muffled chant from a group of demonstrators beyond the fence that surrounded the White House. He couldn't make out what they were protesting. He didn't much care.

A whisper of doubt fluttered in his mind. Maybe he had allowed Christopher Marlowe to play to his infatuation with the world of espionage. Maybe he never should have allowed Tom Chandler to be taken.

Traitor. That was the word Trevor had used, and now it rang like a knell in Christiansen's thoughts. *Tom Chandler was a patriot, goddam it!* Not the black-and-white, love-it-or-leave-it brand of patriotism that Trevor preached. . . . Christiansen caught himself in his own contradiction. Chandler loved his country, and he had left it. But patriotism was passionate. It meant truly loving one's country, being disappointed by her shortcomings, jealous of her errant flirtations, even hating her when she occasionally dressed up like a harlot. It meant never being neutral, never detached, never unconcerned when ideals were not quite measured up to. . . .

The chanting of the protestors took on the quality of a Greek chorus in the President's thoughts. "Oedipus Rex," he said aloud. Maybe one had to be blind in order to see the kind of wisdom he needed now to get him through this crisis.

Christiansen returned to his desk. While he waited for Kevin O'Brien, he must prepare for his afternoon press conference. He took a note pad from a desk drawer and then sat staring at the waiting blankness of its surface. He tried to dismiss the foreboding that nagged at the edges of his mind. What did O'Brien have to tell him? What would tomorrow bring? He was profoundly worried about Tom Chandler.

Then a smile started at the corners of Christiansen's lips as he remembered the way he and Chandler had plotted, almost like fraternity brothers planning a prank. After the decision to go had been made, Chandler had been unafraid, even enthusiastic, as if he were giving new meaning to his shattered life. A freeze-frame image of Senator Thomas Chandler in the Kremlin, being heralded as the Soviet Union's most important spy, clicked in the President's mind. He was smiling broadly now.

It was going to work. His optimism told him so.

ABOUT THE AUTHORS

Senator William S. Cohen, Republican of Maine, served three terms in the U.S. House of Representatives before being elected to the Senate in 1978. Cohen is a member of the Armed Services and Governmental Affairs committees, as well as the Special Committee on Aging and the Select Committee on Intelligence. He is the author of three other books: *Of Sons and Seasons* (poetry), *Roll Call*, and *Getting the Most Out of Washington*. He and his wife, Diana, have two sons, Kevin and Christopher.

Senator Gary Hart, Democrat of Colorado, is a member of the Senate's Armed Services Committee, Budget Committee, Environment and Public Works Committee, and a former member of the Select Committee on Intelligence. He is the author of two other books: *Right from the Start* and *A New Democracy*. Gary Hart and his wife, Lee, have two children, Andrea and John.